THE PALACE OF VARIETIES

James Lear

All characters in this publication are fictitious and any resemblance to real persons, living or dead, is purely coincidental.

First published 2003 by Zipper Books,
part of Millivres Prowler Limited,
Spectrum House, 32-34 Gordon House Road, London NW5 1LP
www.zipper.co.uk

A catalogue record for this book is available from the British Library

ISBN 1-873741-86-3

Distributed in the UK and Europe by Airlift Book Company,
8 The Arena, Mollison Avenue, Enfield, Middlesex EN3 7NJ
Telephone: 020 8804 0400
Distributed in North America by Consortium,
1045 Westgate Drive, St Paul, MN 55114-1065
Telephone: 1 800 283 3572
Distributed in Australia by Bulldog Books,
PO Box 300, Beaconsfield, NSW 2014

Printed and bound in Finland by WS Bookwell

One

1934: I turn eighteen… My father's blessing… A new opportunity… I surrender at Waterloo… Short-changed by a shilling… A chance meeting… I find an opening

I arrived in London the day after my eighteenth birthday. That event, so keenly anticipated by my mother and sister, had passed at home in furious silence. My father – an officer in the French army during World War One, from whom I inherited my surname, Lemoyne, my dark looks and my quick temper – sat down at the breakfast table and fixed me with a lowering gaze.

'What are you looking so pleased with?'

'Nothing.'

'Wipe that smile off your face.'

My mother, as usual, tried to pour oil on troubled waters. 'It's Paul's birthday, darling.'

My father thumped the table. 'His birthday! And what are we going to do about that? Waste more of our money buying him presents? Champagne, perhaps? A silk suit?'

He pushed his chair back and stormed out of the room leaving my sister, a year older than I and already worn out by a lifetime of skivvying and self-sacrifice, holding the bacon tongs hovering in midair.

'Don't stand there like a simpleton, Jane,' snapped my mother, before running after my father making conciliatory noises. Jane and I looked at each other and shrugged. We were used to such scenes: ever since I had left school at fifteen my father had been needling me about my failure to earn a living. What could I do? It was 1934, and work was not easily had.

Jane bent down and kissed me on top of the head. 'Happy birthday, Paul,' she whispered, placing a measly rasher of bacon on my plate. I kissed her hand as, glancing towards the door, she tipped another thin piece of meat my way. 'Go on, enjoy it. He won't be wanting it. No point in waste.' She tucked a stray lock of brown hair up into her bun and hurried back to the kitchen. I attacked breakfast with an appetite, and spent the rest of the morning in my room, reading, daydreaming, sleeping.

My father went out at noon – in principle to collect his war pension and look for work, in practice to meet his cronies at the pub and fritter away our housekeeping. Our income was pitifully small. Father had been wounded at the first battle of Ypres, and recuperated in a military hospital near Hastings, where my mother, a nurse, fell in love with him. Unwilling to return to France (where, in truth, the war left him pitifully little to return to), he married, transferred his pension to England and pursued his former career as a printer. Jane was born shortly after the marriage, and I was hot on her heels. All was well until the Depression, when Father lost his job and began drinking. Since then we had dispensed with all domestic help, and my mother and sister had taken over the running of the house, while my father and I concealed the shame of our parasitic, useless existences beneath a pitiful display of hostility.

His absence restored a festive mood to the house. Mother and Jane gave me presents – an embroidered wallet and a set of monogrammed handkerchiefs, both products of their exquisite needlework – and we enjoyed a pleasant tea together. Father's return soured the mood instantly. He was drunk and maudlin.

'I've been toasting my son's birthday,' he slurred as Mother stared at him with a gloomy countenance. 'Come here, Paul. Come and receive my blessing.'

I kept to my chair.

'Come when I ask you.'

'No.'

'Come here this instant!'

'You stink of beer.'

He flung back his arm as if to strike me, then abruptly sat down, carried off his feet by the momentum.

'Show some respect to your father, Paul,' said Mother in low, deadly tones.

I stood. 'I shall show him respect when he deserves it.' I walked towards the door. Father launched himself at me, grabbing me by the shoulders. Jane laid a restraining hand on his arm, but he shrugged her off so violently that she fell and cracked her temple against the arm of a chair. Her face went white as a bead of dark blood gathered and ran down her cheek, and she passed out. I turned in a fury to face my father, who was cringing beneath our collective opprobrium.

Perhaps I should have struck him then and there, beaten him sober and by doing so replaced him as the head of the household. But at that moment I could see nothing but day after day stretching out in the same sordid, degrading way. I turned on my heel and left.

The train journey to Waterloo took a little over two hours. It was still early in the morning when I arrived. I'd spent the night on a bench on the station, having vowed before my weeping mother and sister never to set foot in the house while 'that man' was under the roof. I slept very little: it was cold, and I had nothing but my patched overcoat to keep me warm. The first up train left at six, and I stretched out luxuriously across the seats in the second-class carriage and slept. I woke when the guard came to inspect my nonexistent ticket; happily, he took pity on my penniless condition and even brought me an enamel mug of thick brown tea that the engineer had brewed up at the front.

'Where are you going, youngster?' he asked as I sipped the scalding tea.

'London.'

'What for?' He was a kind old soul, a good deal older than my father, with white hair and a red face. I'd seen him once or twice on family trips up to town; he'd always been friendly and courteous.

'I don't know. I've just got to get away.'

'Oh, yes?' He looked curious, scenting a scandal, I suppose. 'Trouble at home?'

'Well...' I was in no hurry to share our family problems with a stranger. 'I need a job.'

'A young man like you should have no difficulty making a living in the city, I should think.' He looked at me with an appraising eye.

'Really?'

'How old are you?'

'Eighteen yesterday.' I thought I detected his red face blushing to a deeper crimson.

'Got any ideas of what you want to do? Most lads want to be engine drivers, don't they?' He had a curious half-smile on his face.

'I'm not a child!' I replied, unsure whether he was mocking me.

'No, I should say not. Very much a young man. Eighteen, you say. Lived at home all your life?'

'Yes.'

'Not much... experience of the world, I suppose?'

'No.' I stared gloomily into my empty mug.

'What line of work did you think of turning your hand to?'

I was ashamed to admit that I had never worked a day in my life, that, in fact, my only occupations since the age of fifteen had been reading, swimming and occasional trips to the pictures, whenever I could sneak in without paying. But there was little point in pretending to be something that I wasn't. 'I've no idea.'

'Look,' said the guard, reaching into his jacket and pulling out a small pasteboard card. 'Make a call here when you get to London. Mr Holly is a good friend of mine. He'll find something for you. Say Dudley sent you.'

I held it up to the light.

Mr Nicholas Holly
General Manager
South London Palace of Varieties
Ontario Street SE

'He'll see you right, young man. Now, mind how you go and be good.' He winked, slipped me a punched ticket so that I could get out of Waterloo without detection, and left the carriage.

The great station was quiet and sleepy, the sun filtering through the filthy glass roof, where a few disreputable pigeons fluffed their tatty feathers on the girders. Here and there gentlemen in suits and bowler hats hurried, heads down, across the concourse. With each train that rumbled into the station, more and more of them were disgorged into the metropolis until, within half an hour, the whole area was crowded. I watched in fascination: so many men, dressed identically, moving purposefully, never bumping into each other, keeping their eyes on the floor. I leaned against a coffee stand and just watched. One or two of them looked up at me, struck, I suppose, by this one idle soul in a sea of human activity. Some of them took a tighter grip on their briefcases, afraid that I was bent on theft. Others smiled vaguely, envying my freedom, I suppose.

My rough night left me feeling grimy, and the strong tea I'd had on the train was ready for release, and so I made my way through the hordes to the gentlemen's cloakroom situated near the ticket office. Here one could get a wash and brush-up for sixpence – a serious drain on my meagre resources (I had ten shillings, not a penny more) but important if I was to make a good impression on any potential employer. I had to find work, bread and a roof over my head without delay – before night fell, and before my resolution wavered.

The cloakroom was busy: plenty of businessmen had to relieve themselves after their long journeys up from the shires. I waited my turn, and eventually took a place at the free urinal between two gents in identical black suits. I unbuttoned my fly, pulled myself out, bent my knees slightly and prepared to piss.

Just as I was relaxing and enjoying the relief of my bladder emptying, I heard a slight intake of breath a little above my right shoulder. I glanced up, caught the eye of my neighbour for half a second, and looked quickly down. He appeared to have finished the job in hand, but was in no hurry to move away. I looked up again. This time his gaze was fixed a little lower, watching the thick stream of piss that I was splashing against the porcelain. What was he doing? I stole a glance downwards for answer to my question. In his right hand he was still holding a cock which appeared to be growing rapidly larger.

Somewhat surprised, I looked down and tried to concentrate on my now-dwindling stream. The man to my left cleared his throat; I looked up and caught him smiling at me, one eyebrow raised towards the rim of his bowler. He, too, was holding his prick in his hand.

I didn't know what to make of the situation, but I was intrigued. By now I, too, had finished pissing, and had no reason to stay where I was – but I was unwilling to walk away from this little adventure without discovering the outcome. And so, taking a lead from my neighbours, I stood exposed at the urinal waiting for something to happen. I could feel the heat of their gaze upon me; both were staring down at my cock, which, flattered by the attention, was beginning to stiffen.

I wondered how long the three of us could stand there with our pricks in our hands when, suddenly, a whisper rippled through the cloakroom and, all around me, men shook themselves off and stuffed their engorged members back into their trousers. I followed suit just in time to see a policeman taking his place at a urinal near the door. Where all had been still and silent watching before was now a scene of innocent toilette: running water, hands being washed and dried, hair combed in mirrors. The policeman, unaware of the muted revels he had disturbed, buttoned himself up and remounted the stairs; we could hear his hobnailed boots banging on the metal treads. As they faded above us, the atmosphere changed as if someone had flicked a switch.

My two neighbours, who had been washing their hands at a nearby sink, returned to my side. 'Want to earn half a crown?' whispered one of them – a middle-aged gentleman with a handsome set of black whiskers. He nodded towards a door at the back of the room marked SHOWERS. My other admirer, a fair-skinned man of perhaps thirty, with a thin fair moustache, laid a well-manicured hand on my elbow and guided me through. 'Let's make it the full crown, shall we?' I was guided over to the door, and a sum of money was dropped into the eager hand of an elderly attendant who unlocked the door to admit us. We stepped into a white-tiled room, and the door was locked behind us.

The room was reminiscent of the changing rooms at the school playing fields. Benches and hooks ran down one wall; big dripping chromium shower heads down the other. The floor was wet, and not a little muddy; a smelly mop and bucket stood in one corner, unused, I suspected, since the last occupants.

My companions had, hitherto, been models of patience and decorum; now, however, hidden from the gaze of their peers, they became more demanding.

'Strip,' barked the dark one, removing his bowler hat and hanging it on a hook.

'Come on, boy, we haven't got all day,' said his companion, loosening his tie.

I watched for a moment as they took off their jackets. Both were well built, the older running slightly to fat, perhaps, but powerful nonetheless. They stood before me with folded arms, waiting for me to comply. I suddenly became aware of the perils of my predicament, but trusted to the innate respectability of the English gentleman. I did not know exactly what they had in mind, but I suspected it could not be murder – and I stood to make five bob. I took off my overcoat and jacket, removed my tie and unbuttoned my cuffs. They were watching me like hawks.

'Get the shirt off,' said the dark one.

I undid the top two buttons, tugged my braces off my shoulders and pulled the shirt over my head, a practice that my mother deplored as lazy but that seemed, in my present hurried circumstances, perfectly legitimate. Their eyes widened as they took in my torso, which was hard and defined thanks to my 'wasted' afternoons at the public baths, ploughing up and down the swimming pool.

'I say,' said the younger, blond one, 'look at the skin on him. Like silk.' He took a step towards me and laid a hand on my shoulder, several shades darker than his own fair colouring. For that I had to thank my father's Mediterranean blood. The other took my nipple between thumb and forefinger, squeezing it slightly.

'A perfect Apollo Belvedere.'

'Now the rest, boy.'

They stood back, awaiting the climax of the show. I noticed that both were nursing visible bulges at the fork of their trousers.

I undid my belt, kicked off my shoes, pulled off my socks and stepped out of my trousers, which had fallen around my ankles. Now I stood there in just my pants – rather a threadbare pair, I'm ashamed to say. This did not seem to worry my two companions, who, heedless of their pinstripes, both dropped to their knees and, one at the front, one at the rear, inhaled great lungfuls from my crotch and arse. This dual assault of mouths, noses and hands, which were running up and down my legs, was an entirely new sensation for me, and within seconds my cock was like an iron bar inside my pants.

I have always been aware that I am more blessed than most in that department. On the odd occasion when I saw my father naked, on his way to or from the bathroom or on rare family trips to the seaside, I realised that this was his most welcome legacy to me; he was massively endowed. At the age of thirteen I had simply marvelled at the size of it; by sixteen, I had matched it myself. Joking remarks at the swimming pool made me acutely self-conscious in this respect; now, however, my size seemed to be working in my favour. I was so stiff that my pants could no longer contain me, and I had tented out in the front so that the material was pulled taut across my bum, leaving great gaping apertures around my thighs. Into one of these a hand soon slipped, grasped my prick and drew it out into the open, where it stood, throbbing slightly, for inspection.

The two gentlemen stared in disbelief for a moment, then attempted to outdo each other in efforts to swallow it. One second, two sets of lips were running up the sides of my shaft; the next, my whole cock was buried in the mouth of one while the other had to be content to bathe my nuts with his tongue. My pants were torn off by impatient hands and tossed aside; they lay, soaking up muddy water, a yard to my left. Hands were kneading my buttocks, slapping them, pulling them apart; every so often a finger would brush against a part of my body hitherto untouched by any apart from my mother.

By now both of them had pulled their cocks out of their flies and were occasionally breaking off from their fevered exploration to give themselves a quick wank. The room was permeated with a strong male scent as three bodies heated up in sexual excitement; it was a new smell to me, and one to which I became instantly addicted.

The young fair man was winning the battle to suck my prick, so his older companion stood behind me and took me in his strong arms. I could feel his hairy belly pressing into my back; he was still clothed, but had pulled his shirt up to increase the contact. And that was not all I could feel: his cock, which was shorter but a good deal thicker than my own, was pushing against my buttocks. With one hand, he felt my chest and stomach; with the other, he grabbed my left ear and pulled my head round so that he could kiss me. His whiskers grazed my face; his mouth tasted, not disagreeably, of tobacco and my cock. I held onto the head that was bobbing around my groin and abandoned myself to the trip. I could feel my guts beginning to boil and knew from my own solitary experience that I was about to come. The dark man stuck his tongue inside my mouth and gripped me in a great bear hug; the other held me deep in his throat while my hips bucked and I squirted what felt like a pint of sperm into him. My knees buckled and I was let gently down to the floor. I lay with my legs stretched out in front of me, propping myself up on my elbows.

If I thought the game was over, I was wrong: I had not yet earned my crown. The two men stood over me, one on either side, and began to wank themselves in good earnest, gazing down at me as if they would imprint every detail of my body on their memories. Well, I would give them something to remember, I thought, feeling for a moment utterly sluttish as I lay on the dirty tiles. I ran my hands over my chest and stomach; I waved my still-hard cock in the air, squeezing out a few more drops of spunk. I raised my legs to let them see my arsehole. This seemed to be the trigger, for first one, then the other, started to shoot his sperm, directing it on to my stomach, chest and neck. I rubbed my hands around in it, glorying in the degradation of the moment.

Spent, however, they suddenly became businesslike once more. Each produced a carefully laundered white handkerchief from his breast pocket – placed there, in all probability, by a dutiful wife – wiped his softening cock and tucked it away. Within a minute the jackets and ties were back in place, the bowler hats adjusted, trousers brushed down, and my two friends were ready to resume their journey to the office.

'Thank you, young man,' said the older of the two, reaching into his pocket. 'That was immensely enjoyable.' He handed me a coin; I could tell from the size and the milled edge that it was a florin. His friend gave me another. I was a shilling down on the deal.

'Thank you, gentlemen,' I said, unwilling after all to quibble over the shortfall. In any future transaction, I resolved, I would get the money while they were still feeling generous.

I watched as they slipped out of the shower room, whispering into the attendant's ear as they went. He glanced inside, shot me a toothless grin and handed me a towel.

At last I was able to wash.

By the time I emerged into the now-quiet station, it was approaching half past nine. The sun was stronger, catching the dust in shafts that filtered through broken panes in the roof. I had thirteen shillings and sixpence in my pocket, and I was hungry. I bought coffee and a cake from a stall at the station entrance, and while I stood there munching, enjoying the sun on the back of my neck (where, so recently, a set of bristly black whiskers had been crushed), I asked the old lady who had served me if she could direct me to Ontario Street.

'You want the Sarf, do you?'

'The what?'

'The Sarf. The Sarf London Palace of Varieties.'

'Yes! You know it?'

'Course I do! Just down the road, dear,' she said, pointing along the dreary street where trams rumbled by full of grey-faced citizens. 'Down the end, past the clock tower, past the electric works, it's on yer right. Can't miss it. Ten minutes.'

Delighted to be saving my tram fare, I sauntered down Waterloo Road, gripping the pasteboard card the train guard had given me in my pocket. It took me a good deal longer than ten minutes. Every new building held some interest for me. Ricci Giacomo's restaurant, on the corner of Alaska Street, smelled deliciously of onions. A little further down, a coffee merchant and the next-door confectioner made rival claims on my appetite. There was the famous Old Vic theatre – even I had heard of that from the weekly magazines. A little further, I could see the clock tower gleaming two hundred yards ahead of me. I hurried past hairdressers, theatrical costumiers, greengrocers, bootmakers, laundries, all of them busy and, to my young eyes, fascinating. One or two of the shopkeepers, particularly the women, caught me staring in the window and gave me a smile or blew me a kiss; outside Dean's Fancy Draper's I was asked to move on. I didn't care: the sun was shining, I had a few bob in my pocket and I was on my way in life.

At the clock tower I skipped over a maze of tramlines and continued my journey south – or so I thought. I walked for ten minutes, looking out for Ontario Street – but eventually, crossing underneath a railway bridge, decided I must have taken a wrong turn, and began to look for a friendly face from whom to ask directions.

A young man came whistling out of a pub, a knapsack over his shoulder, his arms thrust into the pockets of loose, green, cotton trousers. He was in shirtsleeves, with a cap perched on the back of his head and a great mop of ginger hair curling out over his forehead. A cigarette was tucked behind one ear. He was, I supposed, about my own age.

'Excuse me,' I said, falling into step beside him.

He looked at me and smiled. 'Now, what can I do for you?' He sounded and looked unmistakably Irish: green eyes, a snub nose, freckles and a quick smile.

'I'm looking for Ontario Street.'

'Oh, yes.' He walked on; I kept pace with him.

'Do you know where it is?'

'Ontario Street?'

'Yes. Is it nearby?

'What might you be looking for there, now?'

I pulled the card out of my pocket. 'The South London Palace of Varieties,' I said.

'Let's see.' He took the card from my hand and inspected it, looked at the back, turned it every way. 'The South London Palace of Varieties, indeed.' We crossed the road and turned left.

'Do you know where it is? I have to see this gentleman.'

'Who's that, then?'

'A Mr Holly, I believe.'

'Do you know this Mr Holly?' He seemed, if anything, to be

quickening his pace.

'No, not exactly. I have an introduction.'

'Ah, I see.'

'So, can you help me?'

'Help you? What with?'

'To find the South London Palace of Varieties.'

'Oh, yes.'

'You can?'

'Yes.'

'Well, where is it?'

He stopped in his tracks, and I bumped into him. 'Why, you're standing right in front of it!' He burst into laughter. I looked up and there, emblazoned over the front of a decaying but impressive building, were the very words I had sought for the last half-hour.

'Come in. I'll find Holly for you. What name?'

'Paul Lemoyne. He won't know me—'

But my guide had already disappeared through a door, leaving me in the dusty foyer, where I beguiled the time by reading through the bills advertising forthcoming attractions. This very evening the South London Palace of Varieties was proud to present Tucker the Singing Violinist, Gilday & Fox, Monarchs of Hebrew Comedy, in their latest success *Ikey Levey's Birthday*, Lorene & Kidd 'The Peach and the Nut' and, top of the bill, Terri Marlo, 'Not Quite a Lady', with musical accompaniment under the baton of Mr Wilfred Wallace.

I was lost in speculation as to what these acts might be, intrigued particularly by the photograph of Terri Marlo that stood on a gilded easel by the box office, when I was tapped smartly on the shoulder and there was my young friend with a prosperous, stout gentleman standing beside him.

'This is the party,' said the boy, as I smoothed down my hair and hoped that my clothes weren't still redolent of my shower-room adventures.

'I see,' said Mr Holly. 'I believe you wish to see me, Mr...?'

I extended a hand. 'Paul Lemoyne. I'm very pleased to meet you, Mr Holly, and grateful for your time.'

'And what can we do for you?' he said, looking at his fob watch.

'I was advised to come and see you by a... friend of mine, Mr Dudley.'

I now had Holly's attention; he put his watch away and grasped my hand.

'Mr Dudley of the Hastings line?'

'The very same.'

'Ah, I see. Thank you, Kieran, that will be all.'

My guide touched his forelock and sauntered off into the theatre, whistling a tune.

'So, Mr...'

'Lemoyne. Paul Lemoyne.'

'Mr Lemoyne. Very pleased to meet you. Dudley sent you, did he? A good friend, would you say?'

'Only an acquaintance, sir. I was speaking to him on the train this morning.'

'Ah. I see. Well, now, I must thank Mr Dudley for his vigilance. It just so happens that I am in need of a stagehand at the moment. I presume you have come here in search of gainful employment.'

'Yes, please, sir.'

'And you're not afraid of hard work?'

'No, sir!'

'Splendid! We shall get along nicely. Now tell me, Paul,' he said, leaning closer and whispering in my ear, 'I don't know what my good friend Dudley told you about me...'

'Nothing at all, sir.'

'Well. That's fine, boy, fine. Just a word to the wise. When I introduce you to Mrs Holly, perhaps it would be best if you were not to mention our mutual friend Mr Dudley. Perhaps you might just say that you answered an advertisement. How would that be? Not overfond of Mr Dudley, is my wife. Takes a rather dim view of... all that sort of thing. If you get my meaning.'

I didn't, but I nodded nonetheless. Mr Holly's breath was quick at my ear. I thought for an insane moment that he was going to kiss me. Instead, he stepped back, clapped me on the shoulder and made a large gesture with a handkerchief.

'Welcome to the South London Palace of Varieties, my boy! Kieran will show you around. Invaluable chap, Kieran, if a little prone to... well, enough of that. I don't suppose for one moment that you have a place to stay?'

'No, sir.'

'Very well, very well. We shall provide. I can't offer you much. A few bob a week, a roof over your head and a pot to piss in. Mrs Holly makes a fine Irish stew, of which this young gentleman is inordinately fond.' Kieran had reappeared in the foyer, and was pulling himself up and down on a brass rail that ran along the top of the box office. He was quite a gymnast; I could see the muscles in great bunches at the top of his arms.

'Good God, boy, don't pull the whole house down! Kieran is practising his strongman act, hoping that one day the great Holly will allow him to tread the boards.'

'Ah, you're full of promises, Mr Holly,' said Kieran, poking the manager in the stomach. 'Full of promises and full of—'

'That's enough now, thank you. Perhaps you could show our latest recruit around. And tell me, is there room at Mrs Tunnock's for another?'

'Without a doubt.'

'Will you run round later and ask her?'

'I will.'

'There we are, Paul. A job and a bed, yours for the asking. And Mrs Tunnock makes delicious Irish stew, too!'

'You'll not mind sharing with me?' said Kieran with a wink. I was too overjoyed at my good fortune to object to anything; I would have happily bedded down in the box office.

'Come on, then,' said Kieran, throwing a heavy arm around my shoulders, 'and follow me into fairy land.'

Two

Backstage... A roof over my head... My first taste of cock... The life of the theatre... First love... My arse awakens... The wisdom of the ancients

Like every theatre that I have been in since, the South looked sad and dilapidated in the daytime. It was dark in the auditorium, where Kieran now led me, and smelled heavily of unwashed bodies, cigarette smoke and perfume. Once my eyes had adjusted to the gloom I saw the tiers of empty seats, the peeling plasterwork and tarnished gilding around the circle, the faded plush of the stage curtain. I was not a starstruck child; I did not feel, as some have recounted, that I had suddenly come home on first stepping into a theatre. But I was alive to the mood of the place, and eager to find out what my duties would be.

Kieran raced down the aisle, cleared the orchestra pit in a single bound and landed on the stage with a flourish. 'Ladies and gentlemen,' he began, 'The Great O'Houlighan!' He struck a strongman pose, and another, and another, then executed a perfect handstand and walked on his palms up and down the boards. I stood in the stalls and applauded laconically.

'Come on up, Paul,' he shouted after righting himself. He was red in the face; his freckles had all but disappeared.

Steps at either side of the stage gave me a safer access to the stage, and soon I was up there with him. 'Ah, yes, my boy, this is where it all happens. All the great and the good have played here. It's a grand life. Don't you believe a bloody word of it! Come on.'

He put a brawny arm round my neck and led me to the wings, past a jumble of ropes and cables and into a high-ceilinged room, where giant wooden frames were stacked against the wall.

'Scenic dock,' he said, pulling on a rope so that one of the frames was lifted into view. It represented a London street with a bobby on a bike, a young woman with a dog, a boy bowling a hoop. 'Let's see what you can do, then. Come on.'

Kieran indicated a rope, on which I pulled to little effect. 'Come on, boy, give it some elbow grease!' I pulled harder, and the frame slowly groaned back into its place in the stack.

'Ah, well, Mrs Holly's Irish stew will make a man of you I suppose. This way.'

Past the dressing rooms, where a lunatic's wardrobe seemed to have exploded; down to the stage door, where a hundred messages were pinned to a baize noticeboard; up to the gantry, where the lights clustered in meaningless profusion.

'You'll get the hang of it, Paul,' laughed Kieran, seeing how crestfallen I appeared. 'Come with me, now, and we'll get you fixed up with Mother Tunnock.'

We passed through the stage door and out into the daylight, which dazzled me after the darkness of the theatre. I expected to return the way we had come, but instead we crossed the road, turned down a little street over the way and up the steps of a narrow terraced house.

'Is this Mrs Tunnock's, then?'

'Isn't it grand?'

'Is this where you live?'

'Indeed it is.'

'But this morning... weren't you coming out of—'

Kieran dug me in the ribs and put a finger to my lips. 'Ah, you saw nothing of the kind! This is where I rest my head and enjoy all the comforts of home.' He rang the bell. 'Mrs Tunnock! Are you within?'

A grey head popped out of the upstairs window, and a hand shook a duster.

'God, Kieran, can't I get a moment's peace to clean up your mess?'

'Now don't be unfriendly, Ma, I've a new friend for you to meet.'

'Oh, yes? Who's this?'

'This is my good friend Mr Paul Lemoyne, who I'm training up in the mysteries of the theatre, Mrs T, and Mr Holly sends him to you saying please can you find him a space beneath your hospitable roof?'

'Well, he'll have to share.'

'I've already told him, Ma. He's to share with me. Aren't you, Paul?'

'Yes, of course.'

'Good lad,' said Mrs Tunnock, drawing her head in; we could hear her lumbering down the stairs. When she opened the door she'd made some attempt to tidy herself and was bundling up her pinny. She seemed to be composed entirely of curves.

'Well, then, Mr Paul, you're very welcome here. Mr Holly will take care of the rent – not that he pays a great deal. Kieran will show you to your room. Did Stephen move all his stuff out, dear?'

'Yes he did,' said Kieran. 'Stephen was your predecessor. Snot-nosed little fellow. Didn't last the course. Couldn't be bothered with him. Went back to his ma and pa. Now, you and I are going to be good mates, aren't we?'

We climbed the stairs to a small room on the second-floor rear. A large iron bedstead and a lumpy mattress took up most of the space, leaving just enough room for a washstand, a chair and a small table. There was a cupboard in the corner, which Kieran flung open with the largesse of a sultan.

'Here you go, all that the human heart could desire.' Inside hung three shirts, a pair of trousers and a coat – his entire wardrobe. Mine was even smaller, consisting of the clothes I stood up in and a spare shirt and socks folded up in my coat pocket. I didn't even own a pair of pants after my adventures at Waterloo Station.

Kieran threw himself back on the bed and put his arms behind his head.

'You'd better get changed, Paul, if we're to get to work.'

'Changed? I've nothing to change into.'

'Ah, you can borrow my trousers. Don't go spoiling your best gear.'

For the second time that morning, I stripped off. I hung up my coat, took off my tie, kicked off my shoes and dropped my trousers. My shirt tails were long enough to conceal the absence of underwear.

During this performance, Kieran kept up a stream of narrative.

'Don't breathe a word of it outside this room, Paul, but I spent the early hours of the morning with a young lady of my acquaintance. Now don't be shocked: nothing of that sort happened. She's a good girl, more's the bloody pity if you know what I mean.' He stretched out on the bed, sighed and squeezed his balls. 'She's the daughter of a publican, and she's up with the lark, sorting out the cellar. That's the only time I get a little private conversation with her. I creep out of here at five o'clock in the morning and she lets me in through the cellar door. We have a talk and a kiss and then I have to leave with my tail between my legs. Jesus! It's not easy for a young man in the prime of his life to be denied the pleasures of the flesh.'

I thought back to my experiences of the morning, priding myself on the thought that, while Kieran had been engaged in his fruitless pursuit of a young woman, I had enjoyed two men and come off four bob the richer.

'Anyway, don't worry, I'll not be disturbing you every morning: it's only once or twice a week that she consents to see me. I fear I snore a little; your predecessor complained mightily of it.'

'Don't worry, I sleep like a log.'

'Well, now, we'll get on just fine. God, Paul, you're not wearing any underpants.'

I had reached up to get Kieran's spare trousers from the cupboard, and in doing so had revealed my bare backside.

'I – I lost them.'

'You *lost* them? Now how did you lose your pants, tell me?'

'Well...'

'What have you been up to? No, don't tell me. We'd better get you fixed.'

He sprang up from the bed and began rummaging around in the bottom of the cupboard. He found what he was looking for and held them up to me; from that vantage point he had a clear view up inside my shirt. He whistled.

'Look at you, Paul! As hairy as a donkey! And hung like one as well, by the look of it.'

'Hung?' I had no idea what he was talking about.

'Your thing! God, you're a babe in arms. What about your chest? Are you hairy there as well as on your arse? Lift your arms above your head.'

I did as he asked, and he pulled the shirt off me, leaving me naked apart from my socks. Kieran ran a hand over the hairs that were beginning to grow in the groove between the two mounds of my chest. 'Ah, you're a dark, furry little bugger, aren't you? Italian?'

'French,' I replied, hoping that Kieran would not be disturbed by the fact that my cock, although so recently drained, was stirring to life again.

'Not like me, though. Irish. Skin like fresh milk, see.' To prove his point, Kieran unwound the scarf from his neck and began to unbutton his shirt. The skin of his chest was indeed as pale as he said, and I could just make out one rose-pink nipple inside his shirt. I had an unconquerable desire to tease it between finger and thumb.

'Take your shirt off, then, let's see what you look like,' I said, surprised at the hoarseness of my own voice. Kieran obliged in a second. Apart from his forearms, which were freckled and golden like his face, the whole of his torso was as pale as could be. A little patch of golden hair, lighter than the hair on his head, fuzzed his stomach; there was a faint dusting of gold across his chest and under his arms. Apart from that, all was white – all but those two pointed pink nipples, fleshy little bumps that stood out ever more provocatively. I could not control myself: I had to touch them. I reached out and caught Kieran's left tit, pinched it gently; it was the sort of gesture that could have been nothing more than horseplay. Goosebumps broke out all across his torso.

'Aah, that's a nice feeling,' said Kieran, buckling slightly at the knees. 'That's something that Holly likes to do.'

'What? Mr Holly? What do you mean?'

'Oh, he's very keen on these,' he said, pinching both his nipples. 'Likes to play with them and suck them.'

I must have looked like a cretin.

'God, Paul, you don't think he employs us just out of the kindness of his heart, do you? He likes a bit of fun. It's all right. I don't mind. I like it too.'

'What does he do with you?' My cock was sticking straight out in front of me.

'Oh, nothing much,' said Kieran, trying hard to sound matter-of-fact, although he cast a nervous glance at my penis. 'You know, he likes a taste of this.' He grabbed his now very swollen basket. I moved a little closer to him; the tip of my cock, with the foreskin half pulled back, made contact with the back of his hand. He flinched slightly, but let it rest there for a moment, looking down at it with a strange fascination. He licked his lips, then cleared his throat and took a step backwards. A string of sticky juice swung for a moment between my cock and his hand, then disappeared.

'How would you like a taste, French boy?'

We stood for a moment, face to face. I suppose I should have played the man, and insisted that it was Kieran who should get down on his knees and take care of me; I'm sure, with the benefit of hindsight, that if I'd stood my ground at that moment things might have turned out very differently for both of us. But I was too eager to get a look at what was inside his pants. So instead I nodded, fell to my knees and buried my face in the warm wool of his trousers. He smelled of soap and sweat, and very faintly of piss. It was like a drug. I gave my cock a quick pump; if I hadn't so recently spewed my load in that sordid Waterloo shower room I swear I would have come straightaway.

Kieran unbuckled his belt and hastily dropped his trousers. Where my cock was long and dark, Kieran's was pale, the blue veins quite visible along the shaft, with a shiny head the same pink as his nipples.

His balls, fuzzy with that same light golden hair, were drawn up tight; I remembered what he'd said about his frustrating experiences of the morning, and suspected that it wouldn't take long to make him come.

'Go on, then, Paul. Help yourself.' Still he spoke with the same light, bantering tones of the morning, but when I looked up I saw a furrowing of his brow that belied this bland performance.

I needed no second bidding. I had never tasted cock before, and after all my experiences of the morning I was eager to take the passive role. While I kissed and licked his thick prick, my hands played with his round white buttocks. I was astonished by their firmness. 'Come on, suck it,' urged Kieran, whose breathing told me that he would soon be shooting. I opened my mouth and let him in, while at the rear I kneaded his bum and pulled the cheeks apart.

At first I could barely contain his prick in my mouth without gagging, but I was a quick study. I relaxed, inhaled deeply and started to suck him properly. As I suspected, my efforts were quickly rewarded. Kieran grasped my head, bent forward and pumped himself into my throat. We remained like that for perhaps a minute, Kieran resting his head against my back, I nursing his softening prick in my mouth, savouring the taste of his spunk. His breathing gradually returned to normal and he stood up, pulled his cock out of my reluctant mouth with a loud plop, and stuffed himself back into his trousers.

'Right, then, we'd better get on with the job,' he said, for all the world as if nothing had happened between us. I was still kneeling stark-naked on the floor, sitting back on my heels with my very hard prick waving in the air. 'What about me?' I asked, hoping that he would return the compliment at least. And I had other thoughts in my head, connected with those two half-moons of his backside and the tight little hole that my finger had found when he came.

'For God's sake, Paul, take care of yourself and come on.'

Disappointed as I was, I still needed to come, and no amount of indifference on Kieran's part was going to make my erection subside.

And so, kneeling on the rug in that cramped bedroom, I took myself in hand. At first, Kieran busied himself with something on the chest of drawers, turning his back to me. But soon I saw him sneaking a look at me in the mirror, or glancing over his shoulder, and finally standing with his back to the furniture, his elbows propped behind him, frankly watching the show. He tried to look scornful, amused, ironic, but there an excited interest that he could not entirely mask. Or was this just my lust-crazed imagination?

Whatever was going on in Kieran's head, I was consumed by the novelty of performing for an audience of one. I used every masturbatory technique that I had learned in five years' solitary practice. I gripped my shaft in both hands and wanked it that way. I held it from above, encircling the head with my fingers just below the ridge and pulled the skin up and down. I tugged on my balls. I spat in my hand and coated my prick with the saliva, which mixed with the fluid oozing from my pisshole to make the whole thing shine. With one hand I reached round behind myself and played with my arsehole; this was always the thing that sent me over the edge. I thought of Kieran's little hole that he'd allowed me to touch at the point of no return. That was enough: jet after jet of sperm flew from my cock and splattered on the rug.

A short silence was broken by Kieran's slow, ironic handclap. 'Bravo, monsieur!' he said. 'Now put the fucking thing away and let's go.'

Ashamed and somewhat angry with my friend, I stood up, wiped my prick on the bedcover and began to dress. But I noticed, to my immense satisfaction, that Kieran was hard once more inside his woollen trousers. I'll get him yet, I thought. I'll get him.

And so began my life at the South London Palace of Varieties. The days were spent in hard physical labour, hauling scenery in and out of the docks, clambering around scaffolds, sweeping the stage, clearing up the debris of orange rinds, nutshells, fag ends and discarded playbills in the auditorium, running errands for Mr Holly and the 'turns'. The nights were spent in uncomfortable frustration lying next to Kieran's sleeping form, basking in the heat from his compact, muscular body, wondering why he refused ever to renew the intimacies of that first day. I was not without relief: as Kieran had predicted, Mr Holly was soon enjoying regular draughts from my cock, and proved himself to be an adept at the art. Often he would stop me backstage, look hastily around to see that he was not observed by Mrs Holly (he didn't care if the other hands saw him at it: they were in the same boat, after all), pull my prick out of my trousers and, with a few expert caresses with hands, lips and tongue, have me erect within seconds and squirting a big load down his throat minutes later. There was never any question of reciprocation, nor could I see that Mr Holly ever took care of himself during these encounters; I presume he went around all day in a state of permanent excitement, guzzling down as much cock as his greedy mouth could swallow, then spending himself on Mrs Holly at night. I didn't begrudge her, and I certainly didn't mind Mr Holly's ministrations – but I was beginning to feel a little like a milk cow, and craved a more mutual arrangement. Holly was not particularly attractive – he was somewhat portly, and a little overdressed for my taste – but often enough, in the heat of lust, I wished to wrestle him to the floor and take him as he was taking me.

And at the back of my mind all the time was Kieran. I watched him every morning as he strip-washed in the bedroom, splashing cold water over himself, winking if he caught me staring at his half-erect prick. 'Look at me,' he'd say, 'I always wake up in this state.' Sometimes I suggested that he come back to the warmth of our shared bed and let me take care of him, but no – he preferred his tryst with Rose, the bar-room beauty, leaving me with nothing to hope for but the reliable attention of Mr Holly. He was the only one who was getting what he wanted from the situation. There was Kieran, randy but frustrated by his chaste courtship of Rose; there was me, desperate to renew my affair with Kieran, with a permanent hard-on in my pants; and there was Holly, milking both of us whenever he pleased, confident that our personal disappointments meant that we always had balls full of cream for him. I make no complaint: he was a generous cocksucker, and often, after he'd wiped the come from his glossy, damp moustache, he'd reach into his waistcoat pocket for a coin 'in token of my gratitude, dear boy'. But he was not what I wanted.

No: what I wanted, all I could think about, was Kieran. Sometimes in the night I would pull back the covers and look at him by the dim light filtering through our thin curtains. Sometimes, if I was very bold, I would touch him. I don't suppose now that he was unaware of this, but at the time he pretended to sleep and I persuaded myself that my actions were undiscovered. Once or twice I took hold of his prick; sometimes, if he was lying on his stomach, I let myself gaze at his arse, and even ran a hand over his buttocks. On one occasion Kieran grunted softly at the touch of my hand, shifted himself so that one leg was crooked and his hole exposed to view. I cursed the lack of light in the room, and would have fumbled for a candle had I not been certain that the noise of a striking match would have woken him. (I am convinced now that Kieran was awake all along, and might have permitted me further intimacies if only I had been bold enough to take them.) This time, however, all I dared to do was press a fingertip gingerly against his hole, feeling it tighten as I made contact, then relax again. My cock, which was at full stiffness, wanted to plough straight in.

Mr Holly got a particularly copious mouthful the next morning, and rewarded me more generously than usual. As he was sucking me, I guided his hand round to my rear and let him know in no uncertain terms that I wanted a finger inside me, which he was delighted to insert. The expression of surprise on his face, as he looked up at me with my cock halfway into his mouth, almost made me laugh out loud; the next moment I was shuddering with delight as his finger entered me and made me come.

I don't know where I got this idea that the arse was a centre of pleasure. During my solitary teenage experiments I had discovered that a little pressure on that part could lead to increased excitement; now, however, I was consumed with the idea of fucking and being fucked. I don't know which I wanted more. I longed desperately to get inside Kieran's succulent arse, to push my cock into him and make him take it. I fantasised constantly about the two men in the showers at Waterloo, and wondered whether, had I permitted it, one or both of them might have stuck their handsome pricks up my backside. I remembered the sensation I had felt when the older, darker of the two held me from behind, wrapping his arms around me, pressing his hairy stomach against my back – and the feeling of his hard prick pressing against my arsehole. If only I had wriggled backwards, I might have had him inside me.

But I had to content myself with Mr Holly's finger (or fingers, as he became bolder) and occasional glimpses of Kieran's bum. He was teasing me, I swear. He would bend over in front of me when he was undressing. He would hang around the room naked – but if ever I made my excitement obvious he'd laugh, cuff me around the side of the head and get dressed. Needless to say, after a few weeks of this I was totally, horribly in love with him.

But there were other distractions at the Palace of Varieties besides the work, Mr Holly's mouth and fingers and Kieran's teasing. I soon discovered that there was a good deal of extracurricular work that could allow an enterprising young man to increase his income without too much trouble. For this welcome news I had to thank our genial, effeminate dresser, an elderly queen known to all and sundry as 'Vera', who sat in the wings in between acts in a canvas chair working industriously at his 'tatting', stitching sweet little handkerchiefs or collars that he gave as gifts to his favourites. I soon numbered myself among this happy band. Vera beckoned me over one night soon after I had arrived at the Palace and confided, in his astonishing drawl, 'I have quite fallen in love with you, young man.

Come and sit on my knee.' I did as I was bidden, expecting at every moment to feel his hands in my crotch, but instead he gave me a friendly hug and slipped a peppermint cream into my mouth. 'Run along, now, you must have work to do!' he said, brushing me off as if I were a cat. Thereafter, though, he always had a kind word and a sweetmeat of some description to brighten up the slog of backstage life.

During a matinée I must have been looking particularly glum – perhaps Kieran had allowed a little more heartbreaking familiarity with his still-inviolate arse – so Vera called me over and gestured with one heavily beringed hand. 'Sit at my feet, child, and imbibe the wisdom of the ancients.' There wasn't much for me to do: it was a quiet house, and Holly had put together a decidedly second-rate programme of jugglers, acrobats and comedy singers that made few demands on stage management. I did as I was bidden, and rested my head on Vera's knee. His hand smoothing my hair was strangely comforting; I realised for the first time how much I missed my mother and sister.

'What ails you, Paul?'

'I'm homesick.'

'And lovesick, too, I suspect.'

'Yes.' Well, it was true, there was no point in denying it.

'I shan't ask the name.' He didn't say 'her' name or 'his' name. 'Just promise me that you won't pine yourself away.'

'What else can I do?'

'Make something of yourself. A handsome young man like you – no, don't trouble to deny it, you've got a lovely mug and a trim little body, as well you know. You should be bettering yourself instead of wasting your most precious commodity on greedy old Holly.' Vera must have seen scores of young men with their pricks down Holly's throat.

'But how can I make anything of myself? I'm not educated.' I silently cursed my father for wasting money on drink that should have been spent on my schooling. 'I've no experience of work apart from this. I've no money – Holly pays for my board and lodging in return for my work backstage.'

Vera rolled his eyes. 'Paul, tell me something. How much does he pay you for that?' He nudged my groin with his slipper.

'Sometimes he gives me a couple of bob.'

'A couple of bob.'

'Yes.'

'Honestly, I despair of the younger generation,' he said, digging his needle into his tatting with unusual vigour. 'A couple of bob! For heaven's sake. And I suppose you say thank you very much and slip it into your pocket and think yourself lucky, do you?'

'I do.' I was indeed grateful to Mr Holly, who thus provided me with the only spending money I ever had.

Vera stood up. 'Come with me, child. Over here.' He took me by the arm and led me to the very edge of the stage, where, by dint of peering through a gap in the wings, we could observe the audience.

'Look, boy. What do you see?'

'A half-empty theatre.'

'Yes. A half-empty theatre. But you're not looking at things the right way. Tell me who is there.'

I peered more intently into the gloom. 'A few old ladies. Some kids, who ought to be in school. A couple of toffs.'

'That's better. A couple of toffs. Describe them to me, dear.'

'All right. Well, up there in the dress circle there's two chaps, both well dressed, middle-aged, I'd say, perhaps forty-five, wearing ties and tie pins, well-cut hair.'

'Anyone else?'

'And up there in one of the boxes there's a gentleman on his own, looks like he might be Jewish, perhaps about thirty, dark, prosperous, quite handsome.'

'Very good. Now, Paul,' said Vera, leading me back to his chair, where he picked up his tatting and I resumed my position at his knee, 'what do you imagine that prosperous gentlemen like that are doing in a music hall at three thirty on a Wednesday afternoon?'

'Watching the show.'

'Watching the show, yes. But don't you imagine they have anything better to do? Places to go? Their clubs, for instance, must be missing them, or their offices. If they've time on their hands, why not spend it at home with their wives? Why come here?'

'I suppose they... like the turns?'

'Warmer, Paul, warmer.' Vera leaned forward and rubbed his hands together. 'Some of the turns in particular are very popular with the gentlemen. Now, your prosperous Jewish gentleman, as you so rightly described him, is a great admirer of Miss Jennifer Bright.'

'Of Bright and Light?'

'Yes, indeed, of Bright and Light, acrobats *extraordinaire,* who are currently entertaining us on stage. You've seen their act, haven't you?'

'Many times. I admire them tremendously.'

'You've noticed, then, the extraordinary positions into which the highly flexible Miss Bright manages to manipulate herself.' I had indeed, and marvelled at the fact that she could get both knees behind her ears.

'Well, now, that talent has won her the admiration of a number of gentlemen, among them Mr Rosenblatt, who currently attends her every performance and afterwards treats her to supper, or a ride in his car, or gifts of jewellery, or an afternoon in an hotel.'

Light was beginning to dawn. 'Ah. I see.'

'Ye-e-e-e-es. In an hotel. Where her extraordinary flexibility is no doubt demonstrated without the benefit of clothing.'

'No doubt.'

'Now, take Mr Larry Light, her partner in the act.'

'What about him?' I had noticed Larry Light several times: he was a graceful, willowy blond young chap with cherry lips and blue eyes, and a shapely pair of legs that he showed to great advantage in his spangled flesh-coloured tights. More than once I had seen him looking at me from beneath his floppy fringe.

'He, too, has his admirers.'

'The two gentlemen in the dress circle?'

'Bright boy! The two gentlemen in the dress circle.' Vera was scrutinising my face for any sign of disgust – although really, as he'd seen me in congress with Mr Holly, he should have known that the idea was hardly repellent to me.

'And what, I wonder, do they get up to?' I could feel a stirring in my pants: the thought of slim, blond Larry Light at the mercy of those two handsome older gentlemen was quite interesting.

'Ah, well, that's not for me to say. Larry did tell me,' said Vera, leaning towards my ear, 'that he could be very accommodating, if you get my drift.' I thought I did. 'And if you look at that arse of his it's not hard to believe.'

I crept over to the wings again to watch Bright and Light's act through new eyes. Larry was, at that moment, holding Jessica aloft as she arched backwards and did the splits in midair; his strong, slim legs and curvaceous buttocks were trembling with the effort. Could it be that he, Larry Light, allowed gentlemen to fuck him? That behind the thin stuff of his tights was a hole that had been regularly abused by one, perhaps two pricks at a time? That he actually enjoyed it, and benefited from it? I put a hand in my pocket to push down the erection that had sprung up, and returned to Vera's chair.

'Now you see.'

'I do. But what's all this got to do with me?'

'Oh, do try to keep up, dear,' said Vera, sounding unusually pettish. 'What I'm trying to tell you is that the theatre is full of opportunities. Now, some of them like the girls, hence the success of Miss Jennifer Bright and her surprising collection of gems. Some of them like the boys. You may have noticed that Larry Light is always very nicely dressed, and comes to the theatre in a car that I can assure you he didn't buy out of the money that he earns on the music hall stages of our great capital. And some of them, my dear (and pay attention at this point) like young men like yourself. Now, look at Larry. He's blond, he's pretty, he's a bit girlie, which suits some of them down to the ground because they get a nice bit of pussy as well as something to hold on to round the front. But you're different: you may be young, Paul, but you look like a man. And there are plenty of gentlemen, believe you me, to whom a young chap like you is just the ticket.'

'And you mean that they'd be... generous?'

'Very generous indeed, I should think, from where I'm sitting.' Vera was looking down into my crotch, where my still-hard cock was clearly outlined. 'They'd probably pay by the yard, dear.'

'And how do I... find these kind gentlemen?'

'For heaven's sake, do I have to hold your hand every step of the way?' asked Vera, sounding, for a moment, incredibly weary. 'The stage door, dear. Where else?'

Three

I embark on the oldest profession... The other side of the river... Supper at the Albany... My oral technique improves... I take it up the arse... Lover or whore?

I would never have used the term 'prostitution' to describe the career that I was embarking on – to me a prostitute was one of the colourful creatures I saw plying their trade outside the theatre – but I suppose that is just what I became. I told myself that I was simply enjoying the generosity of a string of friends and admirers; in fact, it was a straightforward money-for-sex transaction that enrolled me in the lists of the oldest profession.

After the scales had been removed from my eyes during that quiet weekday matinée, I was eager to take advantage of any opportunity. The following day, when Mr Holly tried, as usual, to suck me off ('Time for my elevenses, dear boy') I declined, telling him that I had an engagement in the evening that I was unwilling to imperil. 'Ah,' he said, with only mild disappointment, 'a girlfriend, I suppose. Well, good luck to you, my boy.' He did not suffer for long: a few minutes later I saw Harry, the burly, tattooed delivery driver leaning against a pillar with his eyes closed and his head thrown back, pumping his 'elevenses' down Holly's throat.

During the afternoon performance I kept running to the wings to scan the audience for opportunities, encouraged by Vera, who, in between dressing the turns, nodded and winked and cast exaggeratedly lascivious stares at the front of my trousers. But trust my luck: today there was nobody in the house but faithful Mr Rosenblatt and a few dowdy-looking families. Larry Light's two swains were nowhere to be seen (and I noticed Larry wincing during some of the more energetic parts of his act; perhaps his arsehole had been unusually accommodating last night). I hoped to spot some attractive, well-heeled gentleman to whom I could offer myself, but there was none such to be seen.

I moped around the theatre between the matinée and the evening performance, convinced that I was a failure. 'Chin up,' said Vera, 'the real quality don't come to the afternoon shows. You wait till this evening, love, find yourself something with a bit of handbag.' And so I busied myself with my duties, lent a sympathetic ear to Kieran's complaints about Rose, briefly considered hauling him back to our bedroom and forcing my cock up his backside, but decided instead to concentrate on the more rewarding prospects ahead of me. And it was as well that I did.

The evening brought the crowds, and by half past seven the theatre was packed. People milled around in the foyer and aisles; others scanned the audience for friends; some even concentrated on the show. They had all come to see Terri Marlo, currently fulfilling an exclusive engagement at the South London Palace of Varieties; Mr Holly was doing very well out of this popular (if ageing) female impersonator, who regaled the house with a selection of sentimental songs in a shaky tenor and a string of daringly risqué anecdotes in between. When Miss Marlo came on for her first spot of the night, everyone took their seat. I peered out from the wings into a sea of faces; someone out there, I felt sure, wanted what I had to offer. If only I could get out on the stage and advertise myself in the way that Bright and Light did. For the first time in my life I felt a desire to perform – but not for the reasons that, I understand, inspire most would-be theatricals. This was a far more businesslike ambition.

Well, I would have to trust my 'lovely mug' to do the persuading for me. When the show was over, and the crowds were pouring out of the front of house, I raced through my chores and slipped down the passage past the dressing rooms to the stage door. There was Terri Marlo on the arm of her manager, a dark, handsome gentleman by the name of Albert Abbott – the only person I had ever seen get the better of Mr Holly in a financial discussion. Admirers surrounded her, mostly women, who touched the rich beading of her dress with stunned admiration and stole occasional sidelong glances at the brooding Alfred, who, I'm sure, set feminine hearts aflutter. If only, I thought, he were the sort of man I might find waiting out there for me. There was Larry Light, chatting amicably with a couple of young men in wide-lapelled double-breasted raincoats and soft felt hats, who smoked cigarettes like Gloria Swanson and seemed to be wearing lipstick. I pushed past them; Larry whispered 'good night' and let his hand brush against my thigh. Well, if I wanted his arse, it was there for the taking. I made a mental note, returned his greeting and squeezed past his too-familiar hands.

Outside the stage door, waiting within the circle of lamplight as a fine drizzle fell on the cobbles, there were six, perhaps seven, men, all of them, I fancied, alone. I walked out, stood directly beneath the lamp where they could see me to best advantage, and took the cigarette that I'd stashed behind my ear. Young as I was, I recognised the usefulness of cigarettes in the sport of courtship. I placed it in my mouth, hooked my thumbs into my belt and waited, pulling the waistband of my trousers down far enough to reveal an inch or two of my hairy lower stomach. Most of the gentlemen were indifferent to my presence, watching the door behind me like hawks; they, I presumed, were waiting for the young ladies. Two, however, reached into their jackets for lighters. It was a race as to who could put a flame to me first. One of them – I noticed with regret that he was a handsome if weak-looking man – struggled vainly to produce a spark. The other, a big, open-faced man in a smart suit that showed off his heavy body to advantage, clicked an expensive little gold contraption into instant life, and walked towards me, cupping his hand around the flame.

'May I?' He put the lighter up to my cigarette; I lifted my face, drew on the flame and exhaled a cloud of smoke through my nostrils. For someone who had never tasted tobacco before he left home, I now smoked like a movie star. I had learned much in my weeks at the Palace of Varieties.

'Thanks.'

'You're new here, aren't you?' He was well spoken. I judged from his appearance that he was, perhaps, forty-five. He reminded me of one of my teachers: healthy-looking, well fed, not handsome but pleasant-looking with humorous blue eyes, a big nose and a full mouth that was quick to smile. He had a buttonhole, an umbrella and a suitcase; I imagined that he had come straight to the theatre from his place of his business. On his large, square hand I saw a wedding ring.

'Yes. I work backstage.'

'Hmm. I thought as much. You look... fit.'

'Yes.' There didn't seem to be much else to say. The other gentleman was still watching like a hawk, hopeful, I suppose, that I would reject the bolder suitor and go with him. My new friend, however, was taking no chances.

'Shall we walk? There's an excellent chop house in Bermondsey, if you are hungry.'

I was hungry, but I was in no mood to waste time in a restaurant, however excellent. I grunted and looked over his shoulder.

'Alternatively, of course, we could take a cab directly to my rooms in town, where I'm sure the cook will be able to rustle up something for you.'

This was more like it. A cab, a room in town, a cook – proof that this was a man of means. I smiled, took the proffered arm and walked, casting a look of friendly regret at the thwarted rival – enough, I hoped, to make him try his luck again another night.

It took us no time at all to find a cab. Mr Newsome (as he introduced himself) looked rich and respectable – just the sort of fare that the cabbies were happy to have. He said only one word to the driver – 'Albany!' – and we were away towards Westminster Bridge.

As soon as we were on the move, Mr Newsome turned towards me and laid his left hand on my thigh. 'What a very handsome chap you are. May one ask your name?'

'Certainly. Paul Lemoyne.'

'Not from round here, I think.'

'No, sir. From Sussex.'

'Yes. A cut above the local lads. Most definitely.' He squeezed my thigh; his wedding ring glinted in the light of a street lamp. 'And I hope that we have an understanding, Paul.'

'I think so.' I was struggling to keep my voice under control, not to betray my excitement. My cock, however, I could not so easily master: it was growing inside my trousers, snaking its way down towards Mr Newsome's hand. Any minute now he was going to get a delightful surprise.

'Maybe you're wondering, Paul, why a man like me should wish to go with young men like you. I am, after all, a married man, well off, happy and comfortable in my life.' I had no doubts in my mind why he had picked me up: he wanted my cock, possibly my arse, and he was welcome to both of them – for a price.

'You see, in a man's life there are many crossroads, many different directions, some of them leading to happiness, some of them perhaps taking a more roundabout route.' We were, by now, on Westminster Bridge. Mr Newsome prattled away; I wondered whether he delivered the same speech of justification to all his trade. 'Take, for instance, this river, this mighty Thames of ours.' The water was visible, glinting darkly, from the cab windows. 'Sometimes we are happy to stay in town, on one side of the river, enjoying the many comforts of our lives there – a successful business, a family home in Ealing, a convenient set of rooms in Albany with a competent housekeeper. But sometimes' – and here he increased the pressure on my thigh – 'one has a yen to cross the river, to plunge deep into the uncharted territories, to take one's chance and see what one may find there—Oh, my goodness!'

My cock had, at that moment, reached almost its full extent and nudged Mr Newsome's hand most insistently. Quick as a rabbit, he ran his fingers up its length and whistled in surprise.

'My God, Paul, that's a big piece. Have you ever seen a bigger?'

'No, I don't think so.'

'Possess yourself in patience, then, my boy, for tonight, maybe, you will.'

'Oh yes?'

'You don't believe me?'

'I await proof.'

Mr Newsome's eyes twinkled. He looked towards the driver, who was watching this little drama unfold in the rear-view mirror. Mr Newsome picked up his briefcase and placed it upright on his knees, thus forming a screen between himself and the driver's line of vision.

'Take a look at this, Paul.'

Shifting awkwardly in his seat, he unbuttoned his fly, delved inside and, with some difficulty, brought into the air the biggest prick I could imagine. It must have been a good inch longer than mine, but it was the girth rather than the length that astonished me. It looked like a rolling pin. 'And that's not even fully hard,' he said, with an understandable note of pride. 'My wife, alas, finds it impossible to accommodate. I hope that you will be more successful. Boys generally are.'

So this was it: I was finally to get fucked. And not only fucked, but fucked by what I imagined was the biggest chopper in London. My heart beat hard in my chest, whether from fear or excitement I was not sure. I reached out gingerly and clasped it; my fingers barely met around the thickest part.

'You like it?' said Mr Newsome, evidently delighted.

'Very much, sir,' I whispered, noting the increased stiffness that rewarded my touch.

'We shall have a splendid evening, I think.' By now we were rattling up Haymarket, and Mr Newsome slipped himself back inside his trousers.

The cab let us out on Piccadilly; while Mr Newsome paid the driver I could feel my knees shaking underneath me. Nervous as I was, I would not have run away for the world. I would happily have refused all payment. I was only impatient to get my hands back on that huge, fat cock and to give myself up entirely to Mr Newsome's lust.

That, however, was to be delayed. I followed Mr Newsome into the Albany's entrance hall – where the doorman tipped his cap respectfully – across an exterior courtyard and into an echoing stairwell. My heart was beating so hard, and so much blood had flowed into my painfully stiff cock that I thought I was going to pass out. On the first landing, I stopped to catch my breath.

'Something the matter, lad?' said Mr Newsome, scowling slightly. I suppose he thought I had cold feet, and was about to bolt. The truth was that I wanted him so badly I would have happily given my virgin arse right there on the cold stone of the stairwell.

'Nothing, sir.' He liked it when I called him sir. 'Just...' With my left hand I stretched the fabric of my trousers tight across my groin, so that he could be in no doubt about my continued interest.

'Patience, Paul,' he said, with a twinkle in his eye. 'All in good time.'

'I don't know if I can wait.'

He stood before me and grabbed my balls in a none-too-gentle grip. 'New to all this, aren't you, lad?'

'Yes, sir.' I could feel myself blushing. I rested my head against the fine black wool of his coat. I could hear his heart beating hard from within his great barrel chest; for all his sang-froid, I believe he was as excited as I was.

'You must learn to relax and control this' – he gave my cock a mighty squeeze – 'if you are to be successful in your new profession. You give too much away, Paul. A less generous, er, sponsor might be tempted to take advantage.'

That was all I wanted him to do, but, starved of oxygen as my brain was (I never seem to do my best thinking when my prick is hard), I still saw the wisdom of his words. Well, there was nothing for it: my excitement would not subside, but the waiting would make the release all the sweeter.

I took a few deep breaths to clear my head, and tried to assume the persona of the experienced man of business. Mr Newsome's apartment provided me with some diversion: it was certainly the most comfortable, handsomely furnished set of rooms I had ever been into. There was nothing ostentatious about the arrangements, nothing that screamed of money – but, for all that, it was clear that the inhabitant was a man of wealth and taste. There wasn't much furniture, but what there was – a leather settee with an Indian shawl thrown across it, a matching leather armchair, some good walnut tables and bookcases – matched the room perfectly. Through an open door I could make out a modest divan.

Mr Newsome gestured to me to sit down, and prepared us both a Scotch and soda. I sprawled on the sofa, hoping that the sight would provoke my companion into leaping straight onto me, but I was set to rights by a quiet 'tut' from Mr N and the sudden appearance in the room of an unexpected third party. For a moment it flashed across my mind that I had been lured here to be the meat in some kind of sandwich – a thought that, since my amorous initiation in the toilets of Waterloo Station, only increased my excitement. The other, however, was a servant rather than a player, an elderly man, perhaps sixty, every inch the discreet English valet. I saw his eyes flicker over me for one second before he addressed himself to Mr Newsome.

'Good evening, sir.'

'Good evening, Bishop. We have company this evening.'

'So I see. Good evening, sir.'

'G-good evening.'

'Will you require supper, sir?'

'Yes please, Bishop. Mr Lemoyne has not eaten.'

'Would a chop and some vegetables suffice, sir? And perhaps a piece of apple tart?'

My mouth was watering, not, this time, because I anticipated a taste of Mr Newsome's hard cock.

'Thank you.'

'Will that be all, sir?'

'A sandwich will be enough for me, thank you, Bishop. And you might bring a bottle of champagne.'

'Yes, sir.'

Bishop glided out of the room again; his presence, although friendly, had caused my excitement to abate completely. It was as well: I had a chance to remind myself that I was here for profit as well as pleasure. My host made polite conversation, asking about my job at the theatre, my family background, telling me a little about his work in the city and his home life. We might, to all appearances, have been two distant relatives conversing at a dinner party – except that, every so often, Mr Newsome rearranged his groin as if to remind me of what was in store for me after dessert and coffee.

After twenty minutes, Bishop was back with a trolley from which emanated the most wonderful savoury odours. I have nothing to say against Mrs Tunnock's Irish stew, but this certainly made a change. I wolfed down the chop in six large chunks, while Mr Newsome watched with a smile on his face, chewing through his sandwich in the time it took me to demolish the entire meal, apple tart and all.

'Better?'

'Much better, thank you, sir. Please excuse my manners.'

'They're not feeding you enough at the theatre.'

'I don't complain.'

'Are you full, Paul?'

'Yes, thank you.'

'Sure you haven't got room for something else?'

I may have been a beginner, but I could see which way the wind was blowing.

'Maybe. What's on the menu?'

Mr Newsome smiled and stood beside my chair. The bulge at the front of this trousers had resumed the prodigious proportions of earlier.

'How about a nice fat portion of cock?'

'Mm, yes please.'

Mr Newsome winked, picked up my plate (empty now save for a puddle of gravy) and held it in front of his trousers. He unbuttoned his fly, and drew himself out. His cock rested on the plate, sitting in the gravy, reaching almost from edge to edge.

'Dig in.'

The sight of this ridiculous 'meal' made me laugh out loud – which, I'm happy to say, delighted Mr Newsome. I stroked the top of his prick, tracing the thick blue vein that ran its length and then divided over his foreskin, which was now stretched tight across his bulging knob. The helmet was just peeping out of the end. With the flat of my palm, I rolled his cock gently from side to side of the plate, getting it as messy with the gravy as I could manage.

When it was completely slick, Mr Newsome put the plate down and stood with his hands on his hips, his huge weapon throbbing before him.

'Go on, then, Paul. Show me what you can do.'

I leaned forward in my chair and took the end of his prick between my lips; it tasted of meat and salt and gravy. With one hand I clutched his balls, which weighed heavy and full, while with the other I gripped the base of the shaft to hold it still. I started to lick along the underside and then all around its circumference until it was completely clean. By now Mr Newsome was completely hard, his foreskin pulled right back over his fat knob.

Excited as I was, I was somewhat concerned by the task ahead of me. I could barely get my hands round it, so how on earth was I going to get that huge prick into my mouth – or my arse? I experienced a moment of trepidation – but, being the thrill-seeking little slut that I was, it was soon replaced by mindless, drooling lust.

'Come on, Paul,' said Mr Newsome, 'you can do better than just licking it.'

I could, too. I opened my mouth and took as much as I could in one go. It felt wonderful: hot, smooth and hard. But, as it hit the back of my throat, I gagged and my mouth filled with saliva. I pulled back and swallowed.

'Try again, lad. Slower.'

This time I took it an inch at a time, allowing my lips to stretch around it – at the thickest point, just behind the head, I felt that my mouth would split at the sides. I allowed myself to breathe deeply and slid all the way down to the base. Soon I had my nose buried in Mr Newsome's bush.

'That's what I like to see,' he said. 'A young man with my prick down his throat. Now let's see what you can do with it.'

Fortunately for me, and of course for Mr Newsome, I had learned a good deal about the art of oral sex during those frequent 'coffee breaks' at the Palace of Varieties, when Mr Holly demonstrated a technique perfected over years of practice. And so, imagining that the prick in my mouth was my own, I did all the things that I knew would give pleasure. At first I drew my lips back to the head, licked the pisshole and then slid down to the base again. I repeated the movement a little faster, then faster still, until I had established a good sucking rhythm. This seemed to delight my companion, who cupped his hands round the back of my head and addressed me by all sorts of soft endearments.

I knew, however, that too much of this treatment would make him come too quickly, and so I withdrew my mouth and caught my breath. Mr Newsome grabbed me by the jaw and rewarded me for my efforts by smearing his spit-slicked cock all over my face, then leaning down and kissing me deeply. For a moment I felt that I was in love with this man, that we could perhaps live together, that he would keep me and educate me; at the same moment, I also considered the fact that my show-stopping performance was bound to earn me a good sum at the end of the evening.

Next I paid some attention to Mr Newsome's balls, a handsome pair that it would have been shameful to neglect. I ran my tongue in circular motions round and round his scrotum, then took each egg in my mouth and sucked it like a gobstopper. This was a Holly special, and one that always kindled a terrible lust in my loins; it seemed to be having the same effect on my client. As a finale to this act I took a deep breath, opened wide and managed to take both balls in my mouth at once, moving them around with my tongue so that they churned and tightened in their sac. I felt Mr Newsome go weak at the knees and groan.

'Are you ready now, boy? Are you ready to be fucked?'

In truth I had thought of little else, and had occasionally slipped a hand down the back of my trousers to pacify my twitching arsehole. I thought, however, that a slight show of resistance might inflame his ardour yet further.

'I don't know, sir. It's so... big.'

'You can take it.'

'But... I've never been fucked before.'

'Really?'

'Honestly, sir. The only thing I've ever had up there is a finger or two.'

'Indeed!' Mr Newsome was red in the face and sweating slightly. As I had intended, the thought of my fingering my virgin arsehole was acting on him like a drug.

'Yes, sir, I swear.' I stood, and swiftly pulled the shirt over my head. 'I want you to fuck me, sir, I really do.' I unfastened the top of my trousers and let them drop round my ankles. 'But I just don't know if my arse is ready for it.' I kicked off my trousers and stood before him in nothing but my underwear.

'I see. Well, we'll just have to break you in gently, then.'

'Yes, sir.'

'Lie down on the couch.' I did as I was told, and watched with mounting pleasure as Mr Newsome stripped off his clothes. He was a heavily built man, strong in limbs and chest, well proportioned. His cock stood up with all the vigour of a sixteen-year-old's.

He stood at the foot of the couch. 'Show me, Paul. Show me how you finger yourself.'

Without further ado, I wriggled out of my pants (noticing with gratification that Mr Newsome's eyebrows shot up when he saw my cock) and raised my legs in the air. I stuck a finger in my mouth, wetting the tip, and allowed it to play round the lips of my arse.

'Not like that, boy, I can't see. Turn over.'

Quick to obey, I flipped myself onto all fours, thrusting my bum towards him and spreading my cheeks as wide as I could.

'That's better. God, what a pretty little hole.'

I let my wet finger hover around the edge, and then gingerly stuck it in up to the first knuckle.

'How does that feel, Paul?'

'It feels good, sir.'

'Can you go any further?'

I slipped the finger in up to the second knuckle, then the third.

'How's that?'

'It's nice... sir...' With my other hand I pushed my cock back between my thighs to show him how excited I was.

'Can you get another finger into yourself?'

'I'll try.' I added another finger. 'Am I doing it right, sir?'

'Here, let me.' Mr Newsome sat down beside me on the couch; the heat from his body was like a well-banked fire. He smacked me lightly on each buttock, then pressed against my tight hole with a finger. I tightened up, determined not to make this too easy for him.

'Come on, Paul. Let me in. That's it.' I relaxed, and his finger slid into me. It was thicker than mine, and there was a short blast of pain. My arse clamped around his knuckle and I took a sharp breath.

'Oh, sir!'

'Gently does it.' He saw me wanking myself, and judged that it was safe to proceed. Another finger joined the first; now I really was having trouble accommodating him. But any discomfort was soon replaced by a pleasurable feeling of fullness, and when he started to move his fingers inside me I felt I was going to come instantly. A great dollop of juice spurted from the end of my prick onto the leather of the sofa.

'How do you feel, Paul?'

'I think I'm ready for you to fuck me.'

'Good boy. I'll take it slowly, I promise you. But I must have you now. I must.'

In answer, all I could do was moan. For all that I was trying to put on a good performance, my real feelings had overtaken any masquerade.

Mr Newsome took a dollop of cream from the bowl that had earlier dressed my apple tart, and applied it liberally to my rear end and his cock. Then came the bit that I was dreading: the first breach of my hole. He pushed and prodded until, despite an involuntary resistance on my part, he was inside me. It hurt – much more than I had expected it to. A sharp line of pain shot right up into my stomach. I looked round with surprise on my face.

'Oh, Jesus!'

'It's all right, Paul. Just relax.'

'No, you'll have to take it out.'

'I can't now, Paul. I have to fuck you. Come on, take a deep breath.'

I did as I was told, and the pain began to subside. Within a minute of holding him immobile inside me, it had stopped altogether. My cock, of course, remained as solid as an iron bar.

'I'm all right now, sir. You can fuck me.'

He needed no second bidding. With another thrust he was right inside me – and this time, instead of pain, I felt overwhelming pleasure. The fullness, the sense of having a deep itch well scratched, the slight tinglings of discomfort – all swamped my senses. Mr Newsome started to move inside me, and soon had picked up a good rhythm. I dared not touch my prick, for I felt that I might come at any second.

Mr Newsome must have felt this as well, for he withdrew from my bum and stood awhile catching his breath. My arse gaped, empty and dissatisfied.

'Turn over. I want to see your face.'

I lay on my back. Mr Newsome knelt on the floor before the couch, picked up my legs and put them over his broad shoulders, and was once again inside me. He fucked me gently in this position for a while, muttering endearments that we both believed at the time, stopping every so often to kiss me, to pinch my tits or to play with my cock. By now I was so excited that I felt I could stand it no longer.

'Please, sir,' I said, 'fuck me hard.'

In answer, he extended his legs behind him, braced himself on his toes and started pumping into me with all his force, crushing his mouth against mine, smearing my torso with sweat from his powerful chest. Somewhere along the way I must have come – I wasn't particularly aware of its starting, but seemed rather to enter into a long orgasm that lasted for maybe a minute. The sound of our two stomachs slipping and squelching as my sperm coated them was ridiculously loud. Finally Mr Newsome bellowed, threw his head back and ploughed into me so far that I could feel him somewhere up in my stomach. His cock seemed for a moment to double in size, and then he spewed his load into me.

We lay for a while with him still inside, panting on each other's shoulder. Then he withdrew, wiped himself on his discarded shirt and stood over me like a mighty conqueror. Where some men are enervated by the act of love, Mr Newsome seemed to be refreshed and fortified.

'Well, young man,' he said, 'I can honestly say that you are the best fuck I've had in many years. Congratulations on the finest arse in this great, wicked city of ours.'

'Thank you, sir.'

'I trust you will see me again?'

How strange, I thought, to be discussing 'our future' in such uncertain terms when only a few moments ago we had been so close – almost, it seemed to me, one person.

'With pleasure, sir.'

'Perhaps you are in a hurry.'

'Do you wish me to leave, sir?'

'No – but you have your work.'

'Yes, sir.' I thought, naturally, that he was throwing me out: it was obviously not appropriate for the young man to stay, or to expect further companionship, once the act was over.

I dressed quickly, pocketed the money that he gave me and prepared to say goodnight.

'Perhaps you will come to the theatre again, Mr Newsome.'

'If you will be glad to see me.'

'I would be most happy to see you, sir.'

'Paul?'

'Sir?' He was eyeing me again with a calculating look. 'Do you consider the amount that passed between us sufficient?'

In truth I had not even counted it. 'Certainly, sir. Generous, indeed.'

'Would you consider...'

'Sir?'

'Staying a little longer?'

It was already well past midnight; he clearly wanted my company for the entire night.

'Perhaps.' In truth I was in no hurry to make my way back to Mrs Tunnock's. The only attraction of the place was Kieran, and that was cold comfort after what I had just experienced.

'I thought maybe you would like to... stop here awhile...'

I see. So, those words of affection were not entirely in vain. He wanted to install me. I faced a moment of choice. To surrender to the romance of the moment – and in truth I felt half in love with Mr

Newsome, whatever the circumstances of our liaison – or to play the hard-hearted whore. My better nature struggled for supremacy, and I looked up at his quizzical, half-smiling face. I could feel myself getting hard again at the prospect of a whole night spent riding that mighty steed. And then I remembered something he had said earlier in the evening: 'You give too much away, Paul. A less generous sponsor might be tempted to take advantage.' Well, out of his own mouth the words had come.

'It'll cost you.'

'Ah. Of course.' He looked half disappointed, half delighted. 'How much?'

'Half as much again.'

'Very well.' He put another sum of money on the table. 'You learn fast, Paul.'

'You teach well, sir.'

'Well, if we are not to be friends, we shall be something else – something just as good. We shall take advantage of each other. I am happy with the situation. Yes. Quite happy.'

And over the next few hours he showed me just how happy he was. Perhaps, had I consented to be his 'companion', to accept in payment the freedom of his chambers, the gifts that he would doubtless bestow, our relations might have been more tender, less crude. As it was, with a clear financial agreement between us, Mr Newsome and I could take our pleasure in each other as crudely and as brutally as we liked.

I walked up Piccadilly at six o'clock, while Mr Newsome was shaving by gaslight, with aching legs, a sore bum and £15 in my pocket.

Four

A face in the crowd... A pint in the Princess of Wales... A pint of a different vintage... Fucking in the bogs

Vera was delighted when I blabbed my confession during the interval the following evening. No detail was to be left out – no endearment so intimate that Vera would allow it to pass unexamined. This, I discovered, was how the old creature got his pleasure – by hearing, from the horse's mouth, the most explicit accounts of the actions of which he was no longer capable. My obscene tirade soon had me fully aroused again – how prodigious, then in the first spring of my adult life, were my powers of recovery! – and I wanted badly to have a wank, content that Vera should watch if it pleased him. 'Good Lord, child, what are you thinking of!' he shrieked as a began to fumble in my trousers. 'Oh! My eyes!' He held a pale, papery hand across his forehead, like a heroine in a melodrama. 'That I should see such things at my time of life!' And then, snapping back into the conniving persona that was more truly his own, he added, 'You can't afford to waste it, my dear. That's your stock-in-trade.'

Perhaps if Mr Newsome had returned to the theatre that night and used his considerable powers of persuasion, I might yet have traded a life of stage-door prostitution for the more certain comforts of being a kept boy in Albany. But tonight there was no sign of him in the audience; tonight, I supposed, his 'other' nature satisfied, he returned to Ealing for a spell of domestic bliss from which he would emerge when next he needed me. And so the field was clear for my other admirer, he whom I had spurned in Mr Newsome's favour. I could see him quite clearly in the circle, nattily dressed, his hat placed safely on his lap, gloved hands occasionally turning it by the brim as he stared with scant attention at the acts. By this stage in my theatrical career I had been promoted to scene shifter, and thus made brief on-stage appearances between numbers while Mr Holly oversold the turns to a credulous audience. Tucker the Singing Violinist had just reached the caterwauling climax of his act, and we were to set up for Miss Terri Marlo, whose performance required not only a backdrop of Hyde Park, but also a few items of scenery: to wit, a water fountain, a bench and a tree, all of them rendered in painted plywood by our very own scenic artists. While Kieran improved his muscles by hauling the backdrop into place, I shouldered the necessary items and prepared to take them on stage.

'I've got an admirer out there tonight, Kieran,' I said, blatantly pressing myself against him in the wings.

'Who?' He scanned the house for a rich widow – that was his favourite fantasy, that he would be 'taken up' by a randy society lady. 'Where is she?'

'It's a man, stupid.' I wished there were more light, so I could better see the look of consternation on his Irish mug.

'A man? Jesus, Paul, you're not...'

'Course I am. There's plenty out there will pay for what I've got.'

'You mean you let them have your cock?'

'Certainly. And they're only too happy. You've seen it, you should know.'

'And what do they—'

There was no time to complete this question, as the lights were down and we had only a few moments to recreate a sunny corner of the Serpentine on the South's little stage. Kieran hauled away on the ropes, his magnificent arms fully revealed by his rolled-up sleeves; I noticed with some pleasure that his crotch was bulging in the most interesting manner. Mr Holly, no doubt, would get a bedtime drink.

Out on stage, I swiftly deposited bench, fountain and tree in their appointed places, checked quickly that all was well and then allowed myself to glance up into the house. Without the lights to blind me, I could see the audience quite well – better, in this twilight between the acts, than the artists themselves. And there in the circle was my admirer, sitting bolt upright now, craning for a better view, standing even to take in every detail of my appearance. I nodded slightly, touched my forelock, and ran back to the wings. Vera, with a mouthful of pins and his hands up Miss Marlo's train, rolled his eyes in obscene anticipation. That old crow never missed a thing.

For the rest of the show I ran rings round Kieran, who kept finding excuses to run into me behind the scenes, wanting, I supposed, more details of my new life. Well, I would not satisfy him so readily – partly to punish him for the frustration he had inflicted on me for so long, partly for practical reasons. I knew that if I allowed myself to get intimate with Kieran I would end up neglecting the customer who awaited me in the circle – and that would never do. At one point Kieran, infuriated by my evasions, grabbed me by the wrist and placed my hand on his erect cock. I held it for a while, coolly comparing its length and girth with the mighty weapon that had plundered my virgin treasures the night before. Kieran looked dumbfounded. He had, I suppose, expected me to sink to my knees in gobbling gratitude. Instead I leaned forward, whispered 'later' in his ear, licked his neck and then, when he did not pull away, kissed him full on the lips. He started to move away, so I held the back of his head and drove my tongue into his mouth. His cock did not relax, and so I knew that he liked this as much as I did – and yet, for all his willing flesh, Kieran was not yet ready to cross the bourn. One day I would push him over the edge; one day, I promised, he would beg for my kisses. But that day was far off.

Finally, Terri Marlo was bustling back to her dressing room, the stage was ready to be cleared, and I saw to my immense gratification that my admirer was among the last to leave the auditorium, enjoying my scene-shifting performance far more than he had the 'mirth and song' of the divine Miss M. When the stage was swept and the house was closing for the night, Vera scuttled out of his hiding place with a brush in one hand and a comb in the other. 'Come on, Valentino, let's get you ready to meet your public. I know that sort: he likes his trade rough, but not too rough.' He flicked the brush around my jacket and over my trousers, then, with a few deft swipes of the comb, converted my tousled black hair into a passable coiffure. 'Let's have a look at you, then.' Vera stepped back to admire his handiwork. 'Yes, you'll do. Go and get him. And don't forget: I want all the details tomorrow.'

The usual rigmarole of cigarette and lighter brought us together; I assume my friend had invested in a new flint in order not to be beaten to the prize on this occasion. As he held the flame up to my lips I had opportunity to observe his hands – elegant, manicured, smooth – and the pristine whiteness of his cuffs. Beneath the whiff of my cheap tobacco I could smell something expensive in the toiletry line – a superior soap or cologne. When he dared to look at me from beneath the exquisitely curved brim of his hat, I saw two clear, blue-grey eyes, clear skin, a fine, narrow nose and a neat little mouth, elegantly framed by a neatly trimmed moustache. His chin was shaved to perfection. He must have been barbered just before coming to the theatre. Compared with him, I felt like a huge, unkempt brute. This, I was soon to discover, was the desired effect.

My limited experience of prostitution – one night only – led me to expect that I would, at this stage, be whisked off in a cab to some comfortable apartment, fed, watered and pleasured before being sent off with a few quid in my pocket. This was far from the case with Client Number Two. 'Where can we go?' he asked me, looking shiftily around the ill-lit backstage area. For an insane moment, I thought of taking him back to Mrs Tunnock's, although I am sure that my generous landlady would have drawn the line at seeing her premises used for homosexual assignations of so blatant a kind.

'I... er... I don't know...'

He laid a hand on my sleeve, surreptitiously feeling the muscles beneath, and drew me to the darkest corner of the yard, near the fence that separated us from the tram garage. It was a filthy spot: puddles of oily water had leached through the muddy ground, and there were small piles of detritus swept out of the theatre. Above all, there was an overwhelming stench of piss; this was where the stagehands, myself among them, nipped out during the acts for a quick jimmy riddle, rather than go all the way round to the facilities in the foyer.

'This will do nicely,' said the smart young gentleman, breathing in appreciatively. I began to realise that, despite his appearance, daintiness was not high on the agenda.

Indeed, heedless of his perfectly pressed trousers, he fell to his knees in a stinking puddle and buried his face in my crotch, inhaling so hard that I thought for a moment he meant to ingest me through his nostrils. I could see little of what was going on down there, so complete was the darkness, but I knew that the pressure of his face was causing me to stiffen. This delighted him.

'Get it out,' he mumbled.

I obliged. In one deft movement, I unbuttoned my fly and let my half-hard cock into the air. He lost not a moment: no sooner was I revealed than his tongue dived under my foreskin and began exploring every hidden fold. It wormed around my pisshole, it coated my head with saliva – and of course it brought me to full stiffness.

'May one enquire at the rear?' he asked in his clipped accents.

'Yeah.' I understood that I was not required to be polite or articulate; instead I turned round, pulled my trousers down and presented my bum for his inspection. I hadn't washed since the morning, but my arse was innocent of anything more unhygienic than sweat. He dived straight in, cleaning every crevice. Perhaps he was disappointed that my personal standards were as high as they were.

I assumed that our liaison would culminate in a suck and a hasty farewell, but my friend had other ideas. After gorging himself on my arse, he stood up and took the cigarette from between my lips, where it had been burning down all the while. 'A cheap, nasty brand,' he said, sniffing the smoke, then throwing the butt into a filthy puddled, where it fizzed and went out.

'All I can afford, mate.'

'I see.' And then, without warning, he kissed me voraciously on the mouth, running his tongue over my teeth, around my palate, inside my lips, savouring the taste of low-grade tobacco. Satisfied, he licked a little around my chin and led me back into the light. I just had the presence of mind to tuck my cock back into my pants before it was exposed to the dwindling crowd of stage-door johnnies still waiting for their favourites to emerge.

'Where do you drink?' asked my curious customer.

'Drink?' In truth, I'd had little time to explore the various pubs that peppered the area. Kieran, I knew, occasionally had a lively night at the nearby Princess of Wales, and so I named it.

I saw his eyes light up. 'Oh, yes. A marvellous place.' By Kieran's account it was a fairly low dive, frequented largely by stagehands, prostitutes, labourers and itinerants. A new light was shed on my customer's peculiar tastes.

'Would you do me the honour of allowing me to buy you a drink at the Princess of Wales, young man?'

'Yeah. All right.'

Without further conversation, we crossed the road towards the pub; I noticed that he knew the way better than I, and had doubtless made similar journeys there in the past. On the pavement outside, he slipped some coins into my hand. 'You do the honours, please. I'll have... whatever you have.'

We walked into the pub – a strange pairing, I suppose, except that the unusual was the usual in the Princess of Wales. A few eyes looked up at us, then looked away; at least it was clear that we weren't there to cause trouble. I was relieved to see that Kieran was not of the company tonight; I felt less sure of my ground now than when I had ribbed him backstage during the show. I recognised one or two of my colleagues, as well as Harry the tattooed delivery driver, who cocked an eyebrow when he saw who I was with and buried a smile in his pint.

Well, I should have to play a role again – a role with which I was only dimly familiar. Fortunately for me, I was blessed with a true tart's instinct for divining the wishes of my client. Our earlier encounter in the foul puddles of the yard suggested to me that I was required to be coarse, crude and above all dirty. I thought back to the two gents in the gents' at Waterloo, and realised that there was another side to sex that I had not yet fully explored – one that, I felt sure, was about to be opened up to me tonight.

I swaggered up to the bar, slapped a shilling down and ordered 'two pints of bitter' in what I hoped was a passable imitation of a cockney accent. The barman obliged, gave me my change (which I pocketed) and left me to carry the drinks. My friend – we had not yet been introduced – was standing by a pillar, looking hopelessly out of place in his surroundings. And yet I judged from the flush on his face that the stink of beer and fags and unwashed men, the spit and sawdust on the floor, the hint of broiling sausages from the landlord's quarters above, worked on him more subtly than the finest perfumes. I thrust one glass towards him, clinked mine against it and said, ''Ere's 'ow.'

How Vera would laugh at my ham acting! Oh, well, it was winning the audience over, and it was no worse than some of the turns I'd seen on the stage of the South London Palace of Varieties. True to character, I drained the glass in one go. I could feel those cold grey eyes taking in every movement of my throat.

'Get yourself another, if you wish.'

'I need more money.' This was a blatant lie: besides the change from the previous round, which would have been sufficient for a single pint, I still had a pocketful of coins that he'd given me outside – among them, I suspected from their weight and size, a couple of florins and a half-crown. But I gambled on his taste for abuse – and I won.

'Oh dear! Well let me see what I can find.' He slipped a hand into his coat and pulled out an expensive-looking pigskin wallet. 'Well, now, would this cover it?'

'That'll get you the next round, yeah.' And how! He had peeled off a fiver.

'Go along, then. Nothing for me. Yet.'

I swaggered over to the bar and found another pint ready for me; the barman winked as he took the money. How many times had he seen this scenario played out? 'I've given you the decent stuff,' he whispered. 'Might as well not drink the rot-gut, if the gentleman's paying.'

I rejoined my sponsor and raised my glass to him. He was taking little ladylike sips from his pint, which had barely gone down an inch. 'Well, here's to you, guv'nor!' Again I swigged at the beer; this time I took only half, as I wanted to remain tolerably clear-headed for the rest of the evening.

'Here's to you,' he replied. 'What did you say your name was?'

'Paul,' I said, before I had time to think; a tiny twinkle of disappointment suggested that I should have chosen a more proletarian name, Bert, Fred or Ted.

'Woss your name then, guv?' Any minute now I was going to say 'gor blimey'.

'Oh, me – you can call me Trevor.'

Trevor indeed. Not his real name, but that was none of my concern. 'All right, then, Trev. Here's to you.' I drank more. 'Right, Trev, so, what's it to be?' (He was delighted by the workmanlike shortening of his name; I repeated it often in the ensuing conversation.)

'Finish your drink.'

'You trying to get me pissed, Trev?'

A faint flush of colour appeared on his immaculately shaved cheek – I had hit on a spot. 'Oh, no, not in the sense you intend, Paul. I just know that men like you enjoy a few pints after a hard day's work.'

'Yeah, well,' I said, taking another draught and wiping the foam from my lips on the back of my hand, a gesture that had him crossing his legs, 'I work hard and I play hard, Trev. Get my meaning?'

'Play hard?'

'Yeah, Trev. The harder the better.'

The beer was encouraging me to overact; I hoped it wouldn't mar my performance when the time came. There was only, perhaps, a quarter of a pint left. I saw, or thought I saw, Trevor tipping a wink to the barman.

'Have another, will you, Paul?'

'No, that's—'

'To please me. I insist.'

The barman brought another pint over on a tray. I dug into my pocket for change, but he waved me away; clearly he would profit from his cooperation.

'Oh, well, in for a penny...' I drained my old glass and started on the fresh; by now there was no ignoring the fact that I was far from sober. I hadn't eaten since lunchtime; it was now ten o'clock, near closing time, and the other drinkers were thinning out. My head was spinning from hunger and beer.

'You drink like a real man, Paul.'

'Last orders at the bar please!' sang out the barman, mopping tables and stacking chairs. 'Come on, you lot,' he said to a little knot of roughs loitering by the shove-ha'penny, 'time to make a move.' But he was in no hurry to move us along.

'We'd better be off, Trev,' I said, eager to get on with the job in hand before the beer finally did for me.

'No hurry, Paul. The night is young. I'm sure Mr O'Connor won't mind if you finish off your drink in peace.' My suspicions were correct: the barman was in on it, whatever 'it' was.

'Right you are.' I took another swig.

'Come on, Paul,' said Trevor, all hungry eyes, 'you can do better than that. Show me how a real working man drinks his beer.'

'Right you are, mate,' I slurred, and tipped my head back to take the rest of the pint, a good deal of which ran out of my mouth, down my chin and throat and inside my shirt, wetting it. The rest of the pub was now empty.

'Oh, you messy thing,' said Trevor, plucking at my damp front. 'Never mind.' The wet material clung to my chest and stomach, giving a clear indication of what lay beneath. I didn't mind his looking.

'Well, now...' Trevor seemed in no hurry to make the next move. Surely he hadn't given me all that money just to sit and watch me chuck beer down myself.

'Yeah. Right. Where next, guv?'

'Oh, anywhere you like, Paul. I suppose you'd like to eat.'

'Yeah, I'm starving.'

'Right. Well, we could perhaps go to my hotel.'

At last! A hotel! Out of this dump. 'Yeah, 'snice.'

'If you're sure you're ready.'

'Ready when you are, sir!' I stood up with a flourish – a little unsteady, but not reeling.

'Shall we?' Trevor indicated the door.

'Jus' a minute, then,' I said. 'I have to piss.'

The word worked on him like a charm. 'You have to... piss?'

'Yeah. All that beer. I need to go to the bog.'

'Of course. Well, as it happens, so do I. Let me show you the way.' Gone was any pretence that this was 'my' choice of pub: Trevor was clearly at home here. He held open the door marked GENTS. 'After you, Paul.'

I went into one of the most unsanitary toilets it has ever been my pleasure to frequent. The urinal ran up one wall, but had been blocked by cigarette ends during the course of the evening; as a result the floor was awash with urine. The little frosted-glass window and the cracked mirror were both steamed up with exhalations from this swamp. The smell was overpowering: beer, fags and piss.

'Allow me,' said Trevor, hanging his coat on a hook on the back of the door. He reached down with his pretty, cared-for hands and unbuttoned my fly. Normally this would be enough to have me stiff in a jiffy; as it was I was too drunk and uncertain to respond in the usual way. He reached inside my pants and pulled my prick out, allowing himself a cursory feel as if to convince himself of its length and girth.

'Are you bursting, Paul?'

'Yeah, Trev.' I was, too, although the sensation of another man holding my prick made me uncharacteristically unwilling to let it flow forth.

'Well then, please, go ahead.'

'What?'

'Have a... pee.'

'What?' I couldn't believe this was what he really wanted.

'Spend a penny. Take a tinkle. A jimmy riddle. A slash. Come on, Paul, fucking piss on me, for Christ's sake!'

The light dawned, and all was clear. For a split second I weighed in my mind an aversion to the act with the excitement of a new experience. The reader must know me well enough by now to guess which was the victor.

'All right, you dirty fucker,' I said, 'here it comes.'

And it did. Charging down the length of my cock like a liquid express train came the first flood of a gallon of piss. At first Trevor was content to watch, fascinated, as it shot from the prick that he was holding; soon, as I got into midstream, he was bathing his hands in it, bringing scoops of it up to his nose, even tasting it. Then, to my astonishment, he dropped to his knees in that filthy hole and took the last pint of piss directly in his face. Half of it went into his open mouth, where it was rapidly swallowed; the rest spilled down his neck and over his shirt, just as my beer had done a little earlier. Excited by the novelty of the situation, I would gladly have pissed on him thus all night long, and I am sure that he would have welcomed it. All good things, however, must come to an end, and I shook the last golden drops into his face.

This was the signal for all hell to break loose. Trevor, his prim and proper façade utterly shed, dived down onto my cock and swallowed it in one go. A few strokes of his piss-wet lips and I was fully hard, and proceeded to fuck his mouth. Kneeling on the soaking floor, he was soon wet through: his beautiful grey wool trousers, his shirt, his shoes, his socks were all foul with piss, both mine and the anonymous gallons that sloshed around us. I was sufficiently drunk to find this an aphrodisiac.

Fortunately for Trevor, alcohol rarely softens my cock, although sometimes it delays the climax; thus we had a hard, wet time ahead of us. After fucking his mouth so hard and deep that he had several times been on the point of throwing up, I pulled Trevor to his feet and stripped off my clothes – remembering to replace my boots once I was naked, as I had no great desire to wade barefoot in that puddle.

'Pull your trousers down, Trev.'

'Why?'

'I'm going to fuck you.'

'Oh, I don't know...'

I cuffed him lightly round the ear. 'I said pull your fucking trousers down, Trev.'

His hands shaking with excitement, he fumbled with his button and let his trousers and pants fall round his ankles. His dick was of average size, nicely shaped, and so hard that it pointed straight up to the ceiling.

'Now get down on your hands and knees in the piss.'

'Oh...'

'Do it!'

He did it – and showed how eager he was by holding his arse cheeks open with his hands. At last I was to venture into territory I had only ever dreamed about – for the first time I was to be the fucker, not the fucked. Trevor's arse was a pretty piece, as round as my own but paler, resembling alabaster in the greenish light of the pisser. I assumed that I was not the first to abuse him in this way – although you would never have guessed that from the feel of his hole, which was as tight as a pinprick. I hawked into my hand and applied the spit to him, working it in with one thick finger. Every so often he would cry 'Oh!' or emit some other expression of pain or disgust; I knew by now that these were meant as encouragement. 'Shut up, pisspot!' I said, adding a second finger and a third. 'You're going to get fucked good and proper.'

I reached round and felt for his cock; I knew from last night's exertions that fucking was much more pleasurable if the passive partner was sufficiently excited to deaden the initial pain. I wanted Trevor to enjoy himself – enough to come back for some repeat business. I needn't have worried: he was stiff as a stone.

'Right, here it comes.' I spat again and slicked up my cock, pressed the head against the hole so recently vacated by my fingers, and shoved. The head went in, and I heard Trevor gasp in pain. A moment, and I pushed further, so that his hole was stretched by the thickest part of me. I let him get used to that, reaching forward to tousle his piss-drenched hair and to push his face down onto the mired floor. Then with another movement of the hips I was all the way in. I don't know what I expected it to feel like – my fantasies about fucking had all been connected in one way or another with my feelings for Kieran – but the sensation that overwhelmed we was one of softness and heat. I started to move, as Mr Newsome had first moved inside me, slowly and gently. My cock seemed to be surrounded by satin, by a hundred mouths, all kissing and caressing. I picked up my speed, pulled Trevor upright by placing one hand around his neck and crushed our faces together, caring nothing for the fact that he was still drenched with piss, mine and others'. I pulled up his shirt and felt his firm, graceful body, his smooth chest and his hard nipples, all the while fucking him harder and harder from behind. Then I let myself play with his cock, using it as a handle to pull him back on to me with each inward thrust. Unsurprisingly, during this severe assault, Trevor shot a big, white load of spunk right across the floor, splashing against the ceramic wall of the urinal.

This was my cue to change tack. I would give him a moment to recover – not long, for I had no intention of letting him out just yet. Nor had he: he pulled his ruined shirt over his head, kicked off his shoes and trousers into a filthy pile on the floor and grovelled at my feet, licking my thighs, my balls and my hard cock.

'On your back,' I commanded, waving my dick above him like a sceptre. 'I'm going to fuck you again.'

With admirable agility, he flipped himself over and lay there with his legs drawn up, his arse ready for attack. This, then, was the state to which his lust brought him: naked, filthy, lying with his legs in the air in a pond of piss. My education was galloping ahead.

Three pints of beer is enough to make any man into a fountain, and so I decided to give Trevor another drink. I placed a foot at either side of his head – I think for a moment he genuinely feared violence – squatted down and aimed my cock directly at his mouth. It's hard to make water with a hard cock, but I managed, mustering another generous quantity of recycled beer, which I deposited straight into his open mouth. This time, to my astonishment, he drank every drop. To seal my perversion, I kissed him roughly on the lips after he had swallowed, if only to taste another manifestation of my manhood in his mouth.

This was the final spur to my libido, and, lifting his knees up over my shoulders, I ploughed into him mercilessly. Within a minute he was hard again, wanking away and happily rolling his head from side to side on the toilet floor, mumbling all kinds of obscenities, which I would occasionally silence with another bruising kiss. Finally I knew that I was close, and so I started to slam into him even harder, hoping somehow to empty my whole being into him. I knew from my struggles with Mr Newsome that the 'bottom' is, at this stage in the game, more in control than the 'top', who becomes vulnerable at the moment of climax; I caught a glimpse of myself in the mirror, red-faced, a great vein sticking out on my neck, as I pumped my cream up Trevor's arse. Finally I collapsed on top of him as he wanked out another, smaller load of spunk, which still managed to hit him on the chin. I kissed him again as my cock softened inside him, and we lay for a while on the reeking, steaming stone floor.

The following morning I realised for the first time the true value of having a friend in the wardrobe department. In return for a blow-by-blow account of the evening's entertainment, Vera took in my foul, drenched clothes and returned them to me in pristine condition, dry and pressed and faintly redolent of lavender. I would love to tell the reader that I plunged into an abyss of self-disgust and repentance after my piss-soaked adventures with Trevor in the Princess of Wales toilets, but in fact, on sober reflection, I merely congratulated myself on having added another trick to my fast-growing sexual repertoire.

Five

Introducing Mr Albert Abbott... An Irish rogue... A drain on my resources... Lust betrays me into crime... The sting

Need I spell out the succeeding steps that led me from innocence to experience? Within a year of leaving home I was a hardened prostitute, cynically using my job at the Palace of Varieties as a showcase for my real talents, which lay not in the scenic dock but in a variety of accommodations, from palace to *pissoir*, across London. I was flush with money, and a little flash with it on occasions, but not ungrateful to my first friends. I carried on with my work, grateful for the break it gave me from the uncertainties of life on the game, and I continued to live *chez* Tunnock despite the many offers I had of more luxurious accommodation. Mr Holly was well aware that I was now off the menu as far as he was concerned, but he was pleased if anything: after all, my growing popularity brought more paying visitors to Ontario Street, and that was all that concerned him. I knew from Vera that I was by no means the first Palace stagehand to moonlight as a whore; in fact, from what I could make out, the only one of us who *wasn't* on the game was Kieran, the innocent companion of my increasingly rare nights at home. Those nights when I lay awake and erect beside Kieran's apparently sleeping form were long gone, and I was ready only for one thing when I fell into my bed at Mrs Tunnock's: that was sleep. Now I would be the one who was dead to the world; he could have been offering me his bum, for all I knew. I think he was disappointed; perhaps he liked having a young man fawning over him. I'm sure it was a welcome distraction from his failure in other departments.

'We're good pals still, aren't we, Paul?' he asked me one night.

'Of course,' I answered, yawning.

'You're out and about a mighty lot these days,' he said as we splashed our faces at the washstand.

'Oh, well, you know, a man has to make his way in the world.'

'I know what you do, Paul.'

'I never thought you didn't.'

'I mean, I don't disapprove.'

'Kieran,' I said, standing up to face him, both of us shirtless, 'it doesn't matter to me whether you approve or not.'

That clearly stung him; he mumbled and looked down. I felt like a fool.

'Ah, come on, I don't mean anything by that. I know you don't like what I do, and I know that you're a good enough friend not to tell me.'

'Well, Paul, I don't like to think of a young lad like you going to the bad.'

This should have been the moment when we confessed our true feelings and sank to the bed in a tender embrace, never to part. Romance, however, wasn't on the bill that night.

'I can look after myself,' I said, stepping out of my trousers and pants. If he wanted something, he could have it – for free, I heard the whore in me say. I climbed slowly into bed, giving him ample view of my cock and arse; he stood like a dumb man at the washstand, slowly, sadly folding his shirt.

'Will you turn the light out and come to bed?' I said, my eyes already closing.

What might have happened that night I will never know. I fell asleep almost immediately. Kieran looked a little jaded in the morning, and was less than friendly over breakfast; I suppose I had hurt him. To be honest I didn't give him a moment's thought.

Any time I may have had for reflection was soon taken up with the latest backstage drama at the Palace of Varieties. Terri Marlo's contract had expired; Holly was reluctant to let her go (with reason, God knows: she was the one they came to see) but unwilling to pay the increased wages that her manager, Albert Abbott, was demanding for an extended run. I busied myself with chores, all of them conveniently within earshot of the glass-walled office at the top of the stairs. It was impossible for Holly to conduct confidential business in the Palace: every conversation echoed down the steps and was amplified in the backstage passages. I'm sure he thought he was a genius at business; most of us on the bottom of the show-business ladder did a mean impersonation of his negotiation techniques, which basically boiled down to a refusal to pay. Most acts gave in after a token resistance – the Palace was, at that time, one of the best venues on the south London circuit, and had made a few stars in its time. Holly traded on that prestige, and kept his overheads accordingly low. Terri Marlo, however, was an established success, and could easily have played the clubs of the West End – indeed, as Mr Abbott informed Mr Holly, she had been offered an engagement in a revival of *Charley's Aunt* at the Garrick, which was 'legitimate theatre', a phrase into which Abbott injected oceans of contempt.

'Well,' mumbled Holly, doing a few rapid calculations, 'I suppose we could reach a compromise. Suppose I was to offer...' His voice dipped below audibility; just as well, as I'm sure the gulf between my paltry wages and the star salary of a Terri Marlo would have made me fling my broom across the room with rage. Whatever the offer, it was met with a harsh bark of mirthless laughter. The office door flew open and bounced on its hinges, and soon the large, dark silhouette of Albert Abbott was descending the stairs two at a time. I tried to look busy. I had no desire to get on Abbott's bad side, as he had a reputation as a ferocious opponent. And so I continued innocently sweeping, keeping him within eyesight and earshot, reluctant to miss the next instalment of this exciting drama.

Holly stayed in his office, scared to come down; Albert Abbott calmed his nerves before conveying the news to Miss Marlo by pacing up and down smoking a cigarette. I, the humble stagehand, observed him unawares, or so I thought. Abbott was an imposing man of indeterminate age: he could have been thirty, if his aura of physical force was anything to go by, and yet the set of his face and the grizzling of his hair suggested something closer to fifty. Let us say, for the sake of argument, that he was somewhere between the two. He was tall and barrel-chested; in different costume, he could have passed as the strongman in a variety act. But, instead of leotard and belt, Abbott was immaculately, conservatively dressed. He favoured the styles of an earlier era – the formal suit, the cravat, a suitable hat. His hair, of which he had kept a full head (unlike the balding Holly), was swept back from a pale, architectural forehead, and held in place with some shiny pomade. His eyebrows, side whiskers and moustache were all neat without being overgroomed; many of the theatricals whom I had encountered in my career made ill-advised use of the dye pot and the tweezers in these areas, and ended up looking, in the daylight, like off-duty female impersonators. Of Albert Abbott this could never be said: he was every inch a man. And there were several inches of him: he was a little over six foot.

But what struck one most forcibly about Abbott's appearance was not his stature, his dress or his hair: it was his physiognomy. He might have passed muster as the perfect criminal mastermind, such was the expression of force, of malignancy even, that emanated from that face. In the eyes there was something indescribable, a light that rendered them hypnotic. Miss Marlo occasionally joked that he should work up an act as a mesmerist, and I'm sure he would have packed them in. As the reader will tell from the drooling account of Mr Abbott's physical form, I was powerfully attracted to him, and had occasionally imagined him in the place of one of my less attractive customers (a fantasy that always restored a flagging erection). However, I would never have dared to approach him, even to ask him for the customary light. My attraction was greatly weighted with fear.

Everyone assumed that Abbott was Miss Marlo's lover as well as her manager, and for that we all envied and respected her. Terri Marlo was professional enough never to appear in the purlieus of the theatre except in her female guise, and so it was easy to forget that 'she' was in fact a 'he', and that any liaison between them would have been tainted with the sin of Sodom (to which we theatre folk have always been prone). Greenroom gossip suggested that, out of drag, Miss Marlo was a homely little queen with a taste for rough trade, but in her professional guise she was very much the grande dame, and never so much as laid a finger on me. I assumed that any carnal desires were well and truly catered for by Mr Abbott. They were royalty in our little world of varieties, and I respected them as such.

Now, however, I was about to take the first step on a road that would lead me into an inextricable connection with Mr Albert Abbott, the man who, more than any other, shaped and moulded the adult from the raw stuff of the child. I might have stayed for ever as I was, a young tart on the make, happy with the pounds and shillings that I could earn with my pants down, with little thought beyond the next meal or the next fuck. Female whores, I have found, tend to plan more carefully for their future; they possess the lucky knack of giving pleasure without being its slave. Many of the girls whom I knew at this time, among them Miss Jennifer Bright, used prostitution as one long audition, looking for the man who would take them away from it all and land them in the safe haven of a well-provided marital home. The boys, however, are so ruled by their dicks that they start to see the sex as an end in itself, the money as a welcome by-product. Few of them turn their profession to advantage; few of them, indeed, ever escape it. Inevitably there comes the day when they are too old to turn tricks, when a new generation of trade takes the dicks from their arses and the bread from their tables. That, I am sure, is the road I would have followed had it not been for Abbott.

But I am getting ahead of myself. At the time of which I speak, Abbott was just one of a dozen colourful characters who populated my little world, supporting players in a drama of which I was the hero.

The flattery of my clients had gone to my head, and I truly believed myself to be the most desirable piece this side of the Thames. Men came from far and wide for a bit of it. Encouraged by Vera, I believed myself to be a star in that other firmament. Little did I know how insignificant, how dispensable, I really was.

I thought I had observed without being observed, and yet, as I swept and occasionally watched, I was surprised by an abrupt question. 'What are you staring at, boy? Holly not working you hard enough?'

'I beg your pardon, sir, I was—'

'No wonder this theatre is such a shambles, if Holly employs layabouts like you.'

I was arrogant enough to reply to this. 'I work hard for a pittance, sir. If I appeared to be slacking it was merely because I was waiting for you to vacate the space that I need to sweep.'

I suppose Abbott was surprised by such a mouthful of cant coming from a humble stagehand; at any rate, he stopped pacing, regarded me from head to foot and even smiled slightly.

'Pardon me, my lord,' he said, affecting a deep bow. 'I had no idea we had a scholar in our midst. My goodness. Such eloquence. A veritable flower of the gutter.'

'If you wish to insult me, sir, I can do nothing about it.' I was, at that time, painfully sensitive about my lack of education and the errors into which it sometimes led me. I had read a lot, and it was from books that I picked up my style of speech; Abbott and his class had an ease with words and learning that I could only envy.

'I must apologise.' The timbre of his voice had changed completely. 'I have no right or desire to insult you. Forgive me for punishing you for the faults of others.' He gestured with his cigarette towards Holly's office, then dropped the stub into a fire bucket. 'What is your name?'

'Paul Lemoyne, sir.'

'Well, Paul,' he said, fishing out a card from his breast pocket, 'this is who I am.'

'I know who you are, sir.'

'Do you, indeed?' His eyebrows raised a little. I read the card: it said only 'Albert Abbott' with an office address and telephone number.

'You're Miss Marlo's... manager.' I left enough ambiguity to invite him to say more; he declined.

'That's right.' His mesmeric eyes caught mine; I felt as if he were trying to read my mind. 'Miss Marlo's manager.'

'Should I know you by any other way, sir?' This hit a nerve.

'No, boy, you should not. Manager is what I am. All I am.' Again there was that note of anger in his voice. I offered to return the card to him, eager to bring the interview to an end.

'No, Mr Lemoyne, keep the card,' he said, in kinder tones. 'I should like you to make an appointment with me some time.'

'To what end, sir? I have no theatrical ambitions.'

'Oh, my interests extend beyond the theatrical,' he said. 'Among other things, I am a... financier, let us say.'

'I have no money, and so I doubt I could be of any interest to a financier.'

'There are markets and markets, Mr Lemoyne, some of which deal in commodities more precious than money.'

Ignorant as I was, I could guess what he was talking about. I thought in my egoism that I had picked up another client. I hooked my thumbs into the top of my trousers and gave him a little glimpse of the lower abdomen.

'Right you are, sir.'

'And I see that you are for sale. Good. It is enough for you to know that I am not buying. Call me, however, if you ever need any advice on... investments.'

He replaced his hat, wished me good morning and sauntered out of the theatre, doubtless to secure Miss Marlo's engagement in *Charley's Aunt* at the most favourable terms.

*

This might have been the end of the story, were it not for a cruel twist of fate that betrayed me unexpectedly into material want. I was earning money – more than enough for my needs, as I had not only my income from the theatre, my lodging at Ma Tunnock's all 'found' and my ill-gotten gains to boot. I should have been able to live well and to put a little by for a rainy day. I should also have been sending money to my mother and sister, both of whom could have done with the extra, for there was precious little for the housekeeping after my father had drunk his way through his wage packet, I knew only too well. But, selfish as I was, I got through my money as quickly as I earned it. Occasionally I was surprised to find that my pockets were empty, but it mattered little: if I wanted a drink, I knew where to find gentlemen to pay the bill. With the regular patronage of Mr Newsome, who had broadened my arse considerably with frequent vigorous fuckings with that outsize tool of his, and of 'Trevor', who paid good money for the degradation of our encounters, I should have been comfortably off. But no, I spent money on clothes: nice wool trousers that were ruined on the piss-soaked floors of public toilets; fine silk shirts that were ripped off me and covered in spunk by my more enthusiastic tricks. I bought extravagant presents for my friends: scarves and perfume for Vera; cufflinks for Kieran (I thought they would cheer him up, although he had no shirts to wear them in); even flowers for Mrs Tunnock on her birthday. I paid for drinks and meals when the stagehands went out; nobody ever tried to stop me. They felt – and I agreed – that the good fortune of one was the good fortune of all. Enjoyable and admirable as this way of life seemed at the time, it meant that I put myself at the mercy of any rogue with an eye for an open purse.

This sad little story began, as do so many, with the best of intentions. I had befriended one of the turns at the Palace of Varieties, a ballad-singer by the name of Gerald Fitzgerald, who sang mawkish mother songs interspersed with interminable dirges about 'Erin's green valleys', and who went down a storm with the sizable Irish community. I suspect now that Gerald Fitzgerald had never been nearer to Ireland than a brief engagement at the Kilburn Gaumont, but this didn't stop him from laying it on with a trowel, speaking with an accent so thick that it should have alerted my suspicions immediately. 'Ah, Paul, that's a foine Oirish name,' he said on our first introduction; I was so green that I believed him, and began to wonder if my father was really as French as he made out.

Needless to say – and the reader should know me well enough to guess this – ours was not an entirely innocent friendship. Gerald Fitzgerald had a reputation as a great ladies' man, and indeed I think he supplemented his income in much the same way as I did, except that his patrons were married ladies. Fitzgerald always had nice things: waistcoats, watches, rings, cigarette holders and the like. His pockets were never full (I was to find out why) but he had about him the air of a rich man, which is more important. He never paid for a drink, but such was his charm that none of us ever questioned his motives. We simply thought that he was too grand and successful to think of such things.

I, little opportunist that I was, fell immediately under his spell. I bought him drinks and lent him the odd pound, thinking always that I was getting the better of the bargain as I listened to his long sermons on the meaning of life. 'Paul, my boy, there's only one lesson you need to learn in this life, and that's to recognise opportunity when you meet it. Look at me, for instance.' And he would launch into a lengthy fictional account of his childhood in Sligo, his early ambitions to become a priest, his success as the star singer in the church choir and his subsequent rise to fame in the theatres of his homeland. This was so much blarney, but it persuaded me at the time.

'You wouldn't think to look at me, Paul, but I'm a great one for the ladies. Now, a lady is like an exotic flower. You have to know when to feed them, when to water them, when to keep them warm, when to let them cool off.' And so he would rattle on, drinking my drinks and cadging my money, distracting me from the more urgent business of earning. He realised quickly that I was not a ladies' man myself, but this didn't give him pause. I should have been suspicious that he changed his tack so soon; instead I simply became more and more enamoured of the man. 'Ah, Paul, I could tell you some stories from the seminary, so I could. There was one priest, now he's the archbishop of Connemara, had his eye on me from the first day, told me I was the handsomest young man had ever kissed his ring.' The priest, I was led to believe, had established him in some splendour in a town house in Dublin. And so the stories went on – and on.

Why did I listen to such rigmarole? Well, I suppose I was in love. Gerald Fitzgerald was a charming rogue, and certainly had the good looks of many of his supposed countrymen. Whereas Kieran represented the red-haired, white-skinned variety of Irishman, Fitzgerald had the dark hair and olive complexion that can, in some instances, flower into the most beautiful specimens of the male sex. His eyes were a shocking blue – the colour of forget-me-nots. His eyelashes were long and thick; I can see why the women made fools of themselves over him. And most of all there was his manner: he had a way of making you feel that you were the only person in the world who mattered. I watched him perform a few times from the wings, and saw him focus on a few special people in the audience, singing the song just for them; doubtless they were the ladies who would be lavishing presents on him in weeks to come.

Fitzgerald must have known that I was on the game – it was pretty common knowledge at the Palace – and he would only have had to listen to a little greenroom gossip to find out the details. I flattered myself that he was attracted to me, that the great ladies' man had found a young man of equal, perhaps greater, interest. I found out all too soon that he saw in me only a source of extra cash.

At first he was content to bleed me in small amounts. The occasional ten bob or pound was soon increased to requests for a fiver.

When I demurred, saying (truthfully) that I did not have those amounts to hand, he would consent with a good will and then, when we were waiting backstage for his spot, would come and put his arm around me and kiss me on the neck. This progressed on the second occasion to a kiss on the mouth; the next day there were kisses with tongues, and I was gratified to see that Fitzgerald took to the stage with a large and very visible erection in his trousers. The next day, flush with cash after a particularly filthy encounter with Trevor, I found that I did, after all, have a ready fiver, which Fitzgerald received with great protestations of gratitude and eternal friendship. I expected him to express his gratitude in more than words, and closed my eyes waiting for his kiss; instead I got only a dig in the ribs and a raucous request for more beer.

A week later, he was all over me again. This time I not only saw but felt the evidence of his excitement as he pressed his groin against my backside while he held me from behind, licking my ear and groping my packet. I was too excited to realise that this was simply the prelude to another request for funds, which came later that night. A fiver would no longer do: this time he needed – he absolutely must have – seven pounds. Again, I held out for a couple of days, and his backstage attentions escalated accordingly. He took my hand and put it down his trousers while kissing me; he slipped a hand down my waistband and pressed a finger against my hole. The money was his the next day.

Love-struck as I was, it didn't take me long to work out that I would have to pay for my pleasure. I would never have accepted that this was a form of prostitution, and that I was suddenly cast in the unlikely role of punter: I simply believed that Fitzgerald could rationalise his love and desire for me only if he was doing it for financial reward. I flattered myself that he truly liked me, and that the money was a salve to his guilty conscience. Little did I know that I was just one of many hopeless admirers, male and female, whom he milked in this way.

Increasing sums went from my pocket to his, and our intimacy increased accordingly. On one occasion he took me out for dinner (I ended up paying, as he had forgotten his wallet) and allowed me to suck his cock in an alley behind the restaurant. It was a mild summer evening, and he was content to stand there with his trousers round his knees, his shirt pulled up to his chest, while I made free with his beautiful, muscular body. That encounter concluded with his fucking my mouth as I leaned back against a rubbish bin; so blinded with love was I that I thought the setting positively romantic. A few more similar affairs, and he took the plunge.

'Paul, you and I are the very best of friends, are we not?' Of course. 'I trust you, and I'm going to let you in on a great secret.' To cut a long story short, he announced that he had been left a great legacy by his former admirer the archbishop of Connemara, recently deceased ('God bless him and all the faithful departed, amen!'). The legacy, said Fitzgerald, consisted of a handsome property in Dublin and a sum of money almost sufficient for its conversion into residential and business premises suitable for two young men with enterprise and ambition. Would I care to join him in the venture?

I needed no second bidding. Fitzgerald's smooth tongue, and my willing imagination, supplied the details: a large town house where we could live together in quasi-marital bliss, and where we could 'entertain' the good bourgeoisie of Dublin in profitable style. Nice clothes, nice dinners – even a car. I deluded myself more thoroughly than Fitzgerald could. I cannot blame him entirely for a ruin that I brought on myself.

All that was needed to achieve the dream was a little 'seed capital' – enough to send us both to Dublin and to make an impression on the locals. Fitzgerald would not come into his money until the weary business of probate was complete. 'By then, Paul, the chance will be gone and some other buggers will have beaten us to the trick.' A hundred pounds would set us up in a fair way to make a killing; but where, oh where, were we to get £100? If only one of us could think of a way, he said as he sank his fat, hard prick into my arse for the first time. 'We could be so happy together, Paul,' he said, thrusting into me as hard as he could go, reading the expression of bliss on my face as carte blanche for further swindling. By the time he'd fucked me through two orgasms, then withdrawn and wanked off in my face, I had already formulated a plan for getting hold of that £100. I'm sure he read my mind, and sealed the deal by kissing me full on the mouth, heedless of the fact that he was tasting his own sperm on my lips. That, perhaps, made the experience even more enjoyable for him, perhaps, for Fitzgerald loved nobody more than he loved himself.

And how would I get hold of the money? By working extra hard, perhaps? By whoring myself night and day to anyone and everyone who'd have me? Oh no: there were quicker methods than that. Like all tarts, I was a good judge of the value of material possessions, and it didn't take much reckoning to realise that I could lay my hands on goods to the correct value with just a little petty pilfering. Mr Newsome had nice things in his chambers at Albany – jewellery, clocks, *objets d'art*. Other clients – among them titled gentry – were even more lavishly provided for. They would not miss a miniature here, a fob watch there, and I knew a pawnbroker in Kennington who wouldn't ask too many questions about where the goods came from. And so I robbed my clients blind for a week, and quickly raised the money. So pleased was I with my success that I barely noticed, much less cared, that the victims of these depredations, among them my most loyal and valued customers, ceased to dance attendance on me at the Palace of Varieties. I suppose I should be grateful that they didn't involve the police; such was the shame attached to the circumstances that they were grateful I had involved them in no greater scandal than petty theft.

Finally I had the £100 in my pocket, and a date with Fitzgerald in which I would hand over this token of our love – as I, poor fool, regarded it. I wanted to play him like a fish on a line, forcing him to admit his true feelings before I handed it over. I had fantasised about what might pass: Fitzgerald would admit that I meant more to him than any woman, that he was mine for ever, that I could do to him the things that, so far, he had only done to me. But, when the evening came around at last, I was so excited that I shot my bolt too soon, and handed over the money before we had even had a drink.

Fitzgerald barely said thank you. He counted the money, pocketed it and looked mournful and distracted. I tried to touch him under the table, but he moved his leg away. When I put my hand over his, concealed beneath a napkin, he moved it away with a tetchy gesture of disgust.

We ate in near silence; I was close to tears. Finally, as we finished our steaks (and I paid), I summoned the courage to speak.

'Gerald, what's wrong?' I cringe as I recall these words; they sound so much the staple of the middle-class novel of adultery.

'Nothing. Nothing.' He stared into the middle distance with those icy blue eyes. His brow was pale and furrowed.

'Is it something I have done?'

'God, no, Paul. There's more in this world than just you.'

'Are you in trouble?' I would take any rebuff, and, like a dog, come whining back for more.

'In truth, I'm in a little difficulty.'

'What is it?'

'I had a letter from the executors this morning,' he said, with the air of a man carrying the weight of the world on his shoulders. 'They tell me that all is not well in the house – our house, Paul. There was a burst pipe over the weekend, and the ceiling has fallen in. It'll take a good deal to repair: twenty, thirty pounds. Where am I to get that sort of money? And without it the whole of the ground floor will be ruined. We might as well try to live in a pigsty. Oh, well, goodbye to that dream.' I noticed that, even in this tragic vein, he made no move to return the money that was to have paid for that dream.

'All for the want of twenty pounds?' I said, incredulous. This time, he did not withdraw his hand, but ran his thumb across the back of my fingers in an absent-minded gesture of affection.

'Twenty, thirty – better say thirty.'

'Let's not spoil the ship for a ha'p'orth of tar!' I said.

'But Paul, I'm a poor man.' He held my gaze, presumably to distract my attention from the expensive tie pin, cufflinks and watch that could easily have raised the requisite sum at my 'uncle's' house.

'You give in too easily, Gerald. Meet me here in two hours.'

'But Paul, you've done so much.' He took my hand in both of his, and pressed my knee between his thighs. 'How can I thank you?'

'Thank me when we wake up together in our home in Dublin!' I said, thinking my words very fine.

Thirty pounds was a good deal of money back then, but I knew that I could find it in two hours. I jumped on a tram to Russell Square, and presented myself at an address on the north side where I had been told quite recently that I would be welcome 'any hour of the day or night'. Fortunately, the elderly gentleman who lived there (a politician of great renown, I might add, but I name no names) was as good as his word. A strenuous couple of hours later I was back on the street, my arms sore from the flogging I had administered, my cock and balls aching from the attentions of an extraordinarily greedy mouth. In my pocket, however, I had £25. A quick call to my room at Ma Tunnock's, where Kieran and I kept £5 in a jam jar in case of emergencies, and I had what was needed.

Fitzgerald kept our rendezvous in the Elephant and Castle public house, and greeted me with all the affection I could require.

'I love you, Paul, more than I have ever loved anyone. At first the thought of going with another young chap disgusted me, but you've proved that two men can be as close as a man and a woman. Closer. I'll never forget this.'

He excused himself for a moment, to go to the toilet I assumed, and I never saw him again.

I waited until closing time, I searched the building, I asked everyone on the premises what had happened to my friend. Fitzgerald, master of evasion, had escaped undetected, with £130 in his pocket.

*

Immersed as I was in the world of vice, I was not so far gone that I had lost all moral sense. I could not say with Macbeth that 'I am in blood [or in my case, sperm] stepped in so far that, should I wade no more, Returning were as tedious as go o'er'. I still had a memory of virtue, if not the actual habit thereof; I hoped that, if my mother could ever have understood my circumstances, she would be proud to find that some of her lessons had stuck. And so I resolved at my most desperate hour to do something – anything within my power – to repair some of the harm that I had done, and at least to pay back those benefactors whom I had robbed. This would mean extra work, more cocks up my arse, more mouths guzzling at me, and an all-round tightening of belts – but I was determined to nip my criminal career in the bud. I did not want to end up like Gerald Fitzgerald, despised by all who got to know him, forced always to move on when the game was up.

And so I whored myself with a vengeance. But, even by my calculations, it would take me months to accumulate the kind of money that I owed. My outgoings were modest enough, but to raise £100 was not the work of a moment, at least not if I persevered in the paths of righteousness. (This is a true reflection of how I thought at the time; it amuses me now to observe that I regarded prostitution as a perfectly legitimate way of earning money. Perhaps I was right.)

I was standing in the back alley behind the Palace one wet Monday night, wondering who would blow into my path, and feeling pretty sorry for myself. I'd had an embarrassing public encounter with Mr Newsome the previous evening, during which he'd openly (and audibly) accused me of being a thief, and had not even waited to hear my explanations. The result of this – quite apart from shaming me in front of anyone within earshot – was that a promising catch, a gentleman in his fifties with the physiognomy of the experienced pervert – scuttled off to safety before I could hook him. If my reputation took too many more such blows, my career would be over and I would have little choice but to embrace crime or to return home. Neither prospect seemed appealing.

It was then, as I stood with my hands thrust deep into my pockets, trying to push my basket forward into the light, that my fingers brushed against a square of cardboard, softened and crumpled by constant contact with my legs. I pulled it out and was about to discard it when I saw the name:

Albert Abbott
4 Romilly House
Cambridge Circus WC

Mr Abbott! I had hardly given him a thought since our brief backstage encounter shortly before the termination of Terri Marlo's contract. (She, incidentally, was packing them in in *Charley's Aunt*; I had been unable to procure even a standing ticket.) The details of that conversation were no longer clear in my mind, but certain words came back to me. 'I am a financier,' he had said. Financier. Investments. That could only mean one thing: money.

I placed the card carefully within my breast pocket, pushed my cap back on my head and tried to catch the eye of a stocky middle-aged man – obviously married, and equally obviously hungry for some cock – who had been lurking around the alley for the last ten minutes.

Six

I venture up West… More about Mr Abbott… Marriage prospects… An obedient slut… Novel use for a paperweight… Among the market traders… Buggery in the snuggery… Two into one will go

I arrived at Cambridge Circus bright and early the next morning: there was a matinée at noon, and so I had little time to hang around. It was a pleasant summer's morning, the sky seemed freshly washed and the air somewhat cleaner than usual, even in the West End. The Palace Theatre – not our humble South London Palace of Varieties, but the real posh Palace, where Ivor Novello reigned – looked truly palatial in the early-morning light. Romilly House was on the opposite corner, a substantial but unostentatious redbrick building with a narrow, blue-painted doorway and a number of highly polished brass plaques. I rang the bell for ABBOTT and awaited admission.

I might have been impressed by the smart elderly flunky who admitted me, were it not for the fact that since my first night with Mr Newsome in Albany I'd been admitted to places far grander than this – among them some of the most famous addresses in our capital. (This is not the kind of autobiography that seeks fame by association; if it were I could have made my fortune many times over, and brought down a government or two along the way.) So I sauntered into the lobby of Romilly House and made myself comfortable in a leather armchair on the first-floor landing.

'Will Mr Abbott be long? I don't have very much time.'

'Mr Abbott is a very busy man.'

'Could you tell me how long I'll have to wait?'

'You don't have an appointment, Mr…?'

'Lemoyne. Paul Lemoyne. Perhaps if you were to tell him that

I'm here...'

I was about to deliver some foolish, arrogant speech to the poor old man, who was only doing his job and keeping the hordes of hopefuls away from the holy of holies, when a door at the far end of the passage opened and a familiar face appeared.

'Mr Lemoyne? Did I hear that name?'

'Here, Mr Abbott.'

'Show the gentleman in, please, Frank. He's expected.'

Frank gave me an appraising stare; God knows how many similar young men he had ushered in and out of the building. I am afraid to say I sneered at him.

'Good morning, Mr Lemoyne,' said Abbott, extending a large, square, hairy-backed hand. His cuffs were gleaming white and perfectly starched, in contrast to my threadbare rags coated with two days' grime. I tried to take his hand without revealing the sorry state of my laundry, a gesture that his sharp eyes did not miss.

'I am delighted that you have come to see me. I thought, perhaps, that you did not take my offer seriously.'

Offer? I couldn't remember anything as concrete as an offer, but I fudged the issue. 'I have been very busy, sir.'

Abbott seemed to find this funny. 'Yes, so I gather.' Had the tales of my infamy reached him already? 'Well, I'm honoured that you managed to fit me into your schedule.' I felt, somehow, that he was taking the mickey out of me, but, instead of putting on the surly act that I would have tried with my clients, I looked to Abbott for a lead.

'Don't worry, Paul, I'm not going to bite you!' I rather wished he would: the more I saw or Mr Abbott, the less satisfied I seemed to be with the kind of men who usually ended up pawing me. I made an effort to straighten myself, to appear more like a nicely brought-up young man rather than the street urchin into which I was rapidly turning.

'Now, let me ask you a question, Paul. Are you happy at the Palace of Varieties?'

'Yes, sir.' It was the truth.

'Good. And would you say that you're making a comfortable living?'

I saw no point in lying. 'No, sir.'

'Certainly not from the wages that friend Holly pays you.'

'None of my sources of income appear to be meeting my needs at present, sir.'

'Ah, your other sources of income. I am glad you mentioned them, Paul. It does you credit.'

'You know about me, then, sir.'

'Naturally. I make it my business to find out as much as I can about a promising prospect.'

Was this, I wondered, the preamble to a quick fuck over the desk? If so, I was not averse – my cock was already stirring to life in my pants.

'Would you describe me as such, sir?'

'Most definitely, Paul. The most promising prospect I've seen in a long time.' I noticed that he moved away from the window, in order to allow more light to fall on me. The bulge in my trousers was now clearly visible, and I angled myself so that the morning sun would throw it into maximum relief.

'I think, Paul, that you could do very well for yourself in this town. Much better than you have been doing.'

'How, sir?'

'A wise businessman knows the market value of his commodities.'

'I charge what I understand to be the going rate.' Was this a subtle form of bargaining? I knew punters who had tried to knock the price down before engaging.

'You sell yourself short, Paul. You give yourself too freely. I would advise you to look towards bigger markets.'

'What did you have in mind, sir?'

'Have you considered marriage?'

'Never met the right girl, sir.' I delivered this with a grin, thinking it a fine joke between two gents of the same persuasion.

'Then you are a fool.' Abbott was not smiling, and I realised that he was serious. 'How long can you continue in your current walk of life? How long before Holly throws you out, or before the Palace goes bust, or before your reputation' – here he wiped his lips with a handkerchief, as if ridding himself of an unpleasant taste – 'makes you a drug on the market?'

Ah – so the tongues had been wagging after all.

'I have not looked so far into the future, sir.'

'Not so very far, perhaps, Paul.' He was kinder again; this constant shifting of mood was disorienting me, although it exercised a stimulating influence on my lower self. 'Foolish the boy who thinks that it's going to last for ever, this brief summer when everything is possible, when everyone can be brought to pay.'

'I put myself in your hands, sir. What would you do in my place?'

Abbott looked at me for a moment without speaking, and I knew at once that he found my compliance exciting. Had he surrendered to the moment, I might after all have been fucked across the leather-topped desk and sent on my merry way with another few quid towards my conscience fund. I might have been spared much trouble that was to come. I might also have ended up as just the faded whore that Abbott described. I am grateful to him that he mastered his baser desires at that moment and continued as the cool-headed man of business.

'I will speak frankly with you, Paul. The best thing you can do in your position is to stop selling yourself and set your sights on an advantageous marriage, a marriage that will guarantee you means, position and influence in this world. From that vantage point you can think of further ambitions – in public office, perhaps, or in commerce. You are not, I think, entirely uneducated.'

'I'm hardly fit to mix in polite society, sir. My father was a drunkard and—'

'That's as may be. You do, however, have certain advantages over the young men of the middle classes who are jostling for position in London. Hundreds of them are competing on the marriage market, many of them with as little inclination for female company as you, I suspect. But you are already a frontrunner, Paul, if you did but know it.'

I wasn't so green, or so modest, that I didn't understand what he was talking about. Indeed, I'd had my fair share of advances from the well-heeled ladies who slummed it down at the Palace on Thursday and Friday nights, and I never imagined that it was my conversation they were interested in.

'That seems to me a cynical reason for marriage, sir.'

'On the contrary, Paul: it seems to me a perfectly sound basis for a mutually beneficial relationship. There are plenty of women in this town who would give all they had to secure regular access to a young man such as you. They would not, I assure you, expect utter fidelity, nor would they offer it in return. But to have you by their side at Lady So-and-So's dinner table, to present you as the father of their children, and to welcome you on a regular if infrequent basis into their beds, would be worth a good deal.'

'I see.'

'Do you think you could bring yourself to the yoke, Paul?'

'I suppose I could, sir. But would society accept me? I am not of the right class to be welcomed openly in any of the great houses. I have been into plenty of them, and I've seen how society marriages work. I've been brought in and out of the tradesmen's entrance, I've been entertained while the servants have the evening off and the wife is at the theatre. Gentlemen of the upper classes recognise instinctively what I am. They can tell your origins just by looking at you, by smelling you. I have what they want for an hour or for a night, but after that, sir, they despise me. I could no more pass muster in a sham society marriage than I could at Buckingham Palace.'

'I beg to differ.'

'How so? Look at me!' I shot a hand out from my frayed cuff. 'I'm a guttersnipe. I'm what my gentlemen are pleased to call rough trade. They want this, and this' – I gestured to my cock and my arse – 'but they aren't interested in this.' I tapped myself on the temple. 'The only use they have for my head is—'

'Spare me the details, Paul. They are familiar. I am a man of the world. Your little tirade convinces me of one thing: you have the mental capacity it takes to go far in this world. I know enough of society to assure you that there are titled heads with far fewer brains than you possess. There are gentlemen sitting in Westminster who can barely string a sentence together, who think only of the next weekend's shooting in Hampshire. You wear your origins rather too obviously on your sleeve, Paul. But clothes and manners can be changed.'

'I would rather not practise deception,' I said, thinking ruefully of my recent encounter with Gerald Fitzgerald. 'Besides which, if I ever do get married, which I doubt, I would wish to be able to invite my mother and my sister without being ashamed or untruthful.'

'Your honesty does you credit, Paul, although I fear it will do nothing to *keep* you in credit. Well, well, so be it. I don't think less of you for it, although I had hoped... At Lady Tinderbox's ball... there is a certain second daughter of... Well, enough, enough.'

I thought he would dismiss me, but I could see that he was thinking. Rather than take my leave, I waited for him to speak.

'There are other routes to the top, less direct, less open, darker and more dangerous perhaps, but they reach the same goal.'

'I don't understand you, Mr Abbott.'

Again, he was silent, looking me up and down. And then, out of the blue, he said, 'Strip.'

'Sir?'

'You heard me, Paul. Strip. Take your clothes off.'

I was about to enter into my usual tariff speech, but something in Abbott's eye quelled me, and I decided that to obey was more prudent than to bargain. I started with my neckerchief, a once-white piece of cloth that, despite Mrs Tunnock's best efforts on a Monday morning, was now decidedly grey.

'Stop!'

Abbott walked up to me, placed a hand under my chin and tilted my head backwards. 'A magnificent throat. Magnificent.' He placed his other hand open-palmed against my Adam's apple, and I wondered for a moment whether I had fallen into the clutches of a strangler, or, worse still, a vampire. (You must forgive my lurid imagination: I suppose I had spent too much time watching the entertainments at the Palace of Varieties, where crime and gore were popular elements in those days.) But, instead of throttling, Abbott allowed himself only an appreciative caress before standing back. I caught his eye for a moment, and noticed to my gratification that his pupils were dilated with lust. His trousers were too well cut to reveal much more of his excitement, but I could imagine.

'Continue.'

I removed my jacket, a greasy corduroy affair that had been flung on the floor of many a gentleman's apartment, folded it neatly and placed it over the back of a chair. Then I bent down to unlace my boots. Abbott stood over me – seemed, indeed, to tower over me. He was a tall man, but the impression of height was due as much to personal qualities as to physical size. Kneeling before him, I felt delightfully obedient and vulnerable. I would have happily employed the advantage of the position to do for Abbott what I usually did for gentlemen when I was on my knees. Sucking their cocks in this position, looking up with gratitude and submission in my eyes, usually earned me a few bob extra. I glanced up at Abbott, and this time there was no mistaking the increase in the fork of his trousers. He made no move, however, and simply watched as I removed boots and then socks.

'Put your foot up, Paul.' I did so, balancing rather precariously on my left leg. Abbott took hold of the heel in the palm of his hand and began a close inspection of my foot.

'Ah, yes. A foot that Michelangelo could have sculpted. Good high arches, strong ankles, long toes. The feet of a thoroughbred. I can tell a lot about a young man by his feet.' There was a smile on his face as he said this, but I suspect he was at least half serious. Perhaps Abbott would turn out on closer inspection simply to have a foot fetish. His gentle manipulation of my toes suggested that he was quite at home with the erotic potential of the feet – one of the few portions of my anatomy that had not been comprehensively molested by gentlemen in the last few months.

He let me stand again. 'Continue.'

I dropped the braces from my shoulders and pulled my shirt over my head. Abbott was now walking around me, not touching me but running his eyes over every detail of my torso. He reminded me of the men I had seen once or twice in the British Museum, gazing appreciatively at some piece of Greek statuary. I had already discovered that certain rooms at the museum were useful places to meet potential new clients.

Without waiting to be told, I dropped my trousers, and stood before Mr Abbott in only a threadbare pair of underpants. My cock, of course, was at full extension, a fact that the overstretched material of my single remaining garment did nothing to conceal. There was a small damp patch on the fabric at the head of my prick; I felt half embarrassed, half delighted, that Abbott could see me thus exposed.

'Good. Good.' He pulled the wooden revolving chair from behind his desk and sat down in it. 'Now, come and stand before me.'

I did as I was bidden.

'Turn around.'

I did so, and heard a slight intake of breath as Abbott got the first view of my bum.

'The pants, Paul. Take them off.'

Still with my back to him, I pulled my pants down to my ankles, bending over in the process and giving him what I hoped would be a welcome sight of my hairy arse crack. I stood up; my cock was standing straight out from my body and throbbing with each beat of my heart. If he were to touch it now, I would come straightaway.

'Turn round to face me.'

I did so. Suddenly embarrassment swept over me, and I stared at the carpet. Abbott clearly found the spectacle of my discomfiture pleasant, as he was silent for a full minute. My cock beat time like a conductor's baton, begging for relief. A drop of clear, sticky fluid gathered at the head and caught a ray of sunlight coming through the sooty windowpane. It glistened for a moment like a diamond. I longed to grab my cock and wank myself off all over Abbott's worn Turkey carpet, but I sensed that to do so might have disrupted whatever plan the man had for me.

'Now, Paul...' He paused and cleared his throat. I hoped that this was the moment when I would be required to give myself to him; I could see from surreptitious glances to his crotch that his cock was now as hard as mine, and was making the most obscene bulge down his left thigh.

'Yes, sir?'

'Would you say, Paul, that you are a... modest man?'

'No, sir.' I thought this a strange question, as I was standing before him, completely naked with a dripping hard-on.

'Would you find any requests repulsive, or impossible to follow?'

'No sir. I don't think so. Not within reason. I am not keen on extreme pain, and I am slightly squeamish about the sight of blood.'

'Don't worry on that score. You won't be asked to do anything that involves that kind of thing. But I wonder, in the course of your... travels around London, shall we say, whether you've encountered certain... rarefied practices?'

I felt pretty certain that I could lay claim to most such practices: during my months on the game I'd had just about everything shoved into me that would fit, and had given and received copious amounts of all the major body fluids.

'Try me, sir.' I wished he would give me a chance to show what an obedient little slut I could be. The same game was clearly in his mind.

'I believe, Paul, that you are perfectly compliant. I do not need to test you.'

The look of disappointment on my face must have been more eloquent than I intended. Fortunately, Abbott was not such a monster of self-control as I was beginning to fear.

'And yet, after all, I think perhaps that I will. Just to be able to say to my clients with absolute confidence that you come with Albert Abbott's seal of approval.'

'What shall I do, sir?'

He looked around him for inspiration.

'Come over here first, Paul.' He beckoned me closer, until I was standing directly in front of him, my cock inches from his face. He patted himself on the thigh.

'Lie over my knee.'

I obeyed with alacrity, settling myself so that my toes and nose were touching the carpet, my bum arched up in the middle and my cock pressing as hard as possible against his lap.

'Good. Now, let me see how obedient you can be.' He held the back of my neck with one hand, letting his thumb caress the bristles at my nape (I had been to the barber's only the day before). I pushed against his hand, like a cat responding to its master. The heat from Abbott's crotch was burning into my thigh.

With his other hand he lightly stroked my bum – or not even my bum, but the hair on my buttocks, which he brushed with the heel of his palm. Then, for a moment, he broke the contact, raised his arm and brought the flat of his hand down with a firm and quite audible crack against my arse. A-ha! A spanker! I had, of course, encountered them before, and always found that a well-spanked arse increased my appetite for a vigorous fucking. I squirmed a little and raised my arse a few inches more to indicate my appetite for punishment.

The hand was raised and lowered again and again, first on one buttock, then on the other, until I could feel a glow building up on my poor, beaten bum. My arse lips were twitching in anticipation of more, and my cock was rubbed raw against Abbott's trouser leg; I had certainly oozed a good deal of pre-come into the cloth.

Now, with finger and thumb, he spread my buttocks and started exploring my hole with his middle digit. This excited me even more, and I started to fuck his leg more vigorously. 'If you stick your finger in me, sir, I'll come almost immediately.'

I hoped this would be taken as a request; instead, Abbott regarded it as a warning, and withdrew his hand from my rear.

'Up on your feet, Paul.'

I did as I was told, and noticed that, as I suspected, Abbott's trousers were covered in shiny silver cock trails, as if a large amorous snail had disported itself on his lap.

He tapped smartly on the leather surface of his desk. 'Hop up there, boy.'

I obliged, and sat on the edge of the desk with my feet dangling over the edge. I thought, perhaps, that I was going to be fucked on the desktop just as I had hoped. Abbott, however, had other ideas.

'You see that paperweight?' I had indeed: it was a handsome art deco object carved, I supposed, from ivory, with a round, irregular base and a long, thick stem, somewhat bigger than the biggest cock.

'Yes, sir.'

'Would you be able to accommodate that, for instance?'

'Undoubtedly. Why do you ask?'

'I should like to see that, Paul.'

'Why, sir?'

'It would prove to me your willingness to obey orders. And it would prove, also, that you are capable of taking something... very large.' He pressed his hand into his crotch, and I had little doubt of what he referred to.

'I would prefer the real thing, Mr Abbott.'

'And I would prefer you to do as I ask you, Paul. And you mentioned, I think, that if anything were to go up inside you, it would make you come.'

'Very quickly, I think.'

'Good. Show me.'

This was a direct appeal to the exhibitionist in me, and I have never been able to resist the opportunity to show off. If I was not to have Mr Abbott himself, the next best thing would be to debase myself in front of him. I am unwilling to analyse these responses; suffice to say that anyone who has been in a similar situation will understand them without further description.

Drawing my feet up onto the leather surface of the desk, I squatted back on my heels, my knees folded up on either side of me like a crouching frog. I picked up the paperweight – it was a massive, heavy thing, but curiously warm to the touch – and spat copiously on the end of it, never taking my eyes from Mr Abbott's. He neither smiled nor frowned; he simply watched.

Smearing the saliva over the head and shaft of the thing, I brought it down and stood it on the desk just in front of me. My cock, arching up at exactly the same angle, provided a flesh-and-blood replica of the inanimate ivory object that was about to become a very intimate part of me.

I raised my arse a foot off the surface of the desk and shuffled forward a little, until the tip of the paperweight was resting against my hole. I grabbed my prick and wanked it a couple of times, just to prime myself against the pain that I knew stood between me and fulfilment; then, transferring the weight from my feet on to the head of the paperweight, I allowed it to breach me. I screwed my eyes up tight against the pain, and opened them again to see Abbott blatantly caressing the huge length inside his trousers. That was enough, and I lowered away.

I went slowly, unwilling to damage myself and eager to prolong the show. Abbott reached in with one hand and held the paperweight firmly in place on the desk, allowing me to continue my descent without fear of toppling over. Finally, I reached my nadir, and the huge thing was right inside me. My cock, which stayed fully erect throughout, was now resting on the black wool sleeve of Abbott's jacket, and was spewing ridiculous amounts of juice onto the fabric.

'Shall I?'

'Yes.'

I started to move up and down on the dildo, feeling with each downward thrust a welcome contact with Abbott's fist, clenched as it was around the base of the paperweight. A few thrusts like this and I could feel my orgasm beginning; the tickling along the underside of my shaft from his jacket sleeve was enough to bring it on.

'Here I come, sir.'

I sat right down on the ivory cock and ground my arse against Abbott's hand, which must have been painfully crushed by my weight. As I did so, huge jets of come shot up the length of his arm; some of it landed in his beard. A great puddle pooled on to the desk top, and I was done. I sat back, held my legs open with my hands and allowed Abbott to pull the paperweight slowly from my arse.

'Good lad.'

Was that all he could say? I had just put on the performance of a lifetime, and I was expecting a little more than 'good lad'.

'Thank you, sir.' I looked into his face and read there all the appreciation that had been lacking from his words.

He stood up, put a hand round the back of my neck again and pulled me towards him. As I kissed him, I was aware of a huge glob of my sperm coating our faces and lips.

'Can I finish you off, sir?'

'You want to?'

'Yes, sir.'

'Very well.'

He stood back and unbuttoned his fly with one quick tug, unleashing a cock that was every bit as large as my recent ivory lover, but warm, dark and covered with an intricate network of engorged veins.

This time I didn't wait for orders: I jumped off the desk and swallowed him in one fell swoop. Within a few seconds, he had both hands round the back of my head and was fucking my face in a fury of lust. It took only a few seconds for him to come deep in my throat.

That was the strange, perverse nature of my first real encounter with Albert Abbott Esquire, and, after one taste of his arrogant, manipulative style of lovemaking, I was hooked. I suppose in retrospect that I fell in love with him, but at the time I certainly wouldn't have described it thus: the nearest I had ever come to romantic love was in my friendship with Kieran, towards whom I still had some tender feelings and with whom I could dimly imagine myself being 'together'. But for Abbott my feelings were more confused: there was a good deal of resentment mixed in with the desire and admiration. I resented him not least for the way in which he dismissed me from that first session. After shoving an ivory paperweight halfway up my lower intestine I would have expected some kind of pecuniary reward, if only as a token of his appreciation. I didn't regard Abbott as a client, like Mr Newsome or Trevor or my other regulars – but I did regard him as a man of means who owed a duty of generosity towards those less fortunate than himself. Not Abbott, though: he saw me out of the office without so much as a pat on the bum, let alone a coin (or preferably notes) slipped discreetly into my waiting palm.

I still had an hour to kill before I was due to start work at the theatre; half an hour to play, if I were to walk back to Ontario Street and save the tram fare. I was no sooner out in the sunshine than I was thinking of how I could turn a trick or two, and make up some of the money of which I had been disappointed *chez* Abbott. Waterloo Station crossed my mind as an option; that, after all, had been the scene of my first debauch, and I had often toyed with the idea of returning there as a more experienced trader. But surely there were opportunities closer to hand. I was in the West End, after all, home of theatrical folk, all of them bent from the top of the bill to the stagehands. I trotted round to the stage door of the Palace to see if I could eye up a likely prospect, but at that time of day it was as quiet as the grave.

Disappointed, and unsure where else to go in the area, I started walking disconsolately home, and as I did so the desperation of my situation returned to me. What was I thinking of, giving myself away for free when I should be out there earning every penny I could get to make good my misdemeanours? Who did Abbott think he was, conning me (I imagined) into giving him a free show as if it were I, not he, who should be properly grateful? You can see already how he disturbed my emotions – in addition, I was more than happy to blame someone else as a means of assuaging the guilt that I felt for robbing my customers.

Feeling friendless and hard done by, I cut down to Seven Dials and dropped from there into Covent Garden, where the fruit and vegetable stalls, which had been working since dawn, were beginning to pack up for the day. I was hungry – there's nothing like having an inanimate object rammed into the bowels to sharpen a boy's appetite – and I thought that I might as well spend a few pennies on a cup of tea and a bun at one of the cafés that served the market traders. I stopped at one, a little back from the Piazza, and could dimly see through the fogged windows a cheerful crowd of working men. They, at least, would provide some honest human companionship, maybe a kind word to comfort me in my distress. I opened the door, and was immediately hit by a miasma of steam, cigarette smoke and cooking bacon.

The café was full – that is to say that there were twenty men sitting around the tables, rattling away in their peculiar market traders' argot, downing coffee, tea and beer and huge, dripping bacon rolls that the proprietor, a motherly woman in a stained pinafore, delivered to the tables. I sat down at the only available space, took off my cap and ordered some refreshments. By this time I had abandoned all thoughts of sex, and I certainly had no idea of making money in an establishment like this: these men were no better off than I was. However, as I was fast learning, it's when you least expect something that you should expect it most. No sooner had a bitten into my currant bun and washed it down with a draught of strong tea than I felt a hand on my leg.

Looking up for the first time at the man sitting opposite me, I was somewhat taken aback. He was hardly a great catch: he must have been fifty, and had been a good deal battered by life. His face was heavily lined, and his stubble was more grey than brown. But, despite this weather-beaten appearance, he was very much a man, with the strong jawline and massive neck that I appreciated in my partners. He looked like the very last man on earth who would want any of what I had to offer – and yet his hand rested on my thigh, squeezing appreciatively, and he winked when our eyes met.

'All right, Charlie-Boy?'

'Yes thanks.'

'Hard night?'

'No, just starting.'

'You work on the market? I ain't seen you before.'

'No, I work... south of the river.'

'Oh, yeah.' He winked again. Was I so obviously rent?

His hand was moving up my thigh; nobody else seemed to take the blindest bit of notice.

'Fancy a spot of breakfast?' I guessed that whatever happened between us was not going to include a financial transaction – however, I was not one to turn down a new experience, and I found his direct, friendly approach most comforting. Perhaps there was something fatherly about him, although I won't go too far down that road, as I have no wish to play into the hands of any Freudians who may be reading this memoir, for 'research' purposes no doubt.

'What's fresh this morning?' I asked; I think he knew what sort of produce I was talking about.

'You can squeeze it if you're interested.' He slid forward in his chair so that his groin was roughly halfway under the table; in this position it was easy for me to reach down and get my hands on the prize. Despite the thick denim of his trousers, I could feel a prick of prodigious dimensions.

'And what do you like to do with that, then?' I asked, as brazen as I knew how.

'Sticking it down young a young lad's throat, given half a chance.'

'Is that all?'

'Up his bum if he'll let me.'

'I'll let you.'

'Thought you might.'

'Where do we go?'

He jerked a thumb over his shoulder. 'The snuggery, of course.'

I had no idea what he was talking about, and yet it dawned on me that a door at the rear of the café, which I had assumed led to the toilets, had seen an awful lot of inward traffic, with a disproportionately low amount of egress.

'Lead on.'

By now I was stiff again. I swigged the rest of my tea and rammed the half-eaten currant bun into my jacket pocket; little point in wasting valuable food. My new companion put a hand on my shoulder and led me towards the door; a couple of heads turned to watch us, but that was all.

I was led down a narrow, ill-lit corridor with cracked brown linoleum on the floor, down a short flight of steps and then, just before the door that led out into the rear area, through another door and into a dark room. The shutters were closed across the window, and there was no need for a fire – the room seemed strangely warm. A whiff of decaying vegetable matter blew in from outside – it was the signature scent of Covent Garden at that time, when the streets and yards were constantly full of organic litter. Cutting through that was the sharper smell of cheap disinfectant rising up from the lino; this room obviously got a regular swabbing, and I was not too hard pushed to guess why. Gradually my eyes adjusted to the little illumination that filtered through the broken slats of the shutters, and I realised that I was in a room fourteen feet square, which I shared not only with my new friend but with, perhaps, five other men of various ages and builds. My ears and my nose detected immediately the kind of activity that went on in the 'snuggery', and the first thing I saw was a young man, perhaps a year older than I, leaning over the arm of a broken-down easy chair while a huge man with his shirt pulled up over a hairy paunch and his trousers round his knees slammed a prick the size of a baby's arm in and out of his arse. It struck me that the young man, a snub-nosed, curly-headed chap, had not bothered to take off his cloth cap. His eyes were closed, and he was clearly in heaven.

'Buggery in the snuggery, I see.'

My new friend – I shall call him Ron – laughed quietly and began to unbutton his flies. There were no preambles, no kissing or caressing. I saw that this was a place where older men were serviced by compliant younger men, for mutual pleasure at the end of a hard day's work. It flitted across my mind that I was about to do the one thing I should not do: I was giving it away again, when my need for money was so dire. But there was something kindly in Ron's manner, and so I dropped to my knees, eager to get a closer look at the business in hand.

My sense of touch had not deceived me: Ron was handsomely hung, and his big cucumber of a prick was set off by a nice pair of tomato-sized balls. I can only think of him now in terms of fruit and vegetables, as on our subsequent meetings (and there were several) he always sent me away with a punnet of fresh produce knocked off from the day's deliveries.

After the size of his tackle, the next thing that hit me was the smell, that acrid, ammoniac smell that rises from a man's groin after an honest day's (or night's) labour. I breathed deeply, and was instantly as hard as I could be. I wanted to give him the best service he'd ever had – to show him what a professional whore could do, compared with the amateur attentions of the barrow boys. Mind you, from where I knelt, I could see that my young curly-headed confrère was doing an excellent job of taking his giant lover's prick. I saw a great shower of sperm shoot out of the young man's prick as he took the hardest part of his battering. A moment later his huge fucker was grunting and pumping the lad so hard I felt sure he would hurt him; Curly, however, just pushed his arse further back and squeezed out one more huge glob of spunk, which swung around on the end of his prick like a pearl on a chain.

The sight inspired me, and I was determined to do better. I grasped Ron's cock in both hands – there was enough for both my fists to go round, one above the other, leaving a couple of inches proud at the end – and set about licking his bell end. The foreskin was still only half pulled back, allowing me the exquisite pleasure of running my tongue around underneath it, tasting the manly savours that had built up over the last twelve hours. Then, as I licked and squeezed, Ron's cock grew a little more and the head was fully exposed.

That was my cue to enter into some serious oral action. I took a deep breath, paused for a moment to relax my throat, and then dived down, sliding my lips along every inch of his shaft until he was comfortably lodged in the back of my throat, my nose buried in his soft, warm bush. I thought for a moment that I had overreached myself, that I was going to bring up my cup of tea, but the danger passed and I relaxed again.

Ron was clearly used to being sucked off, but I flatter myself that he was impressed by my performance, for he gasped in unfeigned surprise when I swallowed him whole. This was enough to attract the attention of the rest of the men in the room, who were clearly more used to carrying on their business in eloquent silence. Ron, I suspected, was a man of few words – or grunts, moans, sighs, whatever – and his fellow denizens realised that for him to vocalise in any manner whatsoever meant that something interesting was happening.

I had taken him into my throat only three or four times (and been rewarded with a louder reaction on each downward stroke) when a small crowd gathered in a circle around us. It was show time.

Nothing arouses me so much as performing for an audience; not for nothing had I drifted into the world of the theatre, although my finest moments were not on the public stage. In this small room, however, I could be a star, and I set about winning the hearts of the snuggery 'crowd'. I ran my lips up and down Ron's huge cock, ensuring that the onlookers got the best possible view. With one hand I hefted up his massive balls and squeezed them in their sac, while with the other I unbuttoned my fly and released my prick, so that they could all see what I was made of. I found myself thinking, for one insane moment, that they should install a follow-spot in the snuggery, as some of the details of my act were surely lost in the ambient gloom. It never ceases to amaze me that I can seriously ponder such nonsense while engaged in the most degrading sexual activities.

All other coupling had ceased, and we were the sole centre of attention. Curly leaned against his massive lover, with one hefty arm around his shoulders; he had kicked off his trousers, and was now naked, save for that cap. I noticed that he was already getting stiff again, and I was determined that, before I had finished, each prick in the room, no matter how recently it had ejaculated, should be upstanding. That would be my applause – my standing ovation, if you like. It is often said that theatrical folk crave the approval of the crowd to make up for some lack in their own personal lives; this was certainly true in my case, as by this time I had completely forgotten my troubles and was bathing in the warm glow of love that I felt, tasted and smelled all around me.

Ron was not content to be sucked for ever; if I had continued for much longer, he would have come in my throat, and I knew from our earlier discussion that he liked to stick it up the arse when opportunity arose. I was eager to allow him: it was a chance to show off another of my 'turns'. So when he pulled himself free of my lips I needed no bidding: I turned around, braced my forearms against my thighs and offered him my arse. I made sure, of course, that the crowd had a good look, too, and struggled to remove my left boot from my trousers so that I could spread my legs wide enough to reveal every detail.

Ron spit noisily and copiously into his hand, then smeared his cock with saliva. A couple of thick fingers worked a little spittle into my hole; this was going to be a rough ride, but I was ready for it. I reached round and spread my arse cheeks a little wider for him.

The snuggery waited in silence as Ron paused for a moment; his sense of drama was almost as well developed as mine. And then, with one big calloused hand on each of my hips, he lined his cock head up against my hole and began to push. I opened myself to him, and in he slid.

The yelp of pain and screwing up of my face were not acted. I noticed that it was this detail that kick-started the Big Man's cock, which twitched visibly into life, and began to grow as he watched Ron mercilessly ploughing into me. Curly, still held in the Big Man's embrace, was fully stiff, his cock pointing at the ceiling. I could dimly perceive another four or five men in a similar condition, or well on the way.

My own prick had wilted a little with that first blast of pain, but as Ron hit his stride and started fucking me at a medium pace I soon regained my customary stiffness. Now, I like nothing better than to come while being fucked hard by a well-hung man; that element of pain adds immensely to my pleasure. But it was less than an hour since I had spewed a great load over Abbott's sleeve, and so I was in no hurry to shoot again just yet. Besides, the longer I could keep this up, the longer it would be before reality, with all its depressing problems, closed in on me again. So, stiff as I was, I refrained from touching myself. Instead I raised my torso a bit to afford an unobstructed view of my cock to the rest of the snuggery; I noticed with some pleasure that Curly could hardly take his eyes off it. He, I thought, would get it one way or another.

Ron was contentedly fucking my bum, but my front end was unoccupied. This thought clearly occurred to the Big Man, who stationed himself in front of me, grabbed me by the hair (which had grown rather long in recent months, and was flopping down over my face like a curtain, damp with sweat) and pulled me into his groin. It would be hard to say which was bigger, the cock up my arse or the cock that was now slipping and sliding over my sweaty face; I would have to make a comparative, side-by-side study. I opened my mouth, and allowed Big Man to slide into me. He tasted delicious: of sweat, of spunk, and of Curly's arse, up which he had so recently spent himself. This, I thought, could be a long breakfast.

With each thrust from the rear I was pushed up against the Big Man, who fucked my mouth in time with Ron's efforts. I needed to do nothing; usually, when I suck a man, I like him to lie still and let me do the work with my neck muscles, but on this occasion I simply relaxed and let them use me. I rested my forehead on the Big Man's furry paunch, which was as warm and comforting as a cushion, and let him carry on. His balls slapped against my chin, as Ron's balls bounced off my arse and thighs. I was as happy as could be.

Then I found myself unplugged at each end as the Big Man pulled the shirt over my head and Ron tore the trousers off my legs, leaving me clad only in my boots. I knew that I looked good like this, for several of my customers had requested just such a costume for our sessions. I stood for a while and showed myself to the audience, one or two of whom reached out to slap my arse or squeeze my prick. Curly, I noticed, was drinking in every detail of my body and masturbating casually.

Ron grabbed a couple of burst cushions from a broken-down easy chair and threw them on the floor, then lay down at full stretch, his cock waving in the air like a rolling pin. He beckoned me over and spoke the only words that had passed his lips since we entered the snuggery.

'Sit on it.'

I placed a boot on either side of his hips and squatted down with my knees pointing out on either side, almost at a hundred and eighty degrees. I held Ron's prick in one hand – God, it was thick, and as hard as it could be – and kept him steady while I shuffled into position. Then, when I knew that I was at the right angle to take every inch of him, I released the resistance in my legs and down I went. It was, fundamentally, the same performance I had given for Albert Abbott, but this time the cock in my arse was warm and fleshy, covered in veins and slick with saliva, rather than smooth and lifeless ivory. Ron put his hands behind his head, and the muscles in his arms bunched up on either side – work in the market certainly kept a man in good shape in those days. His armpits were dark and hairy, his chest lightly covered with greying fur, over which I rubbed my hands as I rode his prick. I wondered how he would respond if I kissed him. That kind of pansy behaviour might be taboo in this very masculine environment – but what the hell, he was looking up at me with such affection on his face that I simply couldn't resist. I leaned forward (which meant that his cock battered a very different part of my insides), opened my mouth and placed it over his. My worries were unfounded: within seconds our tongues were entwined and Ron was running his fingers through my hair like the most romantic lover on earth.

Now, to my surprise, I felt an extra intrusion at the rear – a finger had been added to take up what little space was left by Ron's cock. The anal sphincter in the young human male is an amazingly elastic ring of muscle, especially when the young human male in question is as ambitious a pervert as me. I immediately began to wonder just how much further it would stretch. This question was soon answered.

The Big Man – it was, inevitably, he who was fingering me – knelt down between Ron's feet and put his massive arms around my waist. Pulling himself forward, he contrived to get his cock where his fingers had been. I was, I confess, scared – but, as usual, desire won out. For a moment he was content to let his prick rest on Ron's balls, but then, as Ron paused for a moment, he took himself in hand and pushed into me. God knows how it felt for them! I imagine that the sensation of prick crushed against prick up a tight young arse must be exquisite, and I doubt that this was the first time that these two had met in this way. For me it was an extreme mixture of pleasure and pain. Usually when I'm fucked the pain subsides within a few moments as I relax to accommodate whatever's inside me; on this occasion, though, no mental willpower or muscle control could accommodate this absurd intrusion. I cried out in pain, but this bothered no one. Ron reached down with one hand to grope my prick and then, satisfied that I was still hard, began to buck in and out of me. I'm glad he did: I suppose, given the choice at that moment, I might have asked them to withdraw, but my cock was enjoying itself at the expense of my poor, tortured arse. The relationship between those two organs seems, at times, to be one of extraordinary mutual abuse.

Soon the two giants were pumping away, and I knew that my ordeal was almost over. Just when I knew they were close (I had checked their balls with my hand, and found them both tight and ready to shoot), Ron lifted me off.

'Suck us off, lad.'

Ron stayed where he was, lying back; the Big Man entwined his legs with Ron's so that their two pricks were pressed together, underside to underside. Now was my chance to do that comparison of size: the Big Man's was thicker than Ron's, but perhaps half an inch shorter. Little matter: they were both monsters.

I knelt beside them (taking care not to turn my back on the audience and thus spoil the show), grasped the two cocks and began licking all over them. There was no way that I could get both in my mouth at once without endangering my life, and so I sucked them separately then wrapped my hands around them and wanked them together while doing as much work with my lips and tongue as I could. This led us to the inevitable conclusion, and thanks to some careful timing and reading of signs on my part I contrived to make them come at the same time, their cocks crushed together in my hands, both heads against my wet, sticky lips. I was rewarded with a double dose of sperm, particularly copious on Ron's part (he, after all, had not just dumped a load up Curly's bum). I looked up, my face plastered with spunk, and saw a handful of men furiously wanking themselves. I beckoned Curly, who lay down and sucked me off while I reclined on the warm, spent bodies of my two older lovers, revelling in their embraces, caresses and whispered obscenities.

It didn't take me long to come, not least because I found my new playmate so attractive; you will appreciate how rare it was for me to engage in these acts with a young fellow of my own age and class. Curly sucked like an expert, and was rewarded with a mouthful of come, which he swallowed without wasting a drop. When I'd finished, I returned the compliment and wanked him off, making a mental note to return to this one for some more private revels of our own.

The orgy was ended. Ron and the Big Man were stuffing themselves back into their clothes, and I saw from a glance at the clock that I had only ten minutes to get back to Ontario Street for my shift. There was no time for postcoital conversation, nor was any expected.

'Can I find you here again?' I whispered to Curly, uncertain whether I was breaking some unwritten rule by doing so. He grinned, nodded and touched the peak of his cap.

'Any time, mate.'

I rushed through the steamy café and out into the sunshine, and ran all the way over Waterloo Bridge.

Seven

Mr Abbott arranges my future... A close shave...
William Herringham RA in person... A lesson in proportion

No amount of penis could alter the fact that I was in deep trouble, and by the time I was halfway through the matinée my cares hung so heavily about me that it was only by throwing myself into hard physical labour that I could keep myself from weeping. Vera noticed that something was wrong. He took his motherly role seriously, and tried on several occasions to draw me into conversation.

'You've got a face like a smacked arse, Paulette. What's the matter?' This was Vera's way of expressing affection, but I was not in the mood.

'Time of the month, Vera,' I mumbled. I hadn't hung around theatre folk for all this time without picking up some of their camp.

'Please yourself. You always do, even though your mother's heart is breaking.'

'I'm fine, Vera. Really. Just tired. Been burning the candle at both ends.' This was true enough – and burning the candle wasn't the only thing I'd been doing at both ends. I remembered my 'spit-roasting' at the hands of Ron and co. that morning.

The matinée passed without incident, and I was relieved to see that there were no familiar faces hanging around the stage door after the show; nor were there any policemen to see me. I could count on one factor in this whole sorry story: it would be a brave and foolish man who got the police involved after having been robbed by a rent boy. He who made such a complaint would most likely find himself behind bars as a result. Thus, perversely, I was protected by the standards of the age in which I lived.

I was finishing my shift, sweeping the stage and the wings, and looking forward to a couple of hours' rest back at Ma Tunnock's, when my attention was caught by a hubbub coming from the front of the house.

'You can't go in there, sir, not until five o'clock.' It was the voice of Minnie, one of the new box-office girls whom Holly had brought in to add a bit of glamour to the foyer.

'Good God, girl, don't you know who I am?'

The unmistakable voice of Albert Abbott. I carried on with my sweeping, never imagining for a moment that I was the one he'd come to see. After all, any business we had had surely been carried out that morning.

Soon Mr Holly's voice was added to the fray. 'Ah, Mr Abbott! What a pleasure, sir! Minnie, go about your business, and please remember your place when you meet a gentleman of Mr Abbott's quality!' A gentleman of such quality, I reflected, that he got his pleasure by watching young chaps like me inserting *objets d'art* into their rectums.

'I knew you'd come back to the Palace of Varieties, Albert,' babbled Holly, unwisely attempting a note of familiarity. 'They all do! We're the jewel in the crown of the cosmopolitan revue circuit.'

'Please don't quote your own promotional material at me, Holly.'

'Come up into the office, Alb— er, Mr Abbott, and let us talk business.'

'It isn't you I've come to see,' said Abbott, in tetchy tones. I could imagine the darkening of his brow.

'Ah, sir, I hope you've not come here to try to steal any more of my stars away!'

'Your stars, as it pleases you to call them, are perfectly safe, I assure you, Holly. No, I have business with one of your backstage staff.'

Now my ears really pricked up – surely there was only one person indicated by this. I feared for a moment that Abbott hadn't come to the Palace to demand further sexual services; rapid my recovery may have been, but I'd already had yards of cock that day, and needed a nap to refill my tanks.

'Oh, indeed,' said Holly, in a strained and rather effeminate voice. 'And with whom might you have "business", my dear sir?'

Abbott ignored the insinuation. 'Paul Lemoyne, your stagehand.'

'Oh, yes, sir, excellent taste you have. He's a very gifted lad.'

'Spare me the chat, Holly. I've no doubt you've had your fill.'

'Oh, sir, I'm a married man.'

'So was Oscar. Now, if you'll just tell me where he is...'

'I'm not sure if he's in the theatre, Mr Abb— Ah.' I interrupted Holly by bursting through the door and presenting myself in the flesh, broom in hand.

'Good afternoon, Mr Abbott.'

'Hello, Paul.' Abbott smiled – actually smiled.

'Well, I'll leave you two to discuss whatever business you may have,' said Holly, mustering what little dignity he possessed. I knew he wouldn't be angry for long: he could see only profit coming from an association with Albert Abbott, no matter how humble the contact. With that he stalked off to his office, and no doubt comforted himself with a draught from one of my colleagues.

'Please excuse me for bothering you at work, Paul.' Abbott was almost deferential in his manner; it made me blush, and I felt my ears tingling.

'Don't mention it, sir.'

'I hope I have not caught you at an inopportune moment.'

'I'm just finishing off.'

'Good. Can we talk somewhere privately?'

By now I was convinced that he wanted to fuck me, and – surprise, surprise! – my dick was very much in favour of the proposal. It was doomed to disappointment.

'We can go to my room, sir, at Mrs Tunnock's. Kieran – that's the chap I share with – will be out all day.' Kieran, poor lamb, was spending every available hour chasing his elusive Rose, and had just that afternoon taken her for tea in Regent's Park.

'Perhaps not there, Paul.' My hopes of another tumble faded. 'Is there a greenroom we could use?'

'I'm sure you know the layout of the Palace of Varieties better than I do, sir,' I said with a smile, 'and you'll be aware that we boast nothing so grand as a greenroom. There is, however, an empty dressing room at the end of the passage where we won't be disturbed.'

He must have seen the look in my eye. 'Relax, Paul. I haven't come round here to fuck you.' Hearing the word on his lips, in that cultured accent, was a novel experience.

'Oh.'

He squeezed my upper arm, feeling the firm biceps beneath the worn fabric of my shirt. 'Not on this occasion, my insatiable one.' Little did he know what I'd been up to since we met that morning!

'Then... what, sir?'

'As I said to your employer, I wish to discuss business.'

'I see.' I did nothing of the kind.

We shut the dressing room door behind us. 'Please sit down, Paul,' said Abbott, gesturing to the rickety chair in front of the decayed mirror, where a thousand second-rate vaudevillians had applied the greasepaint. I did so; he remained standing, resting one foot on the dressing table, near enough for me to feel the heat from his body, to which I was particularly attuned.

'Do you remember the details of our discussion this morning?'

'Yes, sir.'

'You don't have to call me sir all the time, you know.'

'What should I call you?'

'Mr Abbott. Or Albert would be friendlier.'

'Are we friends, then?'

'I hope so, Paul. I thought this morning suggested as much.' He looked slightly hurt. Evidently that performance had not just been a cynical free ride.

'Of course... Albert. I should like to be your friend. I admire you tremendously.' The words were tumbling from my lips, which felt thick and heavy. It was the nearest I had ever come to a declaration of love.

'Let us keep our heads, Paul, for the time being. I mentioned this morning that there were markets in this town into which you could invest your... stock, shall we say.'

'You mentioned marriage.'

'A state for which you have no great enthusiasm, as I recall.'

'Right.'

'But there are alternatives that could make you equally rich, equally influential, if you're willing to exploit an opportunity.'

'I see. And what is your interest in helping me to these opportunities?'

'Money.' He didn't beat about the bush. 'Money, and the chance to make of you something more than I fear you will become if left to your own devices. I have taken an interest in you, Paul. A beneficent interest, I assure you. I wish to... raise you.'

'You can do that quite easily, Albert.' I squeezed my crotch.

'Not now, please.' He didn't avoid a look at what was in my hand, though. 'I have just come from lunch with a good friend of mine. Have you ever heard the name William Herringham?'

It rang a faint bell. I had seen it on a poster near Mr Newsome's Albany chambers. 'Is he connected with the arts?'

'Very good, Paul. Although he's a little more than connected: he's a prominent member of the Royal Academy.'

Of course, that was where I'd seen the name, outside Burlington House on Piccadilly.

'Mr Herringham is, perhaps, our most famous living artist.'

'And what has he to do with me?'

'Well, Paul, as you would know if you had ever stepped into the Academy instead of just parading your arse up and down the Dilly, Mr Herringham is rightly celebrated for his figure studies. Unlike the modernist school, Mr Herringham paints what we would call "academic" studies of the nude. That is to say, realistic representations of their subject. They are neither original nor, in my opinion, particularly good; however, they are immensely popular and they sell for quite preposterous amounts of money. As a result, William Herringham RA is an enormously wealthy man.'

A light was beginning to dawn. 'Would he by any chance specialise in the male nude?'

'Well guessed, Paul, although it would be dangerous for a man of his position to specialise in that field too blatantly. Herringham is a wily old fox, and leavens his boys with a fair smattering of girls, painted in the conventionally pretty manner, with peaches-and-cream complexions and rosy nipples. These he can sell by the truckload; his male nudes, while far more accomplished and painted with a true passion for the subject, he delivers to a smaller but more enthusiastic audience. To walk round a Herringham exhibition is the nearest we come in this darkened age to a public display of pornography, although he escapes censure by his venerable old age, his wealth and his clever deployment of classical disguise. When Herringham paints a young man clad only in a chaplet of laurel leaves, he dubs him "Apollo Belvedere" and positions a lyre across his cock. These paintings he shows publicly, and he is praised for his classicism. Then there is his private work.'

'For which he requires models.'

'You catch on fast, Paul. His private work features neither laurel leaves nor lyres nor Latin tags. It is, shall we say, commissioned by the cognoscenti.'

'Dirty old men.'

'Dirty, very rich old men, who would probably never dream of lavishing a few quid on a beauty like you, Paul, but who will part with hundreds for a Herringham study of just such a one.'

'And you have mentioned my name to Mr Herringham, have you?'

'I have indeed.'

'And so I am to become an artist's model.'

'It pays a great deal better than the work you're currently doing, Paul. In one afternoon's sitting for Herringham, you could earn more than your week's wages at the Palace. You could earn as much as you'd get from five, maybe ten of your... gentlemen.'

'I see.'

'You might also, perhaps, become one of Herringham's golden boys.'

'And who are they?'

'His star models. Those who end up in classical drag on the walls of the Royal Academy. Those who become the most sought-after young men in the capital.'

'And they, I suppose, have access to great rewards.'

'Absolutely. One young man, no more attractive than you – in fact, far less to my taste in every respect – is now living on the Italian island of Capri in his own palazzo.'

'Clever lad.'

'Very clever lad.'

'And you imagine that I might do the same.'

'I do.'

'And you would take a percentage.'

'Exactly.'

'Once an agent, always an agent.'

'Paul, there is a lot that I would do for you without asking for a commission, but it would be neither to your advantage nor to mine. Love without money is a cold comfort in my book.'

'Some would say that's cynical, Albert.'

'I'd agree with them. But it also has the merit of being sensible and realistic, as I'm sure a lad in your precarious position would understand.'

'Thank you for reminding me of that.'

'What sort of trouble are you in, exactly?'

'You have been frank with me, Albert, so I shall be frank with you. I have stolen.'

'I see.'

'I expect you had heard. I am determined, however, to make it good. I will earn that money and pay it back.'

'You'll earn it quickly if you do well with Mr Herringham.'

'How much could I expect to earn in a day?'

'Thirty pounds.'

This was more – much more – than I had expected. I whistled.

'Now I begin to see the sense of the proposition. When am I to meet him?'

'Tomorrow, if you agree.'

'I agree.'

'And are you content that I should be your guide in all things, your mentor? Your Mephistopheles, if you like?'

I understood the reference, thanks to a bawdy reworking of Faust that had graced the Palace stage over the summer. 'I am content.'

'And we are friends?'

I looked into his deep-set, dark, devilish eyes, and saw my own pale face reflected there. I wondered if we could really be friends, or if he was nothing more than a pimp and I his doxy.

'Friends, if you wish it.'

'I do.'

I nodded in assent. Abbott took me under the chin, held my face in his gaze for a while, then leaned forward and kissed me on the mouth. It lasted only for a second, but I felt my will collapse at that moment.

'Good boy. Now we have to smarten you up. It won't do to turn up at Herringham's studio looking like any old piece of trade from Leicester Square, you know. The man's an academician! He paints princes and poets, not renters. Is there a pair of scissors in the house?'

I rushed off to Vera's lair, where I knew every form of grooming knick-knack was available, and returned to my temporary dressing room well equipped.

'Now, Paul, put yourself in my hands.'

I sat in the chair in front of the mirror, and Abbott took an old calico dustsheet from a pile in the corner and threw it around my shoulders.

'First of all, the hair. You look like a proper hoodlum at present, and, while that great flop of black hair may be very much to *my* taste, it may be a little too wild for the great William Herringham.'

Brandishing a pair of scissors with such dexterity that I suspected he may at one time have worked in a barber's shop, Abbott snipped and clipped around my head until my hair was once more of regulation length, well above the ear and a good inch above my collar at the back.

'And now, a shave. Is there any danger of hot water coming out of that tap?' He gestured to the grey old sink.

'Precious little, but you can try.'

He turned the tap. There was a hiss, a muffled explosion and then a trickle of water, which was soon steaming.

'It's a miracle, Paul! That must be a good omen. Now tilt your head back.'

Soon my face and neck were lathered up, and Abbott was plying a cutthroat razor about me. I felt extraordinarily vulnerable, and wondered, not for the first time, whether my new 'friend' was in fact a crazed killer. However, the shave passed off without incident, without even a nick, and my chin felt much smoother than ever I could get it. Abbott dabbed away a few stray suds from behind my ears, and in doing so pressed his groin against my resting arm. I was pleased to find that he was hard in his pants. This kind of ritualistic behaviour – shaving a young man, or having him fuck himself with a paperweight – obviously added spice to his life.

'You'll do. Just try not to get too bristly by tomorrow at two o'clock.'

'Two o'clock? That's no good, sir! I'm working.'

'Not here, you're not. I'll square it with Holly, never fear. You have a great future, Paul. You needn't worry about Mr Holly and the Palace of Varieties if you don't wish to.'

'But I do. They were my first friends.'

'Well, your loyalty does you credit. I shall arrange for an afternoon off, and don't let Holly trick you into letting him suck your cock as payment.' He flicked me with the end of the towel. 'Save yourself for art.'

'I shall.'

I hoped at that point that we might fall upon each other and add our own contribution to the splashes and soap suds on the dusty floor.

'Here's the address. Two o'clock tomorrow sharp.' He handed me a card, with an address in SW1 and the initials 'AA' in black ink in one corner.

And with that he put on his jacket, gave me a peck on the cheek and was gone.

'Dear boy. Deeeeeear boy!'

The academician's house was situated in a pleasant garden square in Mayfair; he certainly wouldn't have far to walk when duty called at the Academy, although judging by the state of him every step would be torture. William Herringham was a man no longer in the first flush of youth, although a few attempts had been made to subdue nature with artifice. For an artist, he had little notion of the image he presented to the eye: poorly dyed eyebrows failed to coordinate with the white of his hair, while what appeared to be rouge was smudged haphazardly across the cheekbones. No matter: despite these personal idiosyncrasies, there was no doubting that I had been ushered into the presence of a great man. His charisma even distracted me from the character who had greeted me at the door, a great silent brute of a man, clearly of military provenance, who looked as if he could strangle me with one hand, and who wore a uniform that may, indeed, have been purloined from his last regiment. When he announced me, I was delighted to hear that his accent betrayed origins of the very lowest class.

Mr Herringham, however, represented the opposite end of the social spectrum. His accent was of a kind one rarely hears any more:

refined to the point of near-incomprehensibility, the vowels tortured out of all semblance to the original. I shall not attempt to render his speech phonetically; the reader must imagine for himself the peculiarities, often comic, of his delivery. Suffice to say that as a son of the lower-middle classes I was immediately 'put in my place' by his cut-glass tones, such was the drilling that we had in social matters in those prewar days. If his voice had not been enough to instil respect, his dress would have been: he wore an elegant silk smoking jacket over immaculate morning dress. A mother-of-pearl tie pin shone in his cravat. Apart from the misguided efforts with cosmetics, he could have been a venerable member of the aristocracy. (Not all of them so very venerable, as I had discovered when I fucked a few of their arses. Mr Herringham looked far too frail for that kind of rough treatment.)

'Come in, do. Grimes will get us a drink. What'll you have? Whisky? Grimes, fetch Mr Paul a whisky.'

Grimes lumbered off; I caught Herringham casting an appreciative glance at his big, beefy bum.

'Well, Paul, how kind of you to join me, and so punctual as well. Our mutual friend assured me that you were the most trustworthy of types. I do hope that's true.' I must have blushed; Abbott, knowing of my recent history, had little cause to recommend my honesty. 'He also says that you are cooperative. Are you cooperative, Paul?'

So far I had not managed to get a word in edgeways. Herringham understood, I think, that most young men in my situation would feel nervous and out of place, and he provided a torrent of words in order to fill the silence. It also gave him a chance to look me over. I assumed from the twinkle in his watery blue eyes that he was pleased with what he saw. I wondered how much Abbott had told him of my eagerness to please.

'I hope I can give satisfaction, sir.'

He laughed – a silly, effete-sounding laugh to my ears. 'Oh, of that I am quite sure, quite sure! Here is Grimes with the whisky. Pour him a large one, man, he needs warming up!'

Grimes handed me a tumbler almost half full of liquor; there was no water on hand to dilute the spirit. I sipped and immediately felt at ease, and started taking more interest in my surroundings. The room into which I had been ushered was impressive yet modest, along the lines, I imagined, of the smoking room of a gentlemen's club. Its panelled walls were hung with souvenirs of foreign travel: an African assegai and shield, an Indian mask, a brass lamp of Arab craftsmanship. There was, I noticed, no evidence that the occupant was an artist, nothing that I could see of Herringham's work or indeed that of his friends and peers. A large handsome desk was covered with disordered papers – correspondence, invitations, newspapers, catalogues – and, here and there in the margins, small elegant scribbles that were the sole evidence of Herringham's calling.

'This is my office, Paul. I see you appraising it with an expert eye. It will tell you little about me. This is where I receive customers, sponsors, journalists and respectable society ladies and gentlemen. They penetrate no further than this. The sanctum sanctorum is denied them. Thither I take only my acolytes.'

I was losing the thread, and must have shown it in my face.

'The studio, Paul, is through here.' He gestured towards a green-baize door, from beyond which I thought I had heard male voices. 'We shan't go through just yet. First of all there are certain formalities to be gone through.'

I thought perhaps that I would be required to sign some kind of legal document, or would be vetted as to my suitability. The formalities, however, proved to be of a different, perhaps more predictable, nature. Herringham rang the bell and once again Grimes filled the doorframe.

'Mr Paul is ready for his audition, Grimes.'

'Sir.' He was one of those London types who whistle their S sounds.

'Now, Paul, I'm sure that Mr Abbott has explained a little of my background. I am an artist, and I specialise particularly in the young male nude. For my next commission, I am required to produce a painting of Poseidon and Leander. Are you at all familiar with the legend?'

'No, sir.'

'Leander was a beautiful Greek youth. Well, aren't they all? His girlfriend lived on the other side of the Hellespont. To cut a long story short, the God of the Sea saw young Leander swimming across the water one day, liked what he saw and dragged him down to a watery grave. Do not look so dismayed, Paul: the worst that you will be required to do is, perhaps, to have a few buckets of water thrown over you. I will not immerse you, like dear old Millais did to his poor Ophelia. You won't catch pneumonia. The studio is well heated, and, besides, Grimes will keep you warm.'

'May I ask a question, sir?'

'But of course, do.'

'Will Mr Grimes by any chance be representing the God of the Sea?'

'An excellent notion! Grimes has indeed impersonated the elder gods before now. I see no reason why not. Poseidon would, after all, be an exceptionally virile figure, would he not? Grimes, are you willing?'

'Sir.'

'Grimes is my most loyal retainer. The doer of jobs I shirk, or perhaps more properly the doer of jobs of which I am no longer, alas, capable.' I began to understand more of Grimes's position in the Herringham household: Herringham himself could barely be more than a voyeur in any amorous activities. 'He is my factotum, Paul.'

'Your *fuck*-totum more like, sir,' said Grimes, with a smile. Herringham went off into another great peal of laughter.

'Grimes is a man of few words, but when they come they are pearls of great price. Fuck-totum! Indeed, Grimes, you've fucked them all one way or another, haven't you?' Grimes nodded. What a handsome specimen he was! Taller than I by a good six inches, he was almost twice as broad, with his barrel chest and his great tree-trunk arms. If everything was in proportion, this would be a challenging proposition indeed. His face – ugly enough, I suppose, but ferociously masculine with its lines and whiskers – gave little away.

'So, to business. I have high standards – ridiculously high standards, some say, but I try to adhere to certain classical principles of anthropometry.'

He was losing me again.

'Anthropometry, Paul, is the ancient art, or science, of physical proportion. It establishes the criteria by which the ancient Greeks – yes, those Greeks again – judged human beauty. And the Greeks, of course, paid particular attention to the male form, believing quite rightly that it is the more beautiful sex.'

I had heard this kind of rambling from other admirers, and took it with a large pinch of salt. These academic or aesthetic arguments were always employed to lend respectability to a basic craving for cock. Doubtless similar nonsense was spouted by admirers of the female form.

'And thus, Paul, we have to ensure that the proportions of all our models are correct. That the length of the tibia stands in the correct relation to the size of the skull, that the shoulders are exactly so many times broader than the hips, and so on and so forth. I shan't bother you with the details, and I'm quite sure from a cursory inspection that you not only fulfil but indeed embody all universally agreed criteria of beauty, and yet I must be sure.' He picked up a pair of callipers, about two feet long, with polished wooden bases and what appeared to be silver tips. 'My reputation, you see, depends upon these details. So, if you would be kind enough to hand your clothes to Grimes...'

This hogwash might have convinced me six months before. Now, however, I'd heard enough nonsense from male lovers to convince me that Herringham's real desire was not to measure me but to subject my body to a quasi-scientific examination that would cloak his baser desires with respectability. One former client had insisted that he was a doctor, and would give me a complete physical examination, which somehow entailed inserting his fingers up my bottom and testing my semen for 'strength' (in other words, swallowing it). I played along, and earned extra for my troubles.

'Certainly, sir. Would you wish me to remove all my clothes at once, sir?'

'No, no! Good lord, this is a detailed business, we must do it a bit at a time. Your jacket first, Paul. We must measure your head and neck.'

I unwound my scarf, and handed it to Grimes along with my cap, which I had been holding throughout the interview. Then I shucked off my jacket and suspended it on Grimes's extended index finger. A couple of tiny creases at the corner of each eye suggested that his enjoyment of the anthropometrical process would be of a franker nature. The shirt came off next.

'Good, good...' Herringham rubbed his dry old hands together and brandished the callipers at me. 'Yes, as I suspected, splendid, splendid... Grimes, could you assist?'

Grimes positioned himself behind me and grabbed me gently by the wrists, pulling my arms back so that they rested on the top of his thighs. I could feel the rough cloth of his uniform, its cold brass buttons, all the way up my naked back.

Standing thus caused the front of my torso to be slightly stretched, and exposed fully to the master's gaze. He placed the tip of the calliper against one nipple, then, extending the tool at its axis, placed the other over its twin. 'Yes, I see, excellent!' Jotted down some notes, then measured the distance between my hip bones, allowing his hands to brush lightly against the groove that ran down to my groin. 'An excellent formation of the iliac crest, the hip flexors. Now, let us see – the major abdominal groups.' Again he brandished the callipers, this time measuring the extent of my diaphragm and the various small muscles that bunched up under the skin. The cold metal tips, and Herringham's papery old hands, were in distinct contrast to the warmth that I was feeling from the soldier at the rear. Not only were his hands holding mine, but his breath was tickling the recently clipped nape of my neck. Every so often, when Herringham's back was turned, I would feel the tickle of Grimes's moustache against me, or a whisper in my ear: 'I'm going to fuck you, boy.'

'Now, Grimes, if I might turn to the brachium.'

Grimes extended one of my arms at ninety degrees to my torso, holding it at wrist and armpit. I felt like a horse at market, being dispassionately inspected by a potential buyer – and, indeed, that was more or less what I was. Herringham measured the radius, the ulna, the span of the hand, the distance from deltoid to sternum, all the while muttering and making notes and calculations. Grimes continued to keep my pecker up by obscene familiarities.

'Excellent, Paul, really excellent,' twittered Herringham. 'Now, if we might take the rear elevation.' Grimes turned me round to face him, exposing my back to Herringham's ministrations. Once again my arms were bent and stretched, my shoulder blades lifted, my neck tilted from side to side. Standing thus, face to face with Grimes, I could make contact of a more intimate sort, and ensured that our crotches were pressed together as much as possible. Grimes was somewhat taller than I was, and so had to bend his legs slightly to obtain the desired position. When Herringham's back was turned, he kissed me full on the lips, drawing my tongue into his mouth with a savagery that took my breath away.

'Now, Paul, if you wouldn't mind loosening your belt and lowering your, ahm... Ever so slightly.' He balked at mentioning the words 'trousers' or 'pants'. Grimes was not so squeamish, and had my trousers halfway down my bum before I could say Jack Robinson.

'Enough! Enough!' squeaked Herringham, unwilling, I suppose, to rush this strange striptease. Now he could fiddle around with my lower back, wittering on about 'lateral extensors' and so on, which basically seemed to entail a lot of work on the top my buttocks, while Grimes explored the new territory that this partial divestment had opened up to him. My cock, sticking straight towards the ceiling, was at least half exposed over the waistband of my pants, pushed up against my bush; Grimes lost no opportunity to give it a squeeze. His kisses were becoming more frequent and blatant. Herringham must have been aware of what was going on, and made no objection. Remembering what Grimes had said about being a 'fuck-totum', I assumed that this was just one aspect of Grimes's role as surrogate lover.

'Would you mind removing your footwear, Paul? Please, sit down if it makes you more comfortable. Grimes will help you.' I sat in a leather-padded swivel chair with curved wooden arms, pushing my groin forward as Grimes knelt beneath my feet. In this position he could unlace and remove my boots and socks (thank God I'd put on a new pair) while occasionally leaning forward to kiss my lower stomach or the head of my cock. The sight of this uniformed monster in such a servile posture was, for me, quite delightful.

'Thank you, Grimes. And now the rest, please.' Grimes needed no second bidding, and so I lifted my arse off the chair and allowed him to pull off my trousers and pants in one swift movement. I sat there, my legs extended in front of me and a yard apart, stark-naked and stiff.

'Now, Paul, if you could jump down on to the floor and kneel for me... That's it, on all fours. And extend one leg behind you like so... Good. Grimes, hold him steady.'

I must have looked rather like a gun dog, pointing at the kill, one leg straight out behind me. Grimes held my thigh and calf while Herringham plied those bloody callipers over the tibia, fibula and God knows what else.

'Now, to save Paul the trouble of moving, Grimes, would you manoeuvre his *membrum virile* into a more accessible position?'

Grimes dropped my leg, which was beginning to tingle with pins and needles, so that I was crouching like an animal. He pushed my head gently to the floor, and then with one hand reached down under my stomach and pushed my cock back between my thighs. In the hands of a novice, this could have been painful. Grimes, however, knew how to manipulate a horny young fellow, and applied the pressure gently and evenly. Herringham now had a clear view of the underside of my prick as it was pushed back between my legs, with the balls hanging down on either side. Surely he was not going to measure this with his callipers!

Oh yes, he was.

He measured it from tip to base. He measured it across. He even made some pretence of calibrating my bollocks, although this was unconvincing.

Finally he was done. 'Thank you, Paul. You may relax.' In truth, I was close to coming. Grimes had made sure of that with surreptitious squeezes and rubbings of my painfully stiff prick. I had been oozing pre-come for the last ten minutes; Grimes had been gleefully licking his fingers, and Herringham's callipers must have been covered in the stuff. I climbed slowly to my feet, my prick sticking straight out in front of me.

'Well, Paul, you pass with flying colours. An excellent anthropometrical result, according in every detail with the classical ideal as exemplified in the works of Praxiteles.' He was off again. I caught Grimes's eye – he winked and smiled. Would the old man leave us to it now, and allow me to give myself to his giant manservant?

'And now, gentlemen, if you are ready, we will proceed into the holy of holies.'

Herringham gestured towards the green-baize door at the back of the room. Grimes took me by the prick and led me onwards.

Eight

Behind the green door... The holy of holies... Preparatory rituals... A strange baptism... Classical tableaux... A fucking masterclass

Strange how closely the two worlds coexisted in those days, rubbing shoulders, separated only by a door, a curtain, a wall – and yet so far divided that the one was almost wholly ignorant of the other. The good, upstanding citizens of London had no idea that behind the handsome façades of their town houses, within their public institutions and seats of government, things went on for which they had no name. Acts were committed that filled the right-minded bourgeoisie with horror, even if they secretly longed to join in (and, in many cases, secretly did). The law turned a blind eye, intervening only when forced by complaints or stupidity. London, some said, was a wicked city – but for the vast majority of its citizens wickedness was hidden away in the dark, where it blossomed in a thousand exotic forms.

To walk through the green-baize door that divided Albert Herringham's office from his studio was to take a step from one world to another. On one side, respectability: wood-panelled walls, business papers, the artefacts of the British Empire, the trappings of success. Admittedly I had been blatantly nude and aroused in that environment – indeed, the incongruity of my naked form in that stiff, formal room had spiced my interest – but this was nothing compared with the journey I was about to make, padding along in my bare feet, led by the cock.

As a child I often tried to picture the Garden of Eden. I had always seen it as an extension of the birthday parties that I had occasionally attended in the homes of other, happier children. Later I learned to view it through the conventional eyes of artists and theologians, but somewhere deep in my imagination I always thought of paradise as a kind of wild party. Now I was stepping straight *into* paradise.

The studio was a large room with a high ceiling; I guessed from its towering proportions that it was, in fact, an upper and a lower room joined together by the removal of the floor that originally divided them. We entered by means of a stairway; the green-baize door gave onto a small wooden platform, from which perhaps fifteen steps led down to the floor, bounded by a brass rail. The first impression, as I stood on that exposed platform, was one of immensity, and of soft, blending colours, warmth and scent – the unmistakable (to me) scent of young, aroused male bodies.

From the centre of the ceiling above me hung a vast brass candelabra, now rigged up with electric lights, dreadfully besmirched with cobwebs, dust and fly-spots. The light from this dangerous-looking contraption was blinding enough at ceiling level, but did little to illuminate the cavernous space below, providing, instead, an intriguing arrangement of shadows that lent a painterly aspect to the whole. Far more light was available through the tall, high windows let into the upper half of the north wall; these, however, were shuttered at present, allowing only a little daylight to creep in around the edges. Perhaps when Herringham was at work the shutters would be thrown back to afford him the light he needed; indeed, directly opposite the windows was the artist's work area, strewn with easels and canvasses. At the present time, however, there was nothing in the way of work going on in that studio.

Around the brass rod that held the chandelier were tied the ends of several lengths of silk and chiffon, which sagged downwards and were then tied to the banisters of the narrow gallery that ran round the upper half of the room. This arrangement of fabric gave the room an Eastern feel, as if I had stepped into the tent of some nomadic potentate, some travelling tradesman scouring strange lands for spices, jewels and slaves. The impression was fortified by a couple of ornate brass lamps, pierced with the shapes of moons and stars, from within which issued fragrant incense. The walls were hung with rugs, and with pictures – these latter, I assumed, the product of Herringham's brush, as they depicted the young male nude in various stages of sexual depravity. One picture that caught my eye, hung as it was near the stairs, showed a novel variation on the myth of Theseus and the Minotaur – a bending, naked youth being sodomised by a hairy giant with a bull's head. The expression on the youth's face was one of rapturous joy; his cock, which was the focal point of the painting, looked ready to explode. I don't know much about art, but I can say with the authority of experience that Herringham's handling of that cock was absolutely exquisite.

I was just wondering whether Grimes had posed as the Minotaur (I felt sure he had: who else had that barrel chest?) when I found myself the object of a general scrutiny from the dimly lit nether regions of this little Sodom.

'Gentlemen!' announced Herringham in a theatrical voice.

'And ladies!' came a limp rejoinder from below, followed by coarse laughter.

'I would like to introduce to you another celebrant in the sacred mysteries, a new votary at the temple of Priapus, ready to pour forth his libations in the name of true art.' Herringham fluted on in this vein for a minute or so; Grimes, who still had his hand wrapped round my prick, was casually wanking me the while, in full view of anyone who cared to look. 'May I present to you, Mr Paul!'

There was a desultory round of applause from below; my sharp ears also picked out the telltale creaking of furniture and the odd moist, squelchy sound that suggested sexual activity. As my eyes grew accustomed to the inadequate lighting, I could make out a little better the details of the room beneath – and it was, without doubt, full of life. Ten, twelve, perhaps twenty men disported themselves in various stages of undress around the studio. Once the applause had died down (it didn't take long), Grimes led me down the staircase; as soon as the electric lights were above my eye level I could see a good deal more clearly.

Over there, on a battered red-velvet couch, a guardsman in full scarlet uniform, his tunic unbuttoned to reveal a chest covered in blond fur, was kissing a naked youth with the coarse features and wiry body of a barrow boy. The latter kissed with the greed and hunger of his class, then, as I watched, drew the guardsman's handsome cock out of his trousers and started tossing him off.

In another corner, a huge, attractive black man, who looked to me like something out of Rider Haggard's *King Solomon's Mines*, lay on his back with his legs spread, one huge muscular arm dangling heavily off the edge off the divan, while an older gent of military bearing slowly fucked him up the bum. Elsewhere lads of my own age, slightly older or slightly younger, all of them well proportioned (Herringham had been busy with his callipers), lounged on the furniture, read books, slept, drank and masturbated. Some of them watched me with undisguised interest, pointing cocks of all shapes and sizes at me; others were languidly detached from their surroundings, presumably exhausted by pleasure.

A grunt from the corner alerted the room to the fact that someone was coming – and I turned my head just in time to see the black man shooting arc after arc of sperm from his thick ebony cock as his older lover pumped solemnly away at his backside. The spunk landed over his chest and stomach, where it pooled or dribbled away. I was transfixed by the contrast of white on black; this was my first encounter with a naked black man, a phenomenon by no means common to your average London renter in that period. The man on top scooped up a handful of spunk (it was a copious load) and brought it to his mouth, savouring the taste, and then, inspired by the sensation, buried himself to the hilt and proceeded to spew his own load into the black man's guts. They fell into an embrace and presently dozed.

'Now, Paul, you must make yourself at home,' said Herringham, fussing around the place, collecting empty bottles and glasses, stopping occasionally to stare with candid admiration at a hard cock, a smooth arse. 'We have work to do presently.'

'Yes, sir.' I was in a daze, and hardly knew what to answer. Had I been brought here to model, in good faith? Or was I just another inmate of Herringham's peculiar sexual menagerie?

'Grimes, take Paul next door and prepare him as we discussed. I shall make ready with the assistance of one of these kind gentlemen.' Two of the nearest young men sprang to their feet and began setting up a stool and an easel; this was clearly a well-practised routine.

Grimes took me across the room, no longer holding my cock (which remained quite stiff of its own accord; there was plenty to keep it interested) and into a small antechamber that housed a lavatory and a basin.

'What is this place, Grimes?' I asked.

'The studio, of course,' he growled, shutting the door behind us.

'But all the lads – who are they?'

'Models, like yourself. Some of them are working for the old man at the moment. Some just come to... waste time. Some of them entertain Mr Herringham's friends.'

'You mean... like a brothel?'

'Not *like* a brothel, Paul. It *is* a brothel. The best male brothel in London.'

'And what's your job in all this? The eunuch in the harem?'

'I'm not a eunuch, of that I can assure you.' He grabbed my hand and placed it on his groin, where something of a truly alarming length and girth was nestling. I felt certain that I was to become well acquainted with the contents of Grimes's trousers before I was much older.

'So the gentleman who was fucking the black man...'

'Ah, you didn't see him here.'

'Of course not.' I understood the etiquette of the trade well enough. 'But he's a... friend of the master's, is he?'

'Certainly. A very good, very influential friend.' Grimes dropped his voice to a whisper. 'I didn't tell you this, Paul, but he's a very big knob at Scotland Yard.'

'Handy friend to have.'

'You can say that again.'

Grimes was unbuttoning his navy-blue tunic; underneath he wore the standard vest of the period. Dark hair protruded above, around and indeed through the material. The man was a bull.

'So, Grimes,' I said, almost nervous in this strange environment, 'what are we meant to be doing?'

'I'm to get you ready, lad.'

'Ready for what?'

'You're modelling for the master.'

'I know that, but what preparations are necessary, now that he's got my clothes off?'

'I understand we're presenting a mythical subject this afternoon. Don't ask me the name – they all sound the same after a while. I believe it has some kind of nautical theme.'

I remembered what Herringham had been saying about Leander crossing the Hellespont, and said as much to Grimes.

'That sounds perfectly likely to me, lad, but I'm not a scholar. I just do as the old man tells me, and on this occasion I've been instructed to deliver you to the studio soaked to the skin.'

'As if swimming the Hellespont.'

'Whatever.'

'I see. And so you're going to pour water over me.'

'Those were the master's instructions, yes. He don't like a lot of water splashing around the studio, so I brought you into the shitter to do it.'

'I hope it's warm.'

'There's only cold in here, Paul.' Grimes had a naughty look in his eye, and I suspected that he had some perverse plan afoot. My cock, which had gone slightly off the boil, twitched back into life.

'That's most unfortunate. A drenching with cold water will do nothing for my... proportions.' I hefted my cock and balls with one hand, impressing on Grimes their rapid reinflation.

'Well, now, I wonder how we can get round that problem,' said Grimes, who by now had stripped off his tunic and was slowly unbuttoning his fly.

'I think you have an idea, don't you, Grimes?'

He grinned in the most sinister fashion. Had I met with him in a dark alley in a less reputable part of town, I would have been frightened. As it was, I throbbed with excitement.

'Yes, I do. You kneel down on the floor there, Paul, and let's see how you take to it.'

The reader will remember that I was no stranger to this form of activity, although thus far I had always been the provider, rather than the recipient. However, I had seen how much pleasure Trevor and a few other clients got out of being pissed on, and was by no means averse to subjecting myself to such degradation, especially from such a handsome brute as Grimes.

I knelt obediently on the cold tiles, my hands on my hips.

Grimes dropped his trousers, and I saw that he was wearing combinations under his uniform. I have always regarded these as the most unattractive form of underwear known to man; on Grimes, however, they looked good enough. His cock had practically popped the buttons at the fly.

It took him only moments to step out of them. He stood before me, stark-naked, a huge, dark, hairy colossus of a man, his thighs as thick as telegraph poles, his shins shaggy, his belly and chest curving upwards covered in fur as thick as a doormat. And protruding from this dense forest was one of the mightiest pricks I have ever seen – and I've seen some mighty bastards in my time.

'So, Paul, are you ready?'

'I'm ready.' In truth, I was so inspired by the thought of having Grimes piss on me that I was half minded to take the whole lot in my mouth and swallow it, as Trevor had occasionally done. This, however, would have defeated the object of the exercise, and necessitated my douching in freezing-cold water from the basin. 'Fire away.'

He stood over me, his cock throbbing and swaying as he gently rocked his hips – but no piss came.

'I'm too hard, Paul, from looking at you.'

'Close your eyes, then, and think of... I don't know. Think of England.'

'I tell you what, mate,' said Grimes, closing his eyes, 'I'll think of the old man. That should do the trick.'

With a look of intense concentration on his handsome mug, Grimes willed his prick into a state of adequate detumescence – and then, without warning, a flood of yellow piss was gushing on to my chest. I pushed myself forward to meet it, revelling in the heat of the fluid as it made contact with my skin. I watched it flow in snaking rivulets down my stomach, losing itself in my pubic hair and then running in a concentrated stream off the end of my hard cock – as if I myself were pissing.

Grimes walked around me, never breaking his flow, soaking my arms, my legs, and my back, down which the piss ran over my arse and down my crack. He aimed a stream at my cock, laughing out loud when he saw how the force of his flow actually pushed it down from the perpendicular. Then he pinched the end of his cock between finger and thumb, screwed up his eyes in effort and quenched the stream.

'Got to save enough for the last bit, Paul. Are you ready?'

It didn't take much to figure out what he meant: there was only one part of me that was still dry – my face and head. I nodded and bent my neck.

I felt his cock slipping over my forehead as he pressed it against me, and then again came the torrent of piss, first in my hair, which was soon as wet as if I'd just washed it, then over my face, over my closed eyes, running over the end of my nose and down my chin. Finally I felt the stream directed straight on my lips; I could no longer resist, and opened my mouth. Grimes stuck the head straight in, and gave me the last few fluid ounces on to my tongue. It tasted less foul than I had expected – salty, pungent, but by no means disgusting. I swallowed as much as he could give and then closed my lips halfway down his shaft (it was as far as I could take him in that position) and concentrated on sucking out any recalcitrant drops. I was also eager to taste another fluid from his prick...

Grimes allowed me to suck on him for a few moments, stroking my wet hair, but then he pulled back, his dick a great glistening sausage that looked as if it would burst its skin.

'Wouldn't do to let you dry off, Paul,' he said, grinning. 'Better deliver you to the old bugger as wet as he could wish.'

Again he took me by the dick and led me back into the studio.

My first modelling assignment for William Herringham RA is etched on my mind as one of the strangest experiences of my young life. When I regained the studio, it no longer resembled the scene from biblical Sodom that I had witnessed half an hour earlier: now it was prepared for business, the decorative young men were dressed, and either departing or at work as Herringham's assistants, fetching and carrying paper, easels and other paraphernalia of the craft. The senior police officer, whom I had so recently seen pumping his spunk up a black man's arse, was dressed in a formal suit, sitting rather stiffly on one of a row of bentwood chairs set in a half-moon around the dais to which I was led by the naked henchman. There were eight chairs, four of which were currently occupied, besides that on which the inspector was stationed. The rest of the 'audience', as I must call them, were similarly respectable and well heeled; I recognised at least one of them from the illustrated papers, and had the impression that he was either a cabinet minister or a member of the aristocracy. All of them but one were in middle age or more; the exception was a willowy, effetely beautiful blond of unmistakably noble lineage. His hair, long for the day, flopped over his brow in golden sheaves and curled over his ears; his face, as fine as a girl's, boasted alabaster skin, rosy lips and an expression of habitual debauchery. He watched me through hooded eyes, possibly darkened with kohl, while toying with an elaborate malacca cane with which he described arcs on the studio floor.

'Gentleman,' piped Herringham, now attired in smock and beret, the very image of a great artist, 'this afternoon we begin work on a new tableau reinterpreting the legend of Poseidon and Leander. In the person of Poseidon, of course, is a trusty hero, Grimes.' (A muffled round of applause from the gloved hands.) And impersonating Leander is a new Herringham discovery, Monsieur Paul Lemoyne.'

Silence.

'To your positions, please, boys.'

Grimes seemed to know what was required of me, and helped me up onto a wooden block about four feet high, mercifully covered in a black velvet cloth (I did not want splinters in my arse, not even for the Royal Academy). 'Sit there with yer legs spread,' he whispered in my ear, 'and look as if you're swimming up to the surface.'

'We join the story at the point at which Poseidon has seized Leander and is dragging him down into the briny depths of the Hellespont. The poor mortal lad, eager to reach his lady love across the straits, struggles to reach the surface, to fill his lungs with air and to escape the intrusive attentions of the sea god. Poseidon, however, has caught him fast, and will hold him in his fatal embrace until Leander, too, joins the immortals for an eternity of pleasure.'

Grimes reclined at my feet in a pose vaguely suggestive of swimming, and caught me round the calf with one great thick arm.

'Perfect, Grimes. As you will see, gentlemen, Leander is already soaked in... brine.'

'He smells like a cottage,' snipped the perverted young lord, who surveyed us languidly through a monocle.

'Today I will concentrate on sketching the outline, and on

capturing the youth's struggles as he tries to escape the clutches of his divine lover – and perhaps as he struggles against desires that he knows are wrong.'

'Oh, for Christ's sake, Herringham,' said the young lord, 'you don't have to gild the lily. It's quite enough for us that they're naked and have such lovely big pricks. What I want to know is when we're going to see them get up to their dirty tricks.'

Grimes sniggered beneath me, and squeezed my leg. Herringham flapped like an old lady at a garden party annoyed by a wasp. 'Lord Simon, I beg you to have a little respect for the muse! If you have any suggestions about the appropriateness of the pose...'

'Oh come on, mother, you know what we're here for. Do your scribbles and then give us some fun.'

The rest of the audience were pained by the manner of Lord Simon's outburst, but clearly sympathised with its content. 'Perhaps,' added Scotland Yard, 'you might show Poseidon grabbing Leander by the balls.' The seriousness of his tone made me giggle; I had to disguise it as a sneeze. 'Or perhaps,' added another, 'with two fingers up his anus.'

'Or with their members pressed together,' added another.

Herringham tapped on his easel with a pencil, like a conductor bringing an orchestra to heel. 'Gentlemen, please! The composition is already decided by the artist. Let us commence.'

'Well just hurry up, I beg you,' mumbled Lord Simon, his coral-pink lips in a mighty pout.

Herringham scribbled and scratched at his easel, his eyes darting from the paper to the models, while I held my arms above my head in what I hoped was a fair impersonation of a boy swimming upwards. The pose stretched my torso, and showed off my ribs; I made sure to keep my legs wide apart, so that the viewing public got a good view of my cock and balls, my inside thigh. Miraculously, I stayed hard. Perhaps it was the pressure of Grimes's hand on my thigh, or my occasional glances down at his magnificent Lascar body. Perhaps it was the taste of his piss, which I could revive by licking my lips, where the urine had dried leaving a thick mineral deposit. My hair, and the skin on my face, back and arms, felt stiff and tight where the piss had dried, as if I had indeed been bathing in the sea and had allowed the sun to dry me.

Finally, after a painful forty-five minutes of this masquerade, Herringham laid down his pencil, passed a hand across his forehead and turned away from the easel. 'That is all I can give you just now. I must rest, rest, rest.'

'Gentlemen,' said Scotland Yard, 'a round of applause for Mr Herringham.' Again, the gloved hands joined in muffled clapping while Herringham turned the easel to face them and bowed graciously. I was glad to relax the pose, and was about to go and find my clothes, but Grimes whispered, 'Not yet.'

The assistants were closing the shutters and relighting the lamps; Herringham himself took off his smock and was escorted out of the room. The rest of the gentlemen, those five who were sitting in a half-moon around the dais, showed no inclination to leave.

'And now at last,' said Lord Simon, 'perhaps you two fellows would be good enough to give us what we came here for.'

'Certainly, sirs,' said Grimes. 'As you're all regulars, I assume that there are, within reason, no holds barred?'

'As long as you don't hurt the boy, Grimes,' said Scotland Yard, attempting, I suppose, to muster a little professional dignity.

'Naturally, sir, naturally.' Grimes squeezed my bum, cleared his throat and proceeded in the mock-posh tones of a music-hall announcer: 'And now, my lords, ladies and gentlemen...' He nodded towards Lord Simon on uttering 'ladies'; the young aristo simpered like a girl, leading me to believe that he had been skewered by Grimes before now. 'May I present to you the most tragical... classical... erotical... homosexual story of Poseidon and Leander!'

There was another round of applause, more audible than before. Gloves were being drawn off, hands pressed more openly over swelling groins. The mood had been reverential when Herringham was in the room, although I had seen plenty of evidence of excitement beneath the pinstripes; now, however, I sensed that the tone was about to be lowered to that of the smoking room.

'Now, Paul,' whispered Grimes, 'just follow my lead and remember: the better your performance, the more money we get.' The thought of money was enough to rid me of any qualms of modesty I may have had, and my cock sprang back to full life. 'Will you take another soaking?' he whispered, licking my ear. 'Gladly,' I said. The thought of submitting to such humiliation in front of an audience was almost too much to bear. I knelt again.

Soaked once more, I took Grimes's cock in my mouth and this time began to suck with a will. I had him fully hard within a minute, and he took over, fucking my mouth with a display of violence. My lips were stretched to the point of pain, and I was bringing up copious amounts of saliva, which dribbled out the sides of my mouth – and yet I would not have stopped, or disappointed the gentlemen, for all I was worth. For their part, they leaned forward in their seats to get the best possible view of the action, but showed no inclination to join in. Their formality, and my abandoned nakedness, focused my mind on the novelty of the situation to stimulating effect.

Once I had proved my sluttishness to the assembled company with such a greedy display of cocksucking, Grimes hauled me to my feet and walked me off the dais, leading me around the half-circle of chairs like a prize bullock up for auction at the market. My prick was jutting out in front of me, throbbing and swinging with each step; being the show-off that I was, I took delight in waving it in the gentlemen's faces. They stared at it with the rapt concentration of the connoisseur, but so far none of them made a move to touch it.

We stopped in front of one chair, where I was closely inspected by a tolerably handsome man of early middle age, perhaps thirty-eight years old, the very epitome of the respectable city gent, his mid-brown hair neatly cut, slightly receding at the temples and thin on top, his chin freshly shaved and redolent of a good cologne. He wore the cutaway collar and sombre tie of the banker, and looked for all the world like one of the unremarkable hundreds of well-turned-out family men who came up from the shires every day to earn their living in the Square Mile. How many of them, I wondered, took their pleasures thus? He stared at my cock like a rabbit staring at a snake, and I thrust my hips forward like the easiest of whores. A drip of clear, viscous fluid oozed out of my piss slit and hung there, an invitation and a challenge. He looked up at me, and then over my shoulders to Grimes, as if seeking permission.

'Go ahead, sir,' said Grimes. 'It won't bite.'

'It might spit, though, sir,' I added, thinking that a touch of cheeky banter would be appreciated. I was right: Banker smiled, gripped my shaft with a firm hand and licked the diamond off the end of it. His touch, and the sight of his immaculate starched white cuffs moving up and down as he wanked me, set my cock to hardening even more.

And so I was passed around the group, each having a touch here, a taste there. Some of them wanted only to worship my cock; others (Scotland Yard among them) were more interested in the back entrance, and had Grimes turn me round, bend me over and part my cheeks with his huge, square-ended fingers. Every so often I would feel a digit gingerly pressed against my hole, or a tongue fluttering around my crease (this belonged to Lord Simon, clearly the most debauched of the party), as I continued my tour of inspection. As I bent over and submitted to this aristocratic rimming, I noticed out of the corner of my eye that Scotland Yard had fished his prick out of his flies and was slowly wanking himself. The others, surely, would join him before long.

Grimes led me back to the dais, sat on the block, put me over his knee and commenced a firm spanking. This seemed to delight them all; in my experience of servicing the upper classes, I have always found that the punishments of the schoolroom and nursery have a particular significance. I played my part, screwing up my face and yelping as that great shovel of a hand bore down on my downy bum; in truth, Grimes was not too harsh on me, and administered just enough pain to get my cheeks glowing. My cock, stimulated by this general blood-flow to the nether regions, pressed against his sinuous thigh and smeared it with pre-come.

Once my bum was warmed up, it was time for the main event, in which it would be fucked in every conceivable position. We started off doggy style: I knelt on all fours, while Grimes steered himself into me from the rear. Mercifully, I had taken cocks almost as big before; remember, I had been broken for riding by Mr Newsome, who shared Grimes's girth, if he lacked, perhaps, an inch of length. I knew how to control my breathing, to ride through the pain, to relax sufficiently to convert it into pleasure, and by the time Grimes had been inside me for a few moments I was ready to take anything he could give me.

Grimes was a true professional, holding himself upright with his arms out of the way so that the gents had an unobstructed view of his prick moving in and out of my arsehole, pulling the lips back with each withdrawal, then plunging in to the hilt again. I, for my part, tried to show that I was still as hard as before, but gradually I was losing my focus on the act of performance, and simply enjoying the ride. I was gratified to see that all the voyeurs were now wanking openly, and that Lord Simon had persuaded Banker to lend him a couple of fingers in order that he might experience the same sensations, in a lesser form, as I was.

Next I was flipped over on my back, my legs hauled in the air and rested on Grimes's shoulders, and the giant himself bore his whole weight down on me through his cock, resting only on the heels of his palms and his toes. In this position he seemed able to penetrate me even more deeply than before, and to batter my prostate gland to such an extent that I was spewing ejaculate all over my stomach without actually achieving orgasm. I had no idea that so much fluid could be produced in this way; even a seasoned whore like me could learn something new once in a while.

Finally, Grimes lay on his back on the black velvet cloth, stretched his arms above his head and grinned up at me. 'Come on, Paul,' he said, smiling in invitation, 'sit on it.'

I needed no second bidding. Making sure that the audience would get the best possible view, I climbed on, took his weapon in my right hand and steered it into position. As soon as the tip was engaged, I allowed my weight to shift to my bum, and I slid smoothly down his well-lubricated shaft until he was buried right inside me. Grimes put his hands behind his head and enjoyed the ride; I bucked up and down, my thigh muscles screaming with the effort, my cock still drizzling his matted stomach with goo. Finally, Grimes lifted his buttocks off the floor and matched each descent with an upward thrust; this, surely, was the furthest I had ever taken a cock. With that thought, I exploded into orgasm, and shot what seemed at the time to be the biggest load of my life. Most of it landed on Grimes's hairy chest; some of it reached his moustache, where it was quickly licked up. A few pearls fell on the black velvet cloth, now rucked and rumpled beneath us. I squeezed out the last few drops, and Grimes shuffled out from underneath me. I collapsed, completely spent, while Grimes, taking his cock in his hand, brought himself off in three or four casual strokes. His load matched mine, and my slender, panting body was liberally bathed in his cream. Just behind my head I could hear the unmistakable noise of several men reaching orgasm; I craned my head around to watch. Scotland Yard wanked hard and shot a messy load over his trousers – the volume was impressive, given that he'd so recently fucked. Banker tossed himself off into a clean linen handkerchief, which he then refolded and replaced in his trouser pocket. Lord Simon, now fingering himself, shot great ribbons of sperm out of a long, slender cock; most of it landed on the floor, although I was delighted to see one gout hit his neighbour's shoulder, where it sat for a while unremarked before soaking into the fabric. The other two watchers seemed to be friends, and wanked each other in unison while enjoying a long kiss.

And then, refreshed and rebuttoned, they returned to the other world that lay beyond the green-baize door.

Nine

Shameful behaviour... I fuck royalty... The call of modernism... Mikhail Boleslavsky, genius and madman... Debasement in the basement... The artist at work... 'Red Hole'

I had told Albert Abbott that I would never abandon my first friends at the Palace of Varieties; that good intention, like so many of the others that paved my road to hell, was soon swept away as I found myself increasingly caught up with William Herringham and his circle. By the end of that first afternoon, I had more money in my pocket than I had ever seen before; more than I could have earned in a month of renting. Each of my gentleman voyeurs had pressed 'a little something' into my hand upon departing; these mostly turned out to be ten-pound notes. Lord Simon was particularly lavish, and I blush to record the figure.

My head was turned. With new friends like these, what need had I of Mr Holly and his petty tyrannies? Why sleep in Mrs Tunnock's rundown boarding house when I could stay, rent-free, in a small *garçonnière* just off the Strand, courtesy of one of my wealthy protectors? There I could receive callers, and the steady stream of invitations and presents that came with them. I could sleep all day if I chose. I could use any one of half a dozen names to secure credit at the best shops in the West End. I even enjoyed a limited celebrity, among art lovers of a certain persuasion. When Herringham's first commission was complete (it remains to this day in a private collection), I was chosen to 'star' in one of his public works, and posed (without Grimes, on this occasion) as Narcissus gazing into the pond. My buttocks were on view, draped with a wisp of chiffon, but a strange formation in the mossy mound on which I lay suggested to the interested viewer what propriety concealed. The picture was an instant success, and was mentioned favourably in *The Times*. I wondered whether my mother and father would ever see it.

Grimes, I am happy to say, was appointed my minder and general helpmeet. He continued to live with Herringham, but was a frequent visitor to my new address on Adam Street. On his visits here (usually in the afternoon, when Herringham was resting) Grimes would fuck me until I could barely walk. There was never any suggestion that I should do anything other than receive, nor did I want to. I learned a little about his past history. Dismissed from the army after an embarrassing court martial (he had been caught stealing, and I suspect had also been fucking every private who fell into his hands), Sergeant Major Grimes found himself broke and unemployable. He dabbled in crime, and showed me a few scars on his face and arms from the knife fights he got into. But he had no stomach for violence, and so found himself employed as a navvy in and around London. It was during a summer job on Burlington House, where he had been digging drainage ditches in the courtyard, that he captured the attention of William Herringham RA, and found himself installed in the studio. Once or twice Grimes brought his friends to visit me, some of them ex-army, some of them navvies, all of them great masculine hulks like himself, who took turns in topping and tailing me. I looked forward to these sessions with a mixture of fear and drooling lust.

I was less faithful to my other companions. When I left my job at the Palace, I barely said goodbye to anyone – the only people I would miss were Vera and Kieran. Vera was philosophical, and made me swear to write to him once a month (I failed, of course, but Vera's letters, in his crabbed hand, continued to pursue me with their kindly concern). Kieran was sullen and hid his emotions beneath a façade of indifference.

'Well, good luck to you, Paul. I hope your new friends turn out to be everything you hope they'll be.'

'Don't worry about me, Kieran. I'm going to make something of my life.' This was cruel of me, for Kieran worked hard, and honestly – he had never turned to crime or prostitution, unlike me. He continued to pursue his Rose, with blue balls and a growing air of desperation. I could see him, ten years from now, his looks and figure gone, a hopeless nobody like the dozens of others who haunted London's theatres.

'Maybe I'll see you round.' He looked so sad as he said this, turning away from me in the room where we'd shared many youthful dreams, that I thought for a moment of relenting, of taking him with me, or making some declaration of my feelings, for, whatever my new life, I still had a tender spot for Kieran that, had he wanted, could have developed into something like love.

I swallowed the impulse. 'Maybe.'

I turned on my heel and left.

I burn with shame as I write these words; I do not believe, now, that I could be such a callous little tart. Ah, well, I was young, I was surrounded by distracting new friends and experiences, and I was getting my arse regularly stretched and my dick well sucked, often by crowned heads. Can anyone really blame me? I will say in my defence that I deposited a sum of money with Vera to hand over to my various 'creditors', to make good my abuse of their hospitality and trust.

While I was distracted by Lord Simon, William Herringham, Grimes and co., the ruling passion in my life was still Albert Abbott. He was the boss, telling me whom to encourage, whom to flatter, whom to deceive. He came every day, or every other day, to Adam Street to review the latest haul of presents and invitations. He quizzed me about my cash flow, and would always levy a certain amount, which I was only too glad to give him. I received him like every other grand courtesan receiving her lover – *en déshabillé*, lounging around artfully revealing my charms, hoping that he would grab the half-hard cock that dangled within reach, or slap the curved, fuzzy buttock that so innocently peeked from beneath my rucked-up dressing-gown. He seldom did so. Every so often, when I least expected it, Abbott would grab me for a passionate, bruising kiss, burning my lips with his, thrusting his tongue into my mouth for minutes at a time as if he would eat my very soul. Then he would release me, quivering in my legs and stiff in my cock, as if nothing had happened. Of course, this unpredictable treatment made me love him madly – much more than if we'd established regular relations. For this relief, however, I was never lacking, thanks to my friends in high – and low – places.

My success as a Herringham Golden Boy took me to places that I would never have dreamed of going, and along the way I picked up a superficial polish in my manners that enabled me to move through the drawing rooms of Mayfair with a minimum of gaffes. Abbott was delighted with my progress. It confirmed his instinct that I was 'a quick study', and presumably also convinced him that I was almost infinitely corruptible. He never asked me, directly, to steal or to blackmail, but he suggested any number of ways that I could extract money from the wallets of the wealthy without actually committing a crime. Knowing as he did that I was willing to allow almost any man with two arms and two legs to take advantage of my dick or my arse, he realised that our money-making capabilities were almost infinite. And there were many men in London who were happy to play along – for a while.

Lord Simon was closely connected with royalty, both domestic and foreign, and it was through him that I entered into a brief but profitable liaison with a minor scion of the house of Windsor, whose family were only too happy to pay me a very large sum in order to terminate the friendship. 'Think how much worse it would be for them if you'd been a girl,' said Abbott, dictating what I thought were outrageous severance terms in a letter that would bear my name. 'You might have got pregnant, and produced a little royal bastard. Let's face it, he's fucked you often enough to guarantee conception.' The truth was that the Duke of —— had been fucked just as often by me, and in a series of costumes that he'd 'borrowed' from the royal wardrobes and barracks. 'As it is, they're getting off lightly. You haven't even given him the clap, let alone an unwanted heir. Let's remind them just how relieved they should be.'

Another royal connection came in the form of Prince 'Timmy', another connection of Lord Simon's, up at Oxford and preparing to take the crown in his native land of —— in East Africa. 'Timmy' was young – the same age as I was, in fact – and had little enthusiasm for the wife, or wives, that awaited him on his return home. 'When I am at home, I please God and my country,' he told me. 'When I am in England, I please myself.' This involved long, athletic sessions in which we debauched each other in every conceivable position, and with every available inanimate object, sometimes in my rooms, sometimes in his suite at the nearby Savoy, sometimes in the low filthy pubs and baths that he favoured in the East End. Prince 'Timmy', who reigned as king for some years after our friendship until a military coup cut short his life at the age of 35, proved my theory that the higher the social position, the lower the desires.

For a while I became the plaything of Detective Superintendent ——, whom I had met on that first afternoon *chez* Herringham. Visits to Adam Street, where he proved himself a considerate and very passionate lover, were soon supplemented by dinners at his club and even, on two occasions, evening invitations to his home, where his wife entertained a mixture of senior policemen, politicians, artists and writers. The superintendent took me on a tour of the upper floors of the houseon the pretext of showing me some fine examples of French *belle époque* art that he was collecting, and there, on the dusty floors of a seldom-used bedroom, sucked me off while the guests were arriving below. Afterwards he dabbed his moustache with his handkerchief, and descended to continue his duties as host. I even met his children – a daughter of fifteen, and a son of fourteen, whom I had little doubt was following in his father's footsteps, and showed far too great an interest in becoming my little friend. Fourteen, even for one as steeped in depravity as myself, was far too young for comfort.

With *Narcissus* hanging in the Academy, *Leander* and a handful of other commissions nurtured in private collections, and a new circle of wealthy friends, I thought I had made it. Abbott, however, had other ideas.

'Herringham is yesterday's man. The people he knows are strictly second-rate.' Lords? Princes? Chiefs of police? I thought not.

'And another thing: he's losing his talent, what little he had. He's too old. The younger generation think he's ridiculous, a relic from a bygone age. It's time for you to move on.'

'But Mr Herringham has been very good to me.'

'Not half as good as you've been to him. Thanks to you, Paul, Herringham's extended his lease on fame for another five years, maybe more. The people who love his pictures of you will carry on patronising him in the hope that he'll turn up another young Apollo. They'll be disappointed. The old man's losing his touch. Between you and me, *Narcissus* was pretty ropy.'

'But *The Times* said—'

'*The Times* gave it a good review because their art critic is a hardened pervert,' said Abbott, with that cruel smile that never failed to make my balls ache. 'The rest of us know that it's a silly little piece, and that the only good thing about it is your beautiful face.'

'And my arse.'

'How could I forget your arse?'

'You seem to have done.'

I hoped that this coquettish remark would inspire Abbott to molest me, but he turned the subject as quickly as he could.

'And so I have a new assignment for you. One that will seal your position in society.'

I wondered what this could be. 'Please tell me more. Who do I have to fuck this time?'

'Paul, please try to take your mind off sex just for a moment. And please stop playing with your penis, which I admit is the prettiest I have ever seen. It is very distracting.'

'I can't. It needs... relief.'

'Later. Now put it away.' He gave me one of those looks that allow no argument. 'Thank you. Now listen. I have secured you an interview with Mikhail Boleslavsky, the Russian constructivist painter.'

'Never heard of him.'

'That is disappointing, but hardly surprising, given the effete circles in which you have been moving.'

'Is he a communist?'

'Of course he's a communist. But he's left Russia, and is currently living and working in Bloomsbury.'

'Bloomsbury? Why would anyone want to live there, when they could live in Mayfair?'

'Paul, do me a favour and only open your mouth when it can make us some money. Mikhail Boleslavsky is an extremely highly regarded genius. His paintings have already been the subject of books by some of the most famous critics in the country. He is admired by such writers as Clive Bell, Virginia Woolf, D H Lawrence. He is... a force of nature.'

'And he likes young men.'

'Naturally he likes young men. He paints them. Not that you'd ever know it from looking at his canvases, which, by the way, I would advise you to study at the Kunstkreis Gallery in Charlotte Street this afternoon before you meet him tomorrow.'

'Very well.'

'Boleslavsky will not pay you, nor, I suspect, will many of the people you will meet at his studio.'

'What's the point?'

'But what he will give you, which is something money cannot buy, is cachet.'

'Cachet.'

'Yes, Paul. Fame. Notoriety. Call it what you will. To be associated with Boleslavsky and his circle puts you in the epicentre of the artistic world. It ensures you a little place in history. It also significantly raises your market value.'

'In other words, there are plenty of people who would pay a great deal of money to fuck a Boleslavsky Boy.'

'Precisely!'

'More than they'd pay to fuck a Herringham Has-Been.'

'Correct.'

'Very well,' I sighed, already regretting the elegant Mayfair world in which I was beginning to feel quite comfortable. 'I am content.'

And, with that, Abbott grabbed me in one of his absurd, unpredictable embraces. Such was his gratitude that he allowed me certain liberties with his person, and the result was that I held our two pricks in my hand as he kissed me, and, pressing their underbellies together, wanked us off all over both of us.

'You're a good, obedient boy,' said Abbott, letting himself out of my flat. Not quite as obedient as he thought: I could give up Herringham, I could give up royalty and Mayfair dinner parties, but I never could give up Grimes and his enormous friends, who continued to use and abuse me for many years to come.

And so – somewhat late in the day, I now realise – I became a modernist. I shook the dust of the Academy from my shoes, and entered the vortex of experimentation, theorising, frequent pretentiousness and occasional inspiration that was the Modern Movement in London. My entrée into these charmed circles, about which so many books have been subsequently written, was through the legendary Mikhail Boleslavsky. If I had a pound for every time I've been asked to comment on Boleslavsky, I would be a rich man by now. Students, critics and art historians have beaten an ever-broadening path to my door in recent years, since the Boleslavsky 'revival' in the seventies, and to each of them I have trotted out a few pleasant anecdotes about his working methods, his moods, his utterances and his personal eccentricities, which seem to send them away happy. I have read most of the stuff that's been published about Boleslavsky and his 'circle' (perhaps 'ring' would be a more appropriate word, and I shall tell you a thing or two about the great man's ring over the next few pages), and it is at best anodyne, at worst erroneous. Well, let me set the record straight. I don't pretend to understand Boleslavsky's art; I never liked it, in fact, and to tell the absolute truth I derive more pleasure from one of William Herringham's second-rate pre-Raphaelite canvases than I do from Boleslavsky's incomprehensible daubs. I know history is against me on this one, and I do not pretend to understand what brings a painter in and out of fashion. (As a footnote: even poor dear Herringham had his revival – very late, and rather short – in the 1980s, when a number of his works went up for auction and stimulated enough interest for a small exhibition at a London gallery. Again – I was interviewed, and was discreet in my remarks.)

Enough of the art history. Mikhail Boleslavsky worked and lived at this time in a small studio in Bedford Square, which he had been given, free of charge, by the distinguished collector and hostess the Duchess of B——, who was content to be 'fucked like a frog' by the wild Russian genius (this was Boleslavsky's account of the arrangement, and I have no reason to doubt it, especially as I once caught sight of some extraordinary bruises on the dear Duchess's torso). It was to this address that I was directed one pleasant spring morning – the sort of morning when the trees seem impatient to come into leaf, when the sky looks freshly washed and when my balls are always churning with an unusually heavy load of spunk. I had been warned by Albert Abbott not to try to extract any money out of Boleslavsky. The man, I had been warned, was a genius, and not to be troubled with sordid financial transactions. (I later discovered that Boleslavsky's rich patrons, among them the amphibious Duchess of B——, had paid Abbott a large sum in order to procure me for the artist. Thus, while Boleslavsky's hands remained clean, filthy lucre rained down all around him.)

To my astonishment, the studio was in a basement. During my time with Herringham I had heard a great deal about the importance of natural light, about why windows had to face north, and why certain times of day were more suitable for painting flesh than others. None of this seemed to matter to my new genius, who worked in conditions so ill lit that it was hard even to read a newspaper in the studio. The single sash window looked out on an area strewn with rubbish, in which a few etiolated weeds struggled to grow; in any case, the glass was so dirty that precious little light could filter through. Any stray beams were blocked by a grubby beige roller blind, which Boleslavsky kept drawn when he was working. At the rear of the building there was a door leading from a small back kitchen to a little L-shaped garden; this, at least, was kept open, allowing the stench of turps and cigarette smoke to escape. The garden was a rubbish dump, full of broken frames, crates, a rusting bicycle and any amount of junk; it provided a home for the half-dozen semi-stray cats that wandered in and out of the studio at will.

I have suggested to one or two academics that Boleslavsky's extraordinary and celebrated use of colour – his 'savage palette', as it has been called – derived largely from the fact that you could see only the very brightest colours in that Stygian gloom, hence the painter's fondness for white, cadmium yellow and some of the brighter reds. This theory, I need hardly add, was dismissed and never printed in the learned articles. Well, here it is; make of it what you will.

Within a few days, the studio would seem like a second home to me, but on my first visit I have to confess that I was disappointed, disgusted even, by the squalor in which the *soi-disant* genius plied his trade. Remember, I was used to higher things: Herringham's handsome quarters, or the elegant homes of my society friends – even my own little *garçonnière* in Adam Street seemed like a palace compared with this dump. What a snob I had become in so short a time! It was not so very long ago that I was content to lodge at Ma Tunnock's, and to consider anything more than a roof over my head a luxury. Now I found myself turning my nose up at the dirt, and trying to protect my new clothes like a prissy society miss on a charity visit.

I pressed the bell push. Nothing happened. I rapped discreetly with my knuckles on the peeling paint of the door. Again, I was not heard. There was no knocker on the door, just the ghost of one, an unpainted patch covered in rust stains. I could hear movement from within, but could see nothing (the blind was down). I wondered what Boleslavsky was doing. Working? Fucking? I was on the point of walking away. The sordid, below-street-level area was beginning to depress me, and if there was no money waiting for me within I might as well return to Adam Street and wait for the next invitation. Abbott would be angry, but who needed Abbott? I had friends more powerful than he was.

Fortunately, I made one last effort to gain entrance. I took a sixpence out of my pocket and tapped hard on the windowpane. This was heard, and elicited a great cry of delight from within. I checked my reflection in the window (I needn't have bothered: it reflected next to nothing) and waited.

After a certain amount of crashing, the door was flung open and there stood Mikhail Boleslavsky, framed, as it were, like a picture. And I must say, he was much better to look at than any of the canvases he created. My first impression was of energy, and when I think of Boleslavsky to this day I always think of a man brimming, bursting with force. He ran at life. He didn't speak: he shouted. He didn't eat: he devoured. His enthusiasm, his passions, were an education to me. Again, I am running ahead. Let me try to describe what I saw.

It was quite obvious that he had just got out of bed: he was wearing a pair of trousers that had been pulled on in a hurry, the flies unbuttoned, the twisted braces pulled over the shoulders. His feet were bare, his dark red hair was uncombed, and he wasn't wearing a shirt. His vest, which was skin-tight, revealed pale, powerful shoulders and arms, and concealed a torso that was obviously athletic. He was just thirty when I met him.

Boleslavsky had what I would call a Slavic cast of feature: high cheekbones, almond-shaped eyes, a high brow and a large mouth with big, regular teeth. His canines showed alarmingly when he laughed (often) and gave him a slightly vampiric air, if ever a vampire was as healthy and boisterous as he. His hair, as I have said, was rust-coloured, somewhat longer than was normal in those days (well, he was an artist), touching his collar at the back where it curled up, swept back from the forehead and held partially in place with an adhesive pomade. When Boleslavsky was working, he would sometimes absent-mindedly wipe his brushes or his hands in his hair, and I began to suspect that his hair was dressed with nothing other than linseed oil. As he stood there, a lock of hair had fallen over his left eye; he pushed it back with one nicotine-stained hand. I noticed that the nails and cuticles were badly bitten, and grimed with pigment. He looked not unlike one of Grimes's navvy friends, if perhaps somewhat more aesthetically pleasing. Grooming, clearly, was not one of the man's priorities. To complete the image, he was unshaven and sported sideburns that came well below the bottom of his ears. A respectable Englishman (or even an unrespectable one like me) would have pegged him instantly as an artist – or, even worse, a foreigner.

All of this I took in in one moment; I suspect that Boleslavsky was appraising me in the same way, and cataloguing me as a jumped-up little snob with a vicious streak. Fair comment.

'Come in, Paul!' He pronounced it 'Powl', and generally speaking preferred during the course of our friendship to call me Pavel.

I expected an interview, I suppose – an audition of the sort that I had undergone *chez* Herringham. Was I the right physical type? What kind of experience did I have? Could I hold a pose, or express the right emotions or moods through my facial expression?

Nothing of the sort with Boleslavsky. Models, for him, were not so much objects that had to be copied on to canvas: they were, I suppose, an inspiration. Being horny made Boleslavsky want to paint, and painting made him want to fuck, and so it was necessary for him to have someone attractive around him so he could do both simultaneously (quite literally simultaneously, on occasion). When he painted me, he would look often at my body, and encourage me to take certain poses, but I don't think he ever tried to represent me on canvas, at least not in any way I could understand. I was there, I suppose, to put him in the mood and to provide relief.

So the first thing Boleslavsky needed to know was not how well I could perform as an artist's mannequin, but how well I could fuck. Without further preamble, he took me by the upper arm, pulled me inside, shut the door behind me and pressed me up against it. His mouth found mine, and his face rubbed against mine like sandpaper (a sensation that always gets me instantly hard). He grabbed my left hand in his right, and shoved it down his unbuttoned trousers; it goes without saying that an artist of Boleslavsky's stature had long ago eschewed the bourgeois constrictions of underwear. His cock was already half hard, and, the moment my fingers were wrapped around it, it became as stiff as an iron bar. His hips pumped, and he began to fuck my fist like a randy dog.

Well, if he wanted to play dirty, I would go along with it – and win. Giving his tongue one final suck, I pushed him away, leaving his cock sticking up over the waistband of his trousers. He staggered slightly, caught his heel on the edge of his foldaway bed (which was still deployed on the studio floor, the sheets crumpled and grey) and landed on his back on the mattress. It was a most agreeable sight. I like to have a man at my mercy within a few moments of meeting him.

There was something about the atmosphere of the studio, and the violent assault of the artist, that made me reckless. I began tearing off my clothes and throwing them willy-nilly on the floor, not caring whether they landed in blobs of paint or clumps of cat fur. So much for the presents that had been lavished on me by Lord Simon and co.: a fine shirt joined a beautiful linen jacket in the debris of Boleslavsky's apartment. Within a minute, I was stark-naked. I stood over the artist for a while, swinging my hard cock around, wondering what I could do that would really take him by storm.

Inspiration struck. I reached over to an easel, picked up a half-squeezed tube of red paint and squirted a handful into my right palm. This I transferred to my arsehole, then I walked forward, crouched down and, grabbing Boleslavsky's cock, steered him into position and sat. The paint was a rather sticky, heavy lubricant (I remember thinking that I finally understood why it had to be thinned with turps or linseed oil) and so the entry was painful and a little slow – but it was worth it to see the look of surprise on Boleslavsky's face as he found himself unexpectedly fucking me. I flatter myself when I say that I don't think many of his English friends ever surprised him sexually. Well, a whore like me knows when to be coy, and when to take by storm.

In retrospect, I wouldn't recommend red oil paint as an adjunct to anal intercourse, for within a few moments the stuff had spread itself all over my thighs, prick and balls, over Boleslavsky's trousers and bed and halfway up both our stomachs. It looked hideously as if we were haemorrhaging, as if the act of love were also some ghastly act of violence. Of course the imagery was not lost on Boleslavsky, who was clearly inspired and started fucking me so violently that I got the impression he was in a hurry to get it over and done with so that he could commit some atrocity to canvas. Within a couple of minutes he'd pivoted me over so that I was on my back and he was banging into me, resting nearly all his weight on his cock. We kissed throughout the fuck, making odd grunting noises – the sort of thing I was more used to hearing at boxing matches.

I came first, adding several large splashes of white to the red colour field of my stomach. Boleslavsky pumped his load inside me, and made the going a good deal easier as his come diluted the sticky red paint.

I thought that we would wash as soon as we had finished, but no: Boleslavsky was ready to work, and started shouting in Russian. A blank canvas on a stretcher was hastily mounted on an easel; before he'd even picked up a brush it was well covered with red paint from his hands and clothes. Then, of course, he must wipe his prick all over it, adding more red paint as well as traces of spunk (and perhaps a little shit) to the 'background'. I was about to wipe my stomach with one of the oily rags that lay about the place, but he stopped me.

'No! Touch nothing! Today you are my palette!'

He picked up a huge brush, the head about two inches wide, and scooped up the sperm and red paint from my stomach, applying it to the canvas in broad, uninhibited strokes. Then he applied the brush to my arse, picking up yet more red. This carried on until all the usable pigment, and every trace of bodily excretion, had been wiped from my body and transferred to the canvas; I was left an uneven light pink. Then he picked up a jumbo-sized tube of black and began applying it straight to the brush, daubing it over the canvas in seemingly random blocks and swirls.

After half an hour, during which I learned all I needed to know about Boleslavsky's working methods, he was bored of one pastime and wanted another. And so, throwing his brushes aside, he lay down beside me and took me in his arms.

'Now we have a child,' he said, indicating the canvas. 'Let us make love properly to celebrate.'

We kissed and embraced on the filthy sheets, and I learned that Boleslavsky could be tender as well as violent and ridiculous. He stroked my hair, he explored my body with fingers, lips and tongue, he caressed me and called me by many terms of endearment, English, French and Russian. He used his vest to clean me up a bit, shucked off the rest of his clothes and spent nearly twenty minutes sucking my cock – I still count this as one of the five best blow jobs I have ever received. Boleslavsky looked like a wild man, the sort who would never take the passive part in sex, but I soon learned that he could be as yielding, as eager to please, as any man or woman I have known. I wondered where he had learned to suck cock like that. I wondered, also, whether his oral abilities had anything to do with his success as an artist – a success, I still maintain, out of proportion to his abilities.

We carried on like this until I had come twice, once in his mouth and once, half an hour later, while he gently wanked me off, kissing me all the while. He managed just one orgasm. 'I have put the rest of my energy into painting,' he said mournfully, as I gave up playing with a cock that could stay only half stiff. (The reader should not imagine from this account that Boleslavsky had any virility problems. On the contrary, he had the most prodigious powers of recovery, and I have known him to come more than five times in a night.)

We lay together, two men who hardly knew each other yet knew each other intimately, and gazed up at the 'finished' painting in the half-light. It looked to me like something that had been hit by a fast-moving vehicle, but Boleslavsky seemed pleased. I should add, by the way, that this canvas was shown under the title *Red Hole* to great acclaim, and has been analysed as a response to the rising tide of violence in Communist Russia, 'an uncanny foreknowledge of the atrocities of the Stalinist era'. I have, hitherto, refrained from explaining the circumstances of its creation or the altogether more mundane source of its name.

Ten

Sex and symbolism... Slumming it... Bermondsey Baths... Eddie the boxer... Lee the shop assistant... All-in wrestling... An unwilling assignation

I could fill a whole book about my time with Mikhail Boleslavsky, and, if any enterprising publisher is interested in a sure-fire bestseller that would rock the art world to its foundations, he has only to make me a generous offer. In this case, however, I must assume that the reader is interested in my story, not Boleslavsky's, and so I shall restrict myself to just a couple of chapters on the great man and his misdemeanours.

I was caught up in his world like a feather in a whirlwind. Where he went, I went. What he wished, I wished, or at least tolerated. I don't think I ever fell in love with Boleslavsky; I would say, however, that I gave myself to him, body and soul, for a time. I knew that he would tire of me as he had tired of other, earlier lovers, both men and women. I looked forward to the day when I would be free of him, although I dreaded it too. I knew that, for as long as I was with him, I was not my own person – I was merely a piece of source material, a tool to be used. Boleslavsky regularly told me he loved me, particularly when we were fucking. He lavished presents on me, he took me on trips around Europe, he treated me like a prince. But it was not me he loved. He wanted to know nothing about me; if ever I mentioned my past, my family, or my hopes for the future, he would lay a finger against his lips. 'We do not need the past or the future, Pavel, when we have the present!' he would say. Or, 'Our families – our histories – what are these but the inessential dross by which the world knows us? I know you, Pavel, more deeply than this, more deeply than you know yourself.' How silly this all looks in black and white. It sounded good at the time, though, and I was predisposed to believe it and go along with it. Now I think I realise that it was the bar that Boleslavsky set up against intimacy. He wanted me only as he saw me, as the inspiration, the ideal boy, the model – not twenty-year-old Paul Lemoyne from Sussex who had a modicum of intelligence, very little education, a lot of experience and was beginning to worry about his future. He didn't want me to be anything other than the creature of his imagination. And being that, I can tell you, was one of the most exciting, rewarding experiences of my life.

For the first couple of weeks, we spent most of the time in his studio; I returned to Adam Street only to get clean clothes, to pick up correspondence and, occasionally, to sleep and bathe. I had brief meetings with Albert Abbott, who was delighted with my reports of *la vie bohème*, and encouraged me to deepen my intimacy with Boleslavsky, 'if you know what's good for you'. Of course Abbott was pleased: he was husbanding huge amounts of money and property that came to him from the artist's circle of patrons. Ah, well, I must not complain: it all came my way in the end.

So, for most of April and well into May, we turned our backs on the spring weather and stayed indoors, naked for most of the time, heated by a dangerous little oil burner that would occasionally tip over and spill flaming tongues of fuel across the floor. Boleslavsky turned out canvases at the rate of two or three a week, all of them variations on the same theme, with heavy use of red and black, and occasional admixtures of sperm, shit, piss and sweat, depending on what we were doing for inspiration. The bed was seldom folded away; I used it as my model's dais, and of course Boleslavsky would regularly leap across the studio, vaulting packing cases and chairs, to land on top of me.

While Boleslavsky was essentially a masculine man, he was, as I have said, surprisingly adept at taking the 'feminine' role in sex. This I had guessed during our first session, when he displayed such aptitude at fellatio; soon I learned that he loved to be fucked as well.

The element of ritual was what made sex exciting for Boleslavsky; there were few occasions when we made love simply out of randiness or affection. He liked to talk of 'sacrifice' and 'purgation', of acting out his psychodramas through the medium of cock, arse and mouth. I was never a great one for this hogwash, being, I suppose, a mixture of philistine Englishman and pragmatic Frenchman. But Boleslavsky had a Russian soul, and had spent long enough in Berlin and Munich to have soaked up some of the extraordinary sub-Freudian cant of the Expressionist movement. And so, when he surrendered himself for his first fucking at my hands, he talked a great deal about 'symbolical murder' and that sort of thing. Fortunately for both of us, I fancied Boleslavsky enough to keep hard just by looking at him and touching him; had this not been the case, I fear that the garbage that came from his mouth would have rendered me impotent either from boredom or laughter.

So, on that first occasion, he had to pretend to be a simple Russian peasant, and I, draped in a black dust sheet, approached him from the rear 'like cold death'. Then I blindfolded him (with one of my long socks) and forced him to his knees, where my 'love weapon' violated his mouth. After this he had to be 'punished' for his sins, and so I put him over my knee and spanked him until his arse was as red as his canvases. (This puts me in mind of another great Boleslavsky masterpiece, *The Scarlet Hand*, which was inspired by the handprints I left in that tender place, but was once again subjected to all sorts of ludicrous political interpretations). Once he'd been spanked, he demanded the belt – a heavy leather belt which he wore on occasion, which, doubled over, made an excellent flogger. I stopped short of making him bleed, as that kind of excess disgusts me, but I certainly marked his arse for days to come.

Once he was well flogged, he commanded me to tie his wrists with rope and secure them to the bed head. Bound in this position, he could easily be turned on to his back or his front – and it was thus that he wished to be fucked. I started him off on all fours, as I found the sight of his sore bottom extraordinarily exciting, and entered him with nothing more than a handful of spit as lubricant. His arse cheeks were lightly furred, the same colour as his head, and as hard as a pair of footballs. I held them open and pushed into his hole, paying no heed to the bellow of pain that assured me I was inside him. Well, he wanted to be punished for his sins, and he would be. I sometimes think that many artists and intellectuals I have met would have had much simpler lives if they'd stayed within the churches they were raised in; there, at least, they could expiate their 'sins' simply and directly through confession and penance. Admittedly, however, this would have been a great deal less fun for all concerned. Boleslavsky, as a professed atheist, still had a pronounced sense of sin and retribution, and required me to act as God or priest in order to cleanse himself. (Then again it's possible that this was mere shallow play-acting, a kind of fancy dress in which Boleslavsky disguised his desire to be fucked. It would not have been enough for him to have simple carnal appetites: they would have to be something much more interesting to match his inflated self-opinion.)

So I fucked away, greatly excited by the broad expanse of his muscular back as it was thus revealed to me, its detail and proportion worthy of the statues in the British Museum. Then I flipped him over – he was still blindfolded, you will remember – and pulled his legs over my shoulders before continuing my intrusion. Boleslavsky, I was pleased to see, was as stiff as a post throughout; unlike many, he did not soften when his arse was under siege. In fact, so great was the delight he took in the punishment he was getting that he came without touching himself, and the spunk shot out of his arrow-headed cock to land in great white plumes over his hard, ridged stomach, where it mingled with the long, coppery hairs and puddled in his navel. I was not far behind. I pulled out and wanked off in his face, thinking that this final humiliation would put the stopper on his penance, so to speak.

When we weren't working or fucking, we were usually eating.

Boleslavsky had a prodigious appetite, and loved to eat in the workman's cafés around Euston, where we could get huge plates of sausage and mash, or Irish stew, for a few pennies. Boleslavsky would sit there sketching on menus, napkins, tablecloths or (if there were none of these) his shirt or the walls, capturing our fellow diners in thick, black pencil strokes. In my humble opinion, these were his best works, in that they were actually *of* something, and they expressed a wonderful brute force, an animal *joie de vivre* that was completely missing from his abstract canvases. I put this to him once, and he looked at me down his long, flat nose, narrowing his eyes and sneering slightly, showing me his canines. 'I know what's good and what's bad, Pavel,' he said, and dropped the subject. Privately I believe he knew what sold and what didn't sell. Abstracts were all the rage, the angrier and more formless the better; I think his rich patrons enjoyed these great explosions of inchoate rage, in the way that some of them (the Duchess of B——, for instance) enjoyed the violent fuckings that he dished out. His figurative work, for which he had real talent, would not have commanded such prices, and did not sit well with the carefully constructed public image of Boleslavsky the wild Russian modernist. I picked up a couple of these discarded sketches when we left cafés, although I remember that some of the very best were scrawled on table tops and wiped off when we'd paid our bill. So much for the permanence of art.

At that early stage in our friendship, all we did in the cafés was eat and talk and, in Boleslavsky's case, sketch. We stocked up on fuel, we laughed and joked with the waitresses, the proprietors and our fellow diners, who thought we were just another couple of immigrant labourers like themselves. There were plenty of refugees trickling into London at that time, many of them artists like Boleslavsky. In that world, he was far from unusual. I, too, blended in with the scenery. I'd left my high-society wardrobe at home in Adam Street, where it came out only for occasional appearances with Abbott; for 'work' I turned up in an old, worn shirt, corduroys, boots, braces and a flat cap. I could play the proletarian just as well as Boleslavsky, and with far more genuine claim. He, I'm sure, had never done a hard day's toil in his life, and went from his papa's house straight into salon society in one smooth transition. He was lucky that he had the physiognomy and build of a working man – but that was about all.

He certainly had a taste for what I would have called 'rough trade', however. Boleslavsky, like all his countrymen, was absolutely obsessed by the idea of the proletariat. They say the English are a class-ridden race, but compared with Russians we're a nation of levellers. It was this fascination with working men that, to me, most eloquently betrayed Boleslavsky's bourgeois roots. I've never known a real working man who fetishised the proletariat in the way that Boleslavsky did; most of the navvies I knew would far rather fuck a nice clean, posh piece of arse such as mine. (I had the whore's happy ability to 'belong' to any class I pleased.) Not Mikhail Boleslavsky, though: he wanted 'to immolate myself on the altar of the class struggle', which basically meant that he wanted to fuck every porter, builder, stevedore, navvy and scaffolder that we could lay our hands on.

This became apparent to me only after the 'honeymoon' was over. To be honest, I was glad when our horizons began to broaden: after nearly two months holed up beneath Bedford Square, with only occasional breaks in steamy cafés, the daily routine of fucking and posing was beginning to wear me down. Much as I adored Boleslavsky and his wild, unpredictable appetites, I was beginning to tire of him. So when he suggested that we go for an 'adventure' I was more than ready to accompany him.

We were going, he said, 'in search of innocence', which was one of the qualities he associated with his fantasy working man. On this particular safari we took a bus from Russell Square, across Waterloo Bridge, through my old stamping ground (I was happy to see the Palace of Varieties looking prosperous and busy in the early evening) and down to Bermondsey. Why Bermondsey? Well, as any of my contemporaries reading this will know, Bermondsey was the location of Bermondsey Central Baths, a magnet for gentlemen from all over London and, at the time of which I am writing, still a rather impressive new facility, all shiny tiles and grand classical architecture. Boleslavsky and I, I need hardly add, were not going there to marvel at the fixtures and fittings.

No: what drew men like us to Bermondsey Central Baths was its reputation. Here you could pick up young, compliant lads who would happily fuck and suck in the showers and steam rooms, who would give and take favours without hope of financial reward, and would even come away with you for a very small financial outlay. While I had worked a certain circuit in my days on the game, I had never tasted this more informal, friendly form of prostitution – if it could really be called that. I found my tart's sensibilities shocked at the thought that these virile young men would 'give it away'. They were spoiling the game for us professionals. That, however, was before I went there with Boleslavsky.

Our first visit was typical of all the orgies to come, and stays with me vividly to this day. It was a dirty June day: the air seemed heavy with grit, and the sky was overcast, the air unseasonably cold. It was that special London weather when nothing seems clean or colourful; not a smoggy day, not a famous pea-souper, but just a grubby, smelly kind of day when one longs to escape the city and wash its grime from the skin. The bus journey from Russell Square was tedious, although Boleslavsky took a childish delight in every grotesque detail of our fellow passengers, and asked me (in an embarrassingly loud voice) to translate for him some of the more idiomatic cockney phrases. We finally reached Bermondsey at about six. It was still broad daylight, of course, but the air seemed darker than it should be. The bath house, with its elaborate tiled façade, was the brightest thing in prospect.

We paid our pennies at the gate, were given towels – huge white squares that had been washed so often the nap was almost gone – and proceeded to the spacious changing areas, where we quickly undressed, left our possessions in a locker and padded on bare feet to the baths themselves. These were a cross between a modern municipal swimming pool and a giant washing station. Men of all ages, sizes and classes were splashing about in a pool maybe thirty feet long, or standing under the showers that lined one wall, or simply sitting and lying on benches enjoying the view. Some of the older customers were sleeping; I guessed they came to the baths to while away the days in congenial surroundings. Boleslavsky took in the scene with an ardent eye, let out a whoop of joy and ran towards the pool, jumped three feet in the air, tucked his feet up under him and landed in the water with a terrific splash. (This is the sort of behaviour known as 'bombing', which was later discouraged in municipal swimming facilities.) A few of the other bathers laughed and splashed him; most of them carried on unconcerned.

I wasn't far behind him, although my entrance into the water was a little less showy. Soon we were swimming up and down, happily eyeing up the more attractive trade that shared the pool with us. There was no shortage of talent: in the thirties, remember, jobs were hard to come by, and there were plenty of young men with time on their hands. Boleslavsky was delighted by the rich pickings, and found a novel method of telling the young men that he liked them. If he saw one he fancied he would swim up to him, then dive down underwater to take a closer look at any concealed areas, only to surface a few feet away smiling and splashing. If this didn't attract their attention, he would pass them again, this time swimming on his back, his hard cock bouncing around on his stomach, a flagpole advertising his interest. Some of the lads just laughed, but most of them, I could see, were intrigued.

The pool itself was too open an area for much to happen beyond looking and showing, and so after we'd swum for ten minutes we headed for the showers, and soaped off the chemical smell of the water. Boleslavsky was stiff throughout, as were many of the men around the place, but there was a strange absence of sexual tension in the air. I suppose a hard-on was as common in the Bermondsey Baths as a herring at Billingsgate market.

Soon, however, this game of peek-a-boo was not enough for Boleslavsky, who wanted to take things further – a lot further. He tried to feel me up a couple of times, and of course I was as stiff as he was – but I was in no mood to be thrown out of the building by the stern-looking attendant. He, I was sure, had seen it all before, and doubtless took his pleasures where he found them – but, as I whispered to Boleslavsky, at least the appearance of respectability had to be maintained, for the sake of all our fellow bathers as well as the management. Boleslavsky muttered some nonsense about the oppressive agents of religion and capitalism, and then, having got that out of his system, followed me towards the door marked TURKISH BATH.

This led to a short system of corridors occasionally interrupted by double doors – a form of insulation, I suppose, that prevented the entire building from overheating. After the final barrier, we emerged into a dimly lit room about the size of a decent living room. There was a small circular pool at one end, around which sat a few customers, paddling their feet and occasionally splashing the cold water over their faces. The rest of the room was taken up with benches and tables, all of them made from slatted wood. At each end of the room there was a furnace belting out heat, and a system of pipes plumbed around the walls ensured that the entire space was as hot as a baker's oven.

So much for the geography of the room: now for the denizens. Even before my eyes had adjusted to the gloom (the room was lit only by a few dim bulbs, sealed behind thick opaque glass shades) my ears had detected the telltale slapping and squelching, the breathing and moaning, that betray sexual activity. My nose, assailed at first by the heat so that I felt the hairs up my nostrils would fry, picked up the scent of sweat, sperm and cock that mingled with soap and disinfectant. It was an instant aphrodisiac, and my cock throbbed against my belly. Boleslavsky was silent with anticipation – but not for long.

We had wrapped our towels around our waists, trying to conceal our erections, but now there seemed no need for modesty and so we dropped them on a nearby bench. Both of us were stiff, and soon we were sweating. We waited for our eyes to go accustomed to the gloom, and then began our exploration.

On a couple of the benches, pairs of young men were engaged in serious embraces that did not invite participation; it was, however, a delight to see fit lads so amorously entwined, their hard cocks responding to the caress of mouth and hand. On one of the massage tables, an older, grey-haired man was receiving a 'massage' from a chunky young hulk, who was fucking him with a look of intense concentration on his face, his forehead corrugated with effort. He glanced over, caught us staring, held our gaze for a while then carried on pumping away with renewed vigour. Elsewhere bodies were draped over benches or tables content to sweat and relax; these, I took it, were recovering from recent sexual exertions.

But the ones who were of most interest to us were the lads who sat or stood around the room obviously inviting approach. Among these were several to whom Boleslavsky had flagged his interest in the pool, and they seemed more than pleased to see us. Two stand out in my memory, and with good reason.

The first – I shall call him Eddie – was a classic piece of East End rough, at least judging by his appearance. Not overly tall, he would have made an excellent flyweight or bantamweight boxer, and, judging by his broken nose and scarred eyebrows, he may indeed have had a few bouts in his time. He wore his hair cropped close to his skull, which was on the small side and a very pleasing shape. His hairline was low, his nose large, his skin a little pitted with the scars of adolescent acne. He had what my sister used to call a 'teacake chest' – flattish, smooth, with the nipples sitting up on the pale flesh like a couple of currants. But he was far from puny. He was the wiry terrier type, with plenty of strength in that light frame. I would guess that he was a little younger than I, perhaps just eighteen, the age I had been when I first came to London. Oh, and his prick! It hung there between his thighs, not fully hard but just at that stage that promises hardness, standing out at about forty-five degrees to his thighs and moving noticeably outwards. When he saw Boleslavsky and me he wiped his nose on the back of his hand, grabbed his cock by the base and waggled it at us. I have received some direct invitations in my time, but this was one of the least ambiguous.

The other was sitting a few benches away, and was a very different proposition. Although around the same age, he had spent a good deal of his time, it seemed, in hard manual work or some form of sports, for his physique was developed to an extraordinary degree. His chest comprised two perfectly rounded mounds, the muscles clearly defined beneath skin that seemed to be made of expensive silk. There was a little dusting of hair along the sternum and around the nipples, then a little more fanning over the stomach and down to the pubic region (which was, at that point, hidden from our view). The muscles in his arms, shoulders and back were all impressive – not huge melons, as one sees on bodybuilders today, but rather the muscles that come through natural effort. William Herringham would have had a fit if he'd seen him, and would doubtless have whipped out his callipers without ceremony. I prided myself on a naturally developed physique, but I was skinny compared with this paragon. I congratulated myself that I was better looking – he was no great beauty, with a plain face and a bit of an overbite – but his body more than made up for any homeliness in his looks. It excited me to think that, if you saw this young man in the street, in the office or shop where he doubtless worked, you would hardly have given him a second glance. In here, though – in this secret other world of nakedness – he was a king.

Boleslavsky went straight over to the pug-faced boxer and engaged him in conversation; I had caught the eye of my muscled friend, and, when he beckoned me over, went to join him. We sat side by side on the bench, exchanging pleasantries; I was interested to note that he did not speak with a cockney accent, but rather in the lower middle-class tones with which I was familiar. His voice, in fact, was nasal and rather high – again, a feature that would disguise his true attractiveness from the casual observer. He made some remarks about the heat, rubbed a hand across his chest and made the muscles in his arms and shoulders jump. Then he shifted position, spread his legs and turned to face me on the bench.

The muscles on his body were impressive enough, but nothing could have prepared me for the muscle that I now saw. It was large; more than large, it was out of proportion to the rest of him. His legs were by no means as well developed as his upper body, and this relative slimness threw the length and thickness of his prick into even greater contrast. It was, at present, lying across his thigh like a basking whale; I had a fine view of its underside, and a pair of handsome balls in perfect proportion hanging beneath in a sweaty pouch.

I found myself turning on the bench to mirror his position, and we sat there, each with one leg tucked up under the other, the knee resting on the bench, our arms by our sides, taking in every detail of each other's body. My cock, like his, lay on my thigh; the reader must believe that I was hardly a shrimp in that department, but looking down at myself I felt somewhat dwarfed by the monster that faced me. We made more small talk – I learned that his name was Lee, and that he worked (as I suspected) as a sales assistant in a gentlemen's outfitters – all the while gorging our eyes on each other. Within a very few minutes we were both fully hard. The sight of Lee's dick at full extension was enough almost to bring tears to my eyes. It was one of those cocks that are thicker in the middle than at either end – like an elongated rugby ball. I could hardly wait to get my hands on it – or my mouth, or my arse. To add to my excitement, I could just about discern in the half-light of the Turkish bath that Lee was blushing furiously, and nothing turns me on as much as a young man who is slightly ashamed but willing to get over it.

Well, I would happily have spent the rest of the day with my new acquaintance, but needless to say Boleslavsky had other ideas. Just as

I leaned forward to kiss Lee on the lips (he closed his eyes and opened his mouth, like a young girl on a date) I noticed that my Russian friend was engaged in some kind of wrestling match with his boxer on one of the massage tables. It was typical of Boleslavsky that he couldn't just enjoy a bit of straightforward, friendly sensuality: no, he had to turn it into a dramatic struggle. He was a fit, strong man, as I've mentioned before, but I was amused to see that Eddie had got the better of him almost instantly, holding his head in an armlock and playfully pummelling it with his fists.

'Come on, Boris,' he said, in a thick cockney accent, 'you can do better than that.'

Boleslavsky, red-faced from the heat and the fight, attempted to free himself, and in his wriggling exposed his bum to Eddie's view.

'You're a naughty little Bolshevik, ain't you?' said Eddie, belabouring Boleslavsky's tender parts with an open palm. How the artist must be loving it, I thought; surely another half-dozen dreadful 'paintings' would be inspired by this.

All the commotion was causing a reaction in the room. Some of the more timid customers had fled to quieter regions, while the sturdier members were gathering round to watch the bout, and cheered Eddie on in undertones, laughing softly at Boleslavsky's humiliation.

This was an interruption I could do without, particularly as Lee, my muscular little companion, seemed completely lost in the wonder of my kisses, and had just planted a tentative hand on my cock. The uncertainty with which he caressed it led me to think that he had not played this way before. I encouraged him with whispered endearments, and was about to manoeuvre him into a horizontal position when our idyll was interrupted.

'Pavel! Help me! Come to the aid of the revolution!' Boleslavsky, of course – at full volume. Much more of this shouting and we'd be chucked out by the management.

'Wait here,' I whispered to Lee, who broke from my embrace with a look of drugged stupefaction on his face. I went over to Boleslavsky, my prick swinging in front of me, and caught Eddie's eye. He winked.

'What do you want me to do, Mikhail?'

'Get this young brute off me.'

'Now why should I do that?'

'He's killing me.'

'Oh, Mikhail, I should have thought you'd enjoy that.' I could see from the hugely engorged state of Boleslavsky's cock that he was loving every minute of it, and was simply using me as a stooge in the act.

'Aaaaagh!' he yelled, as Eddie brought his hand down in another resounding crack on his arse.

'Mate, stop his noise for me, would you?' asked Eddie, grinning at me.

'With pleasure.' I grabbed Boleslavsky by his long, red, greasy hair, forced his jaw open and fed him my cock. This shut him up. I knew from experience that Boleslavsky liked to be fucked hard in the mouth, and would put up with any amount of gagging and discomfort for the satisfaction it gave him.

Eddie moved himself round to the rear, pulled Boleslavsky into a kneeling position and gobbed into his hand. Before he knew what was happening to him, the great artist was being assaulted at either end by a young, hard cock. Lee watched, disappointment on his face, his prick as hard as iron and dripping at the end. Oh, well, so much for our romantic interlude; he was getting a more advanced level of education than I had planned to give him. I caught his eye and held it; if I could not actually have him, I could at least have his attention. While I fucked Boleslavsky's mouth I stared deep into Lee's soul, and as I felt my orgasm building I forced myself to keep my eyes open. Thus, eye locked to eye, Lee and I came almost simultaneously, one into another man's mouth, the other over his own hand.

I pulled out, allowing Boleslavsky to rest his head on his forearms and give himself completely to Eddie's attack at the rear. The young boxer fucked him with extraordinary vigour, occasionally slapping his arse, spitting on him or cursing him. Boleslavsky, for once, was silent, so far gone in his fantasy of who-knows-what. Eddie was greatly amused by the experience, and every so often would drop his hard-man act to give me a big, gap-toothed smile. Finally, however, even he started to take it seriously, and delivered the last two minutes of the fuck with a savage intensity that impressed even me – and I'd been fucked by some of the most savage brutes in London. Boleslavsky, I noticed, spewed his come long before Eddie had finished, and endured the end of the assault with a look of beatific martyrdom on his face.

Eddie steadied himself with a hand on either buttock, threw back his head, exposing a finely moulded throat and prominent Adam's apple, and buried himself deep inside Boleslavsky's arse. He shuddered, snorted and emptied his bollocks deep inside the man's guts. I almost felt like applauding.

So intent had I been on this endgame that I did not notice that Lee had slipped away. This I was not going to allow, and so, acting on a hunch, I ran back towards the changing rooms, picking up a discarded towel to preserve a pretence of modesty. There, as I suspected, I found Lee putting on his clothes, a crestfallen expression on his beautiful, ugly face.

'Hey! Why did you run off like that?'

'You don't want me.'

'What do you mean?'

'You're with your... friend.'

'I want you.'

'Oh... but I...' Obviously the youth didn't think too highly of himself, and indeed, now that I saw him with his clothes on, I was aware only of his defects: the crooked teeth, the sallow skin, the awful clerk's haircut, parted in the middle. I could feel myself falling in love.

'Come back into the Turkish bath. I want to... make love to you.'

He blushed even more furiously, and I was a goner.

'No, it's late. I have to get home.'

'Please.' I wasn't used to begging, and the experience was a novelty. I could feel myself getting hard again, and the towel started to rise accordingly. Lee noticed it; he was hypnotised by it, like a chicken staring at an adder.

'No... I can't...'

I pulled the towel aside and allowed my half-hard cock to throb in the air. 'Come on, Lee, you want to. You want me, don't you?'

'I've got to go. My mum will be wondering.'

He lived with his parents. My cock stiffened even more.

'Can I see you again?'

'I don't think so.' He was obviously one of the nervous type who, after they've come, want to pretend that their 'unnatural' desires will go away. I, being the shameless sort, find that my 'unnatural' desires are never long dormant.

'Please. I have to. Where do you work?'

'What? No, you can't come to the shop. Please promise me you won't do that.'

'Why not? Why shouldn't I come to the shop? What could be more natural than a gentleman like me coming to a gentleman's outfitters?'

'How do you know?'

'You told me, Lee.'

'Oh, God.'

'Come on, where is it? Round here? I'll find you. There can't be that many shops round here that could afford to employ a young man like you.'

'You mustn't.'

I made my cock throb again, and, checking that there was nobody around to see us, grabbed his hand and wrapped it around me. Lee, I could see quite clearly, was getting stiff in his pants.

'Please, let me go.'

'Very well.' I removed my hand, leaving his holding my erect prick. 'You are free.' He couldn't let go of me; I had him, hook, line and sinker.

'Come on. There are people coming. Tell me the name of the shop.'

'No!'

'Tell me, or I'll find you for myself.' My prick jumped in his hand, and he started wanking it.

'It's...'

'Come on!'

'It's...' He stared down at his hand wanking me off, as if it were something unconnected to him.

'Tell me the name of the shop. You want me, don't you?'

'It's Parke's, on Tower Bridge Road.'

'Good lad.' A fat, white-haired man waddled around the corner; Lee dropped my dick as if it were red-hot, and the towel fell into place.

'I'll be seeing you.'

'Mmm.' Poor boy! He rushed out of the changing room as if his mother herself were pursuing him.

I returned to the Turkish bath, where Boleslavsky was now being serviced by four different men, two in his mouth, one in each hand.

Eleven

Desperately seeking Eddie... We tour the gyms... Terry... The search is over... Boleslavsky counts the cost... The green handkerchief... Vodka and rough trade... Violation in the fitting room

If you imagine you have now reached the romantic part of the book, please brace yourself for disappointment. I often wonder if things might have turned out otherwise, but I'm afraid to say that my burgeoning involvement with Lee the gentlemen's outfitter was never to flourish, thanks largely to the unpredictable whims of Mikhail Boleslavsky.

Such were the masochistic tendencies of that individual that he was obsessed for days after our first visit to the Bermondsey Baths with Eddie the boxer, who, he imagined, was a true, unspoiled proletarian male, a divine innocent, a missing link, Boleslavsky's Sweeney figure. I was too worldly-wise to feel any jealousy at his constant ravings about Eddie, and was rather amused by the fact that he had exalted him to these terrific heights within such a short period. We had to go back to Bermondsey time after time (after the second lengthy bus journey, I managed to make Boleslavsky spring for a cab, even though he said he preferred the 'artisanic authenticity' of public transport), always hoping to see Eddie again. I was privately longing for another encounter with Lee. We were both disappointed, although it goes without saying that we found acceptable substitutes in plentiful numbers on each return visit, and within a couple of weeks we had become minor celebrities in the Turkish baths. I suspect that they never saw, either before or since, such a shameless pair of sluts as we were. I drove Boleslavsky to new heights (or depths) of daring that he would never have essayed without me, and he certainly brought out the pervert in me. Many were the young men we sent waddling away from the baths with bandy legs, sore arses, aching pricks and empty balls.

Boleslavsky threw his frustration into his work, and produced a series of dark pictures with names like *The Fighter* and *Turkish Struggle*, which cost him a small fortune in black oil paint. In one of them I almost discerned a human figure, a somewhat etiolated simian shape that could, and I stress only *could*, have been a portrait of Eddie. It was the nearest thing to a human figure in any of Boleslavsky's 'mature' work. I judged from this momentary lapse into realism the depth of Boleslavsky's obsession with the young fighter.

I thought it would be amusing to engineer a second encounter between the two, and so suggested to Boleslavsky that, rather than search for Eddie in the baths, we would do better to beard him in his natural habitat. And so I dug up the names of a handful of boxing gymnasia in the Bermondsey area, most of them in upper rooms above public houses, and we began a short and most enjoyable tour. Boleslavsky was no fool, and dressed for the occasion like a man of some means; it was not rare, in those days, for gentlemen to frequent these establishments, disguising their interest in seminaked working-class lads as an enthusiasm for the sport, and they usually paid for the privilege by investing a certain sum in the 'training costs' of their chosen champion. It was extraordinary how welcome we were made. The world was more innocent then, I suppose, or more accepting. We were introduced to the lads, even taken into the changing rooms where they happily stripped in front of us. It didn't take much imagination to realise that these young men were casually on the game, and would do whatever it took to fill their pockets. Boxing has always been one of the traditional routes out of poverty – and from my experience it's not just the prize money that enables the boys to achieve a measure of independence. The trainers, or managers, were worldly types, who would not have called themselves pimps. Others might have done.

In gym after gym we saw beautiful young brutes, any one of which might have done better service than Eddie. In one we met a gypsy lad, as dark as an Indian, his bruised face retaining an unquenchable beauty, his ears pierced with small gold hoops, his body as hairy as a young ape. I could see that Boleslavsky was taken with him, and I was pleased – rightly, as it turned out. Terry, as the reader must surely know, was to become my replacement in Boleslavsky's bed, and his most famous model. Their later arrest in Nazi Germany, their hair's-breadth escape on a cargo steamer from Hamburg and their subsequent prosperity in California is the stuff of art-history legend.

Others have written more fully of Terry, but let me add one short anecdote to the body of literature. It concerns our first ever meeting, which was not, as history has recorded, at a prize fight in the Mile End Road. It was at a small, impoverished gym on Jamaica Road, where we watched Terry sparring with his middle-aged coach, who then showed him to us like a slave at auction. The gym was closed for the afternoon; there were only the four of us there, and the manager was bolder than most.

'He's all nicely put together, sir,' he said to Boleslavsky, whom he recognised as the one in charge of the purse strings. 'Come on, Terry, drop your shorts.'

Terry still had a small pair of sparring gloves on, but managed to hook the thumbs inside the top of his baggy shorts and pull them down. By dint of wriggling his bum and hips, he got the shorts round his ankles and stepped out of them, leaving him clad only in shin-high cloth boots and the gloves. He was as hairy round the arse as he was on his chest, stomach and legs; it looked as if he were wearing thin woollen drawers. This, I knew, would appeal to Boleslavsky, who would soon be apostrophising him as some kind of ape man, the ultimate primitive, and so on.

Boleslavsky walked around him, touching him here and there, while the manager listed his 'points' like a professional salesman, which I suppose he was. 'Nice round arse, sir, very strong legs. You'll see he's well blessed in the wedding department. Show him, Terry.'

Terry swiped casually at his cock with a gloved hand, and it began to grow. The sight of this young pugilist pulling at himself was fine entertainment, and Boleslavsky and I sat down to watch the show. Terry was soon wanking away, fucking the glove into which he spat for a little lubrication. When he came, the spunk flew out a good four feet from his body, and landed in a white puddle on the unvarnished wood floor of the gym. Boleslavsky gave a round of applause, slipped a bank note to the manager, and we were on our way. For the rest of the day he was uncharacteristically silent, and failed even to paint; I knew that the naked, hairy, wanking boxer had got under his skin.

And such, gentlemen, is the way in which the loves of the artists begin.

We found Eddie the following day, hanging around outside a gym in the railway arches a mere stone's throw from the Bermondsey Central Baths, where we'd first met him. It was about ten o'clock in the morning, and he was obviously waiting for someone to come and open up. As I suspected, he had no job and nothing to fill his time except training, fucking and causing trouble. When he saw us coming, he stuck his hands deep into his pockets, scowled and stared at his feet, hoping that we would pass by.

'Eddie!' Boleslavsky's voice, at top volume, could carry for up to half a mile. There was no ignoring it. Eddie looked up, but the expression on his face was far from welcoming. Boleslavsky took no notice.

'Eddie, my boy! I have found you at last!' We were now within handshaking distance, but the boy kept his mitts stuffed in his pockets.

'Fuck off, Boris.'

'You remember me!'

'Of course I remember you, you cunt.'

'Aah...' Boleslavsky loved to be insulted, and indeed Eddie had called him this and many other rough endearments when he was plugging him in the steam room. Boleslavsky couldn't tell the difference between an insult used as a sexual caress, and an insult delivered with intent. I could.

'Come on, Mikhail, let's go.'

'After searching for so long, and finally finding him? Never.'

'What do you want, Boris?' Eddie was glancing around nervously; I could tell that he didn't want to be seen talking to foreigners and nancy boys on his home turf. I knew the type: in such dark, secluded places as baths he was willing to give free rein to his true nature; but out in the street, in the daylight, he would play the straight boy for the benefit of his mates.

'I want you, Eddie. I have dreamed of you night and day. I have immortalised you in paint...'

'For fuck's sake, shut up.'

'Come on, Mikhail.'

'No! Pavel, leave me be!'

Eddie was assessing the situation; he was a brute, but he was far from stupid. 'What do you want, mate?'

'I want you to come with me, to live with me.'

'Don't be ridiculous, Mikhail.' I was getting nervous; much as I loved Boleslavsky's directness in these matters, it was dangerous, in those days, to make declarations of love to strange young men in such rough areas as Bermondsey. Indeed, I'd think twice about doing it even today.

'It's all right, pal,' said Eddie, who had obviously seen more gangster movies than were good for him. 'I can handle it.' He was calculating how much money he could squeeze out of Boleslavsky, and I knew that there was at least £30 in his wallet – a small fortune in those days to a lad like Eddie.

'So, Boris, you want a bit of this, do you?' He squeezed his packet, and Boleslavsky practically leaped in the air.

'Yes, I want you, all of you.'

'All right. I know a place.'

'Wonderful.'

'Come on, then.'

'Mikhail, don't be silly.' I knew that I sounded like a prissy little queen, but I was genuinely worried for my friend. 'He can come to the flat some time. Give him your card.'

'No! We must go with Fate wherever she leads us! Leave me, Pavel!'

'You heard him, pal. Sling yer hook. We're all right.'

'Where are you going?'

'To paradise!'

'Shut up, Mikhail. Tell me, Eddie, where you're taking him.'

'Don't worry about us,' grinned Eddie, already leading Boleslavsky down the street. 'We're all right.'

Boleslavsky gestured at me to go. Ah well: he wanted experience. He would get it.

I did not see Boleslavsky again for two days, and was on the point of informing the police when he turned up at the studio, with a bandage on his head, one arm in a sling and a huge black eye. I rushed to embrace him, but he pushed me away. 'My mouth...' he lisped, and I noticed that there was a tooth half broken (fortunately not one of the canines). This, by the way, was how Boleslavsky got the gold tooth that glints out of all his later photographs.

'What happened?' I was not angry. I was too relieved to be really angry. I had to fight back the urge to say, 'I told you so.'

'Ah, Pavel,' he mumbled through swollen lips, 'it was wooooonderful!'

Cutting out the embroidery, the story went something like this. Eddie had taken him back to an empty flat in Rotherhithe, where he'd informed him that he wasn't queer, that he hated fucking queers, and that what's more he hated fucking foreigners and that 'Boris' would have to give him money if he didn't want to have both his legs broken. Boleslavsky gladly emptied his wallet, and was rewarded with a brief but, I imagine, intensely satisfactory fuck, during which Eddie was as passionate as he could wish. His balls drained, however, he reverted to type, and began making threats and demanding more money. Boleslavsky had almost had enough by now, and said that he'd go and fetch more money from his bank in the City. Eddie, however, was wise to this game, coshed him over the head, tied him to a chair and, when Boleslavsky came round, forced him to write a letter to the Duchess of B—— that amounted to a ransom note. Eddie delivered the letter, leaving poor Boleslavsky tied to the chair (I'm sure he was in seventh heaven), and returned with a bottle of whisky, which they polished off between them in the next twenty-four hours while they waited for the reply. Eddie alternated between abuse and violence and the most extraordinary sexual assaults. 'He ravaged me in every single hole I have, Pavel,' said Boleslavsky, proudly, 'and I believe if the ransom had not arrived in time he would have cut a new hole and fucked that.'

Fortunately for posterity, the Duchess of B—— managed to raise the cash (I'm sure she was thrilled to be involved in such a dramatic escapade) and Boleslavsky was released. Even then, he was reluctant to leave, having developed an overnight case of Stockholm syndrome long before it was identified. Even when he was untied, he begged Eddie to violate him one more time, and had to goad him with all his might in order to get the desired response. Eddie, who was practically drained by his efforts of the last two days, pissed a pint of whisky into the great man's face, shoved his dick in Boleslavsky's mouth and then fucked his arsehole with the empty but capped whisky bottle. I can only offer up a prayer of thanks to the makers of that bottle, for had it shattered while in use we might have been deprived of some of the most celebrated abstract masterpieces of the mid-twentieth century.

While Boleslavsky made his doomed pursuit of Eddie, I took advantage of his temporary distraction to follow my own quarry. Usually I forgot my tricks as soon as I'd wiped up the spunk; Lee, however, I could not get out of my mind. I don't know what piqued my interest so much: the fact, perhaps, that there was unfinished business – we never did actually get round to doing it together. Or was it the contrast between his unprepossessing appearance when clothed, and what lay beneath: that magnificent Greek torso that would be revealed only to a few lucky onlookers? His shyness, his blushes, his fear of discovery – all of these things worked on me, as well as the memory of that rugby-ball-shaped cock, which I was determined to possess.

I fought with my conscience for all of five minutes, wondering whether I had the right to intrude on a private life that was so obviously guarded, exposing a young man to the shame of discovery, of being sacked by his employers and possibly disowned by his family. I'm afraid I came to the glib conclusion that what I was about to do was for Lee's own good: that somehow I was liberating him from the oppressive circumstances in which he lived. How easy was it for me – a prostitute, a kept boy, a rich man's plaything – to make those judgments! How soon I would learn the bitter sting that society reserves for those it casts out! Ah, well, I have learned the error of my ways, and that should satisfy any reader so misguided as to search for a moral in these immoral memoirs of mine.

I took a day off from my Boleslavsky duties (he was moody and taciturn, working Eddie out of his system with yet more black paint, and did not notice my absence) and, having spruced myself up in a clean set of clothes from my rooms in Adam Street, strolled along the river until I reached Tower Bridge. How many fine sights presented themselves to me along the way! Builders sunning themselves on scaffolds, some of them fat and ugly, others – plenty of others – young and fit and easy on the eye. In each group, I noted, there was always at least one young Adonis who would return my gaze, wondering what he could get out of (or put into) the young toff with the well-cut morning suit and the shiny shoes. I experienced a delightful confusion of roles in this situation – here I was, the hardened courtesan, being eyed up as a prospective client by pieces of trade perhaps even younger than I was (I was, by this time, nearly twenty-one). Well, it comes to us all: yesterday's trade is today's competition, as the old saying goes, and it was a lesson I was just beginning to learn.

I did not stop to sniff any of these wayside flowers, but was gratified at the number of heads that I turned. As long as I looked like a gentleman, I was more confident that I would succeed in the task that lay ahead of me.

I reached Tower Bridge, and paused awhile in the middle of the span to enjoy the play of the light on the water. And, to be honest, I was a little nervous – I needed a few moments to calm myself, to ensure that I would play my role well in the seduction (so I thought) that was to follow. I don't know exactly what aim I had in view: dragging a submissive Lee to Adam Street in the back of a cab, I suppose, and subjecting him to the full range of my depravity. Well, things were to turn out very, very differently.

Mentally fortified, I continued to walk south, and reached my goal just a few minutes later. Parke's Gentlemen's Outfitters was a grand building at the top of Tower Bridge Road with a double vitrine, a handsomely tiled pavement and an air of solid respectability wafting from its conservative window displays. It was without doubt a family concern, the sort of place that had been going for two generations and was struggling to keep up the standards of its Edwardian heyday in the pinched circumstances of the 1930s. I paused to look at a display of gloves and handkerchiefs in the window, and used the opportunity to glance into the dim interior and spy out my quarry. At first all I could see were a couple of customers – perfect examples of the solid, bourgeois type – trying on coats or being measured up by Parke's employees – all of them old and bald. Where was Lee? Surely it had not been my misfortune to turn up on his day off? Or – worse still – maybe he had lied to me about his place of work. Sudden misgivings overtook me – but I had been so sure that he was telling the truth, when I gazed into his eyes and made my dick throb in his shaking hand. Surely he felt for me something of what I felt for him – or had he simply told me the first shop name that came into his head, just to get rid of me?

And then, with a flood of relief, I saw him, coming out from the back of the shop carrying a stack of three wooden trays filled with accessories for sorting. I noticed with satisfaction the curve that his biceps made against the dull fabric of his jacket sleeve. He looked plain enough in his working clothes, with his hair parted in the centre and plastered down to his skull – and yet, to the trained eye, there was much to hint at the naked glories they concealed: a curve here, a swelling there, the arrogant jut of his bum when he bent down to deposit his load behind the counter. It was time to make a move.

I strolled into the shop, looking around me as if I owned the place. One of the older assistants made a move towards me, but I evaded him with a piece of fancy footwork and pretended to be lost in deep study of a gaberdine. Out of the corner of my eye I could see Lee bobbing up and down behind the counter, sorting out his wares – obviously this was the sort of menial task entrusted to the juniors in such establishments. The thought of his lowly rank caused a prickle in my groin, and it was with half a hard-on that I approached his counter. He did not hear me coming, nor, occupied as he was, did he see me. I had a moment of leisure to observe the top of his head and the full, hard curve of his thighs as he squatted down over his work. But then I noticed that irritating assistant cruising towards me again, and decided to take matters in hand. I coughed quietly.

Lee looked up, his face slightly flushed from crouching (which, of course, reminded me of his furious blushings at the baths), registered my smart clothes and assumed an expression of proper respect – then, a second later, registered my face. All the colour drained from his cheeks as he stood up; I thought for a moment he was going to faint.

I needed to set his mind at rest.

'Good morning, young man,' I said, in my best Mayfair accent. 'I would like to see a selection of handkerchiefs, if you please.'

Lee looked in near-panic towards the senior assistant, who, hearing my request, decided that it was insignificant enough for the junior to deal with. He nodded at Lee, and stalked off to the other side of the shop.

'It's all right, Lee,' I said in an undertone, 'I'm not going to show you up. Just act normally.' Then I added more audibly, 'Perhaps if I could see some of those that you have down there...' And I indicated one of the trays he was sorting, that contained a rainbow selection of silk squares. 'They look just the ticket.'

'Certainly, sir,' said Lee, his voice betraying only the slightest quaver. He had the deferential shop-boy manner off to a tee, and put the tray on the counter. 'Did sir have any particular colour in mind?'

I bent over his wares, and looked through them; Lee bent his head towards mine until our foreheads were almost touching.

'I had to see you again, Lee. I haven't stopped thinking about you.'

'Th-thank you, sir.'

'My name is Paul.'

'Paul...' There was something dreamy in his tone, and I knew he was as hooked as I was. How foolish I had been to doubt him!

'Please come with me, Lee. I want you so badly.'

'I can't, Paul.'

'You must! Don't you like me?'

'Yes, sir – er, Paul. I've not been able to concentrate on nothing since that day. I dream about you.'

The assistant was passing nearby in his orbit of the shop, and was well within earshot. 'This one,' said Lee, producing a spotted, red silk handkerchief with a magician's flourish, 'is a particularly popular line at the moment, sir.'

'Yes, very nice. Does it come in any other colours?'

'Navy blue, sir, and a nice bottle green.' He pulled the relevant hankies from the drawer, shaking them out to show them in all their glory. The senior, satisfied at Lee's salesmanship, drew away again.

The counter was covered in piles of silk and, under the pretence of feeling the quality, my hand stole beneath the fabric and found his. Thus, unobserved, our fingers entwined.

'When do you finish?'

'Six o'clock, but I have to go straight home. My mother's ill and I can't get away. I really want to, you have no idea...' I could see the sweat was breaking out above his upper lip, and he was blushing again. I dabbled my fingers in the palm of his hand; it was all I could do to stop myself vaulting over the counter and taking him in my arms right there and then.

'Then when?'

'I don't know. I don't know what to do. I wish you hadn't come.'

'That's nonsense, Lee, and you know it. Do you want to spend the rest of your life sneaking off to the baths, lying alone in bed wanking?'

'I have been, sir. I've had a wank thinking about you every day since.'

'It's not enough, Lee.'

'No.'

'You want more, don't you?'

'Yes.'

'You want us to be naked together, don't you? In bed, holding each other, kissing, feeling each other's body, our hard cocks pressing against each other.'

'Yes.'

'You want me to take you in my mouth, to feel your arse, to fuck you.'

'Yes.' There was, by now, a very obvious bulge in Lee's trousers; thank God we could both conceal our excitement against the counter.

'You want to fuck me, don't you, with that big fat cock of yours?'

'Oh, God, yes!'

'Then come with me.'

'I can't.'

'Does sir require any assistance?' The sibilant voice of the senior, practically at my shoulder, made me jump.

'No, thank you, I'm quite all right.' I discreetly (I hoped) withdrew my hand from the pile of silk – and from Lee's sweating embrace.

'Did you wish to make a purchase, sir?'

'Yes,' I said, feeling strangely like a schoolboy who's been called in to see the headmaster, 'this one, I think.' I picked up the nearest handkerchief – the one in the 'nice bottle green'.

'Very well, sir. That will be all, Lee, thank you. There is plenty more to be sorted in the stockroom. Allow me to complete the sale for you, sir.'

Lee limped off to the back of the shop like a whipped dog, turning to see me one more time, the outline of his hard-on visible even at that distance. His face betrayed such misery, such hopelessness, that I wanted to go after him. Even I, though, was sufficiently cowed by the strictures of English manners that I remained rooted to the spot, and completed the transaction with a stiff formality.

It was a sober, thoughtful Paul who made the return journey, slowly, staring only at the pavement, across the river to Adam Street, holding to my nose the bottle-green handkerchief, imagining that I could still smell a trace of Lee's sweat in the dotted silk.

That night I made my big mistake. I should have stayed at home and nursed my infatuation alone; that, surely, was the correct course of action for the thwarted lover. I might have prowled the streets, seeing his face in every passer-by. I might have mooched moodily along the river, staring at the water until a concerned policeman advised me to move on. I might, I suppose, have penned some desperate sonnet, although I'm glad to say that I have never been moved to literature until this moment. But what did I do? I went round to Boleslavsky's and confided in him.

I don't know what I thought I was doing. Maybe, subconsciously, I wanted to destroy the little flower of romance that was struggling into life between myself and Lee. Well, if that was my desire, I could not have achieved it more thoroughly.

I found Boleslavsky in ebullient spirits. He had recovered from his post-Eddie tristesse, and was putting the finishing touches to a more-than-usually messy painting (this one had a few bits of blue in it, which was refreshing).

'Aaaaah, Pavel!' he cheered as soon as I walked in the door. 'You are here!' Boleslavsky had a great way of stating the obvious which, in his thick Russian accent, somehow sounded profound.

'Yes, I am here,' I sighed.

'But you are sad! My little Pasha must never be sad. Here! Let us fuck! That will cheer you up!' He was already getting his cock out. Good old Boleslavsky: it was hard as ever.

'No, Mikhail, I don't want to fuck – not just now...'

This caused him real concern. 'You don't... want... to fuck? But Pavel, whatever is the matter? What has caused this drastic state of affairs?'

'Oh, nothing.'

It was pointless trying to hide anything from Boleslavsky. 'But you are in love! I can tell! I can smell it on you! And not in love with me, you unfaithful boy! I should be deeply distressed, I should cause a scene, I should throw you out in the street.' Typical: he was turning someone else's problems into his own drama.

'Please, Mikhail, leave me in peace.'

'Peace? Peace? If you want peace, you do not come to Boleslavsky! Here we do not have peace, only War! Only Struggle!' He was off on one of his rants, but he had a point: if I'd wanted peace I could have stayed at home.

'Oh shut up, Boleslavsky.'

'Now then, now then, let us drink and I will listen.' He poured vodka into two tumblers that, I suspect, had recently contained turpentine. '*Skål!*' He clinked my glass and tossed the spirit off in one go; I did likewise.

And so, of course, it all came out: my feelings for Lee, my doomed visit to the shop, our finger play beneath the handkerchiefs, my growing obsession. It felt so good to be telling someone about it, to be putting into words what had so far only been an ache in the chest, the belly and the groin (for such is how I would anatomise love) that I thought nothing of the consequences of this confession. Boleslavsky, of course, had the answer, and after listening in uncharacteristic silence proposed a remedy.

'Good! First we will get drunk!' I already was: we'd polished off nearly half the bottle of vodka. 'Second, we will pick up a couple of young fellows and fuck them all night. Third, if you still feel this way in the morning, we will go to the shop and we will take what is rightfully yours! We will ravish him if needs be! Love is all! Nothing can stand in its way! Down with the bourgeoisie! Up with the proletariat! Long live love!' And he threw his glass over his shoulder; it landed, as did mine, on a pile of dirty clothes, and did not smash.

Oh, alcohol! How many foolish things have we done under your influence! Drunk as I was, this seemed like an excellent proposition, and I cursed myself for my timidity earlier in the day. Why had I not braved the censure of all and simply kissed Lee on the lips, torn him away from the shop and installed him as my lover? I had the means. I should take him by rights. He was mine, wasn't he? He had told me so.

We carried on drinking, and then repaired to a pub on Tottenham Court Road, where working lads were to be had for the price of a meal and a bed for the night. Boleslavsky found one who suited him (art historians take note that he was a gypsy lad, not unlike Terry: the infatuation was setting in) and I chose one of roughly the same height and build as my beloved Lee. I shall spare the reader yet another account of what two seasoned deviants can do to a brace of willing young men in need of money. Suffice to say that a good time was had by all, as was Boleslavsky.

The pair left early the next morning; unlike us, they had jobs to go to. We surfaced at about ten, both still a little drunk, I think, and

Boleslavsky insisted that we have a hair of the dog for breakfast. I was too thick-headed to refuse, and in truth I did feel a little better for a shot of vodka. We got up, made a whore's bath in the sink and clambered into our clothes, which were crumpled and dirty and still reeked of cigarette smoke from the pub. By the time we were fit to face the world it was midday, and we were most definitely drunk again.

'And so, Onegin, do you still pine over the Tatiana of the handkerchiefs?' asked Boleslavsky.

Lee! I had almost forgotten about Lee. But now, thinking about him, I was lovesick and heartsore once more. 'Yes, yes!' I was beginning to enjoy the role of the doomed romantic rather too much. 'What can I do? He will never be mine.'

'Never say never!' roared Boleslavsky. 'Come! *A l'attaque!*' He hauled me out of the stinking basement and guided me, arm in arm, to the cab rank on the corner. Within moments we were spinning down towards, yes, Tower Bridge Road. I should have resisted. I should have insisted we turn back. But I was drunk, I was caught up in a foolish drama, and I was too weak, selfish and vain to make it stop.

We arrived at Parke's all too quickly, and there, standing in the window rearranging a display of umbrellas, was Lee himself. He jumped when he saw Boleslavsky and me approach, but there was nothing he could do without betraying himself. 'For God's sake, don't cause a scene,' I muttered to my companion; talk about locking the stable door after the horse has bolted.

Boleslavsky was dressed in his most ostentatious rig: an astrakhan coat, gift of the dear duchess, and a Liberty silk scarf tossed casually round his neck. His gold watch chain (which bore an amorous inscription in Russian) glinted on his stomach. The senior assistant practically genuflected when we walked in. Lee retreated behind his counter, and would, I think, have fled from the back of the shop had not Boleslavsky acted quickly.

'We wish to be measured for new suits, my man,' he said.

'Certainly, sir,' fawned the assistant, fingering the tape measure round his neck. 'Perhaps if you would care to step through to the fitting room...' He gestured towards a door to the side of the counter.

'I do not wish to be measured by you,' said Boleslavsky, looking down his nose in such a way as to make the poor old chap tremble. 'I require someone younger and cleaner.' He pretended to glance around the shop. 'Ah! The very thing! Have that young man attend to us!' He snapped his fingers in Lee's direction; I could see the poor lad – whom I was supposed to love, let us not forget – blushing in shame and fury.

'Ce-certainly, sir,' said the assistant, offended but too eager to make a big sale to answer back. 'Lee! These... gentlemen wish to be measured for suits.'

'But Mr Chivers,' said Lee, mustering all his courage, 'I'm not trained to do measurements!'

'Don't be ridiculous, boy,' hissed Mr Chivers. 'He is new, sir, and I'm afraid a little lacking in the professional gloss of which Parke's staff are so justly proud.'

'I despise professional gloss,' spat Boleslavsky. 'Come. We are wasting time. Let us proceed.'

'Lee, take the gentlemen into the fitting room.'

'Yes, Mr Chivers, sir.'

With a look of genuine sorrow on his crestfallen face, Lee gestured towards the door. 'This way, gentlemen.' I should have turned back, stopped the charade – but instead I proceeded, hard cock first.

The fitting room was a glorified cupboard with large mirrors on the two facing walls, a bench and a row of hooks down the other, and a curtain that hung over the door to deter Peeping Toms. Boleslavsky closed the door behind us, and put his back against it.

'Sir, you shouldn't have come here – not like this,' stammered Lee.

'I had to see you. I'm sorry.'

'Nonsense!' said Boleslavsky, rather too loud. 'Nothing should stand in the way of love!'

'Sir,' said Lee, mustering all his courage and turning to face his tormentor, 'I must beg you to keep your voice down. If I lose my job it is not only me who will suffer. I have elderly, sick parents and two younger sisters dependent on me. I don't care for myself, sir, if I'm thrown out – it's probably no more than I deserve for frequenting such places as the baths and being so foolish as to give out my place of work to strangers.' Here he fixed me with a none-too-friendly eye. 'But for the sake of my family, sir, I would kindly ask you to have some pity.'

Even Boleslavsky was moved by this appeal, and kept his voice to a whisper. 'Very well. We shall be silent, if you will. You know, I presume, why we are here?'

'To – to be measured for suits, sir?'

'Ha! We are here to fuck you, Lee,' said Boleslavsky, in menacing tones. I didn't like the 'we'. I was there to fuck him, I suppose, but this was the first I'd heard of Boleslavsky's intended participation.

'I see,' said Lee, hanging his head as if he were about to be punished. 'I suppose there's no point in asking you to let me go? I'll see the young gentlemen at home if he wishes. But not here. Please.'

'Strip,' said Boleslavsky, 'or I will call the manager.'

I was about to intervene, but Boleslavsky turned to me with a familiar look on his face – the expression he wore when he was absolutely determined on some ridiculous course of action.

'Now! Strip! Show us your body!'

Lee, realising the game was up, untied his tie and awkwardly kicked off his shoes. 'Quickly, quickly!' said Boleslavsky, who was blatantly rubbing the hard-on in his trousers.

Lee doffed his jacket and pulled his shirt over his head. There, again, was that magnificent body, so at odds with the rest of him. My cock was as hard as could be, and he had not even taken off his trousers yet.

'And the rest!'

Lee obeyed. I guessed he was used to taking orders. He removed his trousers, folded them neatly and laid them on the bench, then, without waiting to be told, pulled down his pants. His cock was soft. I suppose it would have been easier for me to rationalise my actions if

I could say that Lee was secretly excited by this forced striptease.

'Good. Excellent,' said Boleslavsky, who now had his own dick out of his flies and was masturbating slowly. 'Now come here and suck this.'

Lee knelt in front of him, looked up at him with his sad eyes, and proceeded to suck on Boleslavsky's big fat cock. Such was the power of the man's sexual appeal that Lee seemed at this point to relax a bit, to resign himself to the awfulness of the situation and, perhaps, to enjoy himself. I noticed that his prick was stirring and swelling.

Once he'd sucked Boleslavsky for a while, it was my turn. I'd stripped as quickly as I could, and stood there naked and erect waiting to be serviced. Lee shifted round on his knees and started sucking my cock. I cradled his head in my hands, whispering words of love that, I am sure, fell on deaf ears. He sucked like an angel, by the way, never choking, never biting, never giving short measure, but taking me on each downward stroke right into his throat.

I reached down, put my hands under his armpits (I was delighted to feel his muscles clenching my fingers like a vice) and raised him to his feet. I put my arms around him and went to kiss him, but he turned his head to one side. I suppose that was when I realised that I had killed any love that might have existed between us. I was sad, and sorrow, as so often is the case, led to anger and the desire to hit out at the person who was making me sad.

I grabbed Lee's cock, which was half hard, and tugged him a few times until he could not help but get an erection. 'Now I want you to fuck me,' I said, my voice as merciless as Boleslavsky's. That party, by the way, had sat down on the bench and was happily wanking while he watched the cruel drama unfold.

'Yes, sir.'

'So? What are you waiting for?' Our eyes met, and I could see the mute appeal in them; it was too late for that. I wanted to get fucked, and nothing was going to stand in my way. I lay on the floor at his feet, spread my legs and parted my arse cheeks. 'Come on, Lee.

Fuck me.'

He spat into his hand, slicked up his cock and knelt between my legs. I tilted my pelvis up towards the ceiling so that my hole was offered at the right angle, took a deep breath and allowed him to push into me. He gasped at the feeling. I was a particularly good fuck, or so many men had said. Within a few moments he was up on his toes and pumping into me, his sweaty head resting on my shoulder.

'I wish it could have been different, sir,' he said. That was all he said that could be taken as a personal remark.

The fuck was gathering momentum, partly, I suppose, because he wanted to get it over and done with. Lee was grunting, unaware of what he was doing, and the noise brought a cautious tap on the door.

'Is everything satisfactory, gentlemen?' came Mr Chivers's quavering voice from without.

'Perfectly!' roared Boleslavsky.

'Lee, do you require any assistance?'

There was a pause while Lee came round to the danger of the situation. 'No, thank you, Mr Chivers, sir,' he managed to reply, in a rather strangled tone.

'Are you certain that you're getting the measurements right?'

Boleslavsky, bastard that he was, chose this moment to start slapping the boy around the face with his hard, sticky cock.

'Yes, sir, thank you,' Lee was forced to reply just before the Russian's prick entered his mouth.

'Very well, gentlemen,' came Chivers's voice, still sounding uncertain. 'Do ask if you need any further help.'

Boleslavsky, still fully dressed with his cock sticking out of his flies, carried on fucking the boy's face while the boy fucked my arse. I began to wank, quickly. All of this was reflected in the mirrors, repeated into infinity.

Within a few moments, Lee's face assumed a look of rapt concentration, the veins stuck out in his neck and forehead, and his mouth distorted into a silent scream as he spewed his cream into my twitching arse. Ah, well, if nothing else, he got a good orgasm out of it.

After a brief pause, the excitement was too intense, and both Boleslavsky and I squirted all over the youth's beautiful, ridged torso.

Boleslavsky wiped his cock on Lee's face and shoved it back into his pants. 'Come, Pavel, we must go. Get dressed.' Now he'd come, he was in a hurry to get out. He tossed a couple of bank notes on the floor. I felt ashamed. Too late, you'll say, for that, and you'd be right.

I threw on my clothes, and we left Lee lying on the floor covered in sweat and spunk. I caught his eye one last time, and he looked immediately away. There was a tear gathering at the corner, which he did not want me to see.

Mr Chivers was waiting for us. 'Satisfactory, gentlemen, I trust?'

'Extremely satisfactory, thank you,' said Boleslavsky. 'We shall place a very large order with you. We have left our... deposits with your assistant.'

'Thank you, sir, thank you, gentlemen,' chirped Mr Chivers, rubbing his hands with glee. He must, surely, have been able to smell the sex on us. He spent so long complimenting us on our good taste that, thankfully, we gave Lee time to dress without discovery. Just as we were leaving the shop I saw him emerge from the fitting room, his hair awry, but with no other evidence of the ordeal we'd just subjected him to.

We walked out into the afternoon sunshine, our hangovers just beginning, and returned to town.

I never saw Lee again.

Twelve

A peace conference... Money in the bank... The wilderness years... Absent friends... I tire of sex... The long arm of the law... Fuck the police

Thus far I had pushed my luck, tempted Fate, however you wish to put it. But that drunken, vicious afternoon in the clothes shop, when I used so terribly an innocent young man whom I knew to be in love with me, was too much to be borne. The powers that be – the Furies, I suppose – decided that I should be taught a lesson.

My life with Boleslavsky became a burden to me. Genius is all very well, but he was running out of control, drinking more and more, taking terrible risks and all too often paying the price for them. Perhaps Boleslavsky really was a masochist at heart – there is certainly plenty in his work that betrays a fascination with pain – and I think, at that time, he was pursuing that darker part of his nature. There was nothing I could do to stop him; I was never a morally strong person, and while I might nag him to curb his drinking, or to stay away from the roughs, I was hardly in a position to lay down the law. Why, I was no better than he was: I, who had done that appalling thing to Lee. His tear-stained face haunted me, but I knew better than to go back to the shop, to try to explain. I'm sure he would have punched my lights out, Mr Chivers or no Mr Chivers, and gladly lost his job in order to do so. No, I would have to let that one lie. I can only pray now, in retrospect, that Lee recovered from his ordeal, reconciled himself to his true nature and found a worthier object for his affections than my wicked self.

I was tiring of *la vie bohème*, tiring of being Boleslavsky's sidekick. He was tiring of me as well: we seldom fucked any more; in fact we settled into an almost sexless domesticity like any married couple after only four or five months together. As the summer faded and autumn began to nip the air, I found more and more excuses to stay away from Bedford Square. I don't think I was missed. Boleslavsky was preoccupied with his drinking and whoring, and with the fights that he deliberately got into. Seldom the day at that time when his face did not resemble one of his canvases, patched with black and red from the beatings he took. Mercifully, it was also at this time that his friendship with Terry began to develop, and that young paragon – far more morally upright than I, and less patient with Boleslavsky's self-indulgent nonsense – set him back on the tracks.

Not only was I bored and blue – I was also broke. Gone were the days when upper-class gentlemen would slip me tenners. I no longer had expensive presents from Lord Simon or any of the crowned heads I had fucked. I could just about keep up appearances at Adam Street – and the rent, thank God, was still taken care of – but I was always short of spending cash. I had no heart for renting, and, besides, I was exhausted and almost sick of sex. The vast amounts of alcohol that I was consuming with Boleslavsky were taking their toll on my libido, and I was no longer stiff at the drop of a hat. Ah, age and alcohol: what a dreadful combination. I was only twenty-one, and already I was feeling middle-aged.

I should, at that point, have heard Time's winged chariot at my back, taken stock and pulled myself together. But no: old as I was in experience, I was still a young fool, and any problems that I had were bound to be someone else's fault. It was easy to blame Boleslavsky, but what was the point? He was too far gone in his own world, and, anyway, what did he care if I was suffering? As I have said before, he never cared for me – the person behind the actions and the words. I was utterly dispensable, and my time had come.

No: the person I was keenest to blame was Albert Abbott. He has not appeared in recent pages, and yet, however taken up I was with Boleslavsky, I never lost contact with Abbott, nor did I ever, in my heart, stop feeling something for him. I did not know, at the time, what that feeling was; in fact it was closer to hate than anything else. I held a grudge against him as the author of all my problems, and more than once I accused him of profiting from my misery.

'Why, of course I'm profiting from you, Paul! Why else do you think I threw you at Boleslavsky in the first place?'

'Then where's my share?'

'Come now, what would you do with a wallet full of money? You'd waste it before the week was out. I'm looking after it for you.'

'A likely story. You're creaming off the profits and letting me do all the hard work. You don't care about me. I might as well be back on the streets. At least I saw some honest money for my efforts in those days.' And so on and so forth. This little argument replayed itself several times, and I would usually leave Abbott's office with a few quid in my pocket and a misplaced sense of having got one over on him. He must have laughed at me.

As autumn proceeded, my depression set in deeper. I was at a loss: I had no other friends, apart from occasional tricks. Grimes and his fellow giants would still come and work me over, and once or twice I went back up to Covent Garden for a comforting bout of buggery in the snuggery, but beyond those basic physical transactions I had nothing of love or companionship in my life. I found myself missing the early days at the Palace of Varieties, the amicable arrangement that existed between Kieran and me – he complaining of his frustrations with Rose, I longing for his white arse and pink cock, then sharing a chaste(ish) bed. Ah, well, I had put all that behind me, burned my bridges, as usual, idiot that I was. What little pride I had left prevented me from going back to the theatre. I don't suppose I would have been very welcome: I'd hardly left there under the most auspicious circumstances.

Finally, a few weeks before Christmas 1937, I reached the nadir. I had spoken to nobody for days. I'd argued with Boleslavsky and stormed out, vowing never to return again. I'd gone to Abbott, demanding money and making foolish threats. None of my regular fucks was around, and I was lonely. I found myself sitting in a Lyons Corner House on the Strand dripping tears into my tea as I thought of my mother and my sister. In this maudlin mood I went to the stationers at Charing Cross, bought a Christmas card and a box of chocolates and sent them home with an affectionate message. Nothing did I say about how I was making my way in the world; I couldn't think of a lie glib enough. Ah, well, they would suspect the worst, and they'd be right.

I went back to my room, and sat on the bad with my head in my hands. What was to become of me? What of all the promise of my earlier years, my ambitions, my dreams of success, acclaim, love? All pissed away in a long, pointless orgy of fucking and drinking. How would I end up? One of the sad ghosts who haunt the West End, making advances to young lads they can't afford? One of the sour-tempered old queens who hover round the bars, spitting out their impotent rage against the new generation of bright young things? Surely there was something better for me – but at that time I couldn't see it. This, I now recognise, was a perfectly natural reaction to the amount that I had been drinking, but I didn't realise it, and I longed for a drink to take away the depression that was caused by drinking in the first place.

I lay on my bed and shivered. It was a cold night, the first really cold night of the season, but I was too lethargic to pull the covers over me or to switch on the gas fire. Instead I reclined in an attitude of despair, and thought beautiful thoughts about suicide. (I never really entertained the idea, by the way, just imagined how sorry everyone would be if I died, which is the traditional comfort of pathetic young men through the ages.) Then, just as I was drifting off to sleep, there came a tap at my door. Ah, I thought: Grimes. He was one of the few people who knew the concierge well enough to be allowed straight up to my landing. Well, at least I could forget my troubles for the night while I rode around on his monstrous prick.

'Come in,' I said, hauling myself up to a seated position and trying to snap out of my gloom.

The door opened – and revealed not Grimes, but Albert Abbott.

'Oh, it's you.'

'Can I come in?'

'Why ask me? You pay the rent.'

'Indeed I do.' He came in and closed the door behind him. I knew him well enough to see that he was in a benign mood, and was not going to rise to my needlings. I might as well be pleasant.

'Please sit down. Would you like a drink? I've some sherry in the cupboard.'

'No, Paul. Not for me, but do take a glass yourself. I shall take you out for dinner later, if you wish.'

Surely he hadn't come round for a fuck. I sat down again.

'Oh, very well. That would be nice.'

'Paul, I've come to apologise. I haven't been very fair to you in the last few weeks.'

'Something of an understatement!' I was suddenly ready to resume my chorus of grievances, but he silenced me with a gesture.

'You needn't remind me of my crimes, thanks all the same,' he said with a smile. 'I've come for a peace conference.'

'What do you mean?'

'A stocktaking. A plan of campaign. Time to go on to the next stage.'

'Ah.'

'And, before you ask, I've come to give you some money. Quite a large amount of money.'

'Ah.'

'Lost for words, Paul? That makes a nice change.'

We both laughed, and the mood was cordial.

'I take it that you've finished with Boleslavsky?'

'As good as,' I said. 'I think he's forgotten about me.'

'Yes, that's exactly as I expected. You did well. You lasted with him for... what, six months?'

'Something like that, although it feels a good deal longer.'

'I don't doubt it. Is he as terrible as they say? Perhaps you shouldn't answer that question, I can see from your eyes that he is.'

'Boleslavsky is—' I was going to say 'a monster', but that suddenly didn't seem true. 'Boleslavsky is an artist.'

'Yes. A true artist. Unlike Herringham, who is a skilled draughtsman, businessman and dilettante. Boleslavsky – yes, I think we can say that he is a true artist.'

'I hate his paintings, though.'

'You know what? So do I.' Again, we smiled and laughed, and Abbott sat next to me on the bed. What was this 'next stage' of which he had spoken?

There was a moment of silence, and my body braced itself for a kiss that did not come.

'Paul... have you ever...'

'Yes, Albert?'

'Have you ever... had a bank account?'

It was not the question I was expecting. 'No, never.'

'I see. It's time you opened one.' He reached into his jacket and drew out his wallet. 'I have in here a cheque which I have written out to your account, for a considerable sum. Present this to any of the major banks and they will be only too happy to have your custom.' He presented the cheque to me; it was, indeed, enough to live on for some time in the very height of style. My jaw dropped.

'You needn't thank me,' he said, sarcastically. 'You've earned every penny.'

'But...' I was flummoxed, wrong-footed. 'What... I mean, what's it for? What do I do with it?'

'It's the pay you're owed for your careful tending of Mikhail Boleslavsky. I told you that I was looking after the money for you. I don't think you ever believed me. Well, here it is.'

'I see.'

'Spend it wisely, Paul.'

'Right.'

Again, a silence fell between us. I felt a kind of sadness, I was not quite sure why. There was something… final about the transaction. As if this were a parting of the ways.

'And what next?' I asked, looking up into his eyes.

'The world is your oyster, Paul. You're a young man with a good start in life. You are, to use the common expression, "set up". Do with it what you will.'

'But isn't there another job for me? What about our plans?'

'I think our plans have paid off rather well. Oh, don't imagine, Paul, that I haven't done handsomely out of the arrangement. I can afford to be generous.'

'I'm sure you can.' I was beginning to anger. 'I see. So you've got everything you can out of me, have you? Is that what you're trying to tell me? That I've served my purpose, I'm no longer useful to you, I'm used up, worn out, time to get a fresh boy and ruin him? I see. Well, thank you!'

'Paul, stop acting like a hysterical tart.'

'If that's what I am it's what you've made me.' Oh, God, I blush as I recall these words. What a fool!

'It's for that very reason that I have decided – not, I might add, without long and serious thought – to grant you your independence. That, I would have thought, is the greatest gift that it's in my power to give you.'

That shut me up for a minute. He continued. 'I don't want you to be a whore for the rest of your life, Paul. There's more to you than that. You're intelligent, you have talents – yes, other talents besides the obvious ones, I am sure. You could go far in life. But, as long as we stay together, I am standing in your way. I'm leading you astray. I know it's an easy life that you could have, peddling your wares and putting a good deal of money into both our pockets, but it's not an honest life or a good life, and it won't last for long. You must start thinking of your future.'

'And what would you suggest, oh, wise one?'

'I would suggest you complete your education.'

'My education! That's rich. I've learned all I need to know about life, thank you very much. I know where education gets you: nowhere! I've seen the sad little bank managers and schoolteachers who save up a few shillings so that they can buy a young bit of cock. What's so great about that? In this life you've either got money, or you haven't. The rich stay rich, and the poor stay poor, unless you're prepared to grab what you can get and squeeze every last drop out of it.' I fear that I was running away with myself; even I couldn't follow my own train of thought.

'There speaks the great courtesan. Well, Paul, I have said what I came to say. You may wish to reflect on it. Don't waste what nature has given you. You have a brain as well as a pretty face. You could make something of yourself. There is such a thing as honest work, Paul, although I recognise that I'm hardly in a position to tell you about that.'

'Indeed you're not.'

'I can see that you're building up for a fight, and I don't want to speak bitter words to you. I shall leave you. Sleep on it.'

'Oh yes, that's right, just walk out and—' But he had already gone.

I thought for a moment of ripping up the cheque and showering him with the pieces as he walked down the stairs. Fortunately, I thought better of it.

I would prefer to draw a veil over the period that followed. I was twenty-one when I broke with Boleslavsky and Abbott; for the next two years, supported largely by the money I had earned from those two, I led an aimless life of whoring and socialising. I brushed up a few upper-class connections, inveigled my way into a couple of good houses and practised a little civilised blackmail in order to keep myself provided for. Occasionally, stung by some memory of Abbott's words, I would try my hand at a job, but for what was I suited? Nothing. I had no education to speak of, no work experience save that which I couldn't mention in polite society, and I was far too proud to take a humble job. Why work as a clerk or an apprentice when I could easily earn in an afternoon romping with an earl what it would take me a week of sordid graft to accumulate? I dabbled with theatre, lending my 'talents' to a couple of excruciating experimental productions that took place down Villiers Street, but it soon became clear that the legitimate theatre was not my métier. I traded on my connections with Herringham and Boleslavsky to pick up a little work here and there in artistic circles, where there was always someone willing to be kind to me, but there was no future in it. No: if the truth be told, I drifted for two years. They should have been the best years of my life, the years in which I laid a solid foundation for the future, but I wasted them. I was largely friendless, frequently lonely, given to bouts of depression, which I tried – and failed – to wash away with alcohol. Mercifully, I was of a sufficiently robust constitution to survive this self-abuse, and my face and figure never betrayed the fecklessness of my lifestyle.

I took to visiting the Palace of Varieties, just to be in a familiar environment, but there was no comfort for me there. Mr Holly had gone – I believe he moved into cinema management, and doubtless continued to draw his 'elevenses' from the stiff cocks of his young projectionists and ushers – and with him had gone most of the old familiar faces. Vera had retired (he still wrote to me, but I avoided visiting him), and Kieran had disappeared, nobody knew where. Old Mrs Tunnock was still running her boarding house, and greeted me with good cheer, but could give me no clue to his whereabouts. I even called in at the pub where Rose, Kieran's former sweetheart, was now pulling pints behind the bar. I swallowed my pride and asked after my old friend, but she just laughed and shrugged. 'Oh, Kieran! God, I should think he's married by now! He was going steady with Sally, a lovely girl, you know.'

Married. Yes, well, that was what he always wanted. I wondered if he ever managed to get his strongman act on the stage, or if he was now labouring in another scenic dock somewhere across town, his muscles bunching up under the milk-white freckled skin of his arms and chest. I felt a terrible pang of loneliness, and left the pub.

What did I do for sex at this time? Well, believe it or not, sex was no longer the pleasure it used to be. I felt that I had done it all. I had been sucked by every type of mouth, fucked by cocks large, small, thick, thin, bent to the left, bent to the right, black, white, brown and yellow. I had stuck my prick into every orifice that would take it. I had shoved it into arses so tight that I thought they would strangle me. I had thrown it into holes so sloppy it was like dangling a piece of string in a bucket. I had come over faces, over backs, over stomachs; I had pissed in mouths, I had taken dildos, I had taken multiple cocks and fingers, I had participated in orgies. I had done it in bedrooms, bathrooms, ballrooms, alleyways, studios, shops, steam baths, public houses, public toilets – anywhere with a floor or a wall and a modicum of privacy. In short, I had done it all, and usually for money. I was jaded. I could still get it up, but my performances were mechanical things. I thought back to my first sexual experiences – with Mr Newsome in his Albany chambers, when I was fucked for the first time; with Trevor the pervert, with Albert Abbott, Gerald Fitzgerald, Grimes, Boleslavsky, Lee – all the men I had loved, who had loved me. And it all seemed long ago and far away, like a landscape viewed down the wrong end of a telescope. Now, when I fucked, it was no more pleasurable than taking a shit. If it earned me money, I was pleased. That was all.

Sometimes I could raise a little more interest than usual by introducing a touch of pain to the pleasure. If a man gave me a good spanking, I enjoyed sex more, or, if I could inflict a similar punishment on an innocent lad, so much the better. But real pain repelled me. I was neither sadist nor masochist at heart, just a tourist looking for new thrills. I thought at one point that maybe I was turning straight, and that this disgust with the male sex would naturally give way to 'normal' desires for women. I was wrong, and to this day am a virgin with the female sex. I pursued the traditional homosexual interests in soldiers and sailors, finding that they were, as a class, sexually adventurous and not too greedy. When necessary, I would give my chosen partner a little financial sweetener, just to make the transaction satisfactory all round. It would never have occurred to me that I was 'paying' for sex, that I was transforming, in fact, from whore to client. I saw my money as a means to an end – just as I'm sure every punter down the ages has done.

As well as military personnel, I developed a taste for another sort of uniform – the police. This, I suppose, was just a way of putting myself into danger, of flirting with danger, of courting the punishment that I knew, in my heart, I deserved. That was not how I saw it at the time. I only listened to my dick, and my dick responded more vigorously than usual when it saw a nice bit of trade in a dark-blue uniform. After the first time, when I wanked off a copper in a Covent Garden alley, very late one night when I was pissed and he was in a hurry, I became more and more blatant in my approaches to the boys in blue. One of my bobby-chasing exploits stands out quite vividly in my mind.

I had gone up to Hampstead for the day to visit one Mr Thorne, an old admirer of Herringham's who owned several of his works, including a small series of erotic drawings in which I featured heavily. I had met Thorne at one of the parties, and immediately pegged him as a wealthy old pervert – he must have been at least eighty. He was completely impotent, and asked of me nothing more than the opportunity to look at my body, touching me only in the lightest, most inoffensive way. During this shiftless period of my life, he was a useful source of pocket money and a contact, however minor, with the kind of life to which I was once accustomed. I went to his house once or twice a month, and always came away with a few extra quid in my pocket. He bored me to death with his jawings about 'the Greek ideal', but at least his rooms were warm, and all I had to do was walk around, recline on a couch or do a little gymnastics. Thorne never even required me to perform sexually; I usually had a semierection, and once manipulated myself into full stiffness and started wanking, thinking that he'd like to see me squirt my young load, but the look of startled disgust on his face told me I was barking up the wrong tree. After that I was content to lounge around and let him feast his eyes.

I always left these encounters randy as hell. The old man did nothing for me in himself, but his appreciation was an aphrodisiac, and I usually had to find relief as soon as I could. This was never difficult: even though Hampstead Heath wasn't the hotbed of sin that it was later to become, I could usually pick up some young chap around the men's ponds or in the pubs and cafés who would be willing to fool around and take care of my stiff prick.

On this occasion, I didn't have to look too far. I was walking across the Heath with my hands in my pockets, nursing a promising erection, and whistling a popular tune, when I felt a hand on my shoulder. This was a bold approach, even for Hampstead, and I spun on my heel. There, however, was not some horny builder or degenerate princeling, but a young man in the uniform of the Metropolitan Police, his helmet perched on his head and his buttons gleaming.

'One moment, sir.'

It took me a second to register that he was handsome and well put together, and I framed my attitude accordingly.

'Yes, officer, what is it?' Under the peak of his helmet I could see a pair of twinkling blue eyes framed by indecently long eyelashes. He had a slightly crooked, uptilted nose, a clean-shaven chin already blue with half a day's growth, and the suspicion of a smile round his full mouth. At the base of his neck, round the collar of his tunic, there were a few tufts of hair, suggesting that this young officer was a furry little piece beneath the uniform.

'I've been watching you.'

'Indeed. And what have you seen?'

'You've come out of Mr Thorne's house, haven't you?'

'I have. What of it?'

'We've had complaints.'

Had the neighbours been peering through the curtains? Had someone taken exception to the strip shows that went on behind closed doors?

'Oh dear, I am sorry to hear that.' If he was going to accuse me of something, he'd have done so by now.

'Yes, sir, and I must ask you a few questions.'

'Has there been a burglary?'

'Nothing of that sort, sir, I'm glad to say.'

'Has Mr Thorne been... blackmailed?'

'No, sir...' I began to think that we were on the same wavelength.

'Then what? What sort of complaints? Mr Thorne is a very good friend of mine. Naturally I would do anything in my power to protect him from harm.'

'Mr Thorne is not always... careful in his choice of friends.'

'Ah, that I don't doubt. I know he has a penchant for... rough lads.' I wondered if this young hero had been stripped of his uniform by the old rogue. I couldn't fault his taste if that was the case; already I was at full stiffness, and thinking of ways to capitalise on the situation. My young copper seemed nervous; he ran his tongue over his lips, and eased a finger round his collar.

'What were you doing at Mr Thorne's house this afternoon, sir?'

'Paying a social call.'

'Are you quite sure about that?'

'Why do you ask? Were you watching us?'

'I've been keeping an eye on the property for some time, sir.' That was it. He'd been peeking, the dirty little sod, and now he wanted to touch as well as to look. Well, he'd have to earn it.

'I'm very glad to hear it, PC...'

'Nowell, sir.'

'PC Nowell. My name is Lemoyne. Paul Lemoyne.' I extended a

hand. I could see that this kind of bold behaviour was unnerving him; I suppose most of the lads he picked up in this way were more easily cowed by the law. I, brazen slut that I was, could outface anyone without a blush. He took my hand in a warm, firm grip, and we shook like businessmen clinching a deal – which I suppose we were.

'Now, Mr Lemoyne, I would, er, advise you to be careful. Around these parts, you know, tongues wag.'

'Yes, and there's always the terrible danger of Peeping Toms.'

'Ah...'

'Not that it worries me, of course. I've nothing to hide.' I replaced my hands in my pockets and stretched the front of my trousers tight across my groin. My erection could hardly have been more visible if I'd brought it out into the daylight.

'No, I see that sir.' He was clearly getting stiff as well, and fidgeted around inside his uniform, not quite daring to touch it.

'Will that be all, PC Nowell? I have a pressing matter in hand that urgently needs to be attended to.'

'I had better make sure I escort you away from the area, sir.'

'Very well, I can see that under the circumstances you can't be too careful.'

'Yes. The police car's parked up on the High Street, sir. It might be best if I were to drive you home.'

'That sounds like a very sound idea to me, officer.'

'Very well, sir, if you'd like to accompany me to the car...'

We kept this absurd banter up all the way home, finding ever more loaded phrases to communicate our lust to each other. When he was at the wheel he took his helmet off, revealing a head full of brown curly hair. As we drew nearer Adam Street, further from his beat, he relaxed and smiled more. I could see I'd picked a live one. His cock, which was allowed more freedom when he was seated, stuck straight up at the fly like a gear stick.

'Here we are, officer. Perhaps you'd be so kind as to come upstairs with me. I'd feel so much safer if you would.'

'Very well, sir. Anything to help a member of public.'

'This member is most grateful,' I said, thrusting my groin forward as we got out of the car.

We raced up the stairs to my room, and the moment we were inside the door we fell upon each other with the vigour of starving men. I don't know how often PC Nowell got laid, but judging by the energy of his assault it wasn't often enough for his tastes. He fumbled with my buttons in his excitement, and couldn't wait to get his own uniform off – after a few moments he had his cock out of the fly and was humping my leg like a dog. Our mouths were glued together, my clothes were completely awry, revealing to his eyes and hands my chest and stomach – and it was all too much for him. He grasped his cock and pumped it once, twice, three times – and spunk was flying all over his trousers.

I thought he'd turn tail and run, but no: calmed by his first orgasm, he set about enjoying himself. Now he took his time at undressing me, and soon had me stark-naked before him. The contrast – my bare, olive skin, his coarse blue uniform, covered in spunk stains – was most satisfactory. He fell to his knees and started licking and sucking my balls, while I ran my fingers through those luxuriant nut-brown curls.

Soon his mouth was not enough, and I wanted his arse. I stepped back and took control.

'On your feet, officer.'

He stood.

'Strip.'

He didn't have to be asked twice. The buttons were undone in a mechanical rhythm, and the jacket slung aside. The undershirt was pulled over the head, and I was delighted to see that he was every bit as hairy as I could wish. There was a tattoo on the right shoulder of a rose surrounded by thorns.

He sat down on the bed to unlace his boots, then kicked them off and removed his trousers, leaving only the long, white woollen socks and a pair of button-up trunks between him and the elements. I pulled his pants down in one rapid movement; the socks stayed on, rucked halfway down his shins, a delightful counterpoint to the thick brown hair on his legs.

'Lie back.'

He looked good lying there, a fit, hairy young stud – a police officer no longer. The uniform, however, was close enough at hand if I needed any reminding of the prize I had bagged.

'Legs in the air.'

He pulled his knees back into his chest, and hooked his elbows round them. In that position, his long, hard cock was pressed flat against his stomach; his balls hung obscenely down between his thighs. And his hole was vulnerable to my assault: very pink, very tight, and framed by hair.

I plunged in with my tongue, determined to eat him alive. At the first contact he cried out, and continued whimpering as I chewed on his arse, working my tongue up as far as I could, licking him and tickling him in preparation for what I hoped would be the fuck of a lifetime. Gone was his cocky, nervous attitude of our first meeting, and now he surrendered himself to the feelings, and showed neither nerves nor shame. He knew what was coming next. I hawked into my hand, and was about to spread it over my prick when he stopped me.

'Wait. Look in the right-hand breast pocket of my tunic.'

I did so, and there was a small, half-squeezed tube of Vaseline.

'You certainly travel prepared.'

'You never know when you might need it.'

'So do you get fucked by many members of the public?'

'No, sir,' he said, a naughty smile on his face. 'Usually I do the fucking. But as soon as I saw your prick through Mr Thorne's windows I decided I wanted that up my arse as soon as possible.'

In reward for this shameless speech I slapped him hard across the bum, then squeezed out a generous glob of greeny-grey Vaseline onto my fingers.

'Well, that's what you're going to get, Nowell. I'm going to fuck you with my fingers, then with my prick, and then, if you still haven't had enough, I'm going to stick your truncheon up your bum and fuck you with that.'

In reply, he squirmed and smiled, and I guessed that the party could begin.

My finger slid up easily enough, and soon found his prostate gland. I pushed and prodded this none too gently. I was not in the mood for sensitive lovemaking, and I don't think it was what PC Nowell wanted, either. His cock was drooling goo onto the mat of hair on his stomach, and his head was thrown back, leaving his throat deliciously exposed between the hair on his chest and the stubble on his chin. I reached forward and kissed him hard.

I added a second finger to the first, and fucked him roughly in this way; he was in pain, and scowled a little, but when I pulled back to give him a breather he simply grabbed my wrist and pushed himself back on to me. He was ready for more.

With his hole nicely greased up, all I had to do was refresh the coating of spit on my dick, position myself at the entrance and push. I slid into his arse in one smooth movement, and of all the fucks I can remember this was one of the easiest and yet tightest. It was like wanking in a warm satin glove – his arse had a mind of its own, and seemed to pull me into him. Soon I was banging away as hard as I could, concentrating only on not coming too soon.

Inevitably, it was too good to last for long, and I told him so.

'Go on then – fill me up!' It was all I needed to hear, and I fucked as hard as I could, pivoting my entire weight down into his guts and filling them with cream. At the moment of crisis, I glued my mouth over his.

Finally I pulled out with a satisfying plop; it had been a bigger load than usual. Nowell, however, was not finished with me yet. He pointed down at his hard cock.

'What about this, then?'

I never was one to leave a young man unsatisfied, and I grabbed hold of it and started wanking.

'Hang about, sir,' he said. 'Remember what you promised?'

Could he be serious? He was: he reached over and grabbed his truncheon, still attached to the belt of his trousers.

'You asked for it.' I smothered the head of the long, black tube with another gout of Vaseline and held it out to him. 'How do you want it?'

'Hold it right there.' He jumped up on to his feet, held the tip of the truncheon against his arse and swallowed it whole. It was one of the most impressive anal performances I have ever seen. When it was buried a good eight inches up his arse, he began raising and lowering himself, using his thigh muscles, which were divided by great deep grooves with every movement.

'Now wank me off, sir.'

I had the base of the truncheon in one hand; with the other, I grasped his swollen cock and started slowly pumping. Nowell groaned; he was red in the face, the flush spreading down his neck and over his chest. Finally he rolled on to his back and let me take charge.

I fucked him hard with that truncheon, but he was man enough to take it. With each withdrawal, I noticed the little lips of his outer arse clinging to the shiny black surface of the truncheon, well lubricated with grease, spit, and my own copious spendings, which were smeared up the thing in pearly strings. I was hard again, but I had no desire to stop this violation for something more natural. Fucking a policeman's arse with his own truncheon seemed, at the time, like the point to which my entire life had been leading.

Finally, Nowell swore, grunted and spewed another great load over his stomach, chest and neck. I held the truncheon deep in place while he came, then let go and allowed him to shit it out at his own pace. Finally it clunked onto the floor and rolled under the bed. I lay down on top of the horny constable and held him tight, kissing him for all I was worth. My prick was stiff again, and I jabbed it into his sticky, hairy stomach and between his thighs. For the final act, I lay back in his arms and allowed him to toss me off; he certainly knew his way around a cock. I wondered how many of his brother officers were as familiar with the territory.

After a friendly kiss he jumped up and dressed, checking his uniform in the mirror. It was only when he was on the point of leaving that he remembered his truncheon, which I retrieved after a lengthy search from under the bed. It was disgusting, still sticky and smelly and covered in fluff and pubic hairs. I wiped it on a handkerchief and handed it back to him, but not before sniffing along its length. It still smelled most deliciously of his arse.

Thirteen

To Leicester Square... Kieran... A cruel proposition... Virtue defeated... The wonder of champagne... A happy conclusion

Time drifted on, and I became more and more a solitary creature. My sexual encounters, when they happened, were intense on the physical plane, but they brought me no nearer to another human being. During the act itself I felt love, passion, connection – but as soon as it was over I found myself again with a stranger. I was making love to an ideal, embodied for a few moments in one man, who slipped out of my grasp like a will-o'-the-wisp. Perhaps I was chasing after a real attachment – after love – but, if so, I was looking for it in all the wrong places.

One story will suffice to illustrate how detached I had become from my fellow man. I had taken to picking up trade more frequently, basically because I was lazy. All I had to do was stroll up to Leicester Square or Piccadilly, a mere fifteen minutes' saunter from my front door, where there were any number of idle young fellows willing to be taken advantage of for a small financial outlay. In fact, they competed for my attention: most of the other punters were a good deal older than I, and once it became known that the young, handsome, slightly dissolute man in the fashionable clothes was a customer rather than competition, they preened in front of me, advertising their wares. There were rich pickings for a queer with money in those days: such are the advantages of a downturn in the economy. Young men who would normally shy away from the merest hint of homosexuality were out there peddling their pricks and bums for a few bob a night, and I, with my nest egg still just about intact, was happy to take advantage of them.

One wet, dirty night in March 1938, I was sitting in my snug little room reading a novel by Balzac – I was still, despite everything, trying to improve my mind – when I found my attention wandering. I paced around the room, but I couldn't settle. The familiar itch in my groin would not go away – and I realised it was nearly ten days since I'd last had sex. I'd barely even wanked; the weather, I suppose, had dampened my libido. On that night, though, I found that my cock had awoken from its mini-hibernation, and my arse was hungry. And so, with little thought, I put on a Norfolk jacket and wound a muffler round my neck and set off for Leicester Square.

It was nine o'clock and completely dark. The streets were washed with rain, reflecting the illuminated hoardings of the cinemas and restaurants. The street lights lit the drizzle, which blew around them in flurries, whipping against the still-bare branches of the trees. Odours of steam came up from basement kitchens; the sound of a banjo tinkled over from the north side of the square where a busker entertained the queue outside the Empire. But the cinema was not my destination. I was more interested in what was on show in those darker areas against the railings that bordered the patch of green in the centre of the Square. Around here, any night of the year, you could find a dozen or two young chaps on the game – and tonight, rain or no rain, was no exception.

I strolled once round the Square, and heard my name called out by one or two of the more regular renters, whom I had either had before or who knew me by reputation. (Some of them knew me from my former life as a whore; they must have been even more world-weary than I was.) But I never, at this time, went with the same man twice: after the act of love they bored or disgusted me. They tried to make friends, and could only reveal the shallowness of their personalities (as I saw it, God help me) or the dissatisfaction of my own. Looking back, I can see that I had turned into the typical punter – a man who cares nothing for the young man he's renting, who sees only a collection of physical attributes that correspond, more or less, to his fantasy. At the time, however, I just thought that these youths were a sorry lot and didn't measure up to my lofty personal qualities. Maybe if I'd taken the trouble to get to know one or two of them, rather than just dismiss them, I might have found a kindred spirit.

On the first circuit, there was nobody to tickle my fancy, so I took a seat in a small, cosy café and sipped a cup of muddy coffee. After twenty minutes I was out again; the cinemas had all admitted their customers, and the Square was left to the bad and the sad. There had been about fifteen young men around the railings before; now there were more like twenty. This quiet time of night, when respectable folk were at home, in the cinemas or eating, was the prowlers' time. I did the circuit again, and saw nothing new. I was about to go with a young chap called Matthew, whom I'd had before – an empty-headed creature, but with a hot little arse and no qualms about what he did with it – when my gaze was arrested by a familiar profile, half turned away from me and cast into deep shadow by the street light high above. A mass of curls stuck out from a cap pushed far back on the head; further down there was a snub nose, a full mouth and a strong jaw. I moved nimbly to one side, disappointing Matthew, who was about to walk towards me, and caught my quarry face on.

I was right. It was Kieran.

He had not seen me yet; he had his hands rammed deep into his pockets and was watching a man in a heavy overcoat and bowler hat who was patrolling nervously on the outer reaches of the hunting area. I had liberty to observe him for a moment: yes, the same old Kieran, my Kieran, my first friend in London, looking almost as young and fresh and full of life as he had been on the day we had met, but just a suggestion of some fine lines around the eyes, perhaps a slight drag at the side of the mouth, the signs of age and care.

I coughed, and touched him lightly on the arm. He turned to face me with the familiar rent boy's sneer on his face – and then did the most perfect double take.

'Fuck me! Paul!'

'Good evening, Kieran.'

'Jesus Christ, what are you doing out on a wet night like this?'

'I could ask you the same thing, Kieran.'

'Ah, well, you know...'

'Can I buy you a drink?'

'Now there's a kind offer that I shan't refuse. God, Paul, you're looking well.' He took in my clothes, my general air of financial comfort. 'You're prospering mightily by the look of it. I always knew you'd do well.'

'Ah, I mustn't grumble.'

I steered him out of the Square towards a small restaurant on Panton Street, where I knew we would not be disturbed. We were seated and served with a bottle of red wine.

'Well, it's grand to see you, Paul,' said Kieran, his eyes shining. 'I think often of the old days. God, I miss all the laughs we had at the old South London. What on earth are you doing with yourself? You left in such a hurry. I wondered if you'd... found a friend.'

'No, nothing of the kind.' I was in no mood to discuss my own life – I was ashamed of it. 'But what about you, Kieran? What are you doing hanging around that part of Leicester Square of an evening?'

He blushed, and that sealed his fate. I felt a delicious cruelty rising within me; Kieran would feel its sting.

'Ah, you know, just meeting a friend.'

'Like all the rest of the lads down there, I suppose.'

'Well...' He looked up at me from puzzled brows, unable to interpret the callous tone of my voice. 'We live in difficult times, Paul. It's hard to make ends meet.'

'So you supplement your income with a bit of whoring, is that it?'

'If you want to call it that.'

'That's what it is.'

'Well, Paul, you should know.' He was about to get up; I couldn't have that.

'Don't be silly, Kieran. You mustn't mind me. Tell me: I hear you got married. What's her name? Sally?'

'Ah, she's a grand girl,' said Kieran, lowering his voice and looking guiltily around him. That told me something: Sally didn't know how he was making his money. 'We've a lovely baby girl and another on the way. She's made me the happiest man in the world.'

'But work's hard to come by.'

'Indeed it is. I kept going in the theatres, and I still help out where I can, but everyone's cutting back. There's no room for an unskilled man like me. I do a bit on the building sites and the roads, but the work's seasonal and unreliable unless you know the right people, and so—'

'How much do you earn in a week?'

'A good week? Five pounds, if I'm lucky.'

'And on a night in Leicester Square?'

'God... a quid. Maybe.'

'And what do you have to do for that?'

'Jesus Paul! Well, you know, wank them off, let them touch my whatsit.'

'Do they suck it?'

'Some of them do.'

'What about fucking?'

'Come on, Paul, I'm a married man. I'm not one of those pansies that do it because they enjoy it.'

Another nail in his coffin. 'So: five pounds in a good week. And that's enough to keep the family on, is it?'

'If I can get a little extra down here, yes.'

'How would you like to earn a tenner, Kieran?'

'I'd love to!' His eyes were bright again as the solution to some of his more pressing financial problems presented itself. He had not yet divined the poison at the bottom of the cup.

'I can put you in the way of some good money for just a few hours' work.'

'Would it be working with you, Paul? God, that would be grand, just like the old days!' He ran a great freckled hand through his ginger curls, and took a swig of his wine. Two red spots appeared high on his cheekbones. I'd bring a flush to that face, I thought.

'A tenner, Kieran. More, maybe. Just for a night's work.'

'What is it, Paul? Are you back in theatres?'

'Oh, no, it's nothing like that.'

'What, then? The arts? Something posh, I bet. You're looking so good these days, quite a gentleman! God, you've come a long way from Ma Tunnock's!'

I could tell that he was keen to ramble on about the good old days, and so I cut him short. 'No, Kieran, nothing like that. I'm a man of independent means these days. I'm wealthy. I don't have to work for it.'

'Right. I see.' He clearly didn't. 'So what do I have to do for the money?'

I held his eyes, and paused just long enough to see the expression change from happy hope to fearful dismay. 'You'd have to let me fuck you, Kieran.'

That shut him up. The colour drained from his cheeks, and he went white as a sheet. Then the blood flushed up again from his neck to his forehead – anger, I suppose.

'Don't say that even as a joke, Paul.'

'I'm not joking. I've wanted to fuck you up the arse from the first day I met you.'

'That's not true. We were pals, weren't we? We shared a bed, for Christ's sake. I was never like that.'

'Don't speak like a child. I wanted to fuck you, I wanted you to fuck me. I was in love with you.'

'Then for pity's sake!'

'But that was a long time ago. Now I just want to fuck you. Hard. Up the arse. I want to stick my cock up your bum and fuck you until I come. I want you to suck me and wank me. I want you to get yourself stiff and wank off over yourself. I want you to do everything

I tell you to do.'

Kieran put his head in his hands and moaned. 'Oh, God, Paul. I thought you were my friend.'

'I am your friend. I could give my money to any of the boys out there, and they'd be grateful. I wouldn't offer them a tenner, you know. A quid, that's what most of them get, a guinea if I like them, another five bob if they do something really special. I'm offering you a tenner for old times' sake. Take it or leave it.'

'You know I need the money.'

'Yes, and I know that you want to fuck with me.'

'I do not, Paul.'

'Come on, admit it. You enjoy having sex with men. Why are you down here if you don't?'

'I told you, I have a wife and a child.'

'All right, all right. Have it your way. It disgusts you but you do it for the money. So why not with me?'

'Because... you're my friend.'

'That again. I'm offering you ten quid, Kieran. And for what? What's so bad about this? You've already done the worst thing: you've gone with another man. You're a queer whether you like it or not. Taking it up the arse is just a variation on a theme. What's so difficult about that?'

He was defeated. I am sure he would have left if he could, or hit me, but ten pounds was a lot of money. He straightened up, drained his glass and looked me straight in the eye.

'Right. Let's go, then. I'll be your whore for the night, Paul. But no more talk. Come on, drink up.'

I could feel the hostility coming off him in waves; perhaps he thought I would relent, that it was all a joke, but I am sure that even then he would never have forgiven me. Well, if he wanted to be serious, I could match him.

'I'm ready.' I paid the waiter, making sure that Kieran had a good view of the bank notes stuffed into my wallet, and we stepped out into the street.

We exchanged barely a word as we walked down the Haymarket and along the Strand. Halfway down I decided it would be too pure and simple to take Kieran back to Adam Street, where he would find out more than I wanted him to know about my financial position. And so, instead, I took him by the arm and steered him into the lobby of the Strand Palace Hotel, just across the road from my street. It was a stupid, reckless extravagance, but I knew that, by affording Kieran a glimpse of the lifestyle he could acquire by giving himself over to vice, I could further corrupt him.

I marched up to the desk clerk, and requested a room for the night. He was a very proper old gentleman, one of the old school for whom no customer's request is too far-fetched, and yet I think even he was taken aback by my brazenness.

'A single room, sir? I'll see what we have.'

'No, a double, please. My friend will be staying, too.'

'Very well, sir. I'm not sure if we have anything available at the moment.'

I pulled my wallet out of my jacket pocket and opened it to reveal the large wad of cash inside. 'Oh, I'm sure you do. I've stayed here many times before and never been disappointed.' This was a lie. I'd been in once, the guest of Lord Simon, who managed to lure the young porter up to the room and persuaded him to perform with me while his lordship watched and wanked. Still, I knew enough about the geography of the hotel to boss the staff around.

The desk clerk's eyes sparkled when he saw the money (and doubtless saw a fat tip for himself), and suddenly a room appeared to be free.

'Ah, I think we can accommodate you. Do you have any luggage, sir?'

'None. Don't worry, I shall pay in advance.' I peeled the notes out of my wallet; Kieran and the clerk both watched them like hawks. 'That should cover the bill, I believe,' I said, and then pulled out an extra pound note. 'And here's a little something for you.'

The desk clerk handed us the key with obsequious thanks, and we were on our way. Kieran was still silent, but I detected less hostility than before; like most boys of his class, he was easily overawed by money, and allowed himself to believe that someone as financially successful as I was couldn't possibly be all bad. Perhaps the money smoothed the way to his surrender and (I like to think) enjoyment of what followed.

The room was handsome, a little overdecorated for my tastes with salmon-pink walls and elaborate plaster mouldings, but it impressed Kieran. He was happy again, wandering around and touching the velvet drapes, the gilt mirror frames, the handsome telephone (a rarer sight in those days). 'Good God, Paul, this is really living, isn't it?'

'What will you have to drink?'

'I don't know.'

'Champagne?'

'I never tasted it in my life.'

I wanted to get him drunk, to ensure that he would give himself entirely to the degradation ahead.

'You shall taste it now.' I picked up the receiver and placed my order. While we waited for room service, I employed every subtle device to corrupt him utterly.

'This is the life, isn't it, Kieran?'

'Nice if you can get it.'

'You know how I got it, don't you?'

'No.'

'I allowed men to fuck me. I let them suck my prick. I did everything they asked me to, and most of the time I loved it. They paid handsomely for my cock and my arse, Kieran.'

'Yes...' He sounded slightly dreamy now. 'I remember you had a big prick, Paul.'

'So do you, Kieran. I remember it well. I've thought about it often since that time I sucked you off in Ma Tunnock's. Do you remember,

Kieran? Do you remember what it felt like?'

'Yes, I do.'

'And you never did return the compliment.'

'Ah, well...'

'Didn't you want to, Kieran?'

'It's not so much that I didn't want to...'

'Then why not?' I was lasciviously rubbing the front of my trousers, where my hard-on was blatantly outlined.

'Well, Paul, in those days... I mean, two chaps together... I was younger. I didn't really know the... ways of the world.'

We were interrupted by the arrival of the champagne; the waiter noticed that there were two very stiff pricks in the room, and had to be bundled out of the door with a florin in his palm.

I poured the wine and handed Kieran a glass. 'Here's to the ways of the world, Kieran.'

'Cheers, Paul.'

His tone was friendly again, and we drank. He drained his glass in one go, and I was quick to fill it. He drank a glass for every sip I took, I made sure of that. After two glasses I judged it was safe to proceed.

'And so, Kieran, you're going to be fucked.'

'Ah, God, Paul...'

'Yes, you are. You're going to take my hard prick up your arse.'

'Won't it hurt?'

'Yes. At first. But you'll get used to it.'

'And will you... like it?'

'Oh, yes. I've always wanted to fuck that white arse of yours. Didn't you know?'

He was still stiff at the front; the champagne was wearing down his resistance.

'I suppose I guessed.' He drained his third glass.

'So – show it to me.'

'What?'

'Your arse. Drop your pants and show me your arse.'

Now he looked crestfallen again; he put his glass carefully down on the dressing table and started fumbling with his flies.

'The braces, Kieran.'

'Oh, God, yes...' He dropped the braces from his shoulders, and let his trousers drop round his ankles.

'Now your pants.'

These were worn and rather baggy; they came down easily. His cock was still stiff, and poked through the tails of his shirt: it was thicker and pinker than I imagined it, the foreskin clearly revealing the shape of the glans beneath. At the end, the helmet peeped out, moist and fresh.

'Turn round and bend over.'

He obeyed, bracing his great paws on the glass top of the ornate dressing table and sticking his bum out for my inspection. I lifted his white shirt clear, and there it was – two white globes as smooth as marble, with a little ginger fuzz in the cleft. I took a buttock in each hand and squeezed hard. Kieran gasped a little – I think he was surprised to be experiencing pleasure – and bent his head.

I dropped to my knees, determined to feast on this dish. I pried the cheeks apart and got my first view of his virgin hole, pink and puckered, with its insulating coat of golden hair. I blew softly on it, and watched it tense and relax. Then I went in, very gently at first, with my mouth. At first I kissed Kieran's arse, as I had longed to do many times before, and was rewarded with a groan of pleasure. I felt round the front to check that his cock was stiff: I was not disappointed. I changed from kissing to licking – again, gently at first. Kieran could not believe what was happening to him. I don't believe that his arse had ever been a source of pleasure before, and this was a shocking new voyage of discovery for him.

After I'd tasted the fruit, I decided it was time to up the stakes a little. I started rimming him more vigorously, diving in with my tongue and breaching the first sphincter. Kieran was in seventh heaven – well, what young man wouldn't be on receipt of his first tongue-fucking? There is no pain involved: the tongue is a soft organ, unlike the prick, which can rip into a man's guts like a sword. Kieran could open himself up to this gentle assault as much as he wanted. I remembered the first time a tongue had touched my arse, and I imagined the feelings he was experiencing. Oh, to have something so new and wonderful to discover! I was jealous.

Soon I'd had enough of rimming; it was his turn to do some work.

'Stand up and turn around to face me.' He obeyed, and perched his arse on the edge of the dressing table, letting his cock jut straight up in the air. I suppose he imagined that the tables had turned and that he was in charge now – he, the stud, the cocksman, who could sell his stiff prick and get away without having to earn his money. He expected me to stay on my knees and suck him, as I had done once before. He looked confident; smug, even. He would learn.

'Do you like having your cock sucked, Kieran?'

'Yeah. Go ahead.'

I grabbed his prick – it was admirably hard – and let my tongue run round the head. He groaned again, and it was all I could do to resist swallowing the whole thing. It was a beauty: long and thick, perfectly symmetrical save for the one thick blue vein that ran slightly to the left of centre along the top.

I tossed him gently, pulling the foreskin right back over his head as I tasted the pre-come gathering at his piss slit. Now he was making low growling noises in his belly. I stood up abruptly.

'Now it's your turn.'

'What?'

'Your turn to suck my cock.' I unbuttoned in a hurry, and hauled my prick out into the air. Kieran watched it, fascinated.

'I don't do that, Paul.'

'You do, Kieran. You do that and a whole lot more. And you'll do it right. I'll teach you how to be a good cocksucker. We've got all night.'

He stood up to me for a moment, considering, perhaps, fight or flight. But then he remembered the money, and succumbed to the gentle pressure of my hands on his shoulders. He sank to his knees, and took a hold of my cock.

'Now lick it.'

It's a big step for any young man to take, tasting his first cock – particularly someone who, like Kieran, is to all intents and purposes straight. But sex is sex. He stuck out his tongue and gingerly licked up the underside of my prick.

'It won't bite.'

He licked again, more confidently this time, and was soon doing it regularly and with some enjoyment.

'Now the balls.' This time there was no hesitation: he moved on to my balls as if that were the most delightful suggestion in the world. He licked all over the scrotum, and even took them in his mouth in a tentative, exploratory kind of way.

'Now suck my dick.'

This was the moment he had been dreading, or longing for. He took a deep breath, opened his mouth wide and shut his eyes tight, anticipating pain. Gradually his lips enclosed the head, and he moved them down about an inch. Kieran had received enough blow jobs from Mr Holly, me and his various clients to know how it was done; doing it, however, was a different matter.

I placed my hands on his head and persuaded him gently downwards. He scraped me with his teeth and gagged, trying to back away. I let him off.

'Try again.'

'I can't, Paul. It chokes me. It's too big.'

'Flattery will get you nowhere. Try again. It's the same for all of us. You have to learn, and I'm going to teach you.'

This time he was slower, and took another inch. He looked up at me with an expression of pride and pleasure on his face. The champagne had obviously worked its magic.

'Good boy. Now move backwards and forwards. Mind your teeth.

That's it.' He started to bob up and down on the first couple of inches of my prick, lubricating me well with saliva and neither gagging nor biting. It was time for me to take control.

I took his head again, and pushed in a little deeper. He scowled, but managed to take me. Then, with each downward stroke, I pushed a little further. Kieran breathed heavily through his nostrils, and I'm sure would have come off me if I'd let him, but I was determined to break him. He gagged, but I would not release him.

'Relax. Suck me. Suck me.' He stopped, held me rigid in his mouth and started again. This time he was more open, and took the last few inches into his throat.

'Now you're a cocksucker. So suck my cock.'

And he did: he went for it like an old hand. Occasionally he would falter, gagging until his eyes streamed with tears, but nothing would stop him. He held onto my thighs and allowed me to fuck his face – hoping to make me come, perhaps. Well, I was tempted to blow a load down his throat, but I held back. Empty balls might make me have mercy on him, and I was determined to get my money's worth.

Shortly, as I felt my orgasm building, I pulled out of his mouth and was gratified to see that his tongue came lolling out, trying to prolong the contact.

'On the bed.'

'What now?'

'Lie down on the bed. I'm going to fuck you.'

This time there was no complaint, and Kieran lay on his back and stretched out. I pulled off his boots and trousers, pulled the shirt over his head, and soon had him naked. It was a beautiful sight: he was so pale, his cock stood out like a rose on a field of snow.

I stripped quickly and jumped on top of him, grinding my cock against his.

'How do you want me?'

For once, I was taken by surprise. 'What?'

'How do you want me to be? On my back? On my knees?' He was

playing with his cock, which was still hard.

In answer I picked up his knees and dived into his arsehole again, slicking him up with spit until his arse was slippery enough to enter. Then, without ceremony, I pushed my cock into him.

He bellowed in pain, and his cock went limp like a burst balloon.

'Jesus, Paul, take it out! You're killing me! For the love of God!' I was tempted to play the rapist, but I couldn't: some spark of tenderness had been rekindled, and my better nature was unwilling to snuff it. Slowly I withdrew.

'I can't take it. There's no way. It hurts so much. God, Paul, do you let men do that to you?'

'I do, and it doesn't hurt after the first time.'

'You let them fuck you? Why?'

'Because it feels great.' I started toying with his prick again as a new idea crossed my mind.

'It can't, surely.'

'You should ask a woman. Doesn't it feel good for woman to have a hard prick inside her?'

'Sure it does, but not up there.'

'It's even better up there.'

'How do you know?'

'I'll show you. Fuck me.' My expert manipulation was getting him stiff again. 'Fuck me like you'd fuck a girl. I'll show you how good it feels.'

I held him in my arms and rolled over on my back so that he was on top of me. Now it was my turn to put my legs in the air. I spat in my hand and worked it up my hole, then moistened his prick in readiness.

'You really want me... inside you?'

'Come on. Are you a man?'

'You bet I'm a fucking man!' He grasped me by the calves, steered himself into position and pushed. I allowed him inside me in one go, even though it hurt like hell; unlike Kieran, though, I knew the secrets of breathing and relaxation that would take me quickly through the pain.

'Oh my God, Paul, that's so fucking tight! Does it not hurt you?'

In answer I pushed my erect prick forward so that he could see my excitement. 'Come on, fuck me as hard as you can.'

He wasted no time, and was soon banging like a shithouse door. 'You see?' I said, my voice shaking with every pump. 'It's fucking great.'

'God, it's fantastic! I'm fucking you!' That was stating the obvious, but I wasn't going to remark on it; Kieran was throwing me the fuck of a lifetime. It didn't take us long to come – me all over my belly and then, after he'd pummelled my supersensitive arse a few more times, Kieran in my guts.

He stayed inside me for a long time, until he was soft, and then allowed the tension of my muscles to expel him.

'You came, Paul! You came while I was fucking you.'

'I told you. It's the best feeling in the world.'

'Yeah... God, it was great...' He sounded woozy and sleepy; the champagne had caught up with him. I allowed him to fall asleep, and even dozed a little myself, our bellies glued together with my spunk, our soft cocks pressed against thighs.

I awoke after a couple of hours as stiff as a post. Kieran lay beside me, outside the covers, an arm across my chest; he too was semierect, but sleeping. Now was my chance to get him while he was warm, relaxed and confident. I removed his arm and shifted myself down so that I could suck him. I felt him grow to full hardness in my mouth, and judged that he had woken up when he started bucking his hips in time with my sucking. Then I moved down to his arse, and was gratified to hear that his groaning increased in volume. I removed my tongue and added a finger; it slipped up without resistance, and I added another. This time he winced, but I took it slowly and added a third. His arse, I judged, was ready for more.

'Do you want it?'

'I do.'

'Say it.'

'Say what?'

'Say, "Fuck me, Paul." '

'Fuck me, Paul.'

That was all I needed to hear. I took it slowly, unwilling to scare him again, and this time managed to bury myself to the hilt. Kieran's eyes were closed, his face was flushed, and he took a strange journey into new erotic territory.

I started the fuck slowly, judging by his responses how to proceed. Sometimes he would check me with hand on the thigh, or by biting his lip when it hurt; more often, though, he pushed his arse forward to meet me. We gathered momentum, and soon I was fucking him as hard as I'd fuck the most seasoned sodomite.

He opened his eyes and looked up at me. 'Shall I get on all fours?'

'If you wish.'

'I want you to fuck me in every way you wish.'

'Right you are.' Now it was my turn to feel embarrassed; my cruel, exploitative seduction of such a good-hearted fellow. I might just as well have spared him the humiliation. Mind you, the ends were the same: I was fucking him, and he, to all appearances, was loving it.

He turned over and knelt, holding his cheeks apart. I wet my cock and ploughed straight in without preliminaries; his arse was still relaxed enough to withstand such assault. I could see from the movement of his right arm that he was wanking himself.

I was on the brink of coming again, so I pulled out. Kieran looked over his shoulder in disappointment. 'I was about to come, Paul.'

'So was I. But that's not how I want you.'

'What's next?'

I lay on my back and held my stiff cock in the air. Well, he might as well experience most of the basic positions.

'Sit on it.'

This, for me, was heaven, as I could watch his entire torso as it tightened and writhed, watch him wanking, watch his handsome, puglike face as the orgasm approached. It was his first orgasm with a prick up his arse, I kept reminding myself. The first time. I remembered what it had been like, and started thrusting myself upwards into him. This time I was the first to come, emptying myself right up inside Kieran's belly.

Although I was spent, I held myself rigid inside him and let himself work himself to a climax. He writhed like a bear trying to scratch itself against a tree, using my cock as a dildo, reaching a spot right inside him that would trigger his orgasm. It didn't take long, and another load puddled over my belly. Kieran remained seated until we were both limp.

We slept through the night, and fucked again before breakfast. When we dressed, I gave him the money I had promised: a crisp ten pound note.

'I can't take it, Paul.'

'You must.'

'What we did – that was not for money.'

'It was. That's why you did it.'

'Maybe that's how we started, but not how we finished. We were playing a part, Paul, you and I, but we found our true selves in the end.'

Lest this memoir suddenly become too much like a romantic novel, I shall desist from any further record of the conversation. Suffice to say that we went down to breakfast in friendly mood. I was chastened and ashamed, but hugely cheered by my 'conversion'.

Kieran left the hotel with ten pounds in his pocket.

Fourteen

The shadow of war... Goodbye, Albert Abbott... The Tea Pot... A nice bit of scarlet... Bashed!... Evicted!... Rejected!... The lower depths... Kieran again

That encounter with Kieran marked the end of one phase of my life, the beginning of another. Something had come full circle. The journey that had begun on the day I had arrived in London was over. I didn't seem at the time to have learned very much from my experiences, or to have profited greatly by them; my stock of money was dwindling fast, and I had few friends whom I could rely on. But at least I had been jolted out of the aimless existence that was leading me down to an assuredly miserable fate.

Kieran's kindness, his willingness to forgive me, brought me up short. We parted that afternoon, our roles reversed. Kieran had a spring in his step (what young man wouldn't, having just discovered a whole new sexual playground?) while I was pensive and surly. I felt overwhelmed by guilt and self-disgust. My callous treatment of my fellow man – in particular, my exploitation of Lee and Kieran – haunted me. My former life as a prostitute and model dismayed me. What emptiness! What vice! And for what? I could think of only one thing to be thankful for: that, in all the endless round of fucking and sucking, I had never caught anything more serious than crabs.

Other men might turn to religion at this point in their lives, and I did for a while flirt with the idea of flinging myself on the mercy of the church, blurting it all out in one rosary-rattling confession and then being received into the Roman Catholic Church. Plenty of young men were doing the same thing at the time, attracted by the discipline, the ritual, and no doubt the clothes.

The church, however, was not for me: I lacked the mental capacity to grapple with the catechism. And yet there was a void in my life. Usually, if I detected a hole I lost no time in filling it, but this was an emptiness of a different kind, one that could not be bunged up with cock, fingers or art-deco paperweights.

My spiritual emptiness was not the only trouble: my bank account was dwindling rapidly, and I could see no immediate way of remedying the situation. I wasn't keen on selling my arse again, not least because I was now too well known as a man of means and a punter, and couldn't face the jeers of the boys in Leicester Square if I went back to my old renting ways. Besides which, the new me was squeamish about the business of prostitution. When I was eighteen, nineteen or twenty, I could enjoy myself with practically any man; now, however, I found the thought of sex without love unappealing.

Lest the reader start to think that I turned into a pious goody-goody, however, let me recount just how far my new resolutions took me.

It was, by now, 1939. Wiser heads than mine were troubled by the situation in Europe. In retrospect, it may be hard to believe that anyone with half a brain could ignore the threat of war – but, believe me, I was not the only one to turn a blind eye to it. There were plenty who refused even to think about the situation, and a good few of them were in government – so don't judge my foolishness too harshly.

I was more concerned with how to fill my belly, pay my rent and keep a decent set of clothes on my back, and so of course I ended up back at Romilly House, the business address of Albert Abbott. I had not seen him for some time; occasionally our paths crossed at social functions, when he was always polite and friendly, asking after my progress and giving advice where necessary. But he was never more than that. He never turned up at Adam Street; he never tried to renew the intimacies of the past. I had a chip on my shoulder about that, as about so many things. I told him little of what I was doing – or little of the truth, at any rate. I spun stories about new schemes, I overplayed the extent to which I was educating myself, and I made out that my few pathetic little jobs were actually major, worthwhile projects. I don't suppose Abbott believed a word of it, and I can't blame him. He'd given me freedom and independence on a plate, and if I was the worthless sort to piss it all away then why should he care? He must have been disappointed by me. Perhaps if I really had gone to college, or got a job with some prospects, knuckled down and made something of myself, he would have taken a warmer interest in my person. As it was he remained polite, paternal and distant.

When the squeeze was on, I convinced myself that Abbott had somehow done me wrong, that he had kept back some of the money that I was 'owed' from my previous labours. God knows this was not true: the amount he'd given me in that cheque was far more than I could possibly have earned, and had doubtless been topped up by Abbott himself in order to give me the best possible start. But financial need made me panic, and, every time a letter from the bank manager arrived requesting an interview to discuss my plans, I cast about me for others to blame. And, as usual, it was Abbott.

My reception at Romilly House was chillier than on that memorable afternoon when I got intimate with Mr Abbott's desktop furniture. The old doorkeeper had been replaced by a middle-aged woman of severe mien who asked me to take a seat in a voice that did not invite argument. She announced my presence over the intercom, and I waited.

And waited. Twenty minutes passed, half an hour. Occasionally I would attempt to remonstrate over the delay, only to be quelled by her gimlet eye. 'Mr Abbott is in conference and will see you as soon as he can.' Conference my arse, I felt like saying. He's got his fingers up some lad's bum, if I know my Albert.

At last the door to his office opened, and a young man emerged, chatting brightly to Abbott in a heavy European accent. He was a looker: darker than I, Levantine in appearance, with thick wavy black hair and strong features. I looked him up and down with disgust, imagining him swinging around on Abbott's prick. It was jealousy, no more and no less, but I wouldn't have admitted it at the time.

They completed their farewells, and the young man nodded as he passed me. 'Mr Lemoyne!' said Abbott, in a fair impersonation of good cheer. 'Do come in. So sorry to have kept you waiting.'

I stalked into the office and slouched in a chair.

'What brings you here, Paul?' said Abbott, pouring us both a cup of coffee. 'Good tidings, I hope.'

He looked tired and careworn; too much fucking, I thought.

'I need money.'

His manner iced over. 'Ah. Don't we all.'

'You owe me, Abbott.'

'Indeed I do not, Paul.'

'Oh come on, I know your game.' If the reader will forgive me, I will omit the rest of my tirade; I'm sure you are as weary of my stupidity as I am. I could not see what was in front of my nose – that Abbott was exhausted, worried and in trouble. I could only think of my own concerns – all the result of my laziness and dishonesty. We did not part on good terms.

The endgame went something like this.

'But you still have enough money to run your whores!'

'What do you mean, Paul?'

'I saw him. Don't think I don't know what you were up to. What did you make this one do? Stick the telephone up his bum?'

'You don't know what you're talking about.'

'Oh, don't I? You're nothing but a cheap pimp, Albert Abbott! You're not a man! You're a monster!'

'Paul, please.'

'It's too late for that. Look what you've done to me! You ruined me.'

'If you would only listen.'

'Give me some money!'

'There is no money. It's all gone.'

'Like hell! Where did lover-boy get all his fancy jewellery from? I saw it. I'm not stupid!'

'You'd better leave, Paul. I'm sorry. I thought better of you.'

He opened the door and practically pushed me through. 'Miss Green! No more interruptions today. I will see nobody without an appointment. Good day, Mr Lemoyne.'

The door was slammed in my face, and the clever speech I had prepared died on my lips.

'You'd better leave,' said Miss Green.

'Don't worry. I wouldn't set foot in this whorehouse again if you paid me!' This was patently not true, but it gave me some rueful satisfaction as I turned on my heel and stomped down the stairs.

What would you have done under the circumstances? Gone home and thought long and hard about your arrogance and ignorance, and realised that you'd done someone a great wrong? Or gone out to the nearest queer pub, got pissed and picked up a couple of guardsmen? Good for you; I followed the primrose path.

There were not many places in the West End in those days where a homosexual could knowingly seek the company of his fellows. There were a few pubs with a reputation, mostly for whoring. There were a couple of members-only clubs where you could dance with another chap provided that you were discreet. It was to one of the latter that I bent my steps. I needed privacy, and didn't have the wherewithal for trade. Denmark Street was just across the road from Romilly House, and there, in an attic above a music shop, was an all-day drinking club called the Tea Pot, which catered to the flotsam of the West End. I'd been there once or twice with Boleslavsky, just to cause as much trouble as possible; we'd laughed about it and dismissed the patrons as desperate old queens. Well, I was certainly desperate.

In the Tea Pot (so called because it had a giant urn standing in one corner, from which you could intermittently coax a cup full of brown liquid) a whisky and water cost only a few pennies. By the middle of the afternoon I had reached the talkative stage, and bored the barman half to death with a recital of my grievances. By five o'clock I was morose; by six I was reckless.

I left the Tea Pot after four hours' solid drinking, astonished to find that it was still broad daylight in Charing Cross Road. Naturally, with a skinful of whisky, I wanted to have sex, and wasn't too fussy where I found it. I have mentioned before that I had developed a taste for the armed forces, and I knew, at that time of the evening, exactly where to find them.

I caught a bus at St Giles's Circus that took me all the way down Oxford Street to Marble Arch, where I got off and crossed the street into Hyde Park. The north end of the park was still the province of families; I needed to travel deeper into the park to find what I was hunting. Over on the west side, just across the Serpentine, was a walkway where the guardsmen liked to take the air. This was where I went.

I don't remember the details of the pick-up, except to say that I fell into conversation with two husky specimens, both in scarlet tunics, who ribbed me about my drunkenness and warned me that 'a young gentleman like you could get into trouble wandering around town in that condition'. Had I been sober I might have noticed the sly glance that passed between them; as it was, I registered it only as a manifestation of lust. I told them that I wasn't afraid, that I could handle myself, and that I could handle them if it came to it. This led to more rough humour and much back-slapping, and before I knew how it happened we were in a cab headed for Adam Street. I was in seventh heaven, with a handsome, uniformed soldier on either side of me, and I blatantly handled their crotches, to the disgust of the driver, who was nonetheless too scared of the guardsmen to complain.

We reached Adam Street, and I fumbled with my wallet while paying off the cabby. Then we mounted the stairs, during which I'm afraid to say that I sang loudly and off key when I wasn't telling the two lads just what I wanted them to do with me. Anyone in the house must have heard.

We got to my room, and things turned immediately nasty. One of them demanded my wallet; when I refused, he punched me in the stomach while his comrade held me by the arms. I was winded, unable to cry out, and could only lie doubled up as they went through my pockets. When I caught my breath (and I might add that I had sobered up considerably by now), I tried to reason with them.

'I would have given you what little money I had in any case, gentlemen. I think you will find that I am generous.'

'Yeah?' said the taller of the two, a square-headed Apollo with a thick neck and golden-blond hair. 'And how were we going to earn that money, then?'

'I hoped that we might—' His friend, shorter and less handsome, kicked me in the stomach, winding me again.

'Thought we might what, pansy? Roll over for you? Is that you want? You dirty fucking queer.'

More of the same accompanied each blow, harder than the last; I was afraid that they were working themselves up into a frenzy, and would kill me in the end. I shielded my head with my arms, and drew my knees up around my genitals, but they kicked every other part of me. I was bleeding from the mouth and nose, and there was a nasty pain in my right side, but I was still alive.

My last memory of this visitation was the sight of my two assailants standing against the door, their arms around each other's shoulders, their flies open, waving their cocks at me as I lay bleeding on the floor.

I must have passed out. When I came to I was alone, the door was ajar and one of my neighbours was peering timidly around the frame. When he saw me open an eye, he scampered away, relieved that I was not dead and that he would not have to involve the police. I pulled myself up to my feet and surveyed the damage in the mirror. It was not a pretty sight. My right eye was almost completely closed, my lip was split and my nose was a mass of blood. I felt it gently; it wasn't broken, which was a miracle. My balls were sore but unharmed; I think I may have cracked a rib, for it pained me for some months to come. At the time, however, I didn't think about going to the doctor or the police. I blamed myself entirely for what had happened, and thought of it as nothing more than my just deserts. Such was the mindset of even the most noble homosexual in those days. I'm afraid we all harboured the conviction, hard to shift, that we were somehow doing wrong and that we deserved any misfortune that came our way, which must be borne with stoic silence. We were the children of the Oscar Wilde generation, and martyrdom came with the territory.

On this occasion, I avoided scandal. Nobody who heard the bangs and crashes from my room thought to intervene; after all, they had heard me loudly proclaiming what I wanted to do with my two visitors, and must have assumed that I was having a particularly boisterous session. They were all well used to my bringing home strange men, and lately I had been less discreet. Nobody came to my assistance, nobody asked if I was all right; even the neighbour who had seen me bruised and bleeding on the floor kept his distance. We were all terrified, in those days, of 'getting involved', of guilt by association. We could all go to prison.

Once I'd assessed that I was in no immediate danger, and cleaned up the worst of the blood, I was overwhelmed by a wave of fatigue – the shock, and the whisky, had caught up with me. I lay down on my bed and slept in my clothes for about six hours.

I was awoken by a knock at the door. I stood up painfully (the bruises were beginning to ache terribly) and tried to shake myself fully awake. I opened the door, and there was the landlord, a quiet, fat little man who usually didn't ask too many questions. When he saw my battered appearance he gasped and looked panic-stricken, but then stiffened his resolve and delivered the speech he'd prepared.

'Ah, Mr Lemoyne...' He couldn't look me in the eye. 'I'm glad I've caught you in. I trust it's not an inconvenient time?'

'Of course not. Do come in.'

'No, I won't, thank you. It's just a little matter: your tenancy agreement comes due for renewal again at the end of the week.'

'Oh, thank you for reminding me. Shall I pop down and sign it in the morning?'

'No, that won't be necessary. You see, I'm afraid I shall be needing the rooms. My sister-in-law is coming to stay in London for a few months, and of course you understand that given the shortage of suitable accommodation these days... Well, I'm sure you see that I have no choice.'

'Ah. No. Of course not. Well, she is your sister-in-law.'

'So when you have a moment, if it's not too inconvenient...'

'Of course, I—'

'Thank you Mr Lemoyne, I knew you would understand under the circumstances.'

'Quite. Goodnight.'

'Goodnight.'

Neither of us had said the word 'eviction' or the phrase 'move out'. I wondered, as I closed the door, which one of the neighbours had made the complaint.

My packing didn't take long. By the time I'd deposited my portable goods with the pawnbroker, and sold my larger belongings to a furniture dealer on the Strand, I had only enough to fill a suitcase – the very suitcase that had come with me to London five years ago. The money I raised would keep me fed and watered for a couple of months, and might buy me the odd night in the cheapest of hotels, at a pinch; other than that I was throwing myself on fate. No more extravagance for me. I was back where I started – older, no wiser, and considerably more battered.

Finding permanent or short-term accommodation was out of the question given my personal appearance: I looked like the very worst sort of vagrant. I was reluctant to try dosshouses, although I knew where they were if push came to shove. First of all I had an address book to work my way through. I hadn't whored myself round the upper echelons of society without picking up a few wealthy and influential acquaintances along the way. They could make good some of the airy promises they'd made in moments of passion.

My first port of call was the Albany, home of Mr Newsome, the first man to stick his cock up my arse, the man who set me on the road to prostitution. I enquired for him at the lodge, and was told that he was out. I left a note and waited in the Corner House, nursing a bun and a cup of tea for some hours. When I returned, I was reluctantly admitted by Mr Newsome, who seemed terrified by my appearance. He thought I had come to blackmail him. Perhaps others had before me.

'You had better get out.'

'Mr Newsome, I'm desperate.'

'You stole from me. I've a good mind to go to the police!'

'I paid you back.' I hoped that Vera had delivered the sum that I left in his care to make good my depredations upon Mr Newsome's personal effects.

'Good heavens, Paul, what are you thinking? I can't have lads like you coming round here like this! I have a reputation to uphold!'

A thousand hurtful replies crowded into my mind, but I was too weary to give them voice. Where was his reputation that night when he brought me home in a cab? When he made me finger myself on the leather sofa?

'I have nowhere to go, and no money.'

'I'm terribly sorry, Paul, but I can't help you. Please leave me alone.'

The same scene repeated itself at houses up and down the social scale. Some of my former friends had moved on; others refused to admit me. Those brave enough to see me offered the same excuse: there was no money, they couldn't be seen with the likes of me, I had better go elsewhere. And so, dogged with threats and insults, I continued my rounds.

William Herringham was no use: he was, by now, in a nursing home in Richmond, where an acquisitive nephew, his only heir, made damn sure that nobody could get near enough to persuade him to change his will. Grimes had disappeared altogether, and the premises in Mayfair that once housed that little sodomitical paradise were now let to a banker and his family. Boleslavsky, I knew, was travelling Europe with Terry (and at the time of which I write was experiencing his famous adventures with the Nazi authorities that led to his relocation to America). Lord Simon was in the country; Prince 'Timmy' was back in Africa. Mr Thorne was dead. At the house of my old friend Detective Superintendent —, of Scotland Yard, I was greeted by the man himself, who bamboozled me into sucking his cock for a few pounds and then sent me away with a stern warning that if I ever darkened his door again he would have me arrested.

'Times have changed, Paul,' he said, surveying me like a stern headmaster. 'Society takes a dim view of that sort of thing nowadays.' How he puffed himself up on that word 'society'! How he strutted and preened, when only a minute ago he had been fucking my throat! 'You mark my words, boy,' he said, closing the door on me, 'the party's over.'

How right he was. I went from pillar to post like a pariah dog, spurned by all. There was only one address to which I would not go, however low I fell – Romilly House. Albert Abbott was the one person before whom I would not degrade myself.

After a week of this desperate quest, during which I'd slept in railway stations, on park benches and over cups of tea in all-night cafés, I decided that it was all up with me and that I must join the ranks of the dispossessed. I knew of a spike or dosshouse in the East End, where vagrants could get a bed for the night and a cupboard in which to store their belongings, the theory being that they spent the day looking for work. Work, however, was so scarce that most of the inmates drifted around the streets, drinking and fighting. It was a poor sort of home for a person of such promise, but I had little option. I spent three weeks there, during which time I made a few friends and enjoyed a scrap of physical comfort with a troubled soul called Joe, a man of forty who had left his wife and family and lived on the road. He was a sad creature, dazed and confused by his misfortune, but ready to hold me in his strong arms at night and to make love to me with a tenderness that had been lacking from most of my previous encounters. One day he disappeared, and I never heard of him again.

Why didn't I go home? I was ashamed, I suppose. How could I explain to my mother and my sister, let alone my father, the depths to which I had sunk? How could I tell them that all those things I'd mentioned in my rare letters – the jobs, the friends, the bright prospects – were lies? I was too much of a coward to face them, and preferred the misery of my rootless existence to the pain of confronting them with the truth.

One night, while wandering the streets around Bethnal Green, I heard laughter and song coming from a well-lit pub on the corner of a square. The door opened as someone came out, and I saw a sea of happy, shiny faces, flushed with alcohol; heard a blast of loud, convivial speech; smelled the beer and cigarettes and the warm bodies within. Someone was bashing out a tune on the old joanna, and a woman sang along in a wobbly, fruity contralto. I felt in my pockets for the price of a pint. Well, there was enough for a half. My last money, but it would have to do.

I wasn't used to human company, certainly not to crowds, and I found myself slinking through the door like a criminal. Fortunately, the marks on my face had died down, and I no longer presented such an alarming appearance, but my clothes were shabby and I was in desperate need of a wash and a shave. I bided my time at the bar, in no hurry to get served, adjusting to the light, warmth and noise, mastering a desire to turn tail and run back into the night. Finally, there being no one else waiting, I bought my half-pint of bitter and found a quiet corner in which to sit and watch.

The genial atmosphere cheered me up no end. I found myself tapping a foot in time with the piano, even singing along under my breath. I took my time between sips, wanting to stay for as long as possible, eager to delay the inevitable return to the cold comforts of the spike. I revelled in each overheard conversation, each terrible joke. I bathed in the radiance of simple camaraderie, although I knew myself an exile. This was how my life might have turned out, if I hadn't taken a wrong turn – simple, honest, cheerful, with nothing to be ashamed of.

Mercifully, I didn't have enough money to buy more liquor, or I would have quickly fallen into self-pity, and doubtless set off on another foolish quest for distraction. This time I had to reflect soberly on my wasted life, and to hatch plans for my future. Even with the best will in the world, the future looked bleak. I had tried to find work, but was turned away in favour of men with more experience than myself. Even skilled workers were forced to take menial jobs in those days. I could suck cock like an angel, and fuck like a devil, but those skills were not what got you a decent wage in 1939. I could have gone back on the game, but in my current condition I'm afraid I really was trade of the roughest description, and could have commanded only pennies where once I received ten pound notes.

My glass was empty. I held on to it for as long as I could, trying to conceal it from the pot boy, but eventually he picked it up and wiped down the table. There was little reason for me to stay. I pulled on my jacket, settled my cap on my head and was about to leave when I felt a hand on my shoulder. I flinched. Ever since my bashing I was nervous about unexpected physical contact.

'Paul?'

I turned. It was Kieran.

'Paul! I thought it was you.'

'Hello.' I sounded sheepish. He was with his friends, who stared at me with frank, not unfriendly, curiosity.

'Jesus, you look terrible. What's happened to you?'

'I'm fine, Kieran. I must be going.' I didn't want to give him the opportunity to gloat. It was only a few months since our last meeting, when I'd ground his nose into his poverty, my affluence. I could give it out, oh, yes, but I couldn't take it.

I had not counted on the better nature of some of my peers, however. 'Now then, now then, lad, you're going nowhere,' said Kieran, putting an arm round my shoulder and steering me to the bar, 'not until you tell me what's up.'

He ordered me a beer, and signalled his cronies to leave us in peace. God, after what I'd done to him I deserved only a harsh word and a blow.

'Thanks,' I mumbled, and buried my face in my pint.

'This is a bit off your patch, ain't it? What you doing down here? Looking for a nice bit of East End cock?' He whispered the last bit into my ear; I could feel the heat of his breath.

'Not really.'

'I've been meaning to look you up some time, but I don't often get up West any more. I've got a job now.'

'You're off the meat rack, then.'

Kieran roared with laughter. 'God, yes! Thanks to you, old son. That ten quid you... lent me came in very handy. Gave me a chance to get myself sorted out, go looking for a job without worrying about bringing home the bacon for a week or two. Well, I came up trumps. I'm working as an electrician now. All that fooling around with the lights back at the old Palace of Varieties stood me in good stead, and I managed to sweet talk my way into a job. It's not going to make me a rich man, but it keeps the wolf from the door.'

'I'm glad to hear it.'

'But here I am running on about myself and I haven't got an answer to my question yet. What the fuck is the matter with you, Paul? You look like a tramp. Is this some kind of fancy dress?'

'No, I assure you.'

'What happened to all the posh clobber?'

'They're at the pawn shop.'

'And the jewels and the tie pin and the cufflinks? Don't tell me. God, you haven't even got the price of a haircut, have you?'

'I'm flat broke.'

'Really?'

'Really. I'm living at the dosshouse. I spent my last few pennies on half a pint of beer. Now I'm going home. Home!' I put all my bitterness into that one word, and drained my glass. 'Thanks for the drink, Kieran. Take care of yourself.'

'Hold on one moment there,' said Kieran, banging his empty glass down on the bar top. 'You're going nowhere. God help me, Paul, do you really think I'd leave you down and out like this? Aren't I your friend?'

'Not after what I did to you.'

'What you did to me?' He lowered his voice. 'Ah, you were an arrogant bastard right enough, you silly wanker, but I enjoyed it all the same.'

'Oh.'

'Come on, we all make mistakes. I've made plenty in my time. I don't know how my missus puts up with me. But I've learned one thing in life, Paul, and that's that you've got to stick by the ones that you love, come hell or high water.'

'You mean...'

'Of course I mean you, you great soft shite. Now come on, we'll collect your things and see if Sally's got anything left in the stewpot. I don't suppose you've eaten tonight, have you? No, don't argue! You're coming home with me!'

Fifteen

Employment at last… Bella and Buck… A rude awakening… In police custody… Prison?

I hope, dear reader, that you are not anticipating a renewal of intimacies between Kieran and me to take place under the same roof as his wife. I may have sunk low in the previous pages, but after Sally welcomed me as a long-lost brother, fed me, bathed me, gave me clean clothes and even cut my hair, I could hardly pay her back by shoving my prick into her husband's white arse, however much I wanted to. No: we lived for a while in a state of chaste contentment. Of course, in such cramped conditions, I had plenty of opportunity to see Kieran bollock-naked, and I was far from immune to his charms, but neither of us made any reference to our mutual attraction, nor did we attempt to misbehave. Occasionally, when we went out for a drink, he would whisper a few beery suggestions in my ear, and we'd nip out to a dark corner for a wank and a suck, but that was as far as it went. Kieran wasn't getting his oats at home, with a small child, a pregnant wife and an unpaying guest as witness to his married life, and so I suppose he saw me as a more friendly alternative to masturbation. This was enough for both of us. My libido, for once, was not the motivating factor in my life. I had more urgent matters to attend to: like how, for instance, I was going to make a living and secure myself some kind of a future.

After ten days sleeping on Kieran and Sally's couch, I could no longer allow myself to leech off their kindness. I had been a parasite all my life; it was time that I stood on my own two feet. Despite their protestations that I could stay for as long as I liked (indeed, I helped them out with childminding duties, and 'Uncle Paul' became a firm favourite with baby Margaret), I had to move on. I would have done almost anything in the way of work, but there was very little to be had: it was May 1939, and the country was jittery with war panic. Even I had started to pay attention to the news, and spent some of my idle hours in cafés scanning the papers, trying to figure out whether I might as well join the army.

Yes, that would have been the right thing to do, but for the fact that I was a coward by nature and dreaded the kind of reception that one of my kind would get in barracks. I allowed myself on occasion to imagine life as a kind of army whore, regularly servicing the fit, depraved young soldiers, or pandering to the more rarefied pleasures of the officers – but this fantasy was short-lived, as even I knew that reality would be far more brutal than my foolish imaginations.

Instead of biting the bullet, I found myself following the path of least resistance, and was soon embroiled once again with crooks and perverts. So keen was I to stop being a drain on Kieran's meagre resources that I jumped at the first opportunity to come my way, without looking before I leaped. One afternoon, pounding the beat between Trafalgar Square and Bloomsbury, stumbling at each corner upon some memory of my previous life, I came across a postcard in the window of a newsagent on the corner of Charing Cross Road, just a block or so away from Romilly House (I had crossed the street in order not to pass directly in front of Albert Abbott's door). 'Smart lad wanted,' it read, 'to help run busy photographic agency. Pleasant manner more important than experience. Central premises.' I memorised the number and dashed to the nearest phone box.

Within an hour I was an employee of LensArt Limited, after a brief but friendly interview with the boss, Mrs Bella Batley, in her Goodge Street office. Mrs Batley was the sort of person it's easy for a boy like me to like: she was large, overdressed, and applied the makeup with a heavy hand. Her hair was hennaed and artfully arranged, she smelled of face powder and wine, and she smoked short, stubby cigarettes which piled up in the ashtray, each one vividly stained with her pillar-box-red lipstick. She had an easy, jovial manner, swore freely and offered me a drink the moment I walked in the room.

'Buck's not here, dear,' she said, 'but I'm sure you're just what we want. Can you read and write?'

'Yes.'

'You've got a pretty face and an honest manner. You're not a thief, are you?'

I thought such directness should be paid in kind. 'Not any more.'

'That's good enough for me. I'm a terrible old crook myself, as Buck will tell you, but buggers can't be choosers in my opinion, and he's lucky to have me.'

I should have paid more attention to these apparent pleasantries, but at the time I was too pleased with myself to dig deeply. I could think only of the pride with which I would announce to Kieran and Sally that I had found a job. I would stop off at the Berwick Street butchers on my way home and buy some decent sausages for our supper by way of celebration.

'When can you start, dear?'

'Right now, if you wish.'

'I suppose you're broke. All the best people are, you know.'

'I am.'

She rummaged in a drawer, and pulled out a ten-bob note – frayed and stained, but more money than I'd seen in many weeks. Maybe I'd add a couple of bottles of stout to the menu.

'You can start by working your way through this lot.' She pushed towards me a tray overflowing with paper. 'And match them up with this lot.' Another bundle of papers was produced from under the desk. 'Somewhere in there are invoices and receipts that should tally. If you can make them fit together in any vaguely sensible way, you're doing better than I am. When you get a matching pair, clip them together and sign the invoice somewhere, dear, just so I know that it's one of yours and I can work out how much bonus to pay you at the end of the month.'

That seemed easy enough, and I sat myself on the floor to begin my first honest day's work. Honest! I might as well have gone straight back on the game.

We worked through the afternoon, sipping wine, smoking fags and enjoying the sunshine that came through the open windows. From Bella's confused, anecdote-strewn conversation, I pieced together a picture of my new employers, LensArt Limited. Bella Batley was the business brains; 'Buck', or Buckingham Salthouse, as he was more correctly known, was the creative one. 'He's a genius, dear, and as such a little erratic in his ways, but nobody in London can handle a camera like Buck can. Why, the stars are queuing up to have their likenesses taken. You've probably seen his work in *The Stage*, dear, if you study that august journal.' I didn't, but I nodded as if I had. 'Oh, we've had them all in the studio. Noël, Ivor, John, you name them, the crowned heads of the West End. We are, you might say, intimate friends.'

At last! I thought. An entrée into legitimate show business. If I proved myself a trustworthy employee, I might do well, earn some decent money, return to my family with something to show for myself, perhaps catch the eye of one of those theatrical luminaries and be whisked off to the charmed circles where, I felt, I rightly belonged... My vanity was running away with me as usual, and I had even forgotten that there was a war brewing.

'You're certainly getting through that little lot, dear,' said Bella at length. 'You are remembering to sign your name on them all, aren't you? Otherwise I won't know how much lovely lolly to give you.'

'Don't worry,' I said, holding up an example of my work like a good little schoolboy, 'I'm signing every single one of them.'

'Good lad. Well, time's getting on. It's nearly six o'clock. You'd better run along. Back here tomorrow morning, please. Not too early. Let's say eleven. And we'll fix your wages at... five pounds a week?'

It was more than I could possibly have hoped for, and I shook her hand warmly.

'Of course you'll work a week in hand – you understand that, don't you, dear? Just to make sure that we like you and you like us, before we start putting your wages on the books. Don't worry, though: Bella and Buck will take care of you if you need anything.'

'Thank you.'

'I don't suppose you want to earn a little extra, do you?'

'I wouldn't mind.'

'It's just we had to let our security guard go – he's joined up, silly sausage – and we've got no one to look after the studio at night.'

'Where is it?'

'Just across the road, dear, behind Heals. It's quite comfy. There's a bed and everything. We just need someone there at night to make sure nothing goes astray. Photographic equipment costs a bomb.'

A job and a place to stay! This was too good to be true, and I jumped at the bait.

'We couldn't pay you much, say an extra quid a week, but you'll have a bed of your own and there's all the necessaries: a sink and a lavvie and a place to store your belongings. What do you say?'

I would have signed in blood if she'd asked me to. I rushed home eager to share my good fortune with my friends. That night we toasted my good fortune in bangers and beer.

I must apologise for the absence of sex in this chapter. As I have said, it was not the priority in my life at the time, which you must agree makes a change. What with worries about my future, and more general anxiety about the world, I found other things to occupy my time. Of course, with my own West End pied-à-terre, I could entertain, and it didn't take me long to discover the central London YMCA just a few doors away from my home, but I did nothing worthy of note in either place. There were plenty of attractive young men to be had in town at the time: the coming of war made them less inhibited, and more likely to accept a nightcap from the likes of me. I shan't catalogue these conquests. They were enjoyable, they were transient, and they were mostly with lads of my own age and class. Rest assured, however: there is one more sexual debauch on the way, one that should satisfy even the most jaded appetite.

After a couple of days working for LensArt Limited, I felt quite one of the family. Buckingham Salthouse was a willowy young gentleman of perhaps thirty, with a plummy accent, long, wavy hair and a penchant for monocles, canes and watch chains. He flitted in and out of the Goodge Street office, nodded when we were introduced and gave me a limp, pale hand to shake. Bella and he conducted their business in an adjoining room, and whatever their conversations may have been the result was always the same: another pile of papers for me to sort and sign. The work was dull but it passed the time, and allowed me the mental leisure to dream of my wonderful future and to think over a few highlights of the past. With food in my stomach and clean laundry on my arse, I began to think that life was not, after all, so very bad for Paul Lemoyne. What a swathe I had cut since I arrived in London, five years ago! What adventures I had had! From palaces to pisshouses, I had fucked my way through every level of society. I had been adored by artists, immortalised in oil, fucked and sucked by the good and the great. I had loved, and I had lost. I began to see myself in foolishly romantic terms, a sort of male Greta Garbo, a man with a past.

So busy was I with these reflections that I paid scant attention to the paperwork that I was signing. I suppose I should have noticed the disparity between Bella Batley's sketchy outline of LensArt's business, and the black-and-white evidence in front of me. Most of the invoices mentioned 'photographic supplies', but there were very few references to portraiture, or theatres, or famous people. I presumed that this was a business language which I didn't understand, and carried on signing.

The studio was out of bounds during the daytime. I was admitted at seven, when Buck was clearing up; there were usually one or two of his assistants hanging around the place as well, young men of roughly my age, who seemed familiar with their employer. 'Is he your new discovery, Buck?' said one of them, a pockmarked young hulk who looked as if he worked on a market stall. 'No, Paul is our new office manager,' said Buck, casting a significant look at his young friend and putting an unnecessary stress on the words. Did I catch a smirk on that ugly, butch face as they left me to my nocturnal duties?

It will surprise no one to learn that my career as an office manager was short-lived. I was an employee of LensArt Limited for a little over two weeks, during which time I must have signed nearly a thousand invoices, and spent enough time at the studio to start considering it my home. I never received wages as such – Bella would give me money here and there, but there was never anything resembling a wage slip. I asked if I could sign something to acknowledge receipt of the cash – 'Just something with your name on it, and the company name' – but she smiled and pretended not to have heard.

And so I shouldn't have been so banjaxed when the studio door was kicked in late one night, just as I had dropped off to sleep after enjoying a vigorous fuck with a young man named Brian whom I had picked up at the Fitzroy Tavern. At first I thought we were being burgled – hadn't Bella warned me that there were thieves out there on the lookout for unprotected photographic equipment? – and I sprang to my feet, ready to do battle. I was naked, and liberally smeared with drying spunk, but I was prepared to be heroic.

A light blinded me, and I heard low, dirty laughter.

'Here he is, the little ponce.'

I guessed that there were three, perhaps four, men at the door, which was broken off its hinges. I turned to the bed, where Brian was cowering with the sheets pulled up to his neck, and regretted not arming myself with a knife or a cosh. I could still not see my assailants.

'I – I should warn you that these premises are under police surveillance,' I stammered, 'and if you try to steal anything I will stand up in court and give evidence against you.'

I don't know where I got this bollocks from, but it was the best I could do under the circumstances. In reply I heard laughter.

'Paul,' whispered Brian, who escaped the blinding beams of the torch and could see more clearly who our visitors were, 'they *are* the police.'

That took the wind out of my sails. My instinctive assumption was that they had come to arrest us for buggery; such incidents were not unheard of, even at that time of national crisis. But that was not the case.

One of the officers stepped into the room and turned the light on; the torch was turned off, and I saw four uniformed officers piling towards me. Remember that I was naked and, I might add, terrified. Much as I may have dreamed of such encounters, my penis shrank with terror.

'You,' said the first officer to Brian, 'get some fucking clothes on and fuck off.' Then turning to me, he said, in an official voice, 'Is your name Paul Lemoyne?'

'It is.'

'I am placing you under arrest.' He started to read out my rights. The room spun around me, and I saw Brian hotfooting it down the stairs, dodging a kick to his recently fucked arse.

This was the beginning of the nightmare.

The serious business started in the van on the way to the police station. Remember, I still did not know what I had been arrested for, and assumed that it was something to do with the fact that I'd been caught *in flagrante delicto* with another man. I was too confused to wonder why they let Brian go, or why two of the officers stayed behind at the studio, breaking open locked drawers and loading piles of paperwork into bags. I was dazed and terrified; they had not even allowed me to dress properly, and had thrown me into the waiting vehicle clad only in a threadbare dressing gown.

My wrists and arms were sore from the manhandling I'd received on the way down the stairs, but so far they had done nothing worse to me. The driver, an ugly fat brute whose neck rolled over his collar, glanced back as his two colleagues bundled me into the van. I tried to hide in the darkness, but the driver flicked the light on. There was just room for the three of us in the back: me and the two arresting officers.

Under normal circumstances I would have been delighted to be naked in their company, but at the time fear conquered lust. One of them, the senior, I guessed, was a handsome creature, short, with a deeply cleft chin, deep-set eyes and hair clipped so close to his skull that he appeared bald. He never lost a slight smile, even when he was saying or doing the worst things; he was one of those who enjoy inflicting pain and terror, and would have been much more at home on the other side during the ensuing war. The other looked more like a criminal than a policeman – tall, gangling, with poor posture, broad shoulders and scarred eyebrows, as if he'd been in rather too many fights. His hands were enormous, and he had matching tattoos between thumb and forefinger on both. They represented swallows, and were somewhat blurred, as if done long ago. Strange how such details return so vividly.

I felt that I deserved at least to know what I had been arrested for, and I tried to muster a little dignity – not easy when all you're wearing is a thin piece of material, and you're faced with two jackbooted police officers staring at you across a filthy van. I managed to heave myself into a kneeling position, then sat down on the bench seat as far from my captors as I could manage.

'I didn't tell you to sit.' This was Baldy.

'Please, sir, will you tell me what I have done?' I thought it best to be polite.

'You'll find out in good time, son.'

'I have a right to know.'

'You ain't got no rights.' This was Scarface. 'Get down on the floor like the officer says.'

'What—'

'Down on the floor. On your knees.'

I tried, as I went down, to see where we were; there was a tiny square window at the back of the van, covered by a metal grille. We were heading out of town on the Caledonian Road, I thought. To which police station were they taking me? There were plenty closer to hand.

I got down on my knees, and pulled the dressing gown around me. I had no desire to let them see how shrivelled fear had made me.

'On all fours.'

I had heard tales of prisoners being beaten up in police custody, and assumed that was what was going to happen to me. Faced with the immediate prospect of pain, I found myself remarkably clear-headed. The worst had happened. I obeyed, thinking that cooperation might prevent them from getting worked up into a possibly homicidal fury. After all, who would miss me? A queer, a rent boy, a stranger to his family, with no identification and no friends. All I cared about was getting out of the van alive.

Scarface shuffled down to the far end of the bench and sat down behind me. Baldy extended one boot towards me. I could see what was coming.

'I polished my shoes this morning, Paul,' he said, still smiling, 'but look at the mess they've got into during all that trouble back there.' He sounded as if he was making polite conversation. 'Could you help me out with a shoeshine?'

I must have looked dense, even though I had a good idea what he wanted. Scarface, behind me, started to push against my arse with the sole of his shoe, hooking the dressing gown up so that my bum was exposed to the leather.

'Come on, Paul,' continued Baldy, as I was pushed from the rear towards his boot, 'show me what a boy like you can do.'

There was nothing for it: I lowered my head and started, gingerly, to lick his toecaps. As I licked, he turned his foot to offer each surface to my tongue. Meanwhile, Scarface's kicking in the rear had turned to a regular pounding on my arse. I found myself instinctively coordinating my licking to the rhythm of his assault.

'Now the other one, Paul.' Baldy changed feet, and I got to work. Scarface kicked my knees apart and was rubbing my balls with the toe of his boot. I started to get an erection.

'There,' said Baldy, when both his boots had been well and truly licked, 'you've done a good job there. Now let's see what you can do with this.'

To nobody's surprise, he undid his belt, unbuttoned his flies and pulled out a thick, handsome cock, with a well-moulded head and a deep groove around the piss slit, which, I thought, echoed the cleft in his chin. 'Come on, it won't bite.' Ah, well, they had decided to have a bit of fun with me before we got to the station. They knew I wouldn't complain, after all. And besides, I was getting hard despite myself. I opened my mouth and took Baldy all the way down my throat; I don't imagine he'd ever experienced anything like it.

'Look at that, Scotty,' he said to his junior officer, who was still assaulting me at the rear. 'He's done this before.'

Scarface, or Scotty, scooted along the bench to take a closer look. 'Fuck me, sir, he gets it all in, doesn't he?'

'Why don't you have a go?'

'Yes, sir!'

Another cock, another blow job. The dressing gown was torn from my back, and I was traded between the two. The van seemed to have stopped moving, but I couldn't see where we were. All was quiet, save for the heavy breathing and occasional obscenities of the two coppers.

I hoped to bring them both off in the mouth, and thus hasten to the next stage of my arrest, but they had other ideas.

'You're going to take it up the arse now, boy, aren't you?'

'Yes, sir.'

'You want it up there, don't you?'

'Yes, sir.' I'd heard this kind of talk before from punters who had to work themselves up into a state of hostility in order to pretend that their natural desire to fuck a man was an act of violence or assault. It had never fooled me before, and it didn't fool me now. These two were bum bandits like the rest of us, although they would have killed the man who said it. At least by being as passive and obliging as possible I could channel their hatred into more pleasant channels. I doubted that there was anything they could do with their cocks that could seriously distress me. Thank God for all my years of whorish training: I managed to keep those two psychopaths (and their voyeur driver) busy enough to forget that they wanted to kill me.

I stayed on all fours, dropped my head onto my forearms and offered my bum to whoever wanted me first. Inevitably, they had to slap me around a bit before they would fuck me, as if by doing so they made the act of love an extension of an act of violence. So I submitted to the spanking, knowing that they had to pretend to each other that they wanted to hurt me, to punish me. How much easier life could be for men like that if they would cut out the crap and just enjoy an honest fuck from time to time. Now, however, was not the time to point this out.

Once my arse was red and sore from the slapping, I felt fingers prodding my hole. Baldy was going first; Scotty, I presumed, would get sloppy seconds. And sure enough, with minimal lubrication, he was shoving into me. It hurt me, of course, but it felt good, too, and I was used to such treatment and knew well enough how to deal with it. I comforted myself that it must have been sore for him as well, and I kept my arse clamped tight in order to increase his discomfort. Finally, however, he was inside me; I relaxed and let him fuck me, remembering to whimper and groan the occasional 'Oh, no!' just to let them know they were still in charge. Scotty lifted my head off my arms so that I had to watch him wank. I suppose this was meant to humiliate me further, or to frighten me with a preview of what was to come (he was a very, very big boy), and I went through all the appropriate facial manoeuvres to persuade him that it was working. In fact I was thinking that, if I squeezed my bum tight at the right time, I could almost guarantee that Baldy would squirt within the next three thrusts. I was right: he came inside me, and provided enough lubrication to make the next ride a good deal easier.

Scotty, I imagined, hadn't had an awful lot of arse, and so when he got into mine he was so overwhelmed by the sensation that he came in about two minutes. Afterwards he collapsed on top of me, breathing heavily. Checking that his superior officer wasn't looking (Baldy was silent now, staring out of the window as the van resumed its journey), Scotty planted a few tentative kisses on my neck and reached underneath to see if I was hard. I was.

Ten minutes later, we reached Holborn Police Station, less than a mile from the studio, but nearly two hours since the arrest. Both officers were fully clothed; I was thrown out of the van in my soiled, spunk-sodden dressing gown, placed in a cell and given an ill-fitting set of clothes.

Later that night I learned that I was charged with fraud, evasion of tax and conspiracy to publish obscene materials. I was up before the magistrate in the morning, and faced a long spell on remand. With the political situation as shaky as it was, who was going to worry about one young miscreant locked away, more or less? Particularly when the crime was surrounded with the fetid air of homosexuality. Why, I could rot in prison for all anyone cared.

I spent a miserable night reviewing my situation. So this was the point to which it was all leading – all the promise, the wonderful opportunities, the talents on which I prided myself: prison. If it had been the dénouement of a novel I might have nodded sagely, feeling that any young man who so blatantly flouted the mores of society deserved no better. Rough justice, perhaps, but justice nonetheless. This, however, was not Balzac, I was not Lucien de Rubempré, and I was in no mood to apply the rules of fiction to the realities of life. I would not rot in prison! I would not despair, or hang myself, or just disappear. I would have justice! I had done nothing wrong – or, at least, not deliberately! But of course everyone said that.

Who would listen to me? And who, given my track record, would believe me?

Sixteen

Framed... My night in the cells... Freedom... Southward ho!... A berth at Mrs Tunnock's... An honest living... War... A surprise visitor

LensArt Limited, far from being my gateway to the charmed life of the rich and famous, led in fact to the lowest level of hell to which I had yet sunk. With unerring instinct I had fallen among thieves and worse: Bella Batley and Buckingham Salthouse, it transpired, had been peddling pornographic photographs of spotty, skinny rent boys for the last five years (and it's true that their clientele included some of the famous names of the West End, shame on them!); they had also been racketeering, selling vast amounts of fake perfume on the black market. They were wanted for a ludicrous sum in back taxes as well – or, rather, *I* was wanted, since mine was the name that appeared on all the invoices and payment slips; mine was the name that (unknown to me) had been entered in the company records as 'Company Secretary and Treasurer'. Bella and Buck carefully kept their names off everything, and it was in preparation for such an eventuality as had now befallen that they set me up as their fall guy. They must have known that the law was onto them. I can only admire their sang-froid in the days leading up to the raid, as they cosied me into the job, settled me in the flat and got me to put my fingerprints all over everything. Now, of course, Bella and Buck were nowhere to be found.

The police didn't believe for one instant that I was behind the operation. I was far too green to have cooked up anything so clever – and, besides, officers from the vice and fraud squads must have had their eye on LensArt for months prior to swooping, making sure that they had enough evidence. But it didn't matter to them that the real crooks had got away: they had me to take the rap, and a bird in the hand is worth a great deal more than two birds who have taken the ferry to Calais. I can only say, with all my heart, that I hope something hideous befell those two cheats when they arrived in Europe on the brink of World War Two. Somehow, though, I doubted it.

That night in the cells was not without event. Word must have got around the station that there was a queer boy down in the lock-up, and every rough-arsed copper in the place came down to have a look at me. Most of them contented themselves with gawping through the bars and a bit of verbal abuse, but there were others who went further – a lot further. Baldy returned at about three o'clock in the morning, accompanied as ever by his brutish sidekick Scotty and another, younger, officer, a recent trainee, I imagined. Baldy turned the key in the lock, and the three of them came into the cell. This was not, I gathered, an official visit.

'Settling in, pansy?' sneered Baldy. I had half a mind to spit back a mouthful of accusations, for he was surely just as much a pansy as I was, judging by his enthusiastic performance in the back of the van. He, however, had the steel-capped boots and the truncheon, not to mention the two-man backup, so I held my tongue, lowered my gaze and nodded mutely.

'Ready for another taste?' he said, squeezing his crotch. I maintained silence, and kept staring at the ground. 'Come on,' jeered Baldy, 'you were slobbering all over me earlier like a fucking bitch in heat.'

That makes two of us, I thought. I glanced sideways to see how Scotty was responding to this; he, I knew, concealed a gentler side to his nature, and disliked his boss as much as he feared him. He was scowling, torn between discomfort at the situation and his desire for more action. The third member of the party, who was younger than I at nineteen or twenty, was a homely looking lad of medium height, with yellow hair, bad skin and blue eyes. He looked smart in his brand-new uniform. He was squirming with embarrassment and would have bolted out of the cell, were it not for the intimidating presence of his superior.

'Stand up in the presence of a police officer!' yelled Baldy, working himself up into another rage – the only way he could allow himself to have sex. I had been sitting on the bench, but now, like a sleeper, I stood. Baldy thrust a hand into my groin.

'You're hard, you fucking pervert!' He grabbed my hand and brought it down to his own crotch. Yes, he was certainly hard, too. I could feel his prick like an iron bar in his blue wool trousers. Bullying was clearly his cup of tea. 'You're going to suck me and you're going to fucking well like it!'

Here we go again, I thought, as he hauled his prick out of his pants. The head was red and angry-looking – just like his other shiny, bald head. I saw him, suddenly, as a giant prick in uniform, and the thought cheered me considerably. He stood there for a moment, his hands on his hips, his cock sticking out of his fly, leaning back and sticking his groin forward, making his prick pulse slightly in the air. Lit from above by the single fly-blown bulb that hung unshaded from the cell's ceiling, his head was more than ever domelike; his eyes were deeply shaded by his brows; the shadows around his cruel, sensual mouth and sculpted chin were deep, black pits. He was enjoying exposing himself in this way to his inferiors, anticipating the pleasure of having me again. The youngest of the three, I noticed, was staring with fixed eyes at the throbbing, bobbing dick, beads of sweat standing out on his forehead. I began to understand why Baldy had forced him downstairs to witness the scene: he was another victim of his bullying, much, I imagined, as Scotty had been before.

My suspicions were correct. 'Now, you watch this, Mustard,' he said, addressing the lad. 'This is what those dirty fucking queers do to each other all the time.' And he clicked his fingers and pointed to the floor. I understood the command instantly, dropped to my knees and took hold of his cock in my hand. I glanced up to see Scotty and Mustard (so called, I suppose, because of his yellow hair) suspended in fascination. I opened my mouth, ensuring that they got the best possible view, and took Baldy's lower head between my lips. Then I closed my eyes, tried to block out the unpleasantness of the circumstances and concentrated on what I did best: sucking a big, hard dick. I imagined that it was attached to Kieran, to Abbott, to Boleslavsky, to Lee... Well, it was hard, and it was tasty, and I had an audience. I went about it with professional expertise, and with no small amount of enthusiasm.

Baldy was well pleased with my performance, and increased in hardness in my mouth until I thought he was going to come. But it was not so many hours since I had his last load up my arse, and this was going to take correspondingly longer. With one hand I tugged gently on his balls; I considered moving round the rear, but thought better of it.

'You see how he fucking loves it? The dirty, disgusting little... mmmf!... queer bastard... aaaah...' He wasn't fooling anyone, not even himself. He loved every one of my little tricks: the tickling of his pisshole with my tongue, the stretching of his scrotum, the sensation of my throat closing behind the ridge of his glans. I looked up, and saw his head thrown back, his eyes closed, the veins on his thick neck standing out around his Adam's apple.

Then, just when I sensed he was near climax, he pulled out of my mouth with a slurp, leaving a string of saliva swinging from my lower lip. 'OK,' he said in his stern officer's voice, 'who's next?'

Scotty was already unbuttoning, ready to shove himself where his master had so recently been.

'Stop!' barked Baldy. 'I don't mean that. I mean which of you bastards is going to suck my cock next?'

In the silence that followed, I faintly heard a church clock strike the half-hour.

This, I guessed, must have been a new development in the bullying relationship between senior officer and junior plod. Perhaps they had contented themselves so far with abusing their prisoners; now, with Baldy's sadistic nature in full spate, it was their turn to taste it.

'Come on, I'm waiting.' A drop of juice had gathered at the slit of his cock; much as I hated him, I longed to taste it.

Scotty, the more hardened of the two, was dropping to his knees, preparing himself to taste cock – and, I like to think, willing to spare his junior. But Baldy had other ideas.

'Not you, Scotty. I think we should let the new recruit have a go, don't you? Come on, Mustard. I've seen the way you look at me. You're one of them, ain't you, Mustard? You're a fucking queer, just like this bastard.' He prodded me with his boot.

Mustard swallowed hard.

It occurred to me that there were three of us, and only one of him; we could easily have overpowered him. But an attack of this kind was far too uncertain a venture for me to initiate. Scotty and Mustard were, after all, police officers, and as such programmed to obey.

'I'm right, aren't I, lad? You want this.' He made his penis jump again; he was still as stiff as I'd left him. 'You want to wrap your soft red lips around it, you fucking pansy. You want to suck it and lick it and wank it, don't you?'

Well, this was obviously the truth; I could read it in Mustard's face. He was red, sweating, his lips parted, his eyes heavy as if drugged.

'Fucking suck it, then, boy.' Baldy lost patience. Almost spitting with fury, he grabbed the lad by the collar and flung him to the floor. 'I gave you an order, you fucking scumbag. Now open your fucking mouth.'

Mustard, who had been sent sprawling, and grazed his cheek in the fall, brought himself up to a kneeling position, wiped the dirt from his face with the back of his hand and prepared himself. Baldy grabbed him by the chin and prised his mouth open; this act of violence made yet more juice gather at the end of his knob. Finally the prick was between the boy's lips and making its way into his mouth. Baldy fucked the lad's head, ignoring the gaggings, the chokings, the streaming eyes, the straining veins in the neck. He fucked that boy's mouth until he came, pulling back just in time to spray his load over

Mustard's crimson face. The spunk, of which there was a good deal, was startlingly white against such a dark background. It ran down the lad's cheeks and splashed onto his no-longer-pristine uniform; some of it had landed in his eye, and I saw the poor kid struggling with the burning pain that it caused.

What now? Baldy was spent, but he was far from finished.

'Now we want a show. You, queer boy!' I wondered for a second which one of us he was addressing, as we were, all four of us, sisters in affliction. But, from the contempt in his voice, he could only mean me. 'Do you think you can get that sissy prick of yours hard enough to fuck a man's arse?'

What new madness was this? Who was I going to be asked to exploit this time?

'Yes, sir.'

'You poofs don't just take it up the shitter, then? You do the husband's job as well?'

'Yes, sir.'

'Right, then. Scotty, drop your pants. You're going to get fucked.'

I thought Scotty would protest, but to my surprise he started unbuttoning and unbuckling until he stood with his trousers and pants round his boots, his tunic discarded on the bench, his shirt tails hanging down on either side of a very stiff prick. Obviously this was something he wanted to happen.

'Turn round and bend over.' Scotty did as he was told.

'Right, Flossie,' he said, addressing me, 'show us what you're made of.'

Hate, I discovered, can be every bit as aphrodisiac as love, and it took no time at all for my cock to be ready for the charge. I spat in my hand, stationed myself behind Scotty and shoved it in. He was well trained enough to make no sound, although I sensed from the tightening of his body that he was in pain. I reached round and wanked his cock a few times, just to let him know that there is an etiquette in these matters, a kind of noblesse oblige by which the fucker should ensure that the fuckee is having a good time as well. He was still stiff, and soon he relaxed.

'Well bugger me,' said Baldy, unaware of the irony, 'he goes at it like a real man. I've misjudged you, pansy-boy.' Yeah, I thought, and you'd like me to take care of you next, I don't doubt, you fucked-up bastard. I kept my own counsel, though, and carried on pumping. Mustard, still sitting in the corner where he'd slumped after sucking off Baldy, was watching me like a hawk. Baldy was more upfront in his interest. He reached a hand in between Scotty's bum and my thrusting groin, to feel my rigid prick as it went in and out of the tight little hole. 'How does that feel, Scotty? You're enjoying it, you bent bastard, aren't you?'

Scotty had the dignity to say nothing, but squeezed his arse muscles around my prick. At least we would have a good time. Baldy was excluded from something that he badly wanted to join. We shifted ourselves a little, and he could no longer reach us with his hand.

'Right, Mustard, stand up and get your cock out.' I'd seen it coming. 'Go on, lad. Show me what you're made of. That's it. Fuck me, junior, that's a big one, almost as big as mine. Can't you make it grow any more? Come on, wank yourself a bit, or do I have to do it for you, you fucking wet nelly? All right, give it here, let me show you how it's done.' And by such transparent means, Baldy got his hands, and eventually his mouth, round a stiff prick. Mustard, with a look of surprise on his face, found himself leaning back against the wall, his pants round his thighs, his hated senior officer's face buried in his crotch, pumping a load of cream into his throat. I noticed, as Mustard came, that Baldy had stuck a hand down the back of his own trousers and was secretly fingering himself. I wondered which of the two, Scotty or Mustard, would be the first to be ordered to fuck him.

At that thought, my balls clenched and I squirted a load up Scotty's bum. Then, holding him in a standing position, my cock still deep inside him, I wanked him off until his spunk splashed down the damp bricks of the cell wall.

*

My court appearance the next morning was an anticlimax. During the rest of my sleepless night (by the time Baldy had finished with me, it was light), I had resolved to tell the truth, to confess to the degenerate life I had been leading, but to protest my ignorance (if not innocence) in the LensArt scandal and to shed light on the shocking abuse of my human rights in the police cells. I would be dignified, articulate, vulnerable yet brave. Yes, I had been watching too many films as usual. As it was, my big scene was to be denied me.

I was escorted to the magistrates' court by a very sheepish Scotty, who I think wanted to talk to me but didn't have the nerve, poor sod, and sat in the waiting room starting at his thumbs. After two hours of this insufferable tedium, I was summoned into the courtroom, made to swear that I was indeed Paul Lemoyne, and then told that I was to be released on bail pending the preparation of further evidence. Scotty looked as surprised as I was, and I imagined the bollocking he'd get from Baldy when he got back to the station. Fortunately for me, I was a free man.

I drifted through the formalities of my release, hardly aware of anything except the uncanny sensation of waking from a nightmare. Scotty accompanied me to the street, and shook my hand, holding on to it for a little longer than was absolutely necessary.

'I'm sorry about the misunderstanding, sir.'

'That's all right, Scotty.'

'Are you set, then, sir?' Now I was at liberty there was no more verbal abuse, not that Scotty had been a great offender in that respect.

'I have nowhere to sleep, and my few possessions are all in the studio, but apart from that I'm absolutely fine, thank you.'

'Well, sir,' he mumbled, shuffling his feet and looking awkward, 'I am permitted to escort you to the scene of the arrest for you to recover any personal effects that have not been seized as evidence in the case.' He looked up at me with pleading in his eyes, and so I relented. He took me back to the studio, where, amid the disorder of my former home, we spent two hours energetically fucking the living daylights out of each other. I'm sure Scotty was a better, braver police officer for the experience, and more able to stand up to the bullyings of his craven superior.

I walked down Tottenham Court Road with sore legs and a few meagre possessions in my old suitcase. What had happened? How come the police, so sure of their case the night before (so sure, indeed, that they could repeatedly rape me, confident that I would soon be locked up somewhere and unable to make a complaint), had suddenly had to let me go? What new evidence had come to light? Buck and Bella, surely, had not done the decent thing and turned themselves in. So what?

I found myself heading towards Leicester Square, sticking to the sunny side of the street – and, suddenly, I was outside Romilly House. On an impulse, I walked up to the door, desirous of seeing Abbott again and sharing with him the strange story of my recent life. I was about to ring when the door opened, and a man, Mediterranean in appearance, young, dark, handsome and in all other respects very similar to me, came out on to the street. We looked each other up and down for a moment like twins meeting at the end of a Shakespeare comedy, then we both turned on our heels, each disturbed by the experience of confronting a doppelgänger.

So, I had been replaced, that much was certain. Another, younger Paul was being prostituted round the bedrooms and ballrooms of London. Abbott was creaming his profits from another stiff cock, another obliging arse, and had forgotten all about me. Those protestations of love (were they ever that?), those expressions of concern for my future, were so much hot air. I wondered how many there had been before me, how many more to come.

I walked down to the river with a lead weight in my heart, a few clean clothes in a bag and perhaps two pounds in my wallet. Once again, I had to make a fresh start in life. I didn't have the heart to go back to Kieran. Home was still a closed door. I feared returning to the spike. But what were my options? With that much money, I could just about afford to rent a tiny, squalid room for a week and look for work. It was not an attractive proposition. I still had the tools of my trade, my cock and arse with which to make a fast buck. I balked at the idea of making a poor but honest living.

And yet, dear reader, for the first time in my life, that is just what I did.

The West End was obviously beyond my means, but there were few other areas with which I was at all familiar. Mayfair, Hampstead, Bloomsbury... in none of them would I find the kind of desperate rooming house that would afford me a lousy crib. The East End? Too near Kieran. West London? I had never been further west than Hyde Park – it was a desert as far as I was concerned. But south? Yes, south of the river. That was the way my footsteps tended, through Trafalgar Square, down Northumberland Avenue and on to the bridge, south, south until I reached the scene of my first great arrival on the London stage – the Elephant and Castle. Full circle.

The South London Palace of Varieties was, as I have said, still open, but on its last legs, unable to compete with the cheaper, more fashionable attractions of the three cinemas currently running in the area. Since Holly's departure, it had struggled on under a succession of fly-by-night managers, none of them able to attract the last remaining music hall stars. Audiences were staying away, the quality of the acts had deteriorated (I stole my way in through a fire door and witnessed an ancient old bloke in a bad toupee singing 'A Wandering Minstrel I') and the whole place had the air of a broken-down old whore pissing in a gutter. Happily for those of us who remembered the South in its glorious heyday, it was put out of its misery a couple of years later by a well-aimed bomb.

Well, that would offer me little distraction – which was just as well, as I had not enough pennies to squander on the fripperies of the stage.

What little I had I would need for rent and food – and, in order to find the first necessity, I presented myself at the familiar door of Mrs Tunnock, erstwhile landlady to the profession. She looked older and thinner; the disappearance of her theatrical clients had dented her fortunes considerably. But she was still a dear, maternal soul, and looked pleased to see me as ever, registering no surprise, as if we had met just the previous day.

'Why, hello Paul! You'll be wanting a bed, I suppose.' She could see that I was carrying a bag; little did she know where I'd spent the previous night, since when I hadn't washed, and still, to my nose at least, carried the stench of the cells and of policeman's arse about my person.

'Yes please, Ma.'

'Well, I don't know if I can fit you in just at present – I'll have to check the reservations.' I knew the house was empty except for her and the mice, but I thought it impolite to draw attention to the fact. She riffled through a grimy notebook and pretended to make a few calculations. 'Hmmm, perhaps I can find a corner for you, dear. Would your old room suit?'

My old room! The very berth where I had slept with Kieran, where I had dreamed of a better life, where I had rested after my first ball-draining experiences of life on the game.

'That would do beautifully. I'm afraid I can't pay very much.'

'Good heavens, Paul,' she said, with a good impression of sternness, 'I'm not a charity, you know! You pay rent like anybody else, young man. Let's say... Well, I'm afraid it's going to have to be a pound a week.' I could have kissed her, but my doing so would have drawn too much attention to her generosity. I suspect that a pound meant almost as much to her as it did to me. But I had a week's grace in which to find myself work. I dropped my bag in the old room, whence all of the furniture save the bed, washstand and one broken chair had disappeared, and joined Mrs T for a fortifying plate of her unsurpassed Irish stew.

Within two days it felt as if I had never been away. Within three days I had a job, sweeping up at the Elephant and Castle pub, the famous old coaching inn and London landmark. I resisted the temptation to apply for work at the Princess of Wales, fearing that I would be too readily drawn back into my wicked ways in that den of iniquity, where I'm sure rivers of piss were still regularly squirted over thirsty perverts like my old friend Trevor.

At the end of my second week I was able to present Mrs Tunnock with advance payment for a month's rent, and even to contribute a little to the housekeeping: I was her only lodger, as it turned out, and so we settled into a strange kind of domestic routine. I worked at the pub, sometimes for more than twelve hours at a time; she stayed at home, cooked the dinner and made sure my socks didn't have holes in them. I was a conscientious worker, and was soon promoted from sweeper to pot boy, from pot boy to barman, and from barman to assistant manager. I was polite and friendly to the customers, I turned a blind eye to any blatant come-ons from the passing trade, and I didn't even dip my fingers in the till.

I was working at the Elephant on the day war was declared. We crowded round the wireless set in the landlord's sitting room and listened to the news with a mixture of exhilaration and terror. Blackout precautions went up almost immediately, and we waited in daily fear of the first bombs.

I waited for my call-up papers, although they would be slow coming: nobody, as far as I was aware, knew where I lived. Mrs Tunnock dreaded my inevitable departure, for if I went to fight she lost her income – and she lost a surrogate son, which is what I quickly became to her. (To spare the reader any anxiety on this count, let me relate here and now that Mrs Tunnock survived the war in straitened circumstances, taking in washing and cleaning a variety of shops. Her house survived the Blitz, and she did not leave the area till the late fifties, taking a well-deserved retirement just before the bulldozers moved in on Ontario Street.)

Perversely, the outbreak of war coincided with one of the most peaceful periods of my London life. I had settled into a routine. I was off the merry-go-round of casual sexual encounters – in fact I embraced a period of chastity with real relief. I did not become a monk – I was still a young man in the prime of life, and on most nights, before I fell asleep, I summoned up one of my choice memories as an aid to masturbation. Naturally, it was to the more debauched experiences – my exploitation by Baldy, my experiences with Lee, my piss-drenched performances with Grimes – that I returned most frequently.

The so-called 'phoney war' dragged on into 1940, and still nothing happened. I began to think that my call-up would be delayed forever, that the war was a nonevent. I had time to think about the future, to take stock of my life. One thing puzzled me enormously throughout this strange period: how had I escaped from the clutches of the law, when it seemed certain that I would take the rap for the LensArt affair? What new evidence had been brought? Who was my guardian angel?

The answer to that question will form the last part of this memoir.

Christmas passed, and Easter, and the summer was near. I was happy in my work, happy with my way of life, and had even written a letter to my mother and sister to let them know that their wayward son was alive and well. I contemplated a home visit – my first in five years. Yes, it was five years since I had stormed out of the house on my eighteenth birthday, little knowing into what trouble I was running.

And then, in June, I received a visitor at the pub. It was one of those moments in life that belong more truly in the movies. It was a sunny evening, just after opening time, and the pub was still relatively empty. I was wiping glasses ready for the regulars when the door opened and there, framed against the rays of the setting sun, was a familiar silhouette.

Albert Abbott.

I did a brief double take, then carried on with my work, smiled politely and decided to treat him like any other customer. That's what he'd been, after all – wasn't it?

'Evening, Mr Abbott. Nice to see you. What can I get you?'

He came up to the bar and said nothing, just stared into my eyes. He looked pale and drained, as if he hadn't been sleeping well. Probably fucking some tight-arsed little piece of trade, I thought, but I said nothing.

'Sir? A pint?' There were other customers waiting to be served, and when he maintained his silence I moved away down the bar.

'Paul...'

'Just a moment, sir.' I was playing him along, flirting, pretending that my job called me away, although in truth the other customers were a couple of desperate old gents whom I should have thrown out of the pub. Instead I took my time, served them nicely, even engaged in pleasantries about the weather, before returning to Abbott. He was angry, I could see, but something was holding him back.

'So, Mr Abbott, how have you been? How's business?' I put a bitchy little twist on the word. I could feel my old self coming back, and it was not a pleasant sensation.

'I've come to say goodbye.'

'Goodbye?' I was flummoxed. It was not as if we'd been in regular contact recently.

'Yes. I have to leave the country.'

'Oh? Where are you going? Somewhere nice?'

'This is no time for joking, Paul. I may be in danger as it is.'

'I see.' The silly little queen in my nature was suppressed – for the very last time, as it turned out. The months and years to come were to be serious indeed.

'Can we talk somewhere private?'

'I'm working.'

'It's important.' There was something in his eyes that persuaded me of the truth of his words. I whispered in the ear of my colleague, a friendly barmaid called Joyce, who was more than capable of coping on her own. Abbott and I hotfooted it back to Mrs Tunnock's, which was no more than five minutes' walk from the pub. Out in the street, Abbott kept his coat collar turned up and his hat brim pulled down, despite the fact that it was a beautiful, warm, early-summer evening, and the rest of the world was in shirtsleeves.

We bounded up the stairs to my room; the moment the door was shut he threw off his hat, grabbed me in both arms and delivered the deepest soul kiss I have ever experienced. It lasted for about four minutes, during which time I nearly came in my pants. I was completely taken by surprise. What of all his other trade that I'd seen coming and going from Romilly House – all those handsome, dark young men who had replaced me in his life? What was this sudden outburst of affection all about?

I was speechless; Abbott, fortunately, was more possessed and eloquent.

'I couldn't leave without doing that, Paul. I should have just slipped away, not seen you, not allowed anyone to make the connection between us. I hope to God that we were not followed. But I couldn't leave without telling you, once and for all, that I love you. That I will always love you.'

Was this a joke? A nightmare? It seemed as unreal as the war – the war that had been declared but hadn't happened.

Abbott interpreted my silence as hostility or lack of interest, and backed towards the door. He would have left then and there, I would never have seen him again, but some impulse guided my hand to his arm.

'You... love me? What are you saying?'

'I've loved you from the first moment I laid eyes on you at the Palace of Varieties.' He was blushing – actually blushing – and staring at his shoes like a nervous schoolboy. 'I know I got it all wrong. I treated you like a whore, I was greedy, I saw you as a means to riches and position, and you were. But then I saw what I was doing to you, and I had to let you go. It was the hardest thing I've ever done.' Now he looked me in the eyes, and it was my turn to blush. There was no doubting the sincerity of his words.

'Was it you who—' Suddenly everything fell into place.

Abbott laughed. 'I've kept an eye on you, Paul, with a certain amount of dismay at the bad company into which you keep falling. Yes, it was me who got you out of that scrape with LensArt. I've known Bella Batley for a long time. She's always trying to pimp for me, and she blabbed that she'd got this young stooge set up for her latest job. It didn't take too much to put two and two together. I made sure that I had enough evidence on her and Buck to get you off the hook, at least. And I called in a few favours.'

I put my arms around his neck and kissed him again. 'Why? Why should you care about me?'

'I couldn't let you go to prison,' he said, holding me round the waist so that we were joined from chest to knee. The rest of the conversation was whispered. 'I kept an eye on you all along. I knew it was too late for me to repair the damage that I'd done to our friendship, but I couldn't let you come to harm. Sometimes you gave me the slip, but I knew you'd always pop up again somewhere, usually in trouble.' He kissed me again; we were both hard in our trousers, and I hoped we'd have time to seal this new compact.

'But... what about all those other boys?'

'Aah... yes, you've been keeping your eye on me as well, I suppose.'

'I saw them coming in and out of Romilly House. You've been busy.'

'It's not quite as you suppose, Paul.'

'Isn't it? I don't mind. They all looked like me. I take that as a compliment.'

'Some of them did, perhaps. Some of them had black hair like yours. Some of them had red hair. Some of them were actually blond – you'd never even know that they were Jewish.'

'Jewish? What's that got to do with anything?'

'I – I can't tell you.'

'You must.'

'It's too dangerous.'

I stepped back from him. 'Don't you trust me?'

'I don't see any reason why I should, you being the silly little sod that you are.' The fire flashed in his eyes, then he softened. 'But I will, because I want you to understand me. It's selfish, perhaps, but I'd hate to say goodbye on a misunderstanding. I want you to remember me... well.'

I was beginning to panic. Here was true love, for the first time in my life, and it seemed that I was to lose it no sooner than I had found it.

'What? What's going on?'

'Paul, come close again.' We embraced, and he ran his fingers through my hair while whispering in my ear, punctuating his words with kisses. 'Since long before the war began, Europe has been a dangerous place for my people. Did I never tell you before that I'm Jewish? Didn't you guess?'

'No.'

'Well, I didn't make a big issue of it. I might not have been so welcome in the upper-class drawing rooms of Mayfair if they knew that my surname was not Abbott, but Abrahamson. They're a shockingly anti-Semitic lot, the British upper classes. As bad as the other side.'

'What do you mean?'

'Don't you ever read the papers, Paul? In Germany they've been victimising the Jewish people for years. Now it's spreading. There are terrible stories of families, whole communities being rounded up, disappearing. We've been helping them to get out, getting them into England, providing them with the papers that they need to make the next stage of their journey. I've been back and forth to Europe so many times: Hamburg, Amsterdam, Calais, Rotterdam. Thank God I'm protected by a British passport. But now they're on to me. The authorities in the occupied countries know who I am. If I travel to

Europe again, I'll be one of those that disappear. They're after me. They want to stop me. They don't want any more of their Jews disappearing overseas, telling stories about what the glorious Third Reich is doing at home. I'm too dangerous.'

'So where are you going? Where shall you go?'

'Oh, back to Europe of course. Perhaps to Amsterdam. There are many people there who need help.'

'But you just said—'

'Naturally I shan't travel as Albert Abbott, or indeed Abrahamson. I have a couple of other personalities in this bag of tricks.' He indicated his valise. 'I didn't spend all that time in the theatre without learning how to glue on a false moustache or change my hair colour. Dear old Terri Marlo, God bless her, has been invaluable.'

'But you can't go. You're stepping straight into danger.'

'I know, Paul. But I can't stay here in the knowledge of what's happening just across the Channel. How could I live with myself?'

'Then take me with you.'

'Oh, Paul, it's too late for sentimental gestures. Don't imagine that I didn't think about it a million times. I thought we could run away together, that we could start a new life in America.'

'We could. Why not?'

'Indeed we could, except it would be just that: running away.'

'But lots of people are doing it.'

'Indeed they are. Good luck to them. Not me. I'm bound for Harwich. There's a fishing vessel sailing tonight that may be able to get me across. I don't know. I'm travelling light, as you see.'

'Then this is goodbye.'

'So it seems. Goodbye, until we meet again.'

'We'll never meet again. You'll die.' I was crying.

'Never say die, Paul. You mustn't say that. You must believe that I shall come back to you. That will keep me going if things get tough. I shall think of you here in London, or wherever you may be.'

'Yes, wherever I may be. I shall join up. I shall fight too.'

'Brave lad. Come on, then, soldier, dry those tears. Fighting men don't cry. Courage!' He kissed the wetness away from my eyes.

'Courage. Yes, we'll both need that.'

We kissed again, and suddenly we were both overwhelmed by the desire to make love. Not just to fuck, not to use each other, not to gain power, but to reach beyond words and beyond thoughts to a place where we would be, truly, together, whatever may befall us.

And I fear, dear reader, that this is one fuck that you'll just have to imagine for yourself. Some things, even in my life, are private.

That, really, is where I must end this story, for it marks the beginning of a new era in my life – my adulthood, you might say, after the extended late adolescence with which this volume has been principally concerned. It took the realities of love and war to jolt me from self-centred, blinkered childhood into the maturity of manhood. It happened literally overnight. Abbott left me as night fell, and it was a very different Paul who returned to the pub to hand in his notice, and who reported to the draft office the next morning.

As for my adventures in the war, and my search for Albert Abbott, and the strange fate that befell us both, well, that, perhaps, is for another time. But now, the show is over, it's time to ring the curtain down on a bill of entertainment that has been both comical and tragical, pastoral and historical, in which I have tasted most of what men have to offer and, generally speaking, swallowed every drop.

Thank you, and goodnight.

More sensual reading for the discerning homosexual gentleman

The Masters File

by Jack Dickson

An obsessional journey towards sadomasochism

Living with long-suffering boyfriend Gerry, life is easy for oversexed freelance journalist Gavin Shaw: great job, all his home comforts and the opportunity to indulge in casual sex whenever he gets the itch.

That's when an old flame by the name of James Delany makes him an offer he can't refuse.

While James has varied kinky interests, Gavin shies away from anything which smacks of power-play, and that's why he dropped James like a shot when their brief fling strayed too close to the edge. Still, Gavin is a man who never turns down a dare... A pacy, sexy thriller that travels to the outer sexual limits.

Praise for *Out of this World* by the same author:

'The king of the erotic story' ★★★★ *Out in Greater Manchester*

'WOW!!!! ... I was left breathless. A truly great storyteller and a brilliant headf**k' *Scotsgay*

ZIPPER BOOKS/ UK £8.99 US $13.95 (when ordering quote MAS758)